When Everything Ends

K.R. Brendlinger

Copyright © 2025 by Kristen Brendlinger

All rights reserved.

No part of this publication may be reproduced, distributed, or transmitted in any form or by any means, including photocopying, recording, or other electronic or mechanical methods, without the prior written permission of the publisher, except as permitted by U.S. copyright law.

The story, all names, characters, and incidents portrayed in this production are fictitious or used in a fictitious manner. No identification with actual persons (living or deceased), places, buildings, companies, brands, and products is intended or should be inferred. Any similarities are purely a conscience. The opinions and discussions do not accurately represent the author's personal feelings or thoughts on any single matter mentioned.

Interior Artwork by EUREPHORA

Cover Design by K.R. Brendlinger

First Edition 2023, Second Edition 2025

ISBN 979-8-9907394-2-0

Note From Author:

This book was written from both the first <u>and</u> second points of view. Some *italics* emphasize a word, but for the most part, it signifies Bennett connecting with his audience through the book he's writing. **He's talking to you, the reader.**

Your mental health matters.

The following is a <u>content warning</u>.

Bennett likes to swear, a lot. If you do not appreciate some good ole multi-use vulgar slang, this book may not be for you. You will also experience violence, criminal activity, explicit sexual scenes, and dark themes. It contains *mentions of traumatic experiences*, including rape, drug use, suicide, and abuse. This book is intended for mature audiences of adult age. This book is not intended to be a guide, a reference, glamourize any specific act or trait, or idealize relationships.

It is a work of fiction.

United States: <u>National Mental Health Hotline</u> 866-903-3787

<u>Suicide Prevention</u> Call 988, 998lifeline.org

<u>Crisis Text Line</u> Text HOME to 741741

United Kingdom: <u>Suicide Prevention</u> Call 116 123, samaritans.org

<u>Crisis Text Line</u> Text SHOUT to 85258

Canada: <u>Suicide Prevention</u> Call 1-833-456-4566, talksuicide.ca

<u>Text Line</u> Text 45645

International: <u>Visit</u> befrienders.org

Dedication

To a unicorn in a field full of horses:

They won't say how they feel until your dead, but between me and you, the beauty in your differences make you extraordinary.

This story is for everyone who's felt like they didn't belong.

Contents

PLAYLIST

Demons – Beauty School Dropout
570 – Motionless In White
Look Who's Crying Now – Jessie Murph
Comfort – Nicholas Galitzine
I Miss You – Ivan B, Erika Karina
Tantrum – Charlotte Sands
Bad Things – I Prevail
Stay – Ari Abdul
Eternally Yours – Motionless In White
Just Inhale – Bryce Savage
Cyan1de – nothing, nowhere
Miracle – A Day To Remember

EURE
PHORA

EURE
PHORA

Six Foot Holes Call For Irish Coffee, According To Bennett

"Wait...I'm not dead?" Heavy eyelids challenge my awakening. Straining my neck slowly to the side, the half-naked trees surround me. My focus gradually becomes clear. "Uhh. Fuuuck." The unconscious groans travel up my core and echo through my ears, ricocheting off flaking old trees.

Ever stick your head under a snare drum while someone beats on it? Neither have I, but I imagine it's a similar feeling.

"Nope. Still alive." Wonderful.

The farther I lean on my elbows, goosebumps rapidly disperse over my covered skin. I'm back. Here we go again. "Where is, mm—" Wincing, a striking breeze stops me from looking around again. "Shit," I damn near growl, continuing to talk out loud to myself. "Where the fuck is Cherry?"

This is all too familiar, and it fucking sucks. I'm trying to explain to you how much I hate this moment—waking up in silence, not even the whistle of a bird in the middle of the woods.

It's pointless. You couldn't begin to understand.

The best I can give you is a brief explanation. I'm in the woods, burying a body with the actress that my team hired for the lead in my new film. My sudden rise to fame wasn't premeditated, but it's owed to—well, it's another one of those difficult-to-explain situations. Who the fuck starts a story smack dab in the middle of chaos and confusion? A mad genius, darling.

The rush of floating lights blurs my vision as I push my palms into the cold dirt. Great. Come on. If I could just, uh, fuck, just...dig my feet into the ground. Just stand up without... "For fuck's sake. Ugh." Losing my balance!

Toppling to the right and grappling the surrounding void in my desperate panic, I somehow catch myself before I wipe out. Pure dumb luck.

Besides the massive moon, it's nothing less than miles of trees and cold black night. The bright, round circle looks close enough to touch.

Being showered in dirt and pine needles was a little more than expected. I brush my hands against my jeans and walk up the hill past the hollow.

The wet leaves are silent under my shoes, and I'd be undetectable if it weren't for the twigs and branches crunching against my weight—not that it matters to me. I'm not trying to be sly. I know you've seen a vampire movie or two. Do you believe in them? I don't. It's a load of bullshit. Mankind is the world's biggest threat.

I revert to old habits, taking the smooth surface of my thumbnail to my mouth. It deepens into the skin of my lower lip while I scan the woods. Shit. I cower over, spitting a bead of saliva to the ground. A dribble hangs at the corner of my lip as I stand back up, finding the vale below to search for Cherry. She has me biting my fucking nails, questioning things I haven't thought of asking in years—things I had accepted. "I knew this was—" My spoken thought is cut short as I catch a glimpse of her honey-blonde waves sailing in the wind. It should be alleviating—finding her. It should be. "There she is," I sigh.

"Cherry!" Hell, have mercy; spare me the widened eyes. I'm not gonna shut up.

Nobody is going to hear me out here. Nobody.

It's the middle of the woods, am I right? I am. I'm always right, darling. You better be a quick learner if you're going to keep up.

Overwhelming pressure heats my back, cutting around my ribs and the ever-pounding organ in my chest. It's happening again. Move your fucking legs, Bennett, before your limp body rolls back down this hill. These forsaking fucked side effects.

I told you, mankind is fucked. Pills and potions come with all kinds of downfalls.

Forcefully pushing all the air from my lungs out of my mouth, I blow strands of dark hair from my face. Every time the breeze picks up, the wispy fuckers damn near poke me in the eye. I didn't expect to be doing this tonight, or maybe I would have gelled back the straight coffee-ground-tinged threads. It wasn't what I had planned. Well, there is no better time than the present to dig a hole on a miserable night.

I pinch the ends of cotton fabric along my collar, dragging the hood of my untraceable black sweatshirt over my head, and briskly hike down the hill.

It's not like this was my first time.

"Sorry about that." Reaching her, I have no idea why I'm apologizing. It's not like I owe her one. She's the one who owes me an apology. She just left me, hah...fuck. The humor in it all. "Sometimes that happens." The venomous smirk unconsciously pulls at my somewhat thin lips.

"You just randomly die?" She yells in a whisper, her glare never faltering. She's fuming, and I undoubtedly find it amusing. The rounded apples of her cheeks look sharp when she doesn't smile. The glacier in her eyes could reach my soul and strip it from my body, make it her slave, and return it before I ever countered. It's a cloak covering the panic. I know her heart sank when she couldn't wake me. She had to make the choice to keep going.

The chuckle that escapes my lungs is just as rigid as the air I inhale back into them. "Don't be dramatic. I wasn't dead...well, I don't think I was."

I couldn't tell you at this point. Four months ago, I would have been indifferent. Now things are more...cloudy.

"Just help me," she rebukes.

Following her with narrowed eyes, I can see she's not taking the temperature any better than I am. Bury me. Bury me six fucking feet deep because I fucked up the day she reeled me in and wrapped me around her dainty fucking finger.

"Here." I already regret this. "Take my hoodie." Pulling the sweatshirt over my head, her gaze drifts to my exposed skin as I pull my arms out of the sleeves, catching the end of my t-shirt. Don't...don't do that, Cherry. The stubborn little witch will turn an ant hill into a volcano.

"I'm fine," she insists.

"Bullshit." Extending my hand, I offer it to her again. Take the fucking hoodie. "You'll be *useless* if you're frozen." She unfolds her arms and takes it reluctantly. Her eyes flicker as if her mind began traveling with one triggering word. Ah, Fuck. Change the subject, Bennett. How could I let that word slip?

I should say it's Cherry's story to tell, but I'll indulge you with the details later.

"How long was I out?"

"Max ten minutes." She paces before settling on a log, swinging her leg over and straddling it. Her hands steady on the bark, drawing my attention as it flakes. Man, I want them on me. I wouldn't even wince when the strikingly cold silver wrapped around her finger meets my flesh. I'm almost jealous of Ames. God, that's a disgusting thought.

I'll get to that preppy shithead—Ames—eventually. For now, all you need to know is that Cherry never takes that ring off her finger, even when burying a corpse.

Walking past her, I pick up where she left off. "And you got this far by yourself?" I ask, looking over my shoulder. "I'm impressed." Pushing my boot to the metal step of the shovel's blade, the pressure digs the tip deeper into the earth. Flecks of debris loosen as I toss the dirt to the side. With each scoop, the muscles from my forearm to my biceps tighten.

I am impressed. She's what? A hundred and thirty pounds drenched? I'm telling you, she is. Small, like a fucking firecracker. And she got over that hill and found this interstice. I wasn't sure she had it in her. I should have known she would take the initiative. She's never stopped proving me wrong. She never listens either, unlike you. You're not going to get on my bad side, are you?

"Was that a compliment?"

I straighten to look back at her. She rolls those pretty blue eyes around like I can't see them. Surprising her with a few pleasant words amid calamity is savage—toying with her like that when neither of us wants to be within a five-mile radius of each other right now.

After staring at her for a moment too long, I get back to digging, widening the bottomless pit.

"Are we done here?" The fuzzy scuffing of her shoes earns another glance in her direction, and I find her staring at me, holding her dirty hands out to her sides as if she cares if she gets my hoodie filthy. I swear she has some type of attention disorder. She can't even keep her ass on a log and watch me dig a hole.

Wiping my cheek against the short sleeve of my vintage Black Sabbath t-shirt, I continue piling the dirt to the side.

If this happened a month ago, it wouldn't be this fucking cold. If this happened a month ago, it would be a different story.

I'm waiting for the sweat to freeze on my pasty skin and give me hypothermia, but by all means, volunteer to save the damsel in distress again, as if you could play the hero. For a brief moment, she found a gray smudge in my black soul. It's not like I'm in love with her.

"What's your drink of choice?" I ask breathlessly, standing from my squat and brushing my hands down my thighs again. Towering over her, I take a blonde strand between my fingers, tucking it inside the hood. I trace her soft ivory flesh down her neck, stopping when I reach the bone above her chest. Delicate on the surface, the temptation is an illusion. I exhale, slowly emptying my chest as I still battle to regain control. Then I step away. After everything, how is she doing this to me? Making me want to puke and laugh at the same time, to punch a tree and hold her close, to make every intelligent decision and still let her become my stupid obsession.

"Why?" She asks, her tone hushed.

"Personally, I like a good Irish coffee after I kill someone." I drop my deadpan glare, letting the corner of my lip rise with an airy chuckle.

Come on, Cherry. Stop rolling those pretty eyes around like I can't see them. I never thought you would be one to hold your tongue. Yet here we are, in the dark. It has gotta be close to two in the morning. And you are as stiff as the corpse. You won't even look at me.

She brushes her hands together before bending for the shovel and grabbing it in the center of the wooden shaft. "How'd you find this place?" She mutters.

"I've learned my lesson on where and where not to bury bodies." Water vapor clouds my mouth as I exhale laughter. She hands me the shovel; the same grimace tirelessly stuck on her face. "What's the problem?" I know I'm not everyone's shot of Bourbon, but Cherry and I have an understanding. The sudden cold shoulder is unsettling, to put it nicely. I can't handle it when she's quiet. I know those wheels in her head are turning, and I won't like what they come up with.

"It wasn't supposed to happen like this, Bennett." The way she says my name. It's like daggers to the abdomen. Disgustingly harsh. Her shoulder slams into my arm as she walks past, forcing me to step backward.

Heh, ha, yeah. My faint laughs might disguise my irritation for a second, but they evaporate like my patience. "Cherry! Where the fuck are you going?" She stomps up the hill in her size seven and a half combat boots, her arms swinging with tightly coiled fists, one still wrapped around the middle of the shovel pole. The indents in the dirt leave a trail behind her. I keep yelling, but I don't care if she stops. I'll keep chasing. Slow and steady, waiting for her to slip up. "You asked for this! It's not my fucking fault! You're in it now, Cherry. Whether you like it or not."

Okay…now that you're wondering what you walked into. Let me rewind just a minute. Before Cherry. Before all of it. The beginning.

I've spent my entire life invisible. I'm the wallflower of all wallflowers. Always in the background, never quite memorable.

It's funny how they all say they're my friends now. I always thought it was pretty ironic how many people publicly mourn when someone passes unexpectedly. Yet, those fuckers were nowhere to be found through life's lowest moments. They stand outside my sold-out venue with yearbooks, showing the security how we go way back like they're entitled to a seat. It's too bad your influence only stood a chance in high school and not ten years later.

I know what you're thinking. How did I spend my entire life invisible yet have a sold-out venue filled with people waiting to see me? Also, who the fuck did I kill and bury in the woods? We'll get to the second part later. Yes, I've said that six times in five paragraphs. Patience is a virtue. It's worth the wait.

You get fame in one of two ways. You do something to earn it, or you die more dramatically than you lived. I did both, but wallflower perks—only one of those was noticed.

When everything ends—which it always does—something else begins. Benny died three years ago—and not metaphorically. I literally fucking died. Bennett came from the flames like a rising Phoenix. That is actually a metaphor...mostly. Honestly, it's a long story. Are you sure you're ready for it?

Oh shit. I should've started that entire speel with *Hi, I'm Bennett Larson.* Fuck, no. What's my character's name? Baron? Bradford? Bentley? Um...*Hi, I'm Beckett Landon. This is my miraculous story.*

Yeaaah. The reader already DNF'd.

Hah. No.

For a second, I forgot who I was.

Grab your favorite cozy blanket and caffeinated beverage. You're about to binge-read.

Bennett Larson Is
A Red Carpet God

A deep, coarse voice shouts over the crowd of bodies hovering on the edge of the red carpet. "Bennett! Bennett! Is it true you're starting filming next week for another movie? Can you tell us more about it?"

These reporters—they're all the same. Searching for the next story, the next big lead, one sentence they can use to publish a puff piece full of piss-poor guesses and theoretical what-ifs. Blinding bright lights and at least a dozen microphones pointed at me, I've already become accustomed to this reality. I'm not even sure there was a transition stage. I went in head first, waves crashing over me, swimming to the top, undaunted. That's a lot coming from a guy whose comfort zone was on the stage crew, flicking lights on and off; not the master of the puppets. Now, look at me wearing a fucking five-thousand-dollar tux on a red fucking carpet.

"We're at a premiere. Ask me something about this film," I answer, my glacial mask abiding.

A tall drink of water in six-inch heels shoves her microphone in front of the fluffy blonde *himbo*, interrupting with her question. Too slow, buddy. You had enough time to get those highlights re-frosted and the darling beat you to the pop. Slender from her dark bob-framed face to the hem of her fitted turquoise gown, she's a sight. "What was it like working with Abigail Wethers?"

"She's a terrific actor. Finding the right fit for Journey, I had no doubt when she auditioned. She captured the character with such ease as if I had written it specifically for her. She was an asset for Lost In Nirvana." A smile replaces her previously serious face.

Everyone is captivated by the onyx-haired, blue-eyed Abigail Wethers, except me. Wait, nuh-uh. No, it's not like that. I'm not a picky prick who ridicules women. Abigail was the actor for the job, and, might I say, one with a great rack. Despite my team discovering her, I'll take all the credit for her casting. Perfect for the film and perfect for me are two different things. Let's just say I like my women a little more...crazy.

If you're boo-hoo-ing right now, claiming that's an insult, it's not. Stop what you're doing and pull up the digital dictionary. Scratch that. Keep reading. I'll help you out. Yes, the first definition is foolish, senseless, or strange, but number two states extremely excited and enthusiastic. That's right. The girl for me is as passionate as an influencer-obsessed mom looking for a limited edition tumbler on a Tuesday morning after carpool. Number three does mention mental illness. I'm fully capable of chasing a wildly irrational darling through the woods. I may have been there a few...dozen...times.

I wasn't always this straightforward with people. I kept my opinions to myself and avoided confrontation at all costs. People evolve. Some get a kick in the ass and do it quicker. It's also pretty simple when nobody knows the real you. I don't even need a mask.

I wave them off, walking down the red carpet. Ignoring the camera flashes and the shouting, I make my way into the stone-walled building. It's another standard run-of-the-mill theater with a neon-lit, triangle sign above the entrance: *Zairna Theater*. Glamorous on its own and yet unimpressive. My name glows below the flaxen billboard.

As I enter the small private lounge, Justin greets me. "How is it out there?" The lounge is nothing more than a box. Four tan walls with random old paintings, a small couch, two matching chairs, and...fuck, it's equivalent to the local grocery store employee break room with a few accents to cater to the high class.

Justin's question is redundant as fuck. The TV hangs in the corner, with live coverage from Entertainment Block. The sound is muted, but he could easily see the crowd. Oh, look...the hot reporter. Mm mm.

What...God, what is that smell? It's like a fucking, an uh, what are they called...those fucking little tree car air fresheners—the black ones. Did someone hang them in the air vents in this place? If it's Justin's cologne, there is no fucking way he's following me around all evening. It could give an Aspirin a headache.

"It's a fucking zoo," I answer regardless, letting my compressed muscles relax as I get used to the strong odor. "These animals ask the most idiotic questions. *What's next Bennett?*" I mock, walking past my polished, nerdy assistant—he's only in that three-kay tux because I bought it for him—grabbing a bottle of water from the mini-fridge. "And then I had to dodge the real ridiculous housewives in the vestibule." I had no idea who they were. Just big tits and deep pockets. I heard the fan girls squealing and waving their smartphones. While I'm sure those women have some skeletons in their closets, they're not my choice in red flags. They don't want to fuck anyway. They want attention and pictures for social media. He brushes it off, knowing how I am.

Justin has known me long enough to become accustomed to my ways. He doesn't expect me to smile or act like a kid on Christmas. Don't get me wrong, I'm happy I'm successful. As much as I can be after suppressing my emotions for...Off topic. The film is fucking perfect. I'm just not that guy...and it's one trait I've had in both of my lives. Reign in your emotions, for without fail someone will take advantage of your joy, sorrow, and weakness for their personal pleasure. Fuck, I'm back to that. You couldn't possibly believe I got this far without some kind of trauma. I may be an asshole, a shitty human, an arrogant prick, but there's always someone worse. In all of your nightmares, there is another that could top it.

His eyes stay on his phone until he opens his mouth again. "Theater is full. Are you ready to head to the stage?"

Before I get a chance to reply, a clatter pulls my attention toward the door, leaving me stuck in motion.

"Bennett!" The pulsing beat of tightly coiled fists pounds on the wooden plank, separating us. Did a gorilla escape from the zoo out there? "Bennett

Michael!" Michael? She completely pulled that out of her ass. I'm pretty sure it's not my middle name. The hammering replays like the repeat button got jammed. "Bennett!"

Ah, fuck.

The voice finally resonates.

Cassie.

I let my eyes roll before looking back at Justin. His uneven teeth are pressed into his thin lower lip. I wouldn't blame him if he was trying to find a hiding place for when that door springs open. It's not going to be pretty. I nod towards him, and he tussles his messy blond curls through his thin fingers, ducking my gaze behind his palm and cell phone.

"Let me in! Tell security now or I'm going out to the reporters!" She creates more noise, which is most likely a struggle between her and security at this point.

I know how to pick them, right?

I sigh, rubbing my hand down my diamond-shaped face. "Simon, it's fine," I call out, returning to the fridge. I set my water bottle on the stubby table, pull a packet of mixed nuts from a basket, open it, and shake the salty mixture into my mouth.

As I turn around, Cassie comes stomping in, full speed, gripping her little tan purse in one hand and the other is balled into a fist. She stops halfway through the room before her words fly like shurikens. Instead of dodging them, I casually tuck a hand in my pocket and listen to her quarrel while I eat my snack.

She has every right. I broke up with her via text message. We never had anything serious, and she knew it would come to an end eventually. The timing seemed right with the premiere of Lost In Nirvana being tonight and my new project starting next week. I'll be moving cities again like I always do.

I'm not a rags-to-riches story. I wasn't born into a life of fame either. Death didn't give me a new attitude toward existence or whatever else those wheels in your head are repetitively trying to comprehend.

See, upon being awakened from my not-so-eternal sleep, I discovered a book I had written two years prior had hit the best sellers list. Pretty sick, I know. I never pursued it as a serious career.

Writing was an unlikely hobby for a twenty-year-old man. Well, as far as my friends were concerned. I wasn't out to brag about it. Telling my parents wouldn't have gotten me anywhere either. Unrealistic career paths had divided us long before I considered publishing.

The thrilling story was titled Red Tape. *If it sounds familiar, it's because it is, and not just to those who enjoy novels, but to the millions who love a good flick. I turned it into a masterpiece on film, grossing more than one hundred and thirty-four million dollars in the first weekend. That's more than Slaughter Squad claimed. It's why I'm moments away from presenting the premiere screening of my second film in three years.*

But Bennett, that's crazy! How is it possible? Not much is impossible for me at this point. Death might not have restored my outlook on life; however, it gave me something I wouldn't have imagined feasible outside my wildest fantasies. All it took was finding the right connections, and well, who fucking needs sleep? They don't. At least that's what I make them believe.

Give me the details, Bennett. You're dying to know more, right? Sure. That's why I'm writing this. To tell my story. Let me deal with this short stack, and then I'll explain further.

"Cassie, take a look around." I wave a hand to the side, and she plainly glances around the room. Give me a break, *blondie.*

Fuck. I didn't want her to physically check out my lounge. Hey, I said I know how to pick them, not that they're rubies and diamonds.

"These are your last minutes of associated fame. You can run your mouth to the press, tell them how bad of a guy I am, and let them take pity on you, but it won't last. They take your picture because of me, and soon they'll forget you because of me. Baby, if you ever had a chance, it would be to do something for yourself right now instead of trying to get even with the man you willingly had a fling with for the clout."

I owe her nothing. I'm doing her a favor by even having this conversation. No...no, no. Hah. Don't start thinking "oh, maybe he's actually a good guy" because darling, I'm not. I can reassure you. I don't want to be the bad guy, but I can't deny who I am. Don't put the blinders on. Wrap the fucking caution tape around me.

Take a hard look at the red fucking flags. Tell that little voice in your head to go night-night. You can't save me. Nobody can.

I finish off my packet and toss it into the trash can next to the fridge, picking up my water to rinse it down.

"You are the biggest asshole I've ever…"

I set my water down, cutting her off. "Fucked…or used?" Turning around, I find her delicate, heart-shaped face. With each step I take toward her, she noticeably stiffens. She's afraid all on her own. This isn't my doing. She walked in here looking for me.

I twirl a strand of her loose, curly auburn hair around my finger until I can't twist it anymore, then drop it. "You don't have to tell me what I am. We both know who we are, Cassie, and I have no problem reciting it to you if you need a refresher…" Another short, airy laugh pushes through my crooked smile. In a brief second, the noise outside of the room disappears, and the silence edges me on. A heaviness dulls my eyes, dragging a straightened scowl across my lips. "Desperate for gratification." My whispers echo between us. Walking around her, I brush her hair off her shoulder with the flick of two fingers. "For stature." I round her shoulder and push my chest against her arm. She wants to move, but she's afraid to look at me. I sink closer. "Borderline egomaniac and too numb to give a fuck." I fist her curls, pulling them back from her neck. She flinches, and I press my lips to her soft jaw. Bringing my mouth to her ear, I continue. "The world turned us into these creatures…but we let it." Tilting my head back, I follow the movement of her tongue. She swipes it across her bottom lip and swallows. In a jagged motion, the gulp moves down her throat. "Now own it." I let go of her hair. "Go get what you want. I don't have time for this shit."

I step back, turning toward the door when she grabs my wrist and pulls me to her body. Now, Cassie, that is not a smart thing to do. I may have referred to us both as creatures, but we're different species. That I'm sure of.

She presses her large chest to my suit.

Hmm, don't do that.

She's very good at teasing and using that body of hers to get the things she wants.

Grabbing my stubble-covered jaw, her brown eyes travel between mine and my mouth.

See what I mean by teasing? When a woman keeps looking at your mouth, you either have food in your teeth, or she wants to show you what you can do with it.

"What if I want you?" A siren's song, the sound so angelic and poisonous.

My signature laugh rises from my chest and rolls through my throat. "Quit acting." I grab her pathetic little arms and pull them from my face, turning away from her and adjusting my tie.

I met Cassie at one a.m. in the twenty-four-hour grocery store in Upland. If her heels weren't a dead giveaway, the amount of single bills she counted out in the potato chip aisle was. I paid for her bag of kettle-cooked salt and vinegar, and we had a little talk in the back of my blacked-out Range Rover. I needed someone to entertain me, and she needed an opportunity. She needed someone that cared. A matted gutter cat hoping I was her Pretty Woman moment.

"How much do you need?"

"Fine. Twenty-five."

Yes, you wanted me so badly that you had a number in mind for that question. Gutter cats know how to eat. "Twenty-five hundred?" My lower lip curls as I nod. "Done." I wave two fingers backward, getting Justin's attention, who has been pretending he couldn't see the production unfolding feet away from him.

To be honest, I forgot he was there for a minute. I got swept up in the cinematic lust between the devilish fuck and his puppet. Maybe I should play myself in the film adaptation of this story.

Justin quickly walks across the room, turns the dial on the mini-safe below the table, and opens it. He hands Cassie a stack of money wrapped in a white and blue band.

The look on her face is the one I mentioned earlier: the kid on Christmas.

"Now, get your shit together, and don't come begging me for more." I walk to the door, open it, and turn back to her. "Oh, and Cassie...make better choices. I'm a one-of-a-kind asshole. Keep pounding on the doors of powerful men and you'll live to regret it."

A few smooth pieces of glass remain beside the jagged shards in my blackened heart. If I could peel them out without killing myself, I would. No matter how far I run from my past, I can't escape her. The single most delicate, divine, beautiful soul that keeps me from turning into the most vile shade of morally black. It complicates my life. I have to tell you about her at some point, but I can't do that right now. The emotional deep dive is best suited on a day when I'm not in front of an audience.

I give Simon a nod, and he silently reads my mind, stepping to the side to keep his eyes on Cassie. Justin joins me, and we walk out the door and down the dim corridor toward the stage. He's lucky...the wicked air freshener wasn't him.

"You just handed her twenty-five hundred dollars," he mutters in disbelief.

"I did."

Photos of talented greatness are spaced along the wall, and I try to avoid looking at them, correcting my wandering eyes.

If you've never experienced imposter syndrome, be glad. It's worse than a greedy whore. Takes everything you worked so hard on and tells you it's shit. Repeatedly. Till you surrender...but violence is always my first choice.

"Do you need twenty-five hundred, Justin?" I don't bother looking back, continuing towards the growing noise.

"I...um..." He stumbles over his words.

I stop, and he damn near runs into me. Slowly turning around, I shake my head. "It's just fucking paper. I'll add it to your paycheck next week. Call it a bonus." His astoundingly wide eyes and frozen lips are enough cues of his appreciation. I find humor in most situations anymore, and that's what I was hoping for. I want to chuckle at the dumb look on his face and at how unpredictable he routinely finds me. Instead, I devour my amusement and turn back toward the stage. I'm in a good fucking mood tonight, handing out green paper like it's candy on Halloween.

I've been broke. I've been dirt poor because of the situations I chose to get into. Back then, it was still only paper for me. It couldn't buy me what I truly wanted.

I'm not handing out payoffs to keep their mouths shut. Between what Justin already makes, plus the fact that he's terrified of me, he wouldn't dare talk to the press.

Justin's only twenty-one, and I hired him right out of high school. Never did he imagine taking a part-time assistant job would be worth a gap year. If he hadn't applied for security and given me a laugh, I might have overlooked him. I'm not the buffest of men, but is he ever scrawny. If I dared to get to know him, I might find out he was bullied in school and took on martial arts, or he could come from an established family, used to getting his way, and I taught him a valuable life lesson. I don't care enough to find out. It's difficult to disobey me.

"Bennett Larson, nice to meet you," a tall graying man with a voice made for announcing MMA fights greets me as I approach the side stage. His firm shake grips my hand. I glance from his gray-bearded face to the burgundy curtain, which is beginning to shift. The crew rushes to get out of the way.

Justin prepped me as usual, and still, I'm terrible with names and can't remember the graying man's for anything. Oh well. I'll work around it. My speech is short and to the point.

Another man, much younger with wide square glasses and an outdated polo shirt, approaches us. "We're set if you are ready, Mr. Larson." He waves a hand toward center stage.

"Born ready," I smirk and take the stage.

Bennett Is A Deadman In An Airport

"Alright," I mutter under my breath.

I'm not convinced you can handle what you're about to be told. If I let you in on this secret, what's stopping you from using it against me? Oh, I know. Nobody will fucking believe you. Don't be a silly little duck and run your quacker.

A hint of ground coffee beans lingers from a shop down the terminal. Another layover in another musky airport on my way to the next shooting location. Pulling my laptop out, I run my fingers over the ridges of the leather case before setting it on the empty seat to my left. The sleek black keys light up, flashing a loading screen.

This team and cast have been in pre-production for three months and two weeks. I expect everything to be filmed and wrapped within the next four months. In reality, what I do is unheard of, and the conspiracy theories are amusing. They're quite imaginative, but few over the many. Most viewers are too excited and fanning over the cast to consider all the behind-the-scenes marks.

If you haven't heard of the open chat forum called Runner, they're essentially conspiracy theorists all jammed in one troll-worthy internet black hole. I baited them once with everything from extraterrestrial to government asset of distraction. Focus Magazine wrote a piece earlier this year claiming sources admitted to being threatened to work outrageous hours to meet my deadlines. "Sources." No. That's bullshit. I've never left a brain unwashed or a witness to tell a tale.

Truthfully, they're the first to hit the nail on the head. My expectations are high. Sue me. As I said, most viewers ignore the cause for caution. After all, their new celebrity crushes aren't speaking ill of Mr. Larson.

Most people know nothing of the making of a movie or their favorite TV series. From sound to lighting, to—darling, there's a fucking food stylist, and every single job ties into an artistic design that you ignore while drooling over Johnny Cakes and his juicy...lips. Did you fall for him because of his looks or his lines? The lines invisible people like me wrote for him?

Bennett, you're so bitter. That's jealousy at its finest. I know, darling, and it doesn't change anything. Johnny Cakes does his job like the rest of us. He works hard to turn a paper person into a comfort character that I'm guilty of hiding within under the covers on a rainy fall afternoon. I'm simply connecting all the dots for you and why people tag my name next to the stars in my movies. I gave them a reason to. If conspiracy theories helped, I'm from that generation who casually spent Friday nights catfishing strangers for an hour of trolling entertainment, shit-talked grown men off of Xbox Live, and head-banged to metal music seconds before I had a sudden voice change to tell a customer I'm sorry for the wait—AKA I'm a trained troller.

Am I rambling? Shit, anything to avoid a deep dive into my past. I need to write. Write, write. Do not judge my fucking audience in a four-hundred-page letter. I don't give a fuck if I'm exhausted. I'll sleep when I'm six feet deep. I'll never know when I'm about to take a permanent nap.

While the watching world is amusing, their expectations are as unrealistic as mine. They expect me to come out with the next great story — a great plot, well-developed characters, and some sort of bullshit message of beauty in a world that is clearly on fire. I shall repeat, I am not the worst evil in the world. They wear suits just the same, with clean-shaven faces and kind promises. Sorry, was that too depressing? Speaking on how the problem is our own fault, as a whole. Darling, darling, darling — You let them into office. They're not as clean-cut as they appear.

Many are quite sick. Now you're starting to believe my kind of justice is acceptable, right? You don't know me that well yet.

I'm not in this for the rapid releases and quick payday, even if it appears that way. This, though, this story...it's not any story. It's my life and death...and life again. You're viewing my greatest work of fiction. Something so unbelievably true that it has to be fiction, right? Right.

Now, where should I start? Not from the beginning. I said the beginning, but nobody gives a fuck what I weighed when I was born, except women who've birthed or are close to it. That's a visual. Ah...I got it.

With that nugget of gold, I begin typing.

I'm alive, but I was dead once...or twice. It all started with a girl. The girl.

Two years ago in the month of September, my twenty-fourth birthday came and went. Caleb, my sister's widow, visited from Chicago for a week. Yes, my sister's widow. Anna. The girl.

Of course, you thought it was a girlfriend I was head over heels for. I'll continue to surprise you. Anna passed away two years earlier. It was my second birthday without her, but I didn't know it would be the last birthday I'd spend with anyone I called family.

To explain Anna with one word: lighthouse. My guide when all was dark and bleak. She said Annie and Benny were a dynamic duo. She was right on some level. When we were kids, we got into all kinds of trouble. We'd go for nature walks without telling anyone and show up three hours later covered in dirt, traipsing through the house as Mom and Dad panicked from the kitchen. Then we got a little older, pocketed dollar candy from the gas station and Mom would drag us back in to return it. Annie always managed to get us out of it. Everyone loved the outgoing, charismatic, beautiful doll she was. I did too. I just wasn't like her in that way. I was quiet, reserved, and fine with being her wingman.

In junior high, I tagged along countless times on Annie's dates, being the awkward third wheel. She didn't invite me because she felt bad that it was a Friday night and I didn't have plans. She invited me to be her bodyguard. It's not like she was ever truly alone with them, hanging at Cool Cove. It was basically a supervised game room and pizzeria for the local tweens and teens to hang out at.

High school changed a lot. I wasn't as content as I once was. It was difficult living in her shadow and being "the other Larson." The invisible one. The dirt bag. The kid with the terrible music, unfortunate black wardrobe, and ungrateful attitude.

When I dream, I see the sparkle in her golden brown eyes. Her big, wide smile and the freckles that she managed to inherit, and I didn't. She inherited more than just them, unfortunately. The year before I was born, Annie was diagnosed with cystic fibrosis. It's a pretty rare inherited disorder that fucks with the lungs and digestive system. I'm not an expert. I just know that with her treatment plan, she had hardly any flare-ups. None of us saw it coming. She got sick, and then the infection...got worse.

Let me guess, you assumed it was a car accident? How else would a beautiful, positive, young woman leave this existence prematurely? Some of us are born fucked.

Bennett, I can understand why you're so bitter. That's tough.

Darling, I'm not bitter. I'm better.

This is part of my past that you have to know to understand my life. It doesn't define me. I'm not an asshole because I'm mad at the world or a deity. I'm an asshole because I choose to be.

Would Annie approve of who I've become?

Annie wouldn't forgive the things I've done.

It's been over seven years and...it's going to be the biggest bitch to write about her.

Shit. I don't want to do this.

I delete the second half of the sentence.

The day Annie left, all hope dissipated from my soul. That was the first time I died.

It's taken every ounce of my being to keep living without her. I'll never understand why I got a second chance and she didn't.

She deserved it. She graduated high school with honors a year early. Then she got her associate's in accounting and started working for a local non-profit; Acer Service Animals. To this day, her picture hangs on their wall.

I walked around with my head hanging. Restless nights were a permanent feature on my face. In addition to a split lip from dehydration, my eyes had dark circles and exaggerated creases. Like the plague that consumed my mind, I avoided the mirror. The only thing I could do was write, troll live stream gamers, and smoke.

Annie had this effect on everyone...like—

Fuck. How do I...No. Scrap that.

Annie was a saint, starting with all her volunteer work. She opened countless lemonade stands to raise money for the low-income student meal program. I don't know how we're related. Neither do you, I can tell.

Now, Caleb. He was always around waiting for an opportunity to escape the friend zone. He's what you'd call the good guy. He accepted our relationship instead of trying to push me out of frame. Then Caleb proposed to Annie on her twenty-first birthday. Mom and Dad couldn't have been more ecstatic. I mean, the child who they feared would have a strenuous life was made of sunshine, had more friends than they could remember their names, and they were going to get to walk her down the aisle.

I sound jealous. Hah. I wasn't. Never was.

She deserved happiness. If I could wish for that for anyone in the world, it would be her every time.

Every fucking time.

At their reception, Annie gave me the second dance of the night. Life lesson: if you have a bond as deep as the Earth's core, don't take it for granted. That's not a saying. Cherish every fucking day because when they die, you die, and it's a nightmare walking around like a zombie trying to reclaim a life without them.

When Caleb came to see me the week after my birthday—exactly forty-nine weeks before I died, and don't ask me how I remember that—we talked about that moment. That special dance. It was fucking hilarious. Hell—my black skinny jeans weren't made for stretching.

Annie and I, mostly Annie, made up choreography and practiced it for a month. I was committed to her. Every time I hear the Friends theme song, it takes me back. I'm not a performer, if I must remind you. Now picture my nineteen-year-old emo fit, wild bangs, and less muscle than I have now, next to a Barbie doll. Essentially, a pasty, dark-haired twig, trying to do this cringy choreographed dance in front of a room full of people.

That was close to a decade ago, thankfully, and not in times when every dance is recorded and blasted on social media apps. It's easy to bury a past that barely existed to begin with. Don't believe them when they say the internet is forever. I couldn't find the evidence if I talked this generation's brilliant hackers into scouring the fluorescent clouds.

Back to Friends. Annie was obsessed with that show, to say the least. I always humored her stupid obsession, and in return, she stayed up late with me, yelling into my headset at other gamers. The sweetest fucking insults, too. A smile crosses my face just thinking about it. I can hear her yelling, "Cheap shot, Shifter!" It was always a cheap shot, and it was always Shifter. She had no idea, but she'd yell it into my mic with confidence.

Pure sunshine. Fuck, I miss my best friend. I miss talking about everything and nothing with her. I knew this was going to suck. It's been years. Get a grip.

No, don't do that.

Yes, you. Yes, that. Pity.

I'm not mad I missed my twenty-fifth birthday, or that nobody bothered to question when I didn't respond to their Facebook posts and the few text messages I probably got. When you don't communicate with your family and refuse to respond to them when they reach out, years go by, and they tend not to want to put the effort forward either. Caleb reached that point. He knew how close I was with Annie, and he tried to help me. He wanted to be a stand-in and do right by her. I wouldn't let him. Perhaps a part of me was always an asshole...or self-isolation was my Band-Aid. The past can't break your heart if you pretend it never happened and you won't ever feel that agony again if you put an end to meaningful relationships.

I should probably tell the reader how I died—how "Beckett" died. I'm two chapters in. Fuck that. It's too simple. Let them be consumed with questions, confused, and frustrated. They already know he's dead...undead. That's the most important take at this point. I have more I want them to know first about his/my history. It'll work.

I was twenty-four when I died. My death went unnoticed, and after not paying my phone bill for sixteen months, they shut it off. Lying in the empty woods for over a year, I expected to be a rotted and unrecognizable corpse. I wasn't, if you're falling behind again. I was perfectly preserved. Weirder things have happened — the government admitted aliens exist, you can have live cockroaches shipped to your house over the internet or to an enemy's house now, and have you seen that TV series that's dedicated to bizarre obsessions? The judgemental part of me shouted, "That's fucked up." Meanwhile, another side kept watching instead of changing the damn channel. Some of those people would give me a run for my money in the "what the fuck" department and maybe that's why I tuned in—a sense of normalcy.

Something happened to me that's unheard of. I opened my eyes and...

The first person I called when I got a new phone was Annie. Yes, I called the dead girl before anyone else. I was trying to wrap my head around what had happened. The date was everywhere. I wasn't twenty-four anymore. I wasn't twenty-five. Missing over a year of my life, I chose to call the dead girl that I miraculously didn't run into in the afterlife. That's also bullshit.

Bennett, you're skipping steps. Shh. It's all very complex.

Note to self: Use "find and replace" to change all the Bennetts to Beckett when I self-edit. Double-check before sending it to my editor or risk being questioned.

It's not crazy that she was the first and only number I dialed. Our parents kept her number active to hear her voicemail. Yeah, we do stupid things like pay for a phone line not used to hear someone's voice. Grief is complicated. I needed to listen to her voice more than ever that day. I was lost, confused, and everything seemed fucked. It was fucked. Was anyone looking for me? Would anyone notice my sudden reappearance? Did I lose my apartment? What the fuck! I died! I was fucking dead! How am I breathing? How is any of this possible?

Annie was, and will always be, my voice of reason. Without that single call, I would have stood in the street until someone ran me over...or shipped me off to a mental institution.

It would be amusing to add a recap. No. The reader should get it.

Fuck it. I want it to be true to me. This isn't Red Tape or Lost In Nirvana. It's meant to be different. I'll get some hate for it, but I'd be pissed if I didn't push and poke the reader around a little more.

Recap: I was a quiet kid living in the shadow of my sick older sister, who was my best friend. She died. I stopped living. Then I died, too. And those of you that skimmed a few pages or some shit...I came back to fucking life. Are we good? Let's keep going, and if you skimmed a page, knock it off.

I glance up from my screen and look around the airport. Where do I go from here? I should've made an outline.

The unsettling mixture of rage and pain spirals in pieces as I search my mind for the details of the night that I was given a second chance. Flashes of trees, that first step onto the onyx asphalt, and the putrid scent I'd pray to forget.

My mental death was enough to hold a barrel between my eyes. My physical death was quicker. The pain came when I opened my eyes. An overwhelming mental meltdown accompanied by an indescribable ache and excruciating emptiness. Now you know why I hate waking up in the woods. It's not fun, sunshine. I've done it a few times. It's become easier. The less time I'm down, the quicker I recover.

Yes, I've woken from the ground more than once. I can't confirm my heart stopped. Don't ask me how it happens. I'm not the bird brain who...

I glance up from my screen, catching a glimpse of a woman in my direction. Her beauty calls me back, and I forget my sentence. Blonde pigtails, high on each side of her head, draw me in. She's my dirty schoolgirl fantasy. The generic one that every man wants at least once in their life. She would be delicious in a plaid miniskirt—such an innocent and petite figure. Fuck, that sounds pedo-y. This is definitely a full-grown woman, likely in her mid-twenties.

Her charcoal yoga pants flare wide at the bottom, fitting through her thighs and hugging her hips. Oh, wait. She's giving me modern seventies, dirty hippy vibes. I'm into it. Add a few braids, and I can see her inhaling a shotgun kiss and then preaching something about making love, not war. Would she let me take her to the Buclin Hotel and blow her mind? It's not more than five minutes away and beats sitting here the entire layover. Any excuse not to write.

Oh, hell. Not those bizarre chunky white sneakers that all the basic influencers snap photos with. No dirty reference there. Pass. Hard pass. She's a princess. She's a diva. She's the *it girl*. She doesn't deserve me.

A thin pink button-down sweater cuts off right at the waist of her pants and scoops low enough that a small amount of fabric from her beige bra peeks out. Breasts are breasts. I don't care if they're on the smaller side or if they were three times it. I'm interested again. She's sexy. Buclin's it is. I'll throw the shoes out the window when she takes them off. Bon voyage, buttercup.

Oh, look at her...walking toward me. I bet she knows who I am. Of course she does. She's dying to sit next to me.

The pigtail princess crosses her legs and pulls an older smartphone from her pocket. A phone that's three years old and a seat that's three away. She's introverted. I don't blame her.

Wasting little time, I make my move. "Hello." I'm Bennett, as you already know. The man whore of your dreams.

Shut up...

Yes, you. I didn't ask for your opinion.

What is she doing? Hello?

Her eyes finally meet mine as she pulls her earbuds out. "Oh, hi. Sorry, I had my headphones in." She holds the pink pieces in her flattened palm.

Okay, schoolgirl. Play coy.

"What are you listening to?" I don't care.

"An audiobook. What are you, um, typing?" She points at my dimming screen.

I close my laptop and confidently smile. "Words...for a book."

"A reader and a writer. What a pair to meet in an airport terminal in the wee hours of the morning." Her pink lips pull wide. "Are you on a layover as well? I guess that's a brainless question. Why else would you be sitting here?"

She has this cute aspect to her. Almost pure. With high, rosy cheekbones and a full lower lip, I can foresee being sucked into my mouth, yet the subtle brightness that beams from her is going to be what I enjoy the most. The moon swallows the sun. Her sunshine will vanish beneath me when I'm fucking her senseless.

Why am I like this? My favorite person in the world was a sunshine sweetheart. I should respect the speckle of shared congeniality. Call it a trauma response? I don't know. I'm sure you'll come up with an excuse. I know you didn't listen to my warning. You won't stop wanting to save me.

"Yeah. I like the hair," I say, pointing to my messy fringe.

"Thanks! I tried the brunette thing a few months ago, but blondes have more fun. Oh, or did you mean the pigtails?" She laughs.

It's cute. A little high-pitched, but it feels as petite as her. If she tells me she has daddy issues, she's mine.

I read a book on neurobiology and hereditary influence on sexual kinks a year ago. They have no fucking clue why people like me are into hunting my fuckable prey. It wasn't inherited or from childhood trauma. Shit, backtrack. Yes, I'm giving you the dirty insights into how my brain works when it comes to sex. You want to know my story, right? This is a part of it.

Damn it, why do I keep trying to justify myself. It's coming off desperate.

All species are designed to procreate. Some bite the heads off their mate after they finish the deed. We could talk about that instead of human desires are a taboo subject.

"I'm betting you could have green hair and have fun," I flirt.

I admit, it's a cheesy line. I don't care. It keeps her attention, and it's forward enough that she knows I'm interested, while not overly assertive. Look, I know you're judging me and I keep reminding you to open your fucking mind. However, if you can't tell by now...I. Don't. Fucking. Care. I don't. If you think I'm a disgrace, then you're simply not giving a dime about my life. I can't have that. I've been there. Everyone has this compartment in their think space that contains the most or the least bit of curiosity, hoping they'll catch some of the local gossip while they're at the gas pump. Think of me as the bored cashier.

O.M.G. Did you hear about Bennett Larson? You've heard of him, right? Hold on, let me spit out my double bubble gum. Anyway, he left the airport with a woman and two days later she was reported missing.

Psych, I'm playing.

A single man my age has sex on the brain at least an average of sixteen times a day. Shit, any man of any age and any status has thoughts of getting off. If you can't handle it, skip ahead, but I bet you're wondering where this might go next, huh? Did you skim the trigger warnings too? Actually, no. I'm putting an end to this now. I've given you plenty of time to back out, to walk away from this story, and to cry on the internet about how it sucks booty hole. I'm done pressuring you to run away so I can chase you.

I'm kidding. Chill. I'll move on to my next paragraph before I open an app to check to see if you're talking shit on me. All press is good press for a man of my ability.

"That might be true," she agrees with my bold color choices. "But I wouldn't book many gigs with that look."

Huh. Gigs?

"Are you a model?"

"Oh, no." She giggles. "Not a model. I'm an actor. If the industry was based solely on talent, I could present with a rainbow rat tail."

"Interesting. You're that exceptional?"

"I'm confident in my ability."

I pause for a brief moment, running my pointer down one side of my jaw. "Do you know who I am?" She can cut the demure, bubbly act. She knows exactly who she's trying to fool. If she wants a job, all she has to do is ask. I'll float her as an extra. *Solely based on her looks.*

"A handsome man alone in the airport waiting for his flight," she flirts.

Uh. What? Is she...She's quite believable. I *should* hire her.

"Okay, you're good." I smile stingingly, pointing in her direction. Her expression doesn't change in the slightest.

"What's your name?" She asks.

My smile abruptly fades.

She doesn't know who I am. What the fuck is wrong with her? I call bullshit. She's committed to this bit.

"You really don't know?" Wrinkles cover my forehead, morphing me into a perplexed Pug. Those fucking ugly little things. Hell, what is she doing to me? A foolish woman. I don't believe it. She's got to be fucking with my head. This is, uh, she's joking...the...it's a joke. I'm Bennett fucking Larson. She can't tell me that a black hoodie and a pair of washed-out jeans make me less recognizable. I'm emailing someone tonight to get me more media coverage.

"Should I?"

Still simpering and innocent. Dumb blonde. How the hell does she not know who I am? Forget it. Fucking...forget it.

I relax my jaw, shuffling from the balls of my feet as I stretch my arms behind my head. "Unless you've been dead for the last three years, yes, you should. Especially as someone who calls themselves an actor."

"Nope." Her lips roll inward, tightening. "Been very much alive the last three years. Unfortunately, I don't know all the entitled men in this business yet."

My laugh rolls out thick. It's the opposite of her cute ditzy giggles. A brunt, harsh chuckle straight from the throat, scoffing at her remark.

"Well…" I flip open my bag, slip my laptop back inside, and stand. Wasting another minute here explaining to her why she should know who I am is not on my agenda. I shouldn't have said a word to her. If my dick didn't override every ounce of intelligence, it would be easier to avoid these distractions. "Good luck to you, Miss?"

"Cherry. Cherry Kaas. And apparently, the pleasure was all mine."

I look back at her, exhaling a stifled chuckle through my nose in more of an annoyance than actual amusement. Smiling with the same tight emotion, I walk down the terminal.

Cherry Kaas, of all names to choose for an alias. I shouldn't have left. I should have asked—no, demanded she leave. Judging by her last remark, she would have protested.

I'm too fucking tired. I want to pretend like I didn't set another reckless deadline to stress over and find a cute businesswoman on a layover—not another wildly confident artist—to ease the tension. Fuck my editor's timeline.

The coffee shop is both the perfect place to write and the perfect place to pick up that woman who isn't an irrelevant actor. The smell of freshly ground coffee beans heightens the closer I get to the shop. It's one of those scents that puts warmth in the pit of my stomach all the way to the empty cavity in my chest, taking me back to yesterday. You know, one of those scents that automatically places stupid, grin-worthy memories in your think space. Yeah, I have a few of those left. I imagine you made that assumption with Annie.

Aside from my sister, sometimes the reminiscence of my old life manages to whisper sweet nothings throughout my skull like now. That smell reminds me of my mom. Annie and Mom shared features and I imagine she'd look similar if she made it to her fifties. As for my Mom, she may have worked in corporate America, but she had a creative side. I'll pretend that's where my artistic penmanship originated.

When I was six or seven, we would go to a pottery studio next to her favorite mom-and-pop coffee shop, Barley's Brews. Oh shit, there's a crack in the glass wall. I recalled something from my childhood. Huh. *If we behaved at church, she would reward us with a treat. We always fucking behaved. The incentive wasn't necessary. Their homemade toaster pastries were a thousand times better than the cardboard you could buy in the grocery store.*

Want to know something humorous? My lifespan is unknown, but there is a possibility I could live forever, yet I refuse to consume the toxic shitstorm products this country allows to be placed on the shelves of our grocery outlets. I suppose it's the rebellious state of mind that holds me to it when it would be too easy to grab a microwavable meal.

Oh, Bennett, that's hilarious.

Contain your fake laughter.

I could go for one of their triple-berry pastries. The deep pink frosting derived from raspberries is...fuck, amazing. I could crave one for the next six years and wouldn't go back there. My parents have outlived both their children.

I walk up to the woman at the counter, meeting her caffeine-fueled smile. She snorts it for breakfast, lunch, and dinner. Working night owl hours with a free supply of mood-boosting *fuck yeah*? Of course she's on the hot beans. The young woman is pretty, but a waste of time.

Life lesson: Never flirt with the employees unless you have time to wait for their shift to end.

"Hi, what can I get for you?" Her accent is smooth and slightly guttural at the same time.

"Americano, two shots."

She nods, pressing her yellow-painted fingertip to the images on her touch screen. With a short glance, she turns and begins preparing my order. I scan the room, identifying a couple sitting nearest to me, and farther away are two women—my guess is in their early twenties—sitting along the front of the shop.

That's the thing about coffee shops. Yeah, you might find your early twenty-something hipsters, but you also find the mom group, escaping their kids for a morning, and the elderly couple, enjoying an afternoon pick-me-up. However, the majority of coffee consumers who are willing to spend the extra money at a shop are well-employed women. A single woman passing through an airport on a business trip, perhaps. You catch my drift?

"Here you are, sir." I glance down to see a smiley face drawn in fine black marker on the front of the compostable paper cup. The doodle above the brown textured band must be her go-to for nameless orders. It's not personal.

"Keep the change." I hand her a twenty and take my coffee from the convenience of a white quartz countertop. She smiles and gives me a once-over as I walk away.

I'm well dressed, wearing a tailored suit, and I take care of myself, but if you're picturing a businessman that low-key slings an ax around the woods twice a week, you are mistaken. I don't chop wood. I work out max three days a week, mostly to maintain my lean muscle mass. Contact sports aren't for me. I spent all my free time gaming before, well, you know. You won't catch me going on a hike for fun. A hunt? Perhaps.

Women are attracted to confidence, to the way a man holds himself, not the label making his ass crevasse itch. Cut the tag. Don't be a cat running from a cucumber.

Examining the shopfront again, a woman with porcelain skin and onyx hair sits in the corner with a phone in her hand looking gothic chic in an all-black high-neck blouse with some sort of lacy overlay and sheer sleeve. A circular face with pronounced round cheekbones, deep red lipstick transfers to her white paper cup as she takes a sip. Colorful tattoos sleeve one arm, and I easily can pick one out through the material to win her over by knowing its significance.

Most people recognize an infinity sign. My guess is a sibling or friend has a matching design. My entire left arm is a mural inspired by Annie—not that I'd ever tell a woman that: consent, short arrangements, and distance.

Wait. *Short arrangements* sound like a get-in and get-out ordeal. Wouldn't it be nice if I was an a-typical douchebag who doesn't thrive on watching a woman unfold in excessive pleasure?

Mental note: Pick a false name for Annie and auto-replace all mentions in the manuscript. April? Addy? Eh, I'll come back to it.

She sees me. Hello, darling.

Ready, On-Set, &
Bennett Says Go

"Where is my Samantha?" I shout in the crowded room, looking for someone with an ounce of fucking intelligence in this place as I rub the stubble along my chin. Half of them are grazing the continental breakfast spread. The camera crew, lighting department, and every other person I need are here, yet the leading actor is missing...on the first day of shooting.

I made it through a rocky flight and settled into my good old trailer in time for one night of uninterrupted sleep before joining the production for Sold Secrets.

Ames Heart is in a makeup chair. The dreamy blond spent a solid half hour flirting with what's her face from the AD department. Hope he nails the role as easily as he nails women. So where the fuck is this woman that's supposed to give me the performance of her career?

Life lesson: There is reward in being impatient.

Bennett, you contradicting ass. You said patience is a virtue.

Don't get smart with me. Life requires a balance. I'm teaching you a lot. I should be charging more. I won't sign your paperback copy, although I'm sure Justin would be giddy. Speaking of Justin, where is he?

"She's on her way. I just spoke with her," Justin replies, rushing over to me with his headset on one ear and tablet in hand.

He's panicking, thinking I'm going to lose my fucking marbles on him. It's honestly an insult to his intelligence. He knows better. You've heard of the saying "work smarter not harder", correct? I'll save my energy for demanding more from 'underpaid' artists.

"Why is she fucking late?" I grumble, rubbing my brow bone.

Let's talk production. Typically, one would have a casting director handle the talent. I micromanaged every aspect of both Red Tape and Lost In Nirvana. For this film, I've lengthened the rope. I didn't have a choice if I wanted to finish it within the year.

Mel takes care of everything pre-production. She assigns whoever has to be assigned to whatever. Without her, I wouldn't have made it this far. I admit, the amount of shit that goes into making a movie is insane, as is the amount of people who work on my projects. I couldn't tell you ninety percent of their names.

In toxic Hollywood, Melinda Wright wouldn't let me down. She's one of the few that I conducted a deep dive on before giving her a permanent position. Mel keeps her personal shit away from work and knows how to keep Fifteen Film—fifteen months I was dead—free of scandal. She personally confirmed the casting director and team that would make my vision a reality. After all, this story revolves around the pretentiously secretive underworld princess who's expected to hold the high standards of her wealthy family.

I hate not controlling every meticulous moving part. I haven't stopped in the last three years. Maintaining such a high momentum will ultimately break the camel's back, and I don't want to settle for mediocre.

Why do I throw myself into the art like a psychotic horse with blinders on? Well, what else do I live for? I'm determined to attach my name to impactful films and moving stories. The next time I die, everyone will know and either mourn or celebrate.

I already said it; it's not about fame or money. It's about finally expressing who I am to a world that never noticed before. "Oh, Bennett needs our approval. He's a self-loathing pussy." Hey, I never wanted any of this. I only wanted someone to see me like Annie did. You can hold the confidence of the greatest God, and you'll continuously seek the joy of someone who shares your beliefs and passions and cares about the words you have to speak. You will always want to connect. Whether it's a human, God, or undead mystery, being alone is fucking depleting, despite introversion.

The audible breath fills my head like a mental sigh.

This is all I have left to do.

How did I die, though? That's the big question.

Give me a moment to breathe. If you can't tell, I'm a little stressed the fuck out.

*Some would say I was at the wrong place at the wrong time. I must argue; I was at the right place at the right time. You don't see anyone else coming back to life months after their death, now do you? I doubt you would want to either. A zombie apocalypse would mark the end of the modern-day world. You wouldn't see electric car charging station drama anymore. Oh, they'll keep posting on...*what's that video app? Uh...*Knack. With less of the dramatics and more...*uh, shit. The movie with the masks, where no laws exist for twenty-four hours...Damn it. Whatever.

I tap the backspace bar, deleting the sentence.

My childhood was...

No. Delete.

Most of my childhood is a blur. I blacked it out. In my early teens, my relationship with my parents became strained. I guess most of my old life is behind a smoke screen.

Fuck. How am I going to write this? I can't remember...When did it start? Before I was born? When I became the ugly duck, the black sheep, the weird kid in what should be the million-dollar family? When did that happen? Was I fifteen or twelve or eight? Was it when Annie wasn't doing well? Was it when she was okay again? Was it real or was it in my head? Did I force myself out, or did they overlook my silent suffering?

I started working when I was sixteen at an electronics store called Brite Techs, making enough by the time I graduated high school to afford a small apartment in a not-so-amazing neighborhood. I didn't care. It was perfect. I moved out of my parent's house the day I turned eighteen. I didn't plan on going to college, and we fought about it every time I saw them.

That was clear.

Some kids have disagreements with their parents about financial choices. Try community college for a year or two and then transfer. Mine didn't see cost as a deal breaker. They would have made an Ivy League feasible, and a community college would be just as acceptable. At the very least, go to a trade school. Not going to college wasn't encouraged. They refused to accept that I wasn't going to conform. The day I signed the lease, 'fuck you' was written on the walls. I wasn't going to let them control me with the 'as long as you live under this roof' speech.

If I dug really deep, I'd find that it was more than a single disagreement that pushed me to exit when I did. They created a gulf between their exceptional Annie and her unremarkable brother.

Most days, I worked until six, then went home to my shitty apartment and played Xbox Live with my small group of friends. Kenny came over every Friday, and we got shit-faced, yelled at newbs playing Call of Duty, and by midnight he would have whichever girl he was texting come over, occasionally with a friend who I would awkwardly entertain. Is that game still popular? I'd suck at it now.

Anyway, I saw more of his ass than I want to remember, but I learned one thing from him that didn't connect till I—uh traveled? Yeah—*traveled into this life. Why settle for one woman when you can have a new one each week?*

Bennett, you whore.

Look, I'm not forcing anyone to do anything they don't want to. Alright, I may convince people to do things they don't want to do when it comes to my ideal timeline. You don't believe me. Good. You're finally listening.

Kenny was the closest person I had after Annie. Mike and Carter—my high school friends—found their own means to escape misery. Oh shit, that sounds like they jumped off a bridge into a shallow body of water. *Mike went to a prestigious college out of state, and Carter joined the armed forces.*

Eventually, Kenny shitted on his own advice and settled—and fuck, was she a bitch. Ava Uttler was spoiled by daddy's money and influenced by mommy's high expectations. What she ever saw in my dirtbag friend, I'll never know. It's not like he was the best-looking guy or had the biggest dick—again more than I wanted to see. Kenny was tall and thin with black round glasses matching his short hair, wore shorts all year round, and flannel shirts. He had game. That was it. He always knew the right words to say.

That's the second thing he inadvertently taught me. Attitude and words could wrap the most beautiful woman around your arm. I haven't seen him in years. Last I heard, he was moving to Arizona. I guarantee he's changing diapers and is three years in debt.

After working at Brite Techs for four years, I decided to give online college a chance and attempt my associate's in web development. I know, why didn't I do that shit from the get-go? Stupid black sheep. That's all I can say.

I wanted to make more money and realized it's not going to happen at a dead-end job. Maybe the online classes wouldn't be too bad, and I could keep working. I had to do something. While it was once the perfect escape, after two years I fucking hated my apartment. Every other day it was door pounding, dogs barking, and kids screaming. It was to the point where being at work was more relaxing than being at home. That was all just from the apartment above me.

Angela Meedy couldn't have been much older than me. Her smile was comforting on the occasion I'd catch it warming her face. Most mornings in passing, exhaustion deepened her under eyes as she made her way down the steps as if it were a race, collecting gold stars—AKA fallen kid's toys, she scooped up without the bat of a lash.

She rarely greeted me, too focused on her own hustle. Angela wasn't a horrible woman, but her baby daddy was high all day and, for a lack of verbiage, useless. The only time that piece of trash did anything was when he was in the alley selling. What the fuck was his name? Maxwell wasn't stereotypical. He was a clean-shaven, polo-wearing, professional nothing. You would think I'd stop judging books by their covers. It would be more enjoyable to say it's in the programming of the world instead of crediting my lack of self-growth. It's the truth, darling—pretty privilege.

The fuck boys in 2B would crank up the bass on their sound system at two in the morning, and that alone would start a war between them and 2A. The 2B covers matched their label. Can you smell their apartment?

Apart from my endearing neighbors, the building was piss-poor and run down with terrible water pressure and a lackluster owner who solely focused on collecting his payments. It's not like any of this was new. It was the reason my parents tried to talk me out of moving here. I would never have listened to them. Whether they were right about the apartment, college, or the direction my life was heading didn't matter. They made me feel...less than, and I was either going to be exactly that out of spite, or I was going to do bigger things to shove it in their faces.

School went better than I expected. I graduated and secured a job with Morgan Advertising six months later. That's when my life got majorly fucked.

I skipped too much. Fuck it. I'll detail it in my first round of self-edits.

When it happened, I had all but moved the last two boxes into my storage unit. I'm not sure why or how I vividly recall the events that preceded it. It replays in my head in high definition.

I opened the cardboard box in my trunk, setting the last item on top. The gold frame held a picture of Annie and me from the summer before she got sick. Adjusting the tape, I closed the box again and pulled the hatch down on my eighty-nine red Mazda 323 Hatchback. Can't say I miss that old shitbox.

That's when I heard the yelling in the alley beside the apartment complex. It was more like pleading, begging, followed by arguing, and that last grunted "shut up" before the silence. From my parked car, I could see directly down the dim passage. I tried to ignore it, but as they got louder, I let my eyes wander. Three figures stood for a moment, then one dropped to the ground with the curdling sound of a gunshot. It had to be a drug deal gone wrong. Someone couldn't pay up. It's not the first time it's happened. I told you, mankind is what you should fear the most. Between the war on drugs and the addiction pandemic, everyone knows someone. It was around nine. Standing under the streetlight, I've become a sitting duck. A foolish one.

I should have hidden behind the car or ran—anything other than standing there at the trunk of my car, blankly staring down the alley—but I fucking did, like a deer caught in the headlights, too stupid to move. Benny was a weak little bitch. He let the fear of living be his demise.

Anyway, they shot me. The end.

Jokes. Calm down. I'm a funny guy.

I dropped dead on the pothole-covered asphalt in a puddle of blood. What happened next? I can only assume they threw me in the trunk of a car, probably my own. I can't say I've seen it since that day. Then, they dumped my body in the woods behind the old nuclear waste plant off Shrewsbury. That's where I woke up. It smelled fucking amazing, might I add. The first few days were a little uneasy.

I close my notebook and stand from my chair, heading toward the water cooler.

"Sorry, I'm late everyone!" My Samantha greets us. She hustles from the entrance, pulling her crossover purse from her arm. "I had to stop and help a turtle across the road, but the thing was massive and it kept trying to bite me. I shouldn't have ran to town this morning." She exhales, out of breath. "I'm here now, I'm ready. Where do you want me?" She exhales.

"You were supposed to be there. God leads..." A big mouth amongst the crew excuses her absence as I finally turn from the water cooler to get a look at the diva preaching *save the turtles.*

Mother Francis. I almost drop my tumbler, catching it as it slides through my fingers. She throws her straight blonde hair over her right shoulder and places her hands on her hips. I close my eyes, clenching my jaw.

It's the schoolgirl. You've got to be kidding me. From the look on her face, she's not thrilled to see me either.

You already anticipated this not-so-meet-cute coming. That's the story of how I met my final demise, ladies and gents. The woman you caught a glimpse of in the woods? Yep, that's her. The Cherry bomb destined to blow my life up.

"Hello, Cherry. Do you know who I am now?" I ask as she walks over to me. For someone terrible with names, hers stuck. It has a ring to it in the same way a cheesy radio jingle does.

"Bennett Larson I presume. You're everything I've heard you to be." Small dimples appear at the ends of her tightly drawn lips as she reaches for a cup. She has a nose ring? How did I miss that before? She didn't have that little hoop in it at the airport. I would have noticed it.

I lean back against the counter, crossing my arms over my chest. "Where did you come up with Cherry, uh, what was it?" I snap my fingers.

I strike a chord as she nearly breaks her neck, turning back to me with lightning speed. Her eyebrows furrow, revealing a look of pure disgust painted across her face. "Cherry Kaas is not a made-up name, Mr. Larson. It was given to me at birth and I happen to like it."

"Seriously?" I drop my hands to my sides, standing upright and trying not to laugh. "Was your mother a stripper? No, a parlor temptress. She tied the stems into knots with her tongue."

Her jaw drops, and she flicks her tongue to the corner of her mouth, pressing it to her teeth. "That's not very professional, *Mr. Larson*." She overly pronounces my name, digging her point in further. "I apologized for my tardiness. If we could move past our indiscretions for the remainder of our time working together, that would benefit both of us."

"Fine. Professional. Are you planning on taking that thing out of your nose for filming?"

"I have no problem removing it. You should get on the same page as the rest of your team because this was all discussed months ago." She places a lid on her cup, whipping her hair over her shoulder as she walks away.

Wonderful. I get to spend the next four months with little Miss Sunshine and her snarky mouth.

She better not show up late again. Fuck the turtles.

Cherry Lips And Lies

It's impossible to hide flaws under this heavy lighting...and feeling insecure is not an option, especially when it comes to this character. Samantha was born into wealth and power. Portraying that of a perfect life comes to her as naturally as breathing. Luckily for me, or unlucky depending on how one looks at it, I live in the same neighborhood of false pretenses. I pursued acting for a reason. I'm damn good at playing the part.

I've been told to smile my entire life. Strangers in the grocery store—always men—and people who loved to walk in and out of my life. I don't hear it anymore because I've programmed myself to keep smiling even when the exits are on fire and I'm inhaling smoke. I've used their entitlement to my advantage.

Oh, entitlement...As much as Bennett Larson pissed and moaned and made his narcissistic comments, we both know he was overreacting. A few other actors remain in makeup, some getting final touches or hair pinned in place.

Since Mel handed out donuts, nobody has paid attention to me; they have seemingly moved on. If I look harder, they're coyly listening in the distance. Oh, the gossip circles that roam these sets are amusing. The whispers are of my "stripper mother" this morning. It might land me on a few tabloid covers.

"Don't worry about Bennett. His bark is worse than his bite." Mel tosses her deep mahogany curls from her neck and takes in a mouthful of her donut. She's too distracted to notice the flakes of powder falling to the concrete. "You want one?" She asks, holding her hand over her mouth. Kayla continues running a spoolie over my brow as I rotate in my swivel chair, glancing at the boxed assortment.

"Any glazed?" I ask.

I shouldn't, but the glistening, coated dough and the sweet aroma overtaking my senses, are causing my mouth to practically pooling with saliva. It's strong enough to cloak the fumes of hairspray and scented powders. I haven't had a chance to eat either with making the poor choice of leaving set this morning. I didn't have much choice, though.

"Coming right up." She reaches into the pink box, grabbing the donut in a clear sleeve. "I sent Justin for them last night. *Oh, so good.* If you head into the city, stop in at Sugar Rush. They have a ridiculous menu. Just don't expect anything fat-free or healthy." She raises a finger. "Speaking of Justin, I need to track him down. He's probably up Bennett's butt. I'll catch you on set." Her hips sway as exits the room, the sugar high adding a rheumatic pep in her stride.

"How does she eat like that and not weigh a hundred pounds more?" I mutter, admittedly vain.

"I know, right? She had at least two in the last fifteen minutes and if she got them last night, you know she had to dig in," Kayla agrees, dusting a fluffy powder brush over the apples of my cheeks. "She probably lives on sugar and caffeine with everything she has to oversee." Right. As addictive and energy-boosting as cocaine. Mel is the producer that I've seen the most. Since meeting her during the casting process, I've run into her half a dozen times more. "She's been on the payroll since Bennett's first movie, and they *never stop working*. A few weeks off throughout the year, but between you and me, I'm pretty sure he doesn't take a day off." It's not a secret. Everyone knows he's a workaholic. "I saw him giving her hell once and she dished it right back. She's not afraid to tell him off."

"And everyone else is?" I sneer, unimpressed.

"Well, yeah. Aren't you?"

I glance from the corner of my eyes. "For what reason? Is he going to fire me if I do something wrong?"

"Not only that but he could blacklist you. So-long career." She sets her palette down after swirling the brush around once more and tapping off the excess. Her dark ponytail dangles over her shoulder as she leans to the side, shading my lower lash line.

Bennett Larson isn't worse than any other monster I've endured. The grumpy man won't *destroy* my career.

I pinch the last bite of the buttery dough between my fingers. "Maybe he needs a donut. Sweeten him up." Soft snickering pings off to my right. I act as if I didn't hear them, popping the bite into my mouth and licking my fingers clean.

Kayla flicks her brush toward the mirror with a short burst of laughter. "That may help. Sugar always puts me in a better mood." She looks up and winks at my reflection. "All kinds of sugar." Her shoulders dip with a little shimmy.

Please don't remind me I was flirting with him in the airport. The thought alone turns my stomach. No amount of symmetry and sky-blue eyes can change how repulsive he is on the inside. It was poor judgment from the lack of sleep or…lack of oxygen to the brain. Strategically, it could be my way to his sensitive side—assuming he has one, and I want to pursue that route. A little charm to change his attitude? Eh, no. I'm not going to be the one to sweeten up his day.

"Find another volunteer. The man wants to strangle me." Whimpers and cooing noises rise from the women around us, willing to pay tribute.

"I'm pretty sure my husband would give me a hall pass." She shrugs, and a goofy grin pulls at her lips. I tightly smile back and hold in every ugly word I'd love to get off my mind about the man that they want to keep worshiping. I didn't need to meet him to believe the rumors.

"Oh, I love this song." Soft music plays from a portable speaker on the counter behind us. "Turn it up. Please!" One of the girls increases the volume, giving me a reason to bob my head around as I silently mouth the words.

This week on The Cherry Show, I will attempt to *not* head butt—I mean, butt heads—with the director, become friends with everyone I come in contact with, and make time to *bond* with my co-star, Ames Heart. Most importantly, I will prove I deserve to be here. This will be my greatest performance, opening every door I fought to unlock.

The past affects the present. When I was a kid, I threatened to run away. I packed my duffle, walked two blocks to the park, and hung out for twenty minutes. Then I returned home. I couldn't possibly fail at this point in life because "going home" isn't an option anymore.

Cherry Flavored Heartbreak

"Ames! Wait up." I jog behind him, scooping my arm through his as he turns to me. "Are you going to be at the set dinner?" I brush my hand over the blond strands on his arm.

Plenty of the cast and crew members stay here all weekend; occasionally he's one of them. This incentivized someone on the production team to organize a weekly dinner or buffet—a small token of gratitude, or at least that's what they told us. It's probably a sponsor or something, kind of like the courtesy breakfast spread. Who cares who it is? I'll take it and savor every bite.

Living in a trailer in a parking lot for four months might be annoying to others. For me, it feels better than what I considered home most of my life. It's all mine. I don't have to share it or wonder if someone will try to take it away.

Like clockwork, Ames leaves his trailer for a jog at the same time every day. Studying him for the past few days had set me up to catch him before he got into a groove.

I don't know why people run for *pleasure*. No one is chasing you, and if they were, running will only get you *ahead* of the crazies. You'll need another strategy to win. Fleeing, fawning, and freezing won't protect you against someone who's willing to run through you.

We continue down the path near the perimeter fence. The paparazzi camp out on the other side of the secured barrier awaiting their chance to snap a shot of Ames Heart—Hollywood's latest heartthrob.

"*Dinner?* I think you mean *party*. One of those gatherings where people consume copious amounts of alcoholic beverages and get recorded acting doltish?"

He talks as if I don't know he went to a top boarding school and an Ivy League college while continuously staying active with his acting career. The rumor is he's straight-edge. An incident with an ex or something like that. How dare I ask him to *party*? Thank you, Kayla, for your sharing of everyone's business. Whether that's legitimate or not, who knows, but it would be more likely that he doesn't drink to avoid covering those rock-solid abs with a booze-induced pot belly. His income depends on his beauty as he lacks the common sense to finish his degree from *that quality educational institute.* He probably doesn't think I know that either. I'm judging again, but all that money Mom and Pop put into his education, and he dropped out as soon as his acting career took off? The only thing that explains it is pure arrogance. He could be friends with Bennett. I did some research of my own aside from my onset Gossip Girl.

Ames Heart. Short blonde hair, always styled to perfection in a strategically placed side sweep, soft sapphire blue eyes, a chiseled clean-shaven jaw, a strong, absolutely symmetrical nose, and sharp cheekbones on his wide masculine structure. The man is a walking Armani billboard, and that's all anyone would need to know to understand why he's the opposite of me in the most anticipated Bennett Larson movie yet.

He's not the only one who uses their looks to get ahead. I don't give two licks if this man shows up at the "*party*" *meh meh*. I care that the paps take our pictures together with my hands on his arm.

Welcome to the world of acting. It's plastic blocks stacked on silicone dreams. Authenticity can only get you so far. Nobody held my hand and walked me to the gates of stardom. I had to fight all of my life, and to get here, well...I did what I had to do.

Lies come to me so easily, and it's probably the root of why I decided to take up acting. I've seen some things, but I'm a good person. I'm trying to find joy and balance my karma back out, I guess. If I play the sweet, untouched girl next door long enough, eventually I'll believe it. I'll be her. I'll be happy, successful, and adored. My insides will be as bright as how all of these people see my outsides.

"They'll have soda punch, too." I shrug.

"Will I see you there?" He asks, brushing his buttery hand over my arm.

"I'll be there." I'll be there because we're in the middle of nowhere. This desert studio in Nevada isn't flocking with excitement. It's not like I have the extra money to throw at high fashion stores and whatever *it girls* empty their wallets on. *Judgment again, ugh.* Release the tension. Exhale the frustration.

My morning trip was enough to replenish the basics. It's wild how the paparazzi drive two hours from the nearest city just to get a payday. The closest town doesn't have a hotel. I'm not sure if the idea to build in this location was to keep them at bay or if a rich prick thought it would be fun to travel beyond the city limits.

My activities are limited to either hanging out in my trailer alone or catching the crew gossip after they all drink too much and tell me their secrets...or at the very least, Kayla shares everyone's dirt with me, if she hasn't already given away all the secrets she keeps in her beauty box — directly beside her hair tips and just above the body glitter she always has but rarely uses. It's a distraction; it keeps my mind busy.

"I could use a buddy to walk with to my trailer afterward. I'm not a fan of the dark." Two-thirds of a cup wholesome and zero percent naive, playing the damsel in distress is easy, but I didn't need to travel the world, searching for a man to build my suit of armor. Keep smiling. They like that.

"Maybe I'll stop by...for the soda punch." He flashes me his pretty boy smirk.

"You'll keep my secret, then?"

"Who's afraid of the dark? Not either of us."

"No way," I agree.

"I'm going to pick up the pace. I'll try to stop by later."

"Alright. Have a nice run."

He nods, and I head to my trailer.

Unfortunately, I knew who Bennett Larson was when I met him at the airport. I wish he was a forty-something-year-old man with a creeper 'stache who uses an old-school typewriter and couldn't form a sentence around a woman. I wish all the rational reasons I have to find him repulsive would eclipse his mysteriously captivating exterior. He's apparently my type of attraction. *Mind over matter.* His reputation precedes him elsewhere. He's a man with the ability to make you desired, rich, and famous yet he's demanding, critical, and pompous. If it's not aces, it's garbage. He wants perfection and prosperity. His work is brilliant. I won't deny that. And yet, the next four months would drag, buried beneath his gross personality, if I didn't befriend others so easily. I'm adding two-faced to his Wiki page after the nose-piercing comments. Anyone with basal vision could see he has his ears pierced. At least one of them is.

The fool was right about one thing. Mom was a stripper. It doesn't make her any less, and I happen to like my name. Her best memory is my favorite story. It was always more colorful when she told it. As a child, attending the Redner's Cherry Blossom Festival with her grandmother was her peace. She claimed its beauty and serenity were unmatched. The smiles she exchanged with my great-grandmother couldn't be measured by a photo. That was before *her mother* packed them up and fled to Texas with her new husband *and his cult.* I'm named after a symbolic tree of renewal, moron. I never got to meet the woman who inspired my namesake.

I hate that every beautiful memory comes with one full of sorrow. Mom had more trauma than one should, including me—the undesirable product of rape. Nobody wants to know the dark secrets that live behind the pretty smile. They want you to be a selfish, stuck-up witch that they don't have a reason to feel empathy towards. My success makes unhappy people word warriors, all because I'm not completely hideous. I won't apologize for taking what I deserve. My arrival wasn't ideal for Mom. It didn't help her addiction either.

Could I be angry with her that I was born already addicted to the drugs I've never chosen to try? Sure, I could hold on to that resentment. It wouldn't get me anywhere—hating the only person I called family.

By the time I was six months old, I was a normal, healthy baby. It's amazing—the human body—yet…The brain doesn't make things easy once you feed it something that feels euphoric. Something as plain as revenge can drive you to such an extent. An internal monster fuels every microscopic movement forward, rewarding you with the prospect of making them pay for their wrong-doing. It's a different kind of addiction. Never does it end well.

Addiction is a mite. It's little and ugly and somehow has a monumental power over you. You don't escape it. You learn to live with it one day at a time. That was her journey, and I was along for the ride. While she was seeking treatment, I was living with my grandparents—Mom's mother and stepfather, Rose and William. I was the devil in their eyes. Cult leader and brainwashed wife. Indeed, my life continues to darken while I emit sunshine.

It's amusing how these *holy believers* couldn't turn a cheek at the fact that half my DNA came from a sex offender. Certainly don't abort, but we don't want to raise the half-monster child either. It's hard to believe in a faith when surrounded by individuals who can't see the writing on the walls. It's harder to believe in a purpose when you've seen terrible struggle.

This is mine. In one light, I hate when the past floods my thoughts. In another, I'm here for the reminder of everyone who didn't make it. I will be free of the memories of people who wished me failure.

I've become one of the cackling hyenas at the rowdiest table in *Freedome*—the standalone building next to the studio. *Omphalos*—the sponsor that handed out the money to create this adult arcade—has their red, italicized-style logo all over this place.

It's like a bar in someone's basement or garage with half the elegance of *Realtor TV*. The room features two big screens, a few wooden tables, black leather couches, game consoles, a laptop station next to ring lights, a pool table, and a small kitchen behind the bar that extends along the rear.

It's as if they're targeting the younger actors. *Between takes, they'll be here taking videos and pictures to share on their social media stories.* Imaginably, that's what their marketing team proffered. It's quite a brilliant move. I should get on that train. My social media presence is lacking. On the plus side, unlike an actual bar, smoking is outdoors only. Thank you, *Omphalos.*

Rochelle—and her six feet of luscious jet hair—leans across the table, wiping Dawson's lip with a napkin. I avert my gaze, uncomfortable in the awkwardness of it all.

"They're hooking up," Kayla whispers, cautiously pressing into my arm. Her makeup looks like a filter. It's flawless as usual. *Then, there's me.* I forgot I had lashes on earlier and ripped part of them off when my eye itched. I touch my face too much for false lashes and long pointed nails. The gold and pearly white tips are pretty, and I'll get used to it eventually. I'm adaptable to change. By the time I leave this set, I'll be comfortable in the skin of *Samantha.*

I eyeball the tanned, roan-haired man. "I thought he was married."

"He is—to his wife of six years. And at least five of them he's had a girlfriend, too."

My eyebrows draw inward as I pull one side of my mouth tight. She bats her lashes once and looks around the room casually before adjusting her long ponytail. Maybe it's their thing? An open relationship. "And his wife is cool with that?" I whisper.

"His wife takes care of his love child. She thinks his infidelity was a test for their marriage and that he's committed to *only her* now." She looks past me, Dawson catching her eye. Pressing into my arm again and tilting her chin upward, she avoids his gaze as he continues to eye-bang Rochelle. "Once a cheater, always a cheater," she whispers.

Kayla sits forward, reaching across the table to touch the moody beads wrapping around Garrett's arm. "Where did you get these?" She asks.

She's one of the people who legitimately communicates through touch. That's why she became a makeup artist. So she can casually play with someone's hair without getting a restraining order.

"Are they real gemstones?" She continues. "They're kinda heavy."

Their conversation becomes background noise as my attention lands on the master of the puppets. Bennett Larson in all his pretentious glory. He should have changed. The suit is too much.

What's that along the rolled sleeve of his button-up? *A tattoo.* He has a tattoo on his inner forearm. Wait a minute. Is his other arm a full sleeve?

With all of the reasons he gets under my skin, it's the simple comments he's made, categorizing me as he sees fit. Label me as a blatant, predictable, and common fame-thirsty actor because of a nose piercing and a name while he's modified skin deep. He's clearly projecting his inner issues onto me.

"Is Bennett single?" *Did I say that out loud?*

"Girl, Bennett is always single. He doesn't hook up with anyone on his sets though." Her round eyes roll to the side. "I thought he wasn't your type?"

"He's not. I'm meeting Ames tonight."

"Oooh," she coos. "Ames Heart is a *heart*-throb." She winks, jabbing me in the ribs with her elbow.

My cheeks light up with a smile, unable to keep a straight face. "You're too much," I confess and rise from my chair. She's become one of my favorite people here in such a short time. The thirty-something-year-old mom of three doesn't usually stick around for the weekend since she's away from her family all week. I can't blame her for wanting to escape the twelve-plus hour days of intently waiting to powder the traces of oil on my skin; selfishly, I talked her into hanging out for a few hours. Begged. I *begged* her to hang out with me.

"I'll be back," I say, excusing myself from the group and squeezing behind chairs. As I make my way around the table and pass by the group playing pool, I see Mario Kart on the screen once again.

"Mr. Larson," I greet him.

"Cherry," he responds dryly, looking at me for milliseconds and back to the board to measure up a dart. He promptly throws it, glancing at me once more. "I see the nose ring has returned."

"Are you here to socialize or did you come to be the warden?" I walk in front of him, pausing as he returns my glare. I press my back to the wall, slouching a mere foot from him.

He throws the last dart and turns to me without seeing where it hit. The oxygen stiffens in my lungs as I hold onto my breath. His nose is an inch from mine. An uncomfortable pleasure wraps me in a concealed mantilla, pulling me away from wondering eyes. As much as I try to unlock from his gaze, I'm caught in his trap; a moth to flame.

"Do you think we're here to make friends...*Cherry?*" I let my eyes drift to his meager lips. He speaks again, and I return to his partially hooded eyes. "This is your job. I expect it to come first, but...yes..." He turns away, walks to the dartboard, and leaves me stuck against the wall as I process the sensation that's sent my heart into overdrive.

Stomach-jumping, hair-curling feelings will not be allowed. He is *not* and *will not* become attractive. An ugly interior will always destroy intimate feelings, and I will hang to that with all my will.

I bluntly exhale and speed walk in his direction. He turns abruptly, instinctively causing me to step back. "I'm here to socialize, Cherry. What else do you want to talk about?"

"You say my name after every sentence." I grab the darts from his hand, strutting the length from the board. "You must like stripper names more than you care to admit."

"Why did you want to play Samantha?" He asks, trailing behind me.

I throw the dart when he steps to the side, nailing the center of the board. "It's a lead role in a highly anticipated movie. I don't have to resonate with the character, I only have to play her well, if that's what you're asking, and I do everything well." I throw the second dart, hitting the same spot on the board, and nearly knock the first to the floor.

"Just because you can shoot darts doesn't mean you can win my approval with the same attitude." *I wouldn't expect anything less.* His chest brushes my arm, and a warmth involuntarily tenses me beneath his whisper. "And Cherry, I'll be watching you."

Give me a break.

Disguising my agitation, I throw another dart. His power high will eventually come to an end. The man *determined to scare me into obedience* walks away, and I blink, recalling how eyes wander around here.

"You're good at that." I find Ames standing behind me with a glass in each hand. "Soda punch?" He asks, gesturing.

"Thanks." I take it from him, giving him my back as I face the board. Casually, I dip my painted fingernail in the cup. It's always the clean-cut nice guy that is the serial killer. *This is a movie set with professionals, Cherry. It's a safe environment.* Wrong.

Trauma licorice. Once upon a time, *we* were a stupid seventeen-year-old. I snuck into a club with Elise and Hailey—my best friends. It took the turn of every cheesy daytime teen movie. I wish I didn't recall it at all.

A group of guys from our class had fakes. They had been getting in for a few weeks and bragging about it. The bouncers knew, but Rodney's daddy had deep pockets. I'm sure he made some sort of deal to *let boys be boys.* Ew.

Elise insisted we show up and crash their party all because she had this secret fling going on with Skylar Morgan. To this day, I can't simplify his name into one word. The captain of the douchebags kept it a secret for a reason. He wouldn't let his pathetic friends know he was dating an outcast.

Elise may not have wanted to believe it until she found him with a twenty-something party girl on his lap. She drank herself stupid at the bar, reality taking its toll. While I was playing Mother Goose, Hailey, on the other hand, was being entertained by a lovely young man in a suit, who looked like he recently walked out of a business meeting and stopped for a drink. He was *so lovely* that he slipped her some doozy pills. He would have made it out of there with her too—he even fought with me—until I started yelling about her being underage.

Trauma licorice truth; a guy I went to school with who was a known *dog* was more transparent than the man who appeared to be an upstanding citizen. It's an everlasting reminder.

Regardless of where I am or how people portray themselves, my strong sense of self-advocacy and protection will remain until the day I die, color-changing nail polish in check. If that makes me overly anxious or paranoid…no, no it doesn't. That makes me *alive.*

"Yeah, one soda couldn't hurt these abs." He pats his abdomen. My fake smile stretches softly, humoring him. "What did Bennett want?" He asks, lifting his glass to point in the dictator's direction.

Standing next to the pool table, Bennett chats up two men—his assistant, Justin, and another blond. Is his name...is it Blake? No...I don't. Yeah, I don't know.

"He's sour that his team found me and he didn't himself. He doesn't need to worry. He'll still get all the credit for discovering me," I answer him with eyes locked on Bennet's from across the room.

I turn back to Ames, reaching for anything other than his eyes to cling to. His smile won't suffice. Neither makes me feel the enjoyable discomfort I want; something—*anything* deeper. A unique chewing of his lip, a scar, a mole, a crease—a freaking brow hair unplucked. Anything real that can make me feel a quarter of the depth that's in Bennett's eyes. I'll grip onto anything I can, *anyone*, to feel only empty space between me and Bennett Larson.

"I see. You were amazing all week."

I smile, resting my hand on his forearm. "Thanks. It's kinda my job."

"Well." He clasps his hand over mine. "You're great at that job." As his hand leaves mine, I take a sip of my drink. "How did I do? Mediocre?"

"Oh, come on. We're the perfect Samantha and Jensen."

"You're not at all like her though."

Excuse me. "How so?"

"You're angelic."

I nearly snort. "Okay, I'll take it."

"You are, Cherry. The sweetest, cutest girl I've met."

Stooop. Warmth floods my cheeks. "Thanks, Ames. Really. You kind of made my day." He's not wrong about that. I am the cutest girl he's ever met. My cuteness surpasses that of America's Model Marvel contestant Ellie Hoover, with whom the paparazzi have captured numerous photos hanging on Ame's arm. *Sarcastic thinking at its convenience.*

"A girl like you couldn't be single." He just wants to screw me. And the things he says to me manage to make me giddy. Who is his acting coach?

"Single in every way." I'll lean into the priceless moment that a prince charming turns me into a swoony Ella.

"Every way," he repeats. "Does that mean if I flirt with you, you'll flirt back?"

"What makes you think I haven't been flirting already?" I press into his arm, toying a single fingertip up and back down his bleach-haired arm.

"Okay, my flower." He smirks. "I'll put you to the test. Now think really hard about it first, okay?"

"Sure."

"Okay. Give me your best pickup line."

"A pick-up line." I unfold, holding my cup with both hands. Hmm. "Like a line I would use or a line a guy has tried on me?"

"I was going for a line you would use, but with that, I'm guessing you never needed one. So, best one-liner someone has dropped on you. Very best."

Easy. "You're so beautiful you made me forget my pickup line." I bat my lashes, and the slightest giggle escapes.

His mouth tweaks up at the corner, and he dips closer to me. "I think someone stole the stars and put them in your eyes."

I fight the urge to roll my *starry* eyes, instead glancing to the ceiling. "Okay, we have a new best one-liner."

"Thank you, thank you." He bows while raising his cup. I'm waiting for him to start making a static cheering sound. Instead, he takes a swig of his juice and stares at me.

"Want to go do something fun? More fun than this." Grabbing his hand, I don't wait for an answer. "Come with me."

"Where are we going?"

I pull him along, setting my cup down on the counter as I walk past the pool table and toward the door. "This way." He follows in my shadow, walking to the side of the building. The crisp air is a refreshing change from the french fry odor inside Freedome tonight, and the noise level dropped from a good seventy-eight to a ten.

"Where are we going?"

"We're living a little." I promise I'm not going to shave your head or force you to eat an entire bag of potato chips if you give in to the pressure of stretching your wings.

Facing his reluctant body, I hunch my shoulders forward, drag myself the two feet back to him, and grab his hand to pull the stubborn mule into the shade.

"I thought you weren't afraid of the dark?" I taunt, my teeth cutting into my lower lip. Pressing my hand to his chest, I steer him until his back is against the stucco. I'm unable to hide the shifty grin rising from my lips, sealing it with a giggle.

"You're so cute," he says, running his hand over my jaw.

"I'm not always cute." I peer up at him, weaving my fingers through his.

"What are you then, flower?" His fingertips seamlessly caress the backs of my hands, and his pointer brushes the notched beads on my anxiety ring.

I lean into his neck and murmur. "I can be a *very* good girl."

He takes my jaw in his hand till my eyes meet his. "Oh really? Very good? I don't believe it." He does that thing where he says something sarcastic but smiles. He believes it. He believes that I'm a sugar plum fairy, adorned with braids of sweetness.

"You really shouldn't. I'm not that good. Sometimes I need a nice spanking."

Ah, that face! Oh my gosh, Ames. *I can't.* He looks like a flipping cartoon character with giant buggy eyes. There's no way a woman hasn't said worse things to him. Did I catch him off guard, or does he always turn into a tomato when faced with spicy little words?

With nowhere to go, he sinks backward, pressing his head to the wall. His fingers stiffen between mine. "Damn, Cherry." I girlishly laugh at his stifled whisper. Then, I quickly straighten to ask him what's wrong. "Some things are better left unsaid."

I put on my best pouty face and look up at him with doe eyes. "You don't want to spank me? Won't you even fuck my throat tonight?"

"Seriously!" He cups his hand over my mouth, his thumb pressing to my cheekbone while he looks to the light of the building. "Holy shit."

Oops. Did I go too far that time?

I reach for his wrist, pulling his hand down as I hold in my laugh. "What's wrong?"

"What do you mean, what's wrong?" His buggy eyes return, looking between my gaze and the glow. "You can't be talking like that."

"Are you scared someone's going to hear?" My voice carries purposely, and I almost feel bad about it. I shouldn't. I'm offering a one-on-one arrangement any man would be interested in. What's a little extracurricular activity between co-stars?

"I just don't talk like that." He nervously looks around, back to me, and then again to the lit area. He catches my smile, returning it with his own.

"Okay," I reassure him before he gets any more bent out of shape. "You want to play the quiet game?" I playfully laugh, kissing the left side of his lips before he can answer.

He is quite beautiful. I won't tell myself lies to stay away from him. I don't have to. Between his soft, never lifted a shovel a day in his life hands and how hushed he wants me, I can see his pampered life will never mesh with who I am—only my exterior. When our time here ends, he's easily detachable. We will never have a lasting connection.

Romantic relationships have never been my specialty anyway. Once...I mean...there was one time I thought I finally could commit. He was one of the good ones. Raised in a middle-class family, he was grounded and compassionate, driven by a desire to change the world. He played a mean game of darts too. He was a gentle teacher.

All things come to an end.

"Maybe we should slow down a little," he hums against my mouth. I draw back, taken off guard.

"Are you sure about that?" I take his chin in my hand and bring him back to my lips, tasting the sweetness of the fruit punch that remains.

"Excuse me." He clears his throat. *Not Ames.* Of course not. *Bennett freaking Larson.* It's like big brother is always watching. Except, he's not a brother. He's more of a tyrant.

"Mr. Larson. I was just leaving." The coward snaps my hands off of his chest, forcing me to maneuver in reverse as he hustles off to the light of the building. "See you tomorrow, flower," he yells, looking back before taking off.

"Now who's going to walk me back to my trailer?" I call out.

"Flower?" Bennett huffs with a muffled deep laugh.

"What's your problem?" I shout, edging closer to him.

It's not like we were doing anything wrong. Everyone is terrified of the big bad Bennett. He has the power of money and reputation, but he's not made of intimidating bronze muscles. I shouldn't act so naive. The world spins by who holds the most power. The difference is those powerful men like to disguise their sins with words like *for the safety of the people*. Big bad Bennett over here is transparent in his selfishness.

"It would be wise of you to lower your voice," he replies, casually walking towards me with his hands tucked in his trouser pockets. His placid stature is unaffected by his critical tone. I'm jealous that my anger is more toilsome to control. I've spent years honing in on my emotions, struggling with anger from time to time, and he walks around with this ease.

Call me an *emotional woman*. It has *nothing* to do with struggling to be heard for an extensive period of my life. *No, of course not.* Nor is it that I've been unable to cloak my feelings one more day. A man would experience the same, and they will bottle it up. Vulnerability is for the weak, and men must appear superior.

"What are you going to do, fire me? What I do in my personal time is none of your business."

"I don't like drama," he drawls. "If you want the attention of Press Weekly, kiss him in public, not in the decline. The last thing I need is a breakup mid-shoot or you getting upset because he's screwing two other women on the side. Keep it professional until shooting is complete. Do you understand?"

I stare at him with enmity, my lips pinched tightly together. Who does this jerk think he's talking to?

"Cherry, do you understand?" He asks, his words concealing a burning, dire need that demands my confirmation. His repeated question only tests my will. It would be so easy to just...ugh, no. It's not worth it. My furrowed glare is fixed on his when I notice *it,* and my shoulders sink.

It's not possible. It can't be...

His eyes.

I part my lips, my face creasing with the nearing of my brows. Stepping back farther into the dark, I stop as my back touches the building. The blue color I was becoming familiar with no longer exists. His irises are pure white and glued intently to mine.

I'm hallucinating. The nail polish didn't work. Ames freaking poisoned me! This can't be a thing. It's not.

Dismayed, I don't answer him.

His hands slam against the wall. They border my face, and a tremble takes my breath. My chest tightens. I refuse to blink or cower away. His freaky eyes frantically shift back and forth from left to right, staring into me as if he's never witnessed someone who refuses to bow to his will.

"Tell me you understand," he repeats.

My lip quivers, and I suck it in my mouth to hide the uncertainty. I don't like this. I don't like this *at all*. I am not weak. *I'm not afraid of him.*

"Bennett, back up." His chest rises, my palms pushing into him. I demand my freedom. "I would like to go to my trailer." He doesn't move. "Please. I'm suddenly...not feeling well." I'll text Kayla an excuse and apologize. She most likely already assumed I went off with Ames.

The low shuffle of his shoes moving across the blacktop hit me before my realization. He listened, putting distance between us and stepping to the side. He shakes his head slowly, refraining from looking at me. "I'm...I'm sorry. I'll walk you to your trailer," he mutters. "Can I walk you to your trailer?"

No...I don't accept his apology. He's not capable of remorse. This is a trick.

"I don't believe you."

"I am sorry."

Sorry that I'm not bowing to your will. Don't be stupid. Accept his false engagement and avoid any alternative sketchy action. "How could I say no when that's the first pleasant thing I've heard out of your mouth since the airport when you complimented my hair." A ploy to get into my pants that I ruined amazingly.

I walk into the lit path, and he follows, quickly meeting my side.

"What happened to those pigtails?" He mumbles, unable to look at me.

Moments ago, my boss pinned me against a wall, and his eyes practically glowed. Anyone who's not on a path of self-destruction would have scurried away the moment they broke free. Me? I want to know what makes him tick. I want to understand the depth within the monster.

"Samantha would never." I smile. "Maybe they'll make another appearance, you know, in four months when I fly home." Because he's not going to fire me.

"Where is home?" I narrow my eyes at his sudden curiosity.

"Anywhere and everywhere." Rolling my thumb over the thin silver ring on my pointer, I keep walking, trying to get back to my trailer without the need to make up the fine details of how I got here.

"Where are you from originally?" He presses.

Sure, let's play this game. "I grew up mostly in East Grenton and Arcdale, they're suburbs in—"

"In Southern California, outside of Heather," he interrupts.

That was the truth. How did— "How did you know that?" I fold my arms across my chest, grabbing my elbows as the wind chill gets to me. Digging my chin forward, I breathe in the lavender incense coming from the trailer in passing. I'd recognize that calming scent a mile away. It's one of my favorites to add to the candles I make—one of the few hobbies I manage to fit into my busy schedule.

"I'm familiar." He looks away. "Does your family reside there? The income you should be making would easily get them out."

He is also speaking truthfully. Only someone familiar with the area would know that it's not a place you want to stay.

"No. I don't have any family left. It's just me." I awkwardly smile, as if that's not a big deal or, you know...sad.

"Oh," he replies, kicking loose pebbles across the lot with his high-dollar leather shoes.

"Usually you give your sympathies when someone tells you of their family's passing."

"You don't want my pity. It won't change anything." He looks up at the night sky. Under unearthly stars, he continues walking with his hands tucked in his trouser pockets.

"What about your family? Where are they?" He tilts his head away from the night's sky, and his eyes slowly settle on mine. The stars are gone. The night is empty. He swallowed it and me with the same gravitational pull. I'm trapped like the stars, and he says nothing, but I feel everything he wants me to know. I feel more than I want to feel.

I blink away, and so does he. I want him to say it. I need to know...on the off chance someone...could be waiting for him to come home?

"I thought we were sharing?"

"There is nothing to share."

I directly face him, forcing him to stop. His eyes snap to me as if he's offended that I cut him off. "You asked me if I understand? I understand alright. I understand that you come from a poor place and probably have some unfortunate history, and now you made it big and want everything you never had. I understand, Mr. Larson or Bennett. Whatever. Others…they respect you, they fear you, they worship your work, but *I understand* what it takes to get here. I won't mess with your masterpiece and you won't rain on my parade. Okay? Thanks for walking me this far, but I can handle the rest of the way."

His fixation is short-lived and unlike in the shadows, where I swear his eyes turned whiter than snowfall. The man's heavy brows draw inward. A gap forms between his balmy lips.

Well, I give up. He's a statue. I toss my hands up and spin around, heading to my trailer down the lit path.

"Goodnight, Cherry," he finally answers.

"Goodnight," I reply, twirling and walking backward momentarily. He stands still, hands tucked away, watching me on my way.

I took this job because it's what I want to do and how I want to create a living, but I came here for someone else, and to help them, I have to earn the trust of Bennett. Besides his *wonderful* traits, I do have other reasons to dislike the man. His interruption cutting my fun short with Ames kind of worked out to my advantage. Given our mutual acquaintance, it's not that surprising that he's from East Grenton and the unintentional connection I made with him could potentially be my opening. Keep focused, and everything will work out. *It will.*

Bennett Could Manipulate A Narcissist

"Unfathomable woman," I grumble with an exhale.

Hah, yeah...I've never had a single person immune to my control.

Yes, you heard me. Miss Push-My-Buttons is lucky number one. You already knew this would happen, didn't you? But did you think I would wake up from death without some side effects?

There's an explanation for why I can't get in her head. Some sort of weird gemstone necklace or...an evil eye tattoo! Incenses? Oils? Fucking gargoyles! That's why she was late to set. She was off buying a fucking gargoyle.

Back to my side effects. I'm a comic book feen and not a stranger to the term telepathy. Getting into heads and causally persuading them to agree with me...well, remember? I said there's not much that's impossible for me now.

It's miraculous. Yay. I have the perfect double life, like Super Spider Bat Boy. If only I was trying to save the world, huh?

Sometimes I wonder what Annie would say about all of this. Shit, I know what she would have said. She would have implied that I must have hit my head, adding insult to the injury, and pissed at me for going ghost on her for months. She would have filed a missing persons report if I hadn't texted her within forty-eight hours. Who am I kidding?

Once she came to terms with what I was, she would have told me to use my second chance to make a difference. Hmm, hah. Right. I shouldn't laugh.

I may never know what I am or if I have an expiration date, but I know one thing: telling anyone would sign me up to be the next test subject at Area 51. Do you think I'd have a cellmate? I don't want to worry about getting jumped by an alien for my sexy body.

Unfortunately, I have to make the rough comparison between Annie and Cherry. They're similar in ways. Determined. Outspoken. Magnetic. Her likability makes me weak. Yes, I like her, and maybe that's where the problem lies.

I tolerate people. I don't like them.

It's not the worst thing—to like her. The headaches, dizzy spells, and, well, when I want something, I can't let it go. I'm obsessed and must have it. It's as if I'm not able to control myself. I've had days where I woke covered in blood and can't recall where it came from. That's the worst. The questions stack like books, filling my think space until it feels impossible to breathe. I kick the towers down, telling myself that I wouldn't slip up. I'd cover my tracks, and nobody would know. I would use my birth-given ability—invisibility.

I should add a *life lesson* somewhere...Eh, fuck it. Next chapter.

I slip my laptop back into the case and tuck it beneath my seat. With a twist of a cap, I chug six ounces of water and set off to find Mel.

"No," I groan. "This is wrong. Samantha can't wear this." I grab the bottom of a thin silken dress, pulling it out below the rack. "What is this shit?" I pull the next and the next. "Justin! Where the fuck is Mel? Get her on this, immediately." He hurries over to me with his tablet against his chest, already scrolling his contacts for Mel. "Samantha is the highest of high classes." *Shut up; I don't even know what that means.* "She's put together in every way. Her lipstick must be lined perfectly in petal pink, every diamond on her necklace must blind you when she walks by, and *never*—" I enunciate loudly, drawing his full attention to my face as if I pressed a finger to his chin. "*Ever*, would Samantha wear rustic red, plunging necklines, and fucking spaghetti straps," I lecture. Anxiously, he takes my rath of frustration.

"I sent Mel a message that her appearance is requested immediately. Casandra is um..." He wipes across his task chart, or, uh, what's it called—agenda? "She should be..." The clicking of heels crossing the floor draws my sight to tan stilettos. "Holy gelato," Justin says under his breath.

"I don't think gelato is holy," I softly reply, not taking my eyes off her. "It's full of sugar...addictive and as deceiving as coke in the eighteen hundreds," I softly mutter.

Samantha can not wear that dress but fuck me if I tell *Cherry* to change. Curse the beating in my chest that pulses blood through my veins. A warmth gradually flushes my skin, and I look away. Not her. Anyone, but her.

The six-inch heels make her legs appear as long as a sunflower stem, flawless in crystalline hosiery. Each step across the vinyl floor hollows my cheeks. She's pinching my jaw between her hands, demanding my fixation. She drags my attention up inch by inch until I reach the hem of her skin-fitted skirt. Then the illusion wears. She stands before me as an angel of my nightmares.

A calm steadies my voice. "Cherry, you have to switch outfits. Someone..." I look back at Justin before finishing my sentence. "Fucked up. This is not the correct wardrobe."

If I wasn't looking for Mel, I wouldn't have come in here and seen this disaster—or her. Why is that slit so high? Fucking—shit, did she catch me staring? I snap my eyes away, running my nails over the back of my neck.

I'm overanalyzing. My breathing *didn't* shallow as I glanced over the smooth skin along her thigh. I *never* settled on her hips for a second too long. Her lips *never* looked right in the wrong shade. Cherry is not my next fling. She's not a single night. She's a star...and everyone is going to love her.

"I think you look beautiful, Cherry," Justin chimes in.

I swiftly glare in his direction. "Nobody fucking asked."

"Language, Mr. Larson." Her eyes slowly roll over me. "You wouldn't want your right-hand man to quit." She smiles at him—*stupidly.* "Thanks, Justin. It's nice to know charming men exist."

"Bennett," I correct. "You can call me Bennett. The formality isn't necessary." I glance upward and tongue my teeth, sucking saliva down. "We have a schedule to keep. If I have to be stern to stick with it, I will."

"And you will curse."

Justin snorts, and I scowl at him. Cherry passes me, circling to the rack of dresses, and she pages through them. "Do you think it intimidates people?"

"You think I have to swear to intimidate people?" I ask, glancing back at Justin. He quickly looks away, pulling his phone to his face.

"I'll get Mel right away," he says, scurrying off.

A smile peels from my lips. The power is a tonic feeding me endorphins and flooding my brain with a runner's high unlike any other. It's greater when I use my ability. It wasn't a design flaw. It's a perfectly mastered reward—like procreation; the deed feels good.

I wasn't exaggerating when I said obtaining an obsession—whether it be power, acknowledgment, or catching the girl—has a grip on me. I've never felt anything remotely like it, which makes it hard to explain. And I'm starting to feel that pull when Cherry gets smart with me.

She sighs. "Tell me—how is it that you think you're so charming while being a complete douche?" Her full lips almost meet, rounding with the cutting insult.

"Douche?" I flinch. "Ouch." Leaning my arm along the rack, I look down at her, somehow managing to keep my eyes on her face and not the deepening of her neckline. "That's what I call this popular guy in high school who would pretend to be my friend when my older sister was around."

Skimming the flesh of my lip with my teeth, I bite at the corner, briefly pulling it into my mouth. Why did I tell her that?

"That's it. You weren't popular in school, so you created this ego of a shell housing your sad soul." She pouts, placing her hand on my arm. I glance down, seeing one single painted fingernail. "Sappy stories don't give you the right to treat others poorly. You catch more flies with honey."

"Imagine wanting to collect insects on borrowed time."

"How can someone with such a creative mind take an idiom so literally?"

I take a step back, forcing her hand off of my arm as I straighten my shoulders. "I didn't ask for your opinion to begin with." I glance back at her hand. "Remove all of the polish next time." She covers it with her other hand, surprised I noticed.

Finally speechless, I leave before she opens her mouth again.

It's only chapter seven and I'm blocked. If I continue to sit here and fake type, eventually I'll press the keys hard enough to build a sentence.

Cherry is a pain in the ass.

Not that sentence.

Delete.

Be nice, Bennett. It'll get you farther in life, Bennett.

Delete. Fuck it.

I smack my laptop close and inhale warm air.

I'm not unreasonable. I could say something like, um…"*I appreciate it. I mean*—if it was done correctly the first time, you wouldn't have had to fix it."

"Bennett, don't get sweet on me," Mel replies, tossing her salad to coat it with dressing. "Damn, it's nice out today. Low seventies? Amen, Mother Nature."

I hoped it would be comfortable enough to eat lunch in the courtyard between building entrances as we near October.

"Overcast skies are great for filming."

"Do you want me to change something?"

"No. Keep the schedule as is. We can't have any more delays," I insist.

"Let me worry about that."

I shake my head and adjust my chair across from her, stretching my legs.

"What's going on?" Her tone becomes almost serious as if she verily wants to know, and I'm compelled to say more than our casual conversations.

The fucking princess got under my skin. That's what's going on.

Mel, Justin, and Simon have been with me since the beginning of my, uh...

Backspace.

—Journey. I trust them as much as I could trust anyone, but we are not friends. I'd let them drown before I'd put my own survival at risk. Fuck, I'd drown them if it came down to them or me. Sorry, not sorry.

"That woman," I scoff.

In the past three years, I haven't said a thing about my parents, my sister, or where I grew up. This woman shows up on my set and I run my mouth like an oil spill. I need Mel to talk me off the ledge. That's it. Why else would I be coming to her with anything remotely? I'm having trouble convincing myself for the first time, and if someone I at least trust on a professional level tells me not to free fall, it might relight the fucking lightbulb in my think space.

"Be a little more specific. You have a lot of women come and go." She takes a bite of her salad, dabbing her mouth with a napkin. "How bad is the blackmail she has on you?

"Cherry Kaas," I mumble.

She shakes her head, bouncing her tightly bound curls. Mel's round hazel-green eyes widen.

"She's the star, Bennett."

Say it—don't fuck the actors, dumbass.

Her—not you.

"She doesn't have anything on me. I fucking..." I palm my face, pushing my elbows against the wooden surface of the table. "It's not like I want to sleep with her either." I smack my hands down more aggressively than I intend. Mel looks up from her food, giving me a motherly *knock-it-off* expression. "There's something about her that is throwing me off."

It's probably that she reminds me of my sister whom you don't know exists, and at the same time, I'm attracted to her, which is entirely off-putting. She's...enticing. It's that heart racing, blood pumping, anxious for no fucking reason feeling I get when I see her, when I think about her, and when I fucking talk about her.

I can't remember the last time I felt remotely eager for a five-minute conversation, despite it being a mouth battle. Heh, man, I'm fucked in the head. You—you, shut up. It's infatuation with a woman who isn't easy and is—by my own rules—off-limits.

Give up already, right? Change the rules and fall in love. I'd sooner fall into a hole in the ground. Love makes you weak. It gives you a weakness. When someone comes for me, they come for everyone I have ties with. One mistake, and they'll come for me.

Mel twirls her fork full of crispy lettuce in front of her sunkissed amber face. She constantly talks with her hands—and food. "Did you think that there's a possibility—now, hear me out—you like her as a person? You have to be lonely, and not have any family, and the closest thing you have to friends are me, Simon, and Justin. Simon isn't much for a conversation either. I don't recall it in his job description to remain serious and silent ninety percent of the time."

I raise my brows. "You're thorough at your job."

"People talk." She shrugs, picking up a grape and popping it in her mouth.

You can Google me and you'll find nothing because I was nobody, a wallflower, remember? Yeah, you're keeping up now. I had ninety-seven people on my Facebook page, and over half were in some way related to me. I didn't have any of those other apps, or if I did, I had the mystery gray no-face profile picture and no description. I was a Reddit phantom and a forum ghost, hiding behind a screen name. I deactivated everything.

I look past her, almost dazed. "What have they been saying about Cherry?"

"She's had a handful of roles, nothing this big. Pretty lucky if you ask me." I unwrap my sandwich, falling victim to the aroma of melted cheese dripping down the golden brown bread. "Not one diva, desperate, or bloodsucker comment from the crew yet. I like her," she admits. I bite into my Monte Cristo, bummed there wasn't one complaint to match the names I've been titled. "She's perfect for the role, you know it, and Ames has taken a liking to her." She side-eyes me. After grinding my teeth for a moment, I resume my meal.

Alright, enough about her—about all of them. Back to me. I'm the living dead guy.

I'm the reason you're here and you want to know more, don't you? What else can you do besides mindfuck people into doing your bidding, Bennett?

I have one other ability. I'm still testing its limits, but it's some cool shit.

I can manipulate light.

Oh light, Bennett, how exciting. You're so witty.

I'm a creative man, not a scientist. However, they make these devices now that you can find information on anything and everything at the tap of your finger. You might be reading on one right now. Well, I utilized it and did my research after I discovered I could adjust the lighting in the room without leaving my chair.

Do you want to know what it's called? Alright, drum roll. It's photokinesis! Yeah, it's a big deal. Like a big fucking deal. Without electromagnetic waves, we have no life; no plants, no oxygen, and you couldn't be scrolling social media on your cell phone every night instead of reading the self-help book that's been on your bedside table for months.

One day I might technically be able to make myself invisible, not that I care to. Wouldn't that be ironic? Currently, I can only manipulate what I'm making for the big screen. Anything that omits energy waves, I can control in some fashion.

You what I remember the most about the day I was murdered? Waking up, dripping in this disgusting black muck in the woods behind the plant. The distinctive texture rots a part of my brain to this day. And wouldn't it be amazing if I could tell you I walked through the pearly gates, greeted by angels, and got ripped from that beautiful peace and brought back here?

Wait...would that be amazing?

It doesn't matter; I wasn't in hell either. I don't recall one day of those fifteen months. It was black, like the muck.

It was unbearable to walk with this thick gunk pasted to my skin beneath and overtop of my clothing. Which, by the way, was worn to hell, and I'm lucky I didn't flash anyone while walking down the road looking like a swamp monster. If you think it sucks when you wake up with crusted discharge on your eyes when you get a cold, you would be crying with the amount of shit that was gluing my eyelids down.

A drunk-ass swamp monster, hah.

From the road, a small creek came into view during my wobbly hike. I was just able to make it out. My first instinct was to barrel through the woods below and clean as much of it off as I could. In my good fortune, it panned out. Although, it was simply enough to get me from point A to point B without my eyeballs burning. I spent a steady hour in the shower scrubbing, and don't ask me what it was like when I sneezed.

Getting access to a shower was a task on its own.

My old apartment was locked, and my car was nowhere to be found, making it difficult to get to my new apartment. No, I didn't fucking realize I was missing—or dead or whatever the hell you want to call it—for over a year. My only concern was getting a shower and going from there. But Bennett, how the french fucking fries did you do that? Well, darling, one of the shitty hotels accepted the crusty cash I had in my pocket for a night's stay.

Life lesson: Cash is king.

Stop right there. You're looking for the plot hole, huh? Didn't the guy with the pew pew take my wallet? Indeed, he did, but lucky for me, I was at the gas station earlier that day and shoved my change in my pocket in a hurry. It became buried enough below my wallet that this doofus didn't notice. Bingo. I win.

Well, sorta.

As for my clothes, I had to hand wash those rags the best I could and sleep in the nude while they air-dried. It was the shittiest I've slept in my life—mostly because how the fuck would you sleep when you've woken up in a foreign world? Shockingly, they had a hairdryer under the bathroom sink, which was helpful until it blew the fuse.

*I was flat broke at this point. Until I could get to the bank—*that place requires clothes—I couldn't do anything. I couldn't buy a phone, and in the rare sight of a payphone, my coin purse was empty. *If I was speaking to my parents, I couldn't have paid for a ride to their house. So I waited. I showered, washed my clothes, and had a restless night. The next morning, I walked my ass to the bank, hoping they wrote me off as a blue-collar boy rather than a troubled young man.*

Alright, Bennett, I'm following, but...

Shut up, plothole hunter. I know, I went to the bank with no ID. I'm telling you this part of the story because it was the first place I noticed I have the ability to persuade minds. I didn't have to steal. My account didn't close and I wasn't completely foolish with my money.

My state of mind was quite delusional at that point. At first, I assumed the teller was being extremely nice. Then slowly, logic trickled in. Why would she risk her job to go against policy? What we're the repercussions for this? There's no way she's helping me with those risks. I must have a concussion or amnesia. Why the fuck is she handing me an envelope of cash?

I walked out of there with an arrogance, my head held high as I got away with a crime in broad daylight. As soon as I pieced together what had happened, I didn't care how fucked I was anymore. I was about to change everything.

My Name Is Bennett, Not Benny

"Let me help you." I reach for the large white box from Cherry. She struggles to carry a gift bag while several balloons fly wildly around her face. My fingers brush hers, and the friction shocks me. *Fuck*. I shouldn't have offered to help. I should have opened the door for myself and let it shut on her without a second glance. That would have got her going. It would have been hilarious. "What's all this for?" I ask.

"It's Kayla's birthday," she replies, hurrying toward the Freedome entrance.

"And Kayla is?" I ask before she pulls the door open.

"Seriously Bennett?" She scowls. "She's one of the makeup artists. Hurry up. She doesn't know we're doing this. I want to make sure everything is set when she walks in."

I glance around the room full of life. It quickly dials down as I'm spotted. Metallic red spirals stream from the ceiling as she directs me toward a confetti-covered table.

"You did all of this?"

I eye a platter of bite-size sandwiches poked with toothpicks and a massive charcuterie board next to it. My awkward assistant catches my eye, climbing off a chair below a happy birthday banner. He smiles at the woman who's helping him, and for a lingering moment, his hand caresses her forearm.

Huh, maybe he's not a virgin.

It's not surprising that I didn't know what was going on. For valid reasons, the invitation wasn't extended to me. I consume myself with work. Mel was right—I don't have friends. I don't even know why I went to Freedome the other week or why I decided to come here again.

For the girl, Bennett! No, no...no. I'd rather be destroyed with self-infliction than by people who will only stab you in the back. It's not negative thinking; it's being a realist. I've heard about these *ride-or-dies*, but in this entire room, not one person yells shotgun.

"The cake can go right here," she directs. "What do you think?" Her jaw falls before the box is fully open. Then I see it too.

"Uh, I don't think that's going to make the right impression." I stroke my chin, containing my amusement.

"Oh my...What the hell!" Her arms fly to her sides, and I sense I'm about to see a toddler throw a tantrum. "This was supposed to be white iced cake with a studded diamond brocade along the sides and a powder brush on top, with happy birthday Kayla piped in cursive, not..." She shakes her head, and her cheeks flush red with another swing of her arms. "A giant dong!"

I deeply chuckle. It's definitely, and hilariously so, a *giant dong*. The sheet cake is cut into the shape of a *very* large penis.

"It's not funny!" Her hands fly in the air, and she walks around the table like a different angle is going to make it look any better. "How am I going to fix this in five minutes? This is an obvious..."

"Dick," I interrupt. "Where did you get this from? Despite their screw-up, the detail is quite impressive."

"I'm—" She exhales. She looks like she's about to have a panic attack, fanning her hands over her face and pacing. "What to do, what to do," her voice squeaks. "She's going to be here any minute and I..." Panic-stricken, she gawks at the unwarranted masterpiece. "I have to present her with a cock cake!"

I deeply chuckle again. *A fucking cock cake.*

"What am I going to do?" She mutters to herself. "Would she take it as a prank or be offended?"

"You're blowing this out of proportion."

"No, I'm not," she snaps. "This is for a person I work with. Not my college roommate."

"Everyone thinks the penis is funny." Why am trying to calm her?

"There's a time and place, Bennett. You lecture me about professionalism until it doesn't affect you."

She holds stress and tension in her tone. Her shoulders stiffen, and she fiddles with the silver band on her finger. Her eyes flicker back and forth over the cake, revealing a wildly interesting mix of anger and panic stuck in her throat. She fights it back as much as she can.

"They won't be able to replace it in time." She takes her hips, her thumb continuing to rub back and forth over her ring. "I could..." Her jaw clenches. "How do you mix up orders? Don't they double-check this stuff?"

"I sense some anger."

"Trust me, you don't want to see me angry."

"Don't let anyone catch you admitting you're not an angel."

"How did you come up with that perception?"

"You're whole—" With a squint, I air quote. "*Aura* says America's sweetheart."

"Look, can you—" She huffs and rubs her temples. "Please, tell me that big Bennett brain has an idea?" She reaches for a card from the wicker basket on the table, fanning the air to her skin.

"Don't have a meltdown over a fucking cock cake." She's an adult. She can figure it out on her own. "It's not that difficult to fix," I assert, foolishly implying I could fix it despite my lack of baking and cake-decorating experience. "I'll fix it and then you owe me."

I grab a spoon and a dish from the end of the table, scooping up the, ahem, *white* detail along the border. *Yes, it's cum.*

"Sit down and relax."

"Bennett, this is important to me."

"I'm not going to fuck it up. Sit." With a flex of my brow, I return to the cock cake.

I use the flat edge of the cake knife to smooth over the *details* as much as possible. Then I cut the hefty *circles* along each side, forming an upside-down triangular shape. I put the extra pieces in the center to complete the triangle, fully shaping the bristles of a powder brush. I cover the triangle surface with the white cream I scraped off.

"They should have requested a darker shade. Here's your tan-handled brush with white bristles. Just grab a marker and write happy birthday on the cake board." I lick my thumb. "Mm, it's good."

Cherry walks around the table, rolling her eyes. Her thigh grazes mine as she leans down, pressing her hands to the wooden table to examine my revisions.

She springs up and clings to my neck. I wrap my arms around her waist instinctively as her feet lift from the ground.

Her petite body is in my arms and my hands teeter over her exposed skin from her shirt pulling away from her jeans. Her fingers dig into my shoulders and her chest presses to mine. *Why is she hugging me?*

I'm torn. Should I force her feet to the floor or keep breathing in her body heat—her unlikely comforting touch?

"Thanks, Benny! You're the best," she says.

My face falls flat. I tilt to look at her just as her lips press into mine.

Frozen in silence, I'm unable to unwrap my arms from her waist.

What do I do? I need to get out of here now.

Her shaky breath breaks the thick air. "I was trying to kiss your cheek. I'm sorry."

"An accident. Yeah. It's fine."

"You can set me down now."

"Right." I lower her to the floor and step away, tucking my hands in my pockets.

"Mr. Larson," Justin says. "I didn't expect you—"

"*Bennett.*" He quiets as I cut him off.

"Are you staying?" He asks.

"I don't think so. Cherry needed my brief assistance, but I have to get back to work, unless—you want me to stay?" Cherry and I exchange a steady gaze.

"Are you asking me?" Her brows rise. "If you want to stay, you're welcome. Justin could delicate tasks to you for once." A wide smile takes her lips.

"Wipe the shit-eating grin off your face, Justin. I have better things to do." I walk toward the door, waiting for people to move out of the way. "Have fun with that cake, Cherry," I call out and quickly disappear.

Cherry Might Be Clairvoyant

I made a mistake, and it's going to cost me part of my soul. I kissed Bennett Larson. I kissed him on the mouth. I kissed Bennett Larson on the mouth in a very public place, and I'm trying to convince myself that nobody saw it.

Breathe.

Breathe.

It's fine. Everything is fine. I will not be embarrassed or allow the horrible accident to consume my thoughts. I am better than this minor infraction.

I put on my perfect smile, stand tall, and watch the door for Kayla. With my best effort, I avoid scoping out the room and making eye contact with anyone. It's a good thing she didn't show up early. If she saw my slip-up, everyone would know in the next hour. If Shell saw, she'd judge me and talk behind my back because she's jealous.

I straighten the stack of pink napkins and rearrange the utensils, finding anything to fiddle with to distract my mind. I wanted to get on his good side, not join the *Got Freaky with Bennett* Club.

"She's coming! She's coming!" Soft voices call out.

We collectively yell surprise as the door swings open. "Happy birthday!" I call out. She tussles her fingers through her rich brown hair, smiling from ear to ear.

Greeting her, I playfully bump her shoulder with mine, gaining her attention and pulling her over to the cake table before anyone else steals the opportunity to talk her ear off or vice versa. "Hey, we had a little mix-up with the cake and had to redecorate it. It's a little off, just so you know before you see it."

"Cherry, I'm already wowed. As long as the cake tastes good, I don't care if it says happy birthday Fred." She laughs. If she only knew how much more vulgar it was. "And there are gifts! When did any of you have time to shop?"

I gifted her a Ravenwood soy candle that I bought a few weeks ago when I went into the city. A roughly twenty-dollar, eight-ounce jar is nothing to brag about, but it's the thought that counts. I'd be happy to receive a refreshing peach and cinnamon candle. Mel, and Vanessa—from the makeup department—had picked up small gifts as well; otherwise, it's just a few cards. Then there are people like Darren here. I don't think he has ever said one word to her, and he showed up to play pool and eat free cake. It's unlikely that she will take notice or care. However, I'm petitioning for him to walk around with a camera at all times because he looks naked without his gear.

"Hey, flower," Prince Charming calls from behind me.

I turn around, somehow delighted to see his perfectly quaffed hair and his dreamy eyes upon me. "You made it." He always smells like—rich and spicy. It's reminiscent of creamy nutmeg.

"I'm such a busy guy, you know, but I managed to make the time." He tongues his upper lip. It's adorable when he wants to be sarcastic, yet it always comes with a smile as if he needs me to know he's joking. The man has grown on me, both on and off set in these past few weeks. Withdrawing a bit has only called him closer to me. Gossip Weekly and VIP Magazine both ran stories on our *involvement* this week. Focus Magazine must have me on their radar.

As malicious as my intention seemed, I never wanted to hurt Ames. The more we've talked, the more I've listened. Yesterday, when he was telling me about his niece, Payton, and how she's turning two in a few weeks, his face lit up with a joy I hadn't seen before. She's obsessed with some cartoon with a blue dog. It's the same one I always begged to watch as a child, but when he asked for my opinion on which toy he should get her, it hit me—he's letting me into his world.

I don't know why he would think I had a clue. I guess because *I'm a woman*, I should have some maternal instinct as to what to buy a two-year-old. So I answered—buy them all. His claim that he didn't want to spoil her too much still shocks me.

I don't want to be the reason he needs to heal.

I've been laser-focused on my objectives and ambitions like a robot. Kayla and Ames remind me of…David and Jack. I'm a simple girl enjoying the breeze.

"Did you manage to make time for Kayla's party or was it to see me again?" I shrug and playfully pout.

"Anything for my flower." His eyes seesaw from my mouth and back nonchalantly with a soft smile.

I stroll over to the wall at the end of the bar, picking up a cue and chalking the tip. His eyes follow me the entire time until I get back to him. "Wanna play?" I dip my chin toward the pool table. "Loser sticks around to help with the cleanup." Tilting the cue to him, I wait for him to take it, broadening my eyes.

"And what does the winner get?"

"Besides not having to clean? Hmm," I hum, looking upward in thought. I can think of a few G-rated things and a few more that require adult consenting age.

"If I win—" His hand clasps around mine, holding onto my cue stick. "I want to take you on a date."

"Okay, and if I win, you have to tell me why you keep calling me *flower*."

"Deal," he agrees.

I return to the corner of the bar, find a second cue, chalk it, and return to Ames. Kayla tries to squeeze by, forcing me to press into his chest. She glances over her shoulder with a subtle smile. "Oh, excuse me. Birthday girl on the hunt for champagne."

I lead the way to the empty pool table. Ames pushes up his sleeves; he holds the stick in front of his blue jeans with a twelve hundred dollar black and white high-top on each side. "Ladies first."

The redesigned penis cake was delicious, the celebration was endless, and Ames was attentive, yet I find myself on the rooftop, flat on my back, staring at the stars—something I haven't done since I left that town. Freedom on top of Freedome. I'll be the first to admit that is a weird coincidence. I wish I could point out constellations and erase blinking stars that don't belong.

Remember why you're here. This is for Jack and every other person that stood next to him. Bennett Larson is a nightmare, and I won't forgive his actions. I won't fall for his tricks. I'll stick to the plan.

A shaky sigh pushes through my tight chest and I take another deep breath, letting it out slowly. I haven't had an anxiety attack in a very long time. That's what they called it. It could have been much worse. The last time *was worse*.

I guess because Bennett was already there, I utilized him. It's entirely too difficult to straddle this fence. I need to get close enough to him to get even without empathically letting him change my mind.

He only showed up to Freeform once in the past three weeks...twice now. What can I do to get him to meet me halfway? Invite him? He wouldn't come. I could...no, that won't work. I knew this wasn't going to be easy.

"Shouldn't you be at the party?" Bennett's face blocks my view of the sky. Speak of the devil, and you shall be greeted. His ability to show up at the most inconvenient moment doesn't please me.

My mind should be wandering off to what Ames is planning for our first date—normal things on a young woman's mind despite how I creamed him in our game of pool. Weirdly, he compares me to a skunk that's a boy mistakenly called Flower, and the darn skunk just went with the flow of it because he was a shy little pushover. I haven't watched that movie since I was in single digits. *Dang it, what did Bennett say?* Oh yeah, the party.

"I needed some air. It was getting a little loud and reckless in there." I stretch my neck to the side, trying to look around him as he stands above me. "You make a better ceiling than a window. Your big head is covering the stars." I pat the cold surface beside me and quickly realize the neckline of my pastel shirt is off-center. I adjust it, covering my cleavage. The last thing I need is for him to think I'm trying to make another move. Throwing myself at him isn't the way to earn his trust. He might yeet me off the building, judging by his previous reaction.

"Take in all the air you need because I'm not giving you mouth-to-mouth again today."

I hide my face in the palms of my hands and mumble. "Please, never mention that again. Even if there is a lethal weapon pointed at your jaw, don't say it."

"I would like to say shit happens, but what was that shit...an *accidental kiss*?"

He chuckles and sits beside me, resting his arms on his bent knees over his dark wash jeans. If he's not in slacks and a button-down shirt, he's in jeans and a button-down shirt. For a man who's quite meticulous about what his characters wear, his wardrobe is very plain and predictable. At least I know he owns an actual jacket. The thick black cotton looks good with those jeans. *He* looks good.

It's okay to admit someone has an attractive exterior despite their horrid guts. Opportunity doesn't knock every day. This is the opportunity I've been waiting weeks for.

"Can I ask you a question?" I roll to my side and lean onto my forearm, as I make the request.

There are these little moments on set when he makes a dark comment that raises brows and doesn't affect me and our short morning conversations while grabbing the coffees that connect us beyond my agenda. It's terrifying. I'm opening this emotional level connection with Bennett that I didn't want. For some reason, I had the impression I could pull him in without giving anything in return. It makes everything that much more difficult.

I need to know what's under his shell. It could be the mystery, the excitement of uncovering who he is...or was; I really don't know. Before I move forward, it has to be clear that my next decision won't harm anyone else. Only Bennett's reputation will get dragged.

He stares at the edge of the building, replying without so much as a glance in my direction. "You can ask, doesn't mean I'll have the answer."

"Did you always want to be a famous director *slash writer*?"

"Not even close. I have a degree in IT." I catch his eye for a moment, and then he looks back to the horizon with a sigh of relief and another lofty deep chuckle. He keeps doing that, and oddly enough, it's comforting; it's not worrisome at all.

"Then what led you here?"

"It kinda found me. I had this dream one night, believe it or not. Every detail—the depth—was like a vividly painted mural that I couldn't shake. It's kinda normal for me. I've written short stories for the hell of it a million times to get things out of my head. That was the idea, but you can see what happened."

The side of his mouth curls slightly as if he wants to smile, only stubbornly he refuses to show that he may not be a complete grouch. His laughter could be factual joy instead of amusement. He might *actually* be human underneath it all.

"It unimaginably became a huge sensation. I don't keep up with social media, but a few years ago I was trying to find someone, and it turned out quite a few someones were trying to find me, all for the film rights. It would be fucking stupid to give that away when I had the ability to make it happen from my vision instead of someone else's interpretation."

I hesitate, hoping he can't see how baffled I am by my internal argument. Will he praise my performance today? Why do I need his approval? Will I see him around Freedome? Is it worth having a conversation with him if I do? Does he deserve this life? Why should I care? Why am I here again? Then I remember. The visions come back to me, and I try to block them out. I bury them over and avoid the pain, like I do everything. I climb the rocking wall, leaving the shadows at the base. I'm on top and they can't choke me.

I softly sigh my confliction away. "What's next?"

He leans to his side, and I find his blue eyes return to me. "Why are you asking me all these questions?" My silence prevails over him. He inhales before continuing. "I feel like you're the type to hold grudges and up until now, seemed pretty accurate."

The type to hold grudges? I don't care if he takes my less-than-giddy laugh the wrong way; I have various reasons to—hell, everyone who works with him has more than enough excuses for resentment. "I could say it's the same reason you're sitting here entertaining *my questions*." I rub my thumb over my ring four or five—six times. "Are you happy? I mean, did the money buy happiness?" The weight of my lashes softens.

"Happiness, fuck, is that real?" He chuckles as I try to cover up my sunken smile. "Nothing—not one single choice will guarantee happiness. It comes and goes, those moments that make you feel as if life could never be more perfect, but they are just that...moments. Did the money make parts of life less stressful? Fuck yes, but you can't escape sorrow, anger, or fear. Someone will break your heart, someone you love will die, and someone will treat you less than you're worth. The only way to prevent that is to not have any *someones*."

"Then why keep living?" The morbid reality escaping my lips is not bothersome at all. Not to me and not to him. While someone like my maternal grandmother would go on a rant for an hour if I asked her that. I wouldn't do that since I haven't spoken to her since the funeral. Who am I kidding? Most of my friends would tell me to go see a doctor, respectfully. Am I getting enough sunlight? I'm not overworked, am I? Those are the friends that I have been ignoring their calls and only answering texts since I've been here. Balance is difficult to achieve, and they'd never understand what living beneath the shadows felt like.

"For those moments, I guess...because they're worth feeling everything else. Hah," his breathy laugh entraps me again. "Or because I like the pain. There's a word for that, uh...masochist." Yeah, I get that. "I don't have the answer." He shifts, his eyes detaining mine, and for a second I feel buzzed, like when that third tequila shot instantly erases everything except that moment, the stars looking ten times brighter as you spin around staring into the night in the middle of a half-empty parking lot of a shitty dive bar at eleven thirty with your degenerate friends. Not my mentally stable friends; the friends that are a muffed-up type of family and indulge in your hilariously absurd ideas. That kind of buzz. The one I've only experienced a handful of times because I've been too controlled to let go. His gaze disappears, and I remember what I'm here for. It's not to feel a rush of wild and free. It's not to become infatuated with Bennett Larson because talking to him takes me there for a concise moment in time. "I don't have any goals. I'll keep writing and keep producing. When it ends, it ends."

Step one. "How old are you, Bennett?"

"What is this, twenty-one questions?" He stares at me, hindering. I raise my brows virtuously. When he gets tired of my silence, he finally answers with a grumble. "Twenty-nine." His fingers trace the thread curve at the base of his pocket. He pulls out a blue and white box of cigarettes from his pocket, flipping the top open with his thumb. Between two fingers, he pulls a single smooth stick out.

Well, he's telling the truth; when it ends, it ends—because he has no problem inhaling poison. He reaches into the opposite pocket, pulling out a lighter. He brings the stick to his mouth, cupping his hand over the flame.

I roll my eyes and continue my interrogation.

Step two. "And you don't have family?"

His jaw tightens, looking up at the sky with an uncertain sigh. He draws the lit tobacco to his lips. His cheeks become shallow, thinning his lips as he inhales. He blows out a cloud of smoke before he answers. "I do not."

The one-two punch. I'm going in. "And how often do your eyes turn white?"

"My what?" He readily turns to me. His mouth narrows at each corner, and my chest rises and falls with the racing rhythmic beat beneath my ribs.

"Your eyes were white." I proceed to push, ignoring the indications to get on a flight off this roof. This is dangerous.

"You must have been mistaken," he argues. "My eyes are blue. They can't change colors." Bennett takes another drag of his cigarette, and I'm tempted to snap it in half. The putrid stench lives in my nightmares.

"I know what I saw. At first, I thought I was hallucinating. Then perhaps someone slipped something in my drink, but that nail polish you yelled at me for having on, yeah, that was detection polish, and it didn't change colors. I started thinking about it more and I know what I saw." I don't take my eyes off of him, but he refuses to look at me. "Your irises turn pure white."

"What do you want me to say?"

I want a better lie—at the least, you cold, soulless man. I'm not done yet. He's going to give me something.

"How often do your eyes change colors, maybe?"

"I couldn't tell you. I don't know nor have I ever known of them changing colors," he denies.

With an undertone of skepticism, I question him. "You seriously didn't know?"

He leans forward, an inch separating us. "No, Cherry." My gaze falls to his mouth, then to his bitter glare, and back to his motionless lips. His jaw tightens and his eyes remain the same—blue, malign death traps. When he speaks, it's temperate and smooth—evermore arrogant. "They're always blue in the mirror."

There isn't a change in his tone or fidgeting. He doesn't cover his eyes and he's not any more vague than usual. It's as if he's telling the truth. He had no idea his eyes had iced over.

"How did you know I was on the roof?" I ask.

"I didn't. I've been coming up here every night for the last two weeks. It's not as peaceful tonight."

"I was here first." I sink back to the flat of the roof, meeting the cold surface as I rest my head on my forearms. "I came up here to clear my mind."

"Try harder." His *blue* eyes widen, and he puts the tobacco-filled nightmare between his beautiful lips again, inhaling.

"Bennett, how did your family die?" I sit back up, unable to find comfort as the cooling air hits my skin.

He looks at me with the same wide glare. "Cherry, the questions. This is some personal shit."

"You're closed off. Nobody knows much about you and I'm not talking tabloids and media, I mean you've worked with some of these people for three years or something, and they didn't even know where you grew up." I wrap my arms around my legs, leaning into them as chills bead my arms with bumps.

"Am I to assume they now know?" He briefly glares.

"I was defending you," I lie. I let it slip to Kayla, and I'm confident everyone and the janitor now know. "I didn't know it was a secret." I rub my legs up and down, warming the fabric.

The veins in his hand tauten. "It's not a secret and I don't need you to defend me." My lip pulls in a snarl as I roll my eyes. *Jerk.* "Let them talk. There was a time in my life when I cared about what people thought of me. I cared too much about...too much." He shakes his head, pulling his arm out of the sleeve of his jacket. "My parents are not dead. I don't speak to them anymore." He pulls his other arm out, shaking it till it's no longer covering his body, then drapes the fabric over my shoulders.

"Oh, they're bad people?" I pull his jacket over my arms, refusing to make a big deal out of his gesture. He keeps surprising me with these little *kind* acts, and I hate how it plays with my head. Before I got here, I couldn't imagine he had any ethics. I almost wish he didn't. The more humanity he shows, the less I want to stop him, and the more I want to save him.

"No. Not at all. They're fucking saints." A strain heavies his voice. It must be *torture*...coming from saints. "They've endured too much heartbreak."

I hide my face in my elbow, pretending to scratch my nose. "Okay," I nod. "So...what? You made a mistake? If they're saints, wouldn't they forgive you?"

"I was the mistake."

"Do you honestly believe that?" Tucking my chin, I hold the warmth of his jacket as tight as I can. It doesn't smell like tobacco. It's more like...a campfire and...shea butter. I have very few memories of going camping, but the ones I have were with Mom catching fireflies and roasting marshmallows. Burning wood isn't a smell that I could easily forget...or the little flecks of orange floating around until they disappeared into the night. I should look for a campfire fragrance oil. I'm sure they make them.

"You called me *Benny* earlier." My attention returns to him as his shoulder touches mine. The warmth consoles me, and I decide not to pull away. He gazes deeply into my eyes, and I find it impossible to look away. I should. I want to...and at the same time, I don't. The pain in his expression seduces me. "I haven't heard that name in a long time. My sister used to call me that." His eyes drift away before mine do.

"You have a sister? I wish I had siblings, but it was just me and my mom growing up," I overshare.

"*Had* a sister."

Oh.

I blink away. "Annie," he continues. As I look back at him, his hooded eyes slip away. It's too late. I already saw the sorrow trailing down his face.

This isn't right. None of this is right. The man I came here to stop is a brilliant monster. He's destructive and aggressive and...This man is in agony. It's not who I expected to meet.

"I'm sorry, Bennett. I know loss...and struggle too well, like you."

"No, not like me," he snaps. "I didn't grow up in East Grenton. I moved there on my own free will the day I turned eighteen. It was my choice. Nobody put me there. In fact, they tried to stop me." The anger cracks in his voice. "I'll show them I thought. I don't need to follow their rules and let them judge *my choices.* Fucking irrational." He let's out another airy laugh, seemingly concealing the pain and frustration he'd exposed. His cheeks hollow. "I learned quickly what it was like; how much it sucked and how much it would take. They tried to get me to move back in, yeah. Annie tried." My hand warms with his touch, falling to my fingers. His eyes pity me. "I judged you. It wasn't personal." He sits back and his hand leaves mine.

He needed me to hear that—to really hear that. "I didn't want to be that person," he admits. "The uppity rich bastard who belittles someone *weird*," he says with air quotes. "You said you didn't know who I was, it's because I fucking choose to keep to myself. I don't need to prove to anyone that I'm doing fine."

I search his face, not sure if I scold him for calling me weird or comfort him. An Earth-shattering loss might have been his tipping point. He's broken and critical within it. "I feel sorry for you, Cherry. You grew up with very little and I chose to start from scratch."

"You don't get to do that. Don't feel sorry for me now." I brush the hair behind my ear, shaking my head. "I want you to push me and push me and keep pushing me. I'm not going to break. I'm five-four, *I'm a cute little blonde.*" I raise my voice an octave, dodging my head from side to side. "I know what I look like, but I'm strong and I don't want a director who's going to tiptoe around me because I was dealt a bad hand and had to play with it." I stand up, holding out his jacket. "Here."

Bennett rises, towering over me; his eyes fight for my attention before he lets go and takes it. "Wait." He grabs my forearm, and his fingers clasp the entirety, closing around my arm. "Can we keep all of this between us?"

"Your *not secrets* are safe," I reply, trying to leave. The pressure of his hand deepens when I pull away.

I despise him, and yet I like everything he's doing to me. In sharing ugly memories, he manages to make himself look superior to me. That shouldn't excite me. I shouldn't want to taste his lips intentionally.

"Monday night, meet me up here again."

"Is that a question or a command?"

"Please?" He groans, leaving me.

"What games are you playing?"

"It's not a fucking game."

"At the very least, you're more entertaining than watching another game of Mario where Randy loses his ever-loving mind every time someone slips on a forsaking banana peel."

His lips part with a loss for words.

"I'll figure you out eventually, Bennett."

"Are you going to meet me or not?"

"Fine. I'll be here."

"You should get back to the party. Your Golden Retriever must be waiting for you to throw his bone."

"I'm trying not to make it a habit of judging people before I get to know them. It might be useful for you to do the same."

"Fuck it. Judge them."

With four words, my hope for him diminishes, and I recall why I fought to be on this set.

Bennett's First Trauma Licorice

"You're a sick little disaster." I exhale a deep chuckle. "It's okay. I got you. Tell me what you want." She begins to answer as I cut her off "Ah, ah, ah. I explained the rules very clearly. You tell me what you want without using your words. If you can't do that—" I slide my hands up her thighs, gripping her ass. "Then I guess we're done here." Squeezing her waist, I lift her until only the tip of my cock remains inside of her. As expected, she disagrees, pressing her warm, tanned hands harder into my chest, fighting to slide back down.

"That's right. I like it when you show, not tell." Oh, fuck. "Show me. Fucking show me, baby. Ah, yeah." Moans slip between my husky exhales. Her cries grow as she rides my cock, her hips circling and with every deepening roll I tilt my hips up, pressing into her.

"How's that feel? It feels fucking good, doesn't it? It feels good baby...and it could feel better." I squeeze her ass, slamming her tight against me. "Time to play."

Suddenly, she awakens from a trance and fixes her gaze on me. Her chin tilts to the ceiling, and her eyes roll closed. "Don't." I necklace her throat. "I swear if you fucking cum right now—you agreed. You tell me what you want without using your words—you show, then I—" I effortlessly remind her. "Tell."

I tighten my fingers around her waist, pressing my palms to her heated skin as I lift her naked body off of mine. As I slide to the edge of the bed, I wait for her to stop pouting before finding my white button-down on the floor. I hand it to her. "Put this on."

"Why?"

I sigh. She has a difficult time following directions. My fingers trail over her jaw, down her neck, and I press my palm to her chest—an eager thud pounds against my skin. I didn't choose this cabin for the aesthetic.

"Would you like to go outside completely naked or would you like to be covered up?"

"Outside?" Her voice trembles.

There's a fine line between pain and pleasure. If your dream is to fuck Bennett Larson, you might want to reconsider. Show and Tell isn't the only kid game I distorted into something sick. Hide and Seek is my favorite.

"You can have a flashlight."

"You remembered I'm afraid of the dark?" She reaches for my shirt, picks it up, and pulls it over her head.

"Yes. When I find you, I'm going to take each one of those perky little pink nipples into my mouth as your body shakes beneath me. You'll endure my teeth and you'll fucking love it."

"What if I don't?"

They're never worth the chase, but the chase is always fun. I wouldn't say I have a specific kink for this shit; it's the adrenaline I crave, the power, and control. It ties into the knot I call my newfound existence. I always had a mouthful of dirty words, but I couldn't always cash the checks I made out, if you get my drift. Finding someone who can actually keep up with me is the challenge now.

I booked this little rental cabin an hour from set a month ago. Molly was one of those fangirls who kept sending me emails and messages. Or was it Maggie? Marcy? Regardless, she's a one-night commitment with no strings attached. I set the rules. She agreed, and now she's going to disappear into this wooded forest surrounding us, and I get to hunt.

"Oh, my little disaster." *It's a stupid pet name, like baby girl, that gets them going because they're always fucked up and I can't piss the correct name out. It's better than slut, but if the shoe fits, fucking own it.* "Are you scared?" With my feet on the floor, I sit at the edge of the mattress and run my thumb over her stained lip. A thick black ring wraps around my thumb and on my third finger—the coldness startles her as I graze her chin. That's the point of them. "You feel it? Let it take over you. Don't fight that rush. The fear only makes it better. Feed on your pain and run, baby. And when I catch you it will all make sense."

She puckers her lips together tightly, and I remember how annoying it can be to convince some women that they can do this. Oh, how some of them talk a big game, and when it comes down to it, they're timid and nervous or have a difficult time giving up control. I grab her jaw, demanding her brown eyes.

This is the moment I should be telling her how I can't wait to devour her sweet pussy. Right now, I should be—but I freeze. I fucking freeze.

Fuck. Fuck, fuck, fuck. God damn it, *Cherry. Your eyes are white. I've seen them turn white, Bennett.*

Yeah, I use my abilities to ease their anxiety. Why wouldn't I? What if Melinda sees white? I don't know enough about her to understand what repercussions she'd bring. Could I be powerless with her? With all women?

I went days without mind-bending. Then, I took a shot. I convinced that young, tall guy from maintenance—whatever his name is—that working on the weekend would benefit him more than the rest of the team. It was a fucking lie. There was no way in hell I was going to let that clogged toilet sit until Monday.

Justin had left for the evening with an excuse about a doctor's appointment—soundly ludacris. He was going to hook up with that woman he had been flirting with. Despite all else, it proved a theory; I'm not completely broken. I manipulated him.

The man had to outsource plumbing and wait for them to fix it. I couldn't have ruined his day as much as it would have if he pointed out my proclaimed white irises. Now, I waste time pondering if I'm incapable of manipulating the female brain.

"Mindy, you're—"

"Mindy? My name is Melody." She bobbles her head in a pissy fashion and pulls away, my hand falling to her thigh.

Fuuck. I slipped. Cherry has poisoned my brain and I forgot *Melody's* fucking name. I knew it started with *M* and ended with *Y.*

I rub my hand over the shadow along my chin. "You know what? Fuck it." Quick to my feet, I grab her ankles and jerk her to the edge. Her life dangles in my hands as her eyes trace mine. If this doesn't go well, she's not leaving here with a beating heart.

The control heats the blood in my veins, my impassive stare locking her in as the electric current puts me in a chokehold. I told you before, this is difficult and, frankly, exhausting to repeat myself—let's just say it's a merciless intensity.

"Melody." A grit capsules my tone. "I'm about to give you what every man you've wished could have given you. The most enticing experience of your fucking life. My darling disaster, oh beautiful *Melody*," I repeat. "If you want that, *show me.*"

She slides her ass off the bed, between my legs, and my erection presses against her hip. She falls to her knees, deep doe eyes glued intently. Her palms take the hardwood floor and crawls between my legs, stealthily into the living quarters. Her naked ass arches as she smiles over her shoulder.

I walk to the threshold, rest my hands over the frame moldings, and wait for her to reach the front door.

"You're sexy as fuck. You know what you're doing, baby."

With a sultry dance, she reaches for the doorknob. Her eyes meet the darkness as she pulls it open, stuck in her fear. Fuck, I forgot to tell her the flashlight was on the kitchen counter.

She takes one step outside, followed by another.

This means Cherry's the only one that breaks me. Hah, fuck me.

My chuckles never stop while I pull my jeans on, then my socks, and walk to the door to lace my boots. Now, where's my little disaster?

"I'm here. Why did I need to meet you? Also, I didn't appreciate being called out for *poor posture* today." Cherry runs her mouth the moment her head peers over the ladder. I exhale a cloud of smoke and return to the sunset.

Oh, did you want to hear all the details with Missy or whatever the fuck her name was? I fucked her. It was mediocre. You didn't miss much. Anyway…

"You said you wanted me to push you. You want to be the best, right?"

She walks past me to the ledge. "Yes," she groans. *I'd bet money she rolled her eyes.* "Who's playing music tonight? Is that…Elvis?"

Cherry is mine now, and it doesn't matter if I like it or not. She has a hold on me that nobody else has, and it's not as simple as immunity.

"That is indeed Elvis." I reach for her, extending my arm out. "Take my hand." She doesn't contend. Her hand slides into mine, sending a wave of shock through my arm for the second time. Her giggly laugh fills my ears, leaving me with little time to react.

"Oh, thank the heavens. For a second I thought you were going to sing."

Narrowing my eyes in amusement, I reel her away from the ledge. "Do you believe in that…*the heavens*?"

She hesitates. "I guess."

"You don't sound too convincing."

"Well, what do you believe?"

As I stroll to the center with her hand in mine, a sudden wave of nausea hits me, and I let go of her. Fuck. I slowly exhale. Masterful timing—fucking side effects. "Mm…" I clear my throat and count to ten.

"I promise not to preach."

"Yeah, uh—" I refocus, pushing my hair from my face. "If there is a heaven, I'll never reach it."

When I face her, she nods and her lips take a thin line. "You're set on going to hell?"

"Hah, I'm already here." I abduct my arms to the sides, widening my chest, as I point out the obvious. "This is the hell. You gotta pass the test to move on to the heavens. I failed a long time ago."

"You're probably right. You would be rejected."

"Smart ass." Her brows raise, and she does that chin tuck, where she glances up at me, pretending to be innocent in her amusement. "While you're hanging out in hell with me, the least you could do is practice this dance. Give me a little entertainment, since we both know the *save the turtles* girl is going to make her way to the pearly gates...if they exist."

She exhales, slapping my hand and not letting go. "It was one turtle." I side-eye her, and she continues without skipping a beat. "Remind me, the ballroom scene is in what—two weeks?"

"Yes, dear. The dance is simple. I'm not doubting you will pick it up quickly. Staying in character and on step is what you should be thinking about."

I'm making shit up. Cherry doesn't need reminders and instructions. We pay other people to handle this stuff, not me. I'd tell her ten lies if it brought her back up here every night. I'd make up anything to listen to her talk outside of a crowded room. Would you enjoy it if I admitted it? If I told you that she's the first actual connection I've made with another person since, well—I'd like to give the answer I do for everything else—since I died, but that's a lie too. Annie was the last person that I allowed to see me. I haven't opened up to anyone; I haven't wanted to. Honestly, I don't know if it's her I'm interested in or her immunity.

My hand slips lower, and my fingers skim the skin peeking from the bottom of her cropped shirt. Another fucking crop top. I don't get the appeal of short shirts and high pants. Here's my rib cage, sexy, huh? I won't insult her right now. "Let your left hand rest on my shoulder and your right hand stay in mine." I press one finger to her chin, forcing her to look at me instead of her feet—or hands—or wherever else that didn't include my eyes. "Look into the eyes you like so vastly."

"They are pretty."

"Posture."

"Again?" If looks could kill, Cherry would be the death stare champion.

"You'll hear it till you perfect it. Shoulders back." I squeeze her waist, pulling her hips closer. *Was that a gasp?* "Don't hold your breath. Three steps, okay? Step backward with your right foot when I step forward. Think of following the lines of an invisible box on the floor." She relaxes slightly, and I understand. "I feel it too," I mutter.

"What?"

"Uh, your posture is better." With a fucking knife, I cut the tension.

Bennett, how did you become so suave on your feet? Besides that wedding moment, as soon as I got my permit, I drove Annie to dance class every Thursday at six. We couldn't be a minute later or I'd hear about it for a week. Some days I would hang out in the parking lot and wait for her, watching her class from the side viewing window. I had an innocent crush on Kelsey Rodner too—a girl in Annie's class who was made of shiny ebony hair and pretty green eyes. The ballerina never gave me the time of day.

"You're a natural. Annie taught me how to dance." *Well, fuck it. I'm telling her.* "Being with you, it's familiar...I'm trying to say this the right way..." Shit.

Her eyes wander to the side. "I remind you of your dead sister?" Her lips curl inward, pressing together. Then she puffs her cheeks out like a poisonous little pufferfish, holding in her laugh.

"Um...yeah." The merest simper pulls at the corner of my mouth. She stumbles forward, stepping on my foot. "Ouch." My low growl erases any chance of an authentic smile.

"Oh shoot, was that supposed to be a moment?" The tilt of her chin emphasizes the skyward look in her eyes. I glare at her briefly, sucking at my teeth.

Don't do it. Be nice.

"Look, I'm going out of my comfort zone here. I want to be friends...That's what I'm trying to say," I disdain.

Her smile fills half her face as she holds her hand to her chest. "Bennett Larson's first ever on-set friend, possibly *only friend* in existence? I'm honored."

"You can keep it to yourself." I grab her wrist, my hand fully clasping around it as our palms skim against one another. I place her hand back on my shoulder. "Please."

"Secret friend, check." She nods. "So friend, how do you think tomorrow is going to go?"

"I should ask you that. Are you nervous?"

I don't want to admit it, but I am pressing myself thin. Between filming and writing, I'm drowning. The weekend away would have been exactly what I needed if she wasn't in my head. Saturday morning I planned on telling her I changed my mind; I didn't need to meet with her on the roof. By then I already knew it would eat at me. I needed more. Why is she different? What's it about her? As for tomorrow—it's a sex scene.

"I can handle it, Bennett. It's my job and it's going to get *steeamy*," she hums.

"It's not going to be you, Ames, and the intimacy directors. There's going to be multiple cameras in your face, and the entire crew. It'll be more awkward than steamy."

"I'm not worried." Her hand leaves me, and she walks two feet away, spinning in a circle with her arms out. Her fingers wiggle and lace in the breeze. Not a dime of stress. It's like watching a captive animal being released into the wild.

"Good, just like Samantha," I say a little louder, finding the cool surface at the edge of the building where I sit, leaning my arms against my knees. "Plus you did sign a contract."

"I live and breathe *Samantha*, Bennett," she asserts. "It's almost hard to turn her off and my brain back on. Then I remember, I'm not a rich cutthroat heiress." She parks her ass beside me, dangling her feet off the side of the build-ing. "You've met a lot of Samanthas' in this business, haven't you?"

"Hah, no. Many wealthy, strong women, but not *my* Samantha." She doesn't settle for long. Cherry rises, and I wrinkle my brows, as I continue to talk. "Would you believe I met her in another dream?" I rub my eye with my palm, realizing how stupid it sounds. "Corny as sin, I know. It's my process. I keep a notebook next to my bed at night." She balances on one foot, pulling her sneaker off, and her hands slide down her leg. She pushes a multi-colored sock off her pointed toe and switches to the opposite. She's... "Beautiful." I breathe out. "And heart-shattering. When I woke up, it dawned on me. Everyone loves a Samantha. Beauty and purity on the surface and full of demons under-neath, like the rest of us fucking sinners. We all have something—it's at least one thing—that we battle. When someone we hold to a higher standard has a breakdown, it's either deeply soothing, knowing they struggle too or it's a finger-pointing party full of gossip and bullshit, but nobody actually feels sorry for the rich gorgeous woman who seemingly has it all."

Barefoot sunshine stands motionlessly feet in front of me. Her arms at her sides, she looks down, climbing into my soul, or whatever is left of it, with her light eyes. "You're brilliant."

A warmth reddens my cheeks and takes me away from her bare feet, bringing me back to the skyline. "Don't hold me to the Samantha standard. I'm plenty flawed with more demons that I can try to drown."

"You share, I'll share?" She asks although it sounds like a dare. Her knees rest in front of me, and she sits back, crossing her legs. I feel like we're in some fucked up summoning circle and we're about to hold hands to chant and call the dead. *I'm already here.* "I call it trauma licorice."

"You want to trade demon stories?" I lean forward, my voice deepening.

"Sir, I encourage it," she counters, leaning inward. Her heated breath reaches my face. It's tempting—lips I've tasted, close enough for the taking.

"Um…okay." I sit back, somewhat straightening my posture. "I have mommy issues, so I sleep around."

"One up. I have daddy issues, so I occasionally sleep around."

I knew it. "How's that a one-up?"

"Daddy issues always trump mommy issues."

"Says who?"

"Me. We could take it to a vote, but considering there's only two of us up here, the conclusion won't be unanimous."

"How do you choose?"

She veers off to the side. "To sleep with? It's not premeditated if that's what you're asking."

"Random selection, then? Whoever's available?"

"My type is the *nice guy*, Bennett. I'm not going to take the time to morph a guy that's presenting a challenge. I'm not going to waste my energy. Anyway, it's your turn."

I glare at her but continue. "My parents favored my sister more than me."

"My dad was a sex offender."

"Fuck." She's not holding back. "I moved out the day I turned eighteen because I was tired of being the forgotten kid. I couldn't live up to Annie's accomplishments, and I didn't excel in anything of my own. Nobody would miss me."

"I'd miss you." Fuuck, stop looking at me like that. "I watched my mom in an abusive relationship with the same piece of garbage twice." She stares at me deadpan, her teeth barely touching and a gap between her full lips. Her words flow with ease. "He came back for thirds, but that was after I found her and her suicide note."

I close my eyes as soon as the words *found her* escape. "Cherry..." I avert my eyes. Without sympathy, I'm speechless. I said her name like I would any other day. If anything, I say it more breathy, like I want to pull her closer. As if it turned me on to know of her damage. Did she find her in a pool of blood or hanging from a door frame? Is the image etched in her head?

I know, I know. Sick fuck, it doesn't matter. That's her mom. It was her fucking mom.

"It's your turn," she demands.

My eyes promise to continue with a single look. "Um, Annie shouldn't have been the one born with a genetic condition. I should have."

She doesn't give me pity or hesitation, firing back with another demon of her own. "My grandparents had custody of me for a few years while my mom was in and out of treatment centers, working on recovery. They thought I was half evil because my father was a rapist."

"What?" I nearly break my neck.

This is not the woman who my team hired, who Mel signed off on. She's not sweet tea and everyone's girl-next-door crush. She's far more fucked up and I have no idea why she's putting her confidence in me. A few days ago, the woman could insult me with a fucking look, and now her darkest nights have spilled into my lap. Mine for choosing what I do with, and you know what? I don't want to share them. I want to keep them in a jar locked away for only my eyes, for only my ears. I want to walk around set every day, watch her perform every fucking day, and know that I'm the only one who sees who she really is. My second best-kept secret.

"Bennett. Go." She nudges me.

"Cherry, I'm a fucking asshole."

"It's your turn," she grimaces.

"That's it—I'm an asshole."

If anyone could be borderline insolent and still respectful, that was her. "Tell me another demon besides that you're an asshole," she pressures.

"I died once."

Fuck!

Avoiding her eyes, I crack my knuckles one by one. What am I thinking? Oh, let me one-up the abused girl with my death tale and, in the process, drive myself into the poke-and-prod lab. I may want to keep all of her demons locked in my bedroom, but that doesn't mean she'll keep mine.

"Drugs? Did they narc you?" She asks, unphased as if this is normal. It's easy to forget she grew up in East Grenton until we're alone and she tells me horrible things that...I get it now. She's telling me about this shit because she knows she can without being pitied or judged. I lived there. I know how rough it is and how much struggle surrounds you.

"Never touched a drug."

"That's my only guess. Any hints?"

"I got shot," I confidently answer, not moving a muscle.

"East Grenton life, huh?" She smirks.

No wonder I'm drawn to her. Misery loves company.

"It was the day I was moving out, too." Finally, a different reaction. Her reverse smile is comforting.

"Do you want to know my story, *Benny*?"

I don't answer.

"I was separated from my mom early on. She got full custody back when I was five. You were right. She was a stripper *and an addict*. She quit dancing for a cashier job at a local supermarket. It wasn't paying nearly what she made at the club, even with The Kitty being a small run-down shack filled with low-life men." She exhales and goes on. "It was okay though. She was clean, and we were on our own, finally back together. I *always* knew she cared and loved me. She alone showed me that I am worthy and deserving, even when she had a hard time believing in her own worth."

"It's hard being a single parent with no support and with more trauma than one should hold inside. The hospital helped at first. Then came the bills for therapy. She could barely pay rent, put gas in the car, and put food on the table. She tried to hide it, but I saw her…" She hesitates, no longer looking at me. "I saw her crying over scattered bills on the kitchen table often. The memories hurt. They make me feel weak. Do you know what that's like?"

"Once," I admit.

"I can't burn off any of the layers I've spent years building to protect myself. I refuse to let those images seep through the cracks and make me feel that pain again. I guess you could say I had to grow up pretty quickly."

"You don't seem to let it keep you from creating friendships."

"Yeah, well most women are hoping to find love too, like my mom." She tucks hair behind her ear and elaborates. "A woman wants love, companionship, a partner to hold down the fort, and of course, sex, so when my mom started dating again, I couldn't blame her. As early as seven years old, I could understand the desire of a husband until Greg. I hated him. He was nice at first. Then came the constant arguing, and eventually, it progressed, if that's the word for it. By the time I was fourteen, I had met a Stan, two Johns, Greg again, and a Harvey." A gentle smile takes her rage. "Harley Harvey. He was my favorite. He stuck around through the first relapse, but as much as it pained him to leave me, her second relapse was too much for him. He had no legal ability to take me and had twin daughters of his own whom he had partial custody of. He had to put them first. I get it. Oh, my life of little horrors," she plays it off. "Finding her five months after I graduated high school was…" She blanks.

We sit in silence. The breeze wraps our shoulders and twists hair in our faces until she picks up her chin to find me studying her.

"I don't want to let myself open that wound. It wasn't the drugs or the men that took her. It was herself and everything she couldn't bear to fight through daily anymore." She deeply inhales and lets it free. A light rekindles with her. "I'm an onion. I let others do the crying for me. I've seen more in those eighteen years than a child should ever witness. I cried then, I mourned then, and I picked my broken pieces up again because that's what I was taught to do. *Baby girl, we are born fighters. We fight till we don't want to fight anymore.*" She smiles. "My mom used to say that. You know how you can see a photo and hear it? That's what I feel when I think of *baby girl; we are born fighters.* She didn't want to fight anymore. Her choice." Cherry's fingers graze the top of my hand. "It's a lot."

"I want you to tell me everything," I insist. "How'd you get here?"

"Before I turned eighteen, my mom always made sure I was fed, my education came first, and I never went without something to open Christmas day, yet our long early morning walks...those talks, free of judgment, no fear, they're what I miss."

"A few months later, cue Greg for the third time. The moron had no idea Mom was gone. He thought I was covering for her, and we had this huge argument. My landlord had a fit and threatened to evict me if I caused another scene on the property, disturbing the peace or some bull."

"He was just looking for a reason to get me out of there so he could up the rent for some new unsuspecting fool and it didn't take long. I didn't do anything wrong, but the bastard claimed I withheld rent and evicted me. I wasn't in a position to fight it. I didn't even want to. Living out of my car was better in one way; I never had to be nice to that jerk again. I was so tired of being weakened. I wanted something more. Everything more."

"So you decided to get into acting?" I scoffingly ask.

"No." She glares. "Cindy, one of the managers who worked on my shift at Wen Market and whom I became close with when Mom passed, told me about her son's friend who had a temporary position for this company that provided short-term housing. I was going on two weeks of living in a box on wheels with no running water or appliances at this point. I missed work shifts because I overslept. My phone died often. Here was this opportunity I couldn't have dreamed up being served to me as the break I finally needed." Her arms cheer.

"I ended up on her son's friend's team. He was such a flirt and a twerp. Um, uh..." She fades off like she had before, eventually resurfacing. "I left Arcdale when I talked my way into a meeting at Averd Management with Alice Yucain. I had several supporting roles over the past two years and I'm making a healthier living than I once was, but Bennett Larson—you—you're the biggest name in film right now."

"You didn't give a full answer. Why acting?" I ask.

"I should be getting paid for what I've been doing my whole life."

"You're life was fucked." A stifled laugh escapes her lips. Then another, until she's giggling. I slide my fingers across the palm of her hand and grab her wrist. "Come on." I spin her as she stands and rest my hand on her waist. "The music's still playing. One more dance."

"With perfect posture," she mocks, bobbling her head.

"There's always room for improvement and don't worry, I won't step on your feet."

"I know, that's my job."

Stop Being
A Green-Eyed
Monster, Bennett

A tall brunette with a tight bun on the top of her head holds up the slate board, relaying to film and audio what scene is being shot. "Action," I call.

"Samantha, wait." Jensen grabs her hand.

"Why would I wait, Jensen?" She looks at him, ready to walk out the door.

"Because I love you." Jensen pulls Samantha closer.

"Love doesn't swallow lies." She looks into his eyes, unshaken.

"Please, give me one more chance...baby?" He begs on his knees, wrapping his arms around her legs. Samantha pulls him back to her level, kissing his lips softly.

"I've lied to you so many times and never once did I confess and cry for forgiveness, clinging to your body. You knew exactly who my father was the day you met me. You won't get in the way, Jensen." She pushes him back down and walks to the door. "I'd apologize, but everyone lies...because not everyone can handle the truth. I can't spare your feelings anymore, Jensen." Samantha exits.

"Cut! Fuck yes. Perfect," I announce, tossing my headset at Justin.

He fumbles with it and his phone, managing to catch them from falling. "You have a video meeting set up for tomorrow at three. Is that going to be fine?" He asks.

"Yeah, send me an email with the details and that podcast thing; send me a copy of that email too." I begin to walk away, stopping a few feet before facing him. "Hey, did you see where Cherry went?" She was here a minute ago.

"She probably went off with Ames. They've been seen together a lot lately." He looks up from his phone. "I don't think they're dating."

"I didn't ask. Confirm the details before you email me."

I walk away, unbuttoning my white shirt and rolling my sleeves. I contemplate getting another cup of coffee before I head out. To my distaste, it smells like pumpkin or what the fuck is that spice—something of the nutmeg range. The liquid swishes around the glass as I remove the lid, and I can tell it's not a dark roast either. Fuck it. I'll write on fumes until I pass out on my laptop again.

Ignoring everyone dismantling their day, I reach the exit through the main lobby and pull the door open, turning the corner. I stop and clear my throat, making the couple against the wall aware of my presence.

"Mr. Larson." Ames stiffly steps back, and I see her face. She tilts her head, clearly annoyed that I interrupted.

"Take it somewhere else," I reply, watching her creased lips soften.

"Sorry, won't happen again," Ames calls as I walk past them.

I didn't want to say that. I don't. I'm...no. Stop. Don't stop. Keep walking. Do not fucking turn around. *Fuck.*

You know what's going to happen, right? I'm about to fuck shit up.

There are no life lessons. There is no sound of reason. This is one of those moments where I remind you who I am because Cherry is mine. She's not his toy. She's my person. Mine. I can't let it go. I won't. I refuse. He doesn't get to put his hands on her. Not on her hands, not in her hair, and I'll chop them the fuck off if I see them on her waist again.

I turn around, walk up to Cherry, and wrap my hand around her arm just below her shoulder. Leaving Ames outside, I pull her into the building.

She jerks away, her hands coiled tightly. "Bennett, what? You said to take it somewhere else. What's the problem?" She flicks her thumb backward as she looks toward the glass door with a scrunched nose—piercing missing.

"I can't unsee you kissing him."

"What?" She wrinkles the length of her face. "You've watched me kiss him for months."

"No. I watched you kiss him as an actor, for the screen—not for pleasure." I search the room, avoiding her soul-capturing eyes.

The greatness of the building is plain and lacks vibrance. It's ideal when scenes and films are being changed. It's fucking ugly when you stand in a small, blank canvas made of off-white drywall, windows, and doors. Its empty state is a pleasantry.

"I know you said to keep it professional. It won't be a problem. We're adults, Bennett. We talked about it." She steps toward me, and I counter, using every ounce of willpower to keep my hands to myself.

"It *is* a problem. You're better than him."

She's fearless, raising her chin to me as I tower over her. "Do you think I would allow a man unworthy to touch me?"

"I don't know. You weren't very clear on that the other night," I overstep.

"Oh." She nods, flicking the tip of her tongue over her teeth. "You're going to take our personal conversation and twist it as you see fit."

"It's not like that, Cherry."

"Then what? What is it like?" She snaps, resting her fingers on her hips.

My fingers lace over the back of my head, and the distance of empty white walls call me. When I turn back to her, it's over—any logical reasoning.

The odd street clothes accompanied by heavy set contouring muddies. I don't take the time to study her lips. I don't analyze her eyes. I don't think about placement or her taste. I don't care about my prolonged pleasure.

I press my fingers to the sides of her neck, roughly taking her jaw in my hands. Her warm, painted lips softly melt under my convincing pressure. Ounce by ounce, adrenaline floods my nasal cavity, her honied scent telling me to devour her. This is right. I don't want to let her go. I want to slap her against the wall and taste every square inch of her body.

This one time, I don't fucking care. I had to have her.

My blackened heart pounds hard against the walls of my chest, sending chills over my back. A liquid heat coats the underarms of my shirt with every second that Bennett fights with Benny—a dark wrestling match deep within my soul. For the millionth time since she walked onto my set, the part of me with morals argues with the part that doesn't give a fuck.

She was meant to be mine like I was meant to become the undead.

Her mouth finally breaks from mine. She slowly backs away, putting enough distance between us to free her lips. She's close enough to let me do it again.

My grasp on her jaw tightens and I take her bottom lip between mine, sucking her into my mouth.

"Your eyes," she whispers.

Fuck.

I drop my gaze to the floor. *Why does this keep happening?* Her darling hand encircles my throat; the curve of her thumb ellipses my Adam's apple. With a crooked squint, a shaky smirk crosses my face.

"You can smile."

Her lips attack mine as her nails claw at the back of my neck. Fiery, unfathomable heat divides us and brings us closer. The deeper her lips swim into mine and her tongue flicks in my mouth, the harder it is to stay in control. If I reach for her thighs—if I pick her up...She has no idea what would happen—the secrets she would discover.

"I see what's going on," a tentative voice interrupts.

Our lips unlock, and I look to the doorway. The annoyance becomes painted across my face as the pretty boy comes into view.

"The cast can't have any fun, but Bennett Larson is above the rules," he bitches. Ames holds the door open. "Keep her," he yells. "She's a tease anyway." He lets go of the door, walking away as it slams shut.

"I guess your eyes don't *just* turn white when you're frustrated." Her words are hushed and threaded in amusement.

"They do not turn white," I grumble and encase her wrists with my hands to pull her fingers off of my neck.

As I reach the door, it appears Ames was alone and long gone.

"What happened to being friends?" She asks.

Returning to face her, I slip my hands in my pockets and look down at my Oxfords. "I didn't plan that." Her poison-filled eyes pin me. "I don't want anything more than friendship, Cherry."

What the fuck are you doing, Bennett? Shut up. Don't you think I know what I did? I open the gates to a new realm so I can walk away with an everlasting curiosity of what lies beyond the threshold. I fucked up, and this time there's nothing I can do to reverse it.

"Okay, fine." She strides toward the door. "I'm going to go after Ames."

I rush to cut her off, putting my arm across the doorframe. Her eyes dart back to me.

"I told you he doesn't deserve you. Didn't you hear him?"

"I *have* been teasing him. It's not a lie, although he essentially asked for that." She shrugs. "Ames is not a bad guy. *You are.*"

"You're a strong, amazing woman and he's an entitled asshole." Heaviness takes my brows.

"And so are you!" She shouts.

"I'm not the same," I deny.

"*Of course not* and you *didn't* pull me aside, kiss me, deny me, and then continue to tell me I'm an amazing woman. Those are the type of games a manipulative, narcissistic asshole would play. Ames doesn't do that." A burdensome sigh breaks her vexation. "Be straight with me, B. What do you want?"

I step away from the door, finger-combing my hair from my eyes. "I shouldn't have kissed you." Fuzzy spots light my vision, one by one forming a cloud of panic. *Fuck!* Not now, come on! Are these stress-induced? It's happened more often.

I close my eyes as I tuck my chin, hoping she doesn't notice as I slowly release the air from my chest. *Come on, come on. Let this work.*

"Now what? Where do we go from here?" She closes her arms over her body, her fingers tapping stiffly to her radial nerve. "You did and I kissed you back. What happens now?" She asks, less apprehensive than I would expect.

"Nothing. We forget it." I open my eyes and try to move closer to her. "It was a mistake. You made one and I made one."

"That's not fair." She unlocks her arms. "I didn't want to kiss you on the mouth. That was barely a kiss! But that…" She thumbs toward the door. "That was burning inside you for a while. How long have you wanted to kiss me like that?"

Closing the gap between us, I bow to her level and look her in the eyes. "You're right. I wanted that." *She's mine. Friends or…whatever that was. I don't want anyone taking her time besides me.* "I didn't want to walk away and leave you with Ames. I don't want to share you." *I want to grab a handful of her hair and yank until I can taste her once more.* "Nothing can happen between us. It's too messy, no matter how much I enjoyed it."

Looking back at her mouth, I know this is the most bullshit I've ever spoken. It's too messy. I don't want to ruin our friendship. It's cliche, and yeah, fucking bullshit. It's not the reason I can't keep her. I couldn't keep an angel from Heaven.

She wraps her hands around the back of my neck, and her thumbnails dig into the skin below my jaw as she pulls my mouth back to hers. I don't want to stop her. I don't. Fuck. It feels good. She feels—no. Fuck. Fuck, fuck.

I reluctantly pull away, the undeniable growl repeating between my ears. I remove her hands from my neck, left empty of the pressure of her nails.

"Cherry," I hum. "I need you." The words don't surrender to the filter in my head. I don't believe it myself. Her gelid eyes soften, taking me in as her teeth tug the skin of her lower lip. "I like your vibe."

"You need me because you *like my vibe.*" She nods, her lips thinning. "Okay. Fine. I'm going to go shower…I'll see you later." She walks around me, pushing the door open. Her eyes gleam, and a subtle irritation from my explanation remains. "Rooftop."

The deepest sigh escapes my lungs. *The rooftop.*

"Have you seen this?" Cherry yells as soon as her shoes hit the roof.

I blow a cloud of haze out of my mouth, scanning her body in full length. "I'm betting you're about to show it to me."

She rushes to my side, holding up her phone as if I could read it in her shaking hand. "It's not a joke, Bennett. Look at this photo. How did they get this, yet publish it within hours?" I wrap my hand around her wrist, stopping her from moving.

"Son of a bitch," I mumble, pushing the dark stands from my face.

I wasn't exaggerating when I said the press would do anything for a story. They don't give a fuck if it's the biggest load of bullshit. It's a picture of me and Cherry, tongue-tied and sexy as sin.

"Now I'm a director-sucking, talentless whore. Listen—" She draws her phone back to her face as amusement pulls at my lips. I take a puff of my smoke, waiting for the angry little bumblebee to continue. "*Cherry Kaas is the newest leading lady in a bound-to-be hit film from director and writer Bennett Larson. Larson is known for acquiring upcoming actors, although this is the first that one has taken a starring role. So how are indie actors getting his attention? It appears Ms. Kaas has been using her lip-smacking skills.*" She shows me the screen again—as if I could see it. "It's been reposted, shared, and the comments...they're *fucking disgusting*," her voice cracks.

She said *fucking*. "Easy princess. You'll taint that good girl rep even more with a potty mouth."

"I told you." She strides to the ledge, and her hair covers her face with a gust of wind. She fights it off angrily. "When I'm angry, you don't want to be around me."

"One curse word and I'm terrified." I trail behind her, a single hand tucked away. "Don't throw a tantrum this close to the edge."

"It's not funny. They're dragging my name as the newest Hollywood whore."

"Welcome to the public eye, dear." I blow another cloud of smoke out through my nose.

"Can you put that *nasty*—" She flares her nose, prepared to vomit. "—*thing* out?"

"You don't want a hit?" I ask, holding the cigarette out. "You could use it." My eyes fall over her body again, stopping at her exposed navel. Sweatpants and another pink crop-topped t-shirt ruined by the ugly white chunky sneakers.

"I hate that smell."

"I hate those shoes." I point, and her eyes follow.

"Says the man whose wardrobe looks like he never changes clothes." She glares. "It's the smell. I hate the smell. I can't detach it from the piece of shit that beat my mom half to death." She looks down like she's contemplating jumping before returning to her original dilemma. "You have to fix this."

"What about weed?" I inhale again, not doing as she asked. "You gotta cool it with the dark joke. *He beat my mom half to death*," I mock. "Your pretty little white wings will burn."

She hastily walks up to me, snatches the cig from my lips, and snaps it in half. She throws it down and stomps the heel of her ugly sneakers on it until it's flat. "You kissed me. This is your fault. Fix it, B." With the wave of her bare finger directly in front of my face, I laugh through a smile, slip my now-empty hand into my other pocket, and capture the full carton in my palm.

"Think about it, Cherry. How did the media get a photo of us in the lobby? Even with the best lens, it would be blurry from the gate, although it's quite logically impossible."

Her brows furrow and her lip twitches slightly. If I wasn't constantly staring at them, I wouldn't have noticed. "You think it was an inside job?"

"Fuck, Cherry. It was Ames. Like I said, he doesn't deserve you."

"I'm going to kill him," she replies, grinding her teeth.

"As much as I'd like to see that, I can't have it. I'm not reshooting. I forbid the execution of Ames Heart." I pull the carton from my jeans pocket and slide my thumb across a stick until it separates from the rest. "I'm learning so much about you, Cherry bomb," I scoffingly laugh. "You are a bit of a hot head."

Her jaw drops, and then she clenches her teeth together. In her fury, she grabs the box from my hand, throws it down, and stomps three or four times on it before picking it back up and walking to the edge of the roof, where she throws it off.

Well, fucking shit. I stand corrected. She is very much a monster when she's angry.

"You want me to pretend that asshole didn't drag my name?" She yells.

Asshole. Hah. But *he's a nice guy*.

"No." I hold my lighter to the cigarette between my lips until it catches. "I want you to be smart." My cheeks hollow as I take a drag, inhaling the chemicals that give me a short buzz.

She slowly walks back to me, twirling a golden strand around her finger. "Benny," she pleads, far too sweet for a woman who was fuming a second ago. A little light bulb lit in her head. She thinks when she's yelling and swearing, I should duck for cover when the truth is...this calm, collected, sweet tone is far more terrifying.

"Don't call me that." Flicking ashes to the side, I entertain her, wanting a look inside her mind. "What is it?"

"Help me fix this and get back at Ames."

Life lesson: The best revenge is doing nothing to them and everything for your-self.

It's watching your weak-minded wrongdoer melt when you succeed after they tried to make you fail. And the-fuck if I can say I've been living to that lesson. I've destroyed anyone who has gotten in my way and I'd do for her too.

"What do you have in mind?"

"Pretend we're dating." Her shoulders shift and her blue eyes get bigger.

Fuck no.

But why Bennett?

It's cliche and overdone, plus Bennett Larson doesn't "date." I thought she had something a little more fun in mind—defacing his trailer with a thousand banana hammocks or, you know, lighting his house on fire. I'm sure one of those paparazzi out there has his address. How many do you think he owns?

"Look..."

"Eh uh." She tsks, holding her finger up for the second time and I swing my upper body, shielding my cigarette from her. *She's not swiping my last one.* "This won't exclusively benefit me. You get me all to yourself, at least until we part ways."

I didn't think about that—her leaving. The wheels in her head spin more. It's obvious by the way her tongue skims over her upper lip and her brow wrinkles. The master plan is unfolding before my eyes as she slowly wanders back and forth, her arms wrapped around her body.

"What are you implying?"

She stops, her eyes deadpan mine. "You're selfish, B. You want my full attention, but only as *friends*," she scoffs. "You get what you want and I change the conversation. I won't look like I slept my way to the top when I post photos of us on social media with the story of how we met on set for the first time and you had nothing to do with casting my role."

"And on set? Who's to say Ames doesn't contradict your claims with his own? Everyone knows we didn't hit it off at first sight. You showed up late the first day for fuck's sake. Nobody knows we meet up here at night or, frankly, that we talk to each other. I like it this way."

"I'm not saying we tell them that. You don't want to share me and I don't want to share this place. This is ours." *The way she says ours...* "Please. You're the writer. Write our story."

Our story. Cherry and I are on *our* now? She's in my fucking book. Damn it. "I won't compromise on the film. If you're fucking up, I'm calling you out."

"As you should. Just...flirt a little. Hold my hand on occasion. Elementary stuff. Like, you direct actors all day, and you're telling me you can't play the part? I'm willing to give you my undivided attention with zero orgasmic benefits. This has to be a two-way road."

My gaze drifts into a smoky cloud rolling across the moon. I take every puff that my last cigarette will offer, knowing what's to come.

"It's not if I can, it's if I'm willing. *Fuck.*" I sigh. "I guess I owe you some batteries too?"

"Batteries?" She wrinkles her nose.

"For the vibrator you're replacing Ames with."

A big smile lights up her entire face. "You're in?"

"I don't know why, but yeah...I'm in."

She jumps and clings to my body. I take the abuse of her arms around my neck and her hair in my face. I press my nose to her skin, honied gardenia drowning my senses. I unfasten her arms, letting her feet hit the ground.

"And you owe me a carton," I contend.

"The hell I do. I did you a favor."

I bow my head, pinching the bridge of my nose. This debate would go on for hours. I should surrender now.

Bennett Is The Vocabulary Police

"**H**it me." I press my tongue to my hard palate and swallow.

Dear Diary, it's been ten hours since I've written—psych. Did you think I was serious? I've been preoccupied with Cherry and making less progress elsewhere. By elsewhere, I mean talking about myself.

I don't know if I'm going to keep this. It might not make the second draft.

I'd imagine, you're hung up on her horrific childhood. I've moved forward—perks of being a zombie or curse?

"Bennett, are you listening?" She asks.

I close my laptop and lean back from the edge of the roof. "Start over."

"*I first met Bennett Larson in an airport. I didn't like him and it was obvious he didn't like me when I showed up late on the first day of shooting. I had a good explanation!*" This turtle girl. I smirk. "*I had to spend the next four months dealing with him. I didn't plan to enjoy his dark humor. I didn't expect to have deep conversations to the point of spilling my guts on the floor. And I didn't think I would have to make an announcement that I'm dating the one and only Bennett Larson, but when someone decided to take our intimate moment and make it an entertainment piece, trying to make me look less than, I had to make a statement,*" Cherry reads aloud.

"*At an airport*, not in," I correct. "I don't like the last sentence either. Try, *An intimate moment was stolen from me for a story. My private life is mine to share. Yes, I'm dating the one and only Bennett Larson.*"

"*The one and only.*" She laughs. "Okay, conceded, take a picture with me." I stand next to her as she holds her marbled pink phone by the PopSocket. "Loosen up. You're so stiff."

"This isn't exactly natural."

I don't know how I got here. I am the one and only Bennett Larson, and she's the one and only person on this planet who can cut me open and find a shred of the guy I used to be? Ugh, fuck. I can't figure it out. She brings something decent inside me to the surface. She has no idea of the blood I have on my hands. She wouldn't ever be alone with me again if she knew the anguish I was capable of.

"I have an idea." Her unmistakably bright yellow purse rests on the ledge. She retrieves it and pulls a small bendable tripod out.

"That's smaller than what I'm used to seeing."

"Do women often tell you that, too?" She fucks around with her phone and steps back, looking at herself as she adjusts her leggings.

"Never."

She grimaces at my wide smile. "Dance with me," Cherry insists.

"Right now? Without music?"

"Play something on your phone," she orders like I'm an idiot.

Vacantly glaring, I pull out my phone and click on my last playlist. I adjust the volume and sit it next to her tripod.

"Come on, gorgeous." With her hand in mine, I twirl her until her fingers rest between mine. "This is a nice dress." The red floral sundress flares as she spins.

"It was a gift."

"From who?"

"You don't them." I choose to let her vague attitude slide. "Is this what you like to listen to? It's like R&B or—is it rap?"

"Sometimes."

"It's kinda sad. I guess I would have picked you to be a classic rock kind of guy."

"I thought you gave up judging for religious beliefs of something." With a twirl, I bring her back to me, keeping one hand in hers and the other on her waist, like before. "It is a sad song. It's about missing someone and struggling with your shit by yourself."

I have a whole playlist like this. I wouldn't admit it to anyone else. I'll tell her how fucked up I am, all about the demons in my head, and shit, I'd tell her about the lives I've taken before ever letting her see that I am the unlikely curator of a sad boy playlist.

Her soft nod changes the subject. "See, not as stiff."

"Posture," I fuck with her.

One of the days I'm going to get her fired up enough to see this manic side she likes to bullshit about. I wonder what else she hides behind that smile.

"My posture is perfect."

"You're right, but I had to say it." I close my eyes as the chorus hits and mouth the words *Tell me why?*

"Are you going to sing?" My gaze meets hers, and I smirk as realize I got caught. "No way, you can sing? *Doo it!*"

"No..." I exhale a rigid chuckle. "Not happening."

"Come on, B." She pokes me in the ribs, and I twist to the side. "You can smile!" Is she trying to fucking tickle me? "Now you look like you like me."

She has a point. Somehow she managed a genuine smile. A smile that only Annie and my dumbass friends would get. I can't remember the last time I smiled like that. "This was a smart idea," I admit, reeling her back by the wrist.

"*Be smart, Cherry. Posture, Cherry,*" she mocks. "Was your sister as structured as you?"

"No. Annie was..." She earns another smile—not with teeth and more powerful—fueled by the thought of my big sister. "Sunshine and free-flying. Believe it or not, I wasn't always this *structured*," I lower my voice an octave. "I was a mess."

As much as I miss parts of that life—parts of the man I was—if I had the opportunity to choose today to stay this way or to go back, I wouldn't change it. I'd stay this monster over the invisible man. I'd rather be talked about for being an asshole than lost in existence.

"I can't picture you as anything else. *So serious.*" She knuckles my cheek and I level my eyes at her, holding her hand out to twirl her away from me. "I know some really good jokes. Bet I can put another smile on your face."

"Okay, try me," I accept her challenge, crossing my arms in front of my chest.

"What do you call a blind dinosaur?" She pauses, and I shake my head. *Is she fucking serious?* "Do-you-think-he-saur-us."

I chuckle. "That was awful."

"But you laughed!" Her eyes widen with a smile twice the size of mine.

"That was barely a laugh."

"It was a laugh."

A thought slips through my filter. "You're just as bright as she was. I don't know how you do it; how you're still positive with everything you've gone through."

She answers without hesitation or hitch in her tone. "It's pretend. It's what I do. I play the part." She evades my eyes, chewing at her lip.

"That's the thing. Don't do that shit around me."

"If I stop acting, will you?" A crisp breeze catches her hair, and she backs away more.

"What's that supposed to mean?" I'm not pissed, but I have no doubt my face looks it.

"Nothing."

"No, what does that mean?" I repeat with more bite. "Cherry."

She hastily closes the distance between us, brushing her body against my chest. "You're into me. Be into me."

"I'm attracted to a lot of women." I lower my mouth directly above her ear. "It's not a big deal."

She tips her head back, fixated on my rejecting scowl. "You're full of it."

"What do you expect me to say?" I look away, my jaw inflexible, before I meet her intense glare. "That I can't get that kiss out of my head?" The heat of her increasing breath caresses my skin. "That I want to throw you over my shoulder right now and...eh, no." A hardened chuckle takes my words. "I couldn't even tell you what I want to do to you." She presses into me, and I want her to make her scream so fucking bad. "The—" I exhale loudly. "Fuck. Cherry." I take her face in my hands, my thumbs wandering over her smooth skin, tracing the outline of her pouty lower lip. "The fucking world would shift." I let go of her and walk to the ledge, visually chasing the clouds and hiding my hands in my pockets. "Would it change anything? Don't answer. It won't. There is no winning."

"What do you consider winning?" She follows. "Because of this." The sound of her hands hitting against the sides of her thigh makes me briefly glance back at her. "Talking to you, dancing with you, it's pretty good from where I'm standing."

"We're arguing. Cherry if this is happiness then I don't want to know what a relationship would be like with you." Saliva pools in my mouth, and I tilt my head to the side to spit. A fucking relationship? I liked talking to her. I wanted to fuck her. Now I'm thinking longer-term. She's only mine *right now*. Not in two months, two years, or two more lifetimes. "Maybe this wasn't a good idea."

"Then maybe I should change my post and tell everyone about the freakish eye thing you have going on," she boasts.

I glare at her, disgusted with her taunt. "Dry threat. You have no proof that happened."

"*Happens.* It happens." She steps closer.

Do it, Cherry. Come closer, so I can dangle you from the side of this building until you come to your fucking senses. I can see the fear in her eyes as she grips my palms for dear life.

"Maybe you don't want to tell me why it happens, B," he continues. "But you'll have to answer when everyone else starts asking questions."

"Again, you have no proof." The more she fucks with me, the more irate I get.

"You know my secrets, Bennett. I'll find the rest of yours out sooner or later."

Won't she shut the fuck up? No; she keeps edging. "Why are you being like this?" My focus is uncertain, shifting between her eyes.

"Oh, am I a bad friend, or did you give information away to someone you don't know very well? Telling the world how much of a loser Bennett Larson really is, that his parents don't want him."

I rush her, getting back in her face. "You are a work of art." I glare ferociously into her eyes, my chest rising and falling with each heavy inhale taking over my demonic soul. My jaw tightens more with every exhale.

"Proof." Her lips pillow as if she blew out a fire.

"What?" I grunt.

A calm smile highlights her cheeks. *I told you the calm was worse than the storm.* "I never turned the camera off, B. It's recording and your eyes are stark white."

"That was your plan?" I stand in her face, bending enough that my nose touches her temple. "Piss me off? Get my reaction?" I grumble against her skin. "I'll call it an edit job."

She looks up forcing me to move. Her arctic eyes dare me over and over like she's waiting for an opportunity. An opportunity to do what?

"Relax. I'm not going to talk." Her undisturbed and calm words only continue to add to my frustration. *I won't touch her.* She brushes against me, walking toward her phone, and I wait. Making a rash decision right now would only expand the mess I've led myself into. "Don't get mad at me, but..."

"I'm already furious, Cherry."

"Look." She holds out her phone steadily. The screen is paused on a zoomed-in shot of exactly what she's been describing to me. "You see it, don't you?"

"Fuck." My eyelids fall shut, and my hands fall to my head.

Why her? Why? Why! I've lived like this for years, and not a single person has noticed it, and not a single day has gone by where I had any reason to question it. Is it blood type? Does she have some rare blood or some shit? I want answers. What does she expect me to say?

"You honestly didn't know?"

"Fuck no." An airy breath distorts my words. "Why should I talk about it with you? You were gaslighting me to get what you wanted. You got me. You are very good, terrific acting. Bravo! A job well done." I pace.

What the fuck am I going to do? I can spin this. Contacts and a disgruntled ex. I could use it to my advantage for marketing. My team would be able to come up with something brilliant.

"How else was I going to prove it, other than provoke you or seduce you."

"Well by all means *fuck me.*"

"Don't tempt me." The rounded apples of her cheeks soften, pushed up by her smile.

"Give me the damn phone first so I can throw it off the roof. I'm not having you leak a sex tape next." The wind cloaks my body, pimpling the sweat on my arms.

"Boo. Where's the fun in that?" She taunts me, and I'm fed up. I want to squeeze the life out of her.

"Fucking your frenemy not hot enough for you?" I return in a rush, hovering over her. She trapped me. She wanted to humiliate me and now she wants to watch me beg. It's not fucking happening. "I don't trust you."

"Aren't you even the least bit curious?" She pushes her hands to my chest, tilting her head as her torment continues, tonguing her lip.

"Keep your nose out of my business. I'm not hooking up with you now *or ever.*" My luck, she would harvest my semen.

"You're hiding something." Her pathetic hands shove into my chest.

"If I was, there is no chance in hell I would tell you."

What in the fuck is she doing now? Judas fucking Priest. Why is she taking her shirt off? Do you see what I attract when I'm not trying? Crazy ass women.

Isn't that your specialty, B?

Ay, don't start calling me that now. It is my drink of choice, and I can admit when I've found a shot that's too damn strong for me.

"Cherry," I grumble. "What are you doing?"

She drops the crop top and wraps her arms around my neck. I take her wrists in my hands, pushing her away, the instant cold scowl painted on her face.

Mm. Can I insert six question marks here? Add that as a note to the editor. Fuck that, I make the final call. ??????

This is one of those times I think you need a recap, and I myself, am having a hard time searching for the appropriate language. Cherry has lost her fucking mind. Lost that shit. It's gone. Finito. Peace out, Cub Scout.

"Cherry, this is fucking insane. One minute I'm helping you stage a re-lationship, the next you're threatening me, and now you're hanging on me half-naked." Raising my hands in surrender, I take a few steps backward before dropping them. "Are you on drugs?" *Who's your supplier?*

"Um..." She blinks rapidly. "I've been feeling off," she replies, palming her forehead, dazed and hesitant.

"Maybe you should go get checked out. This is kinda fucking terrifying."

"Says the monster."

I need her head on solid. Not just with my sensitive information, but we're days away from wrapping. I pick up her shirt and flip it right side out. "Here, put your shirt back on."

"I can't do it anymore, Bennett," her voice cracks. Her lip quivers as her waterline starts to flood.

What the hell is happening now? Is this a hormonal thing, or is she a lunatic? Fuck. I wrap my arms around her, pulling her against my chest. *I'm ruining my shirt for her. Tears soak through the fabric, and I don't even want to see if her mascara transferred. I run my fingers through my hair, pushing the strands from my face.*

Stop. No. I told you not to do that shit. You think I'm not that bad of a guy? Like, darling, we are over halfway through this book. With all due respect, you know I'm a killer, for certain, and I've given you no reason to see past me being an asshole, yet I'm tugging at your heartstrings because I covered up the half-naked girl?

"You need to talk to someone. The mood swings from hell aren't going to work for me." I let go of her, and she looks up at me. Her puffy, save-me eyes attempt to rewire me. They want me to be the hero. For Cherry, I wish I could.

The corner of my lip twinges, wanting to offer a smile. My memories of saving the day for my darling sister and her friends flood my mind. Following her dewy eyes to her hand, she traces her ring and her skin pebbles.

She licks the salty drop from the corner of her mouth. "You hate me now, don't you?"

"Honestly, I want to. *I want to.* And I don't, but I'm not a fucking doctor. I can help you fix a fucking rumor. I can't bandage up bipolar or depression? Is it depression? Did all of that shit we talked about cause—"

"I'm not bipolar or depressed. I'm not normally like this, and since last night…I don't know. I can't focus. It's like…I don't know. These emotional spurts."

Since last night? *Since last night. And she's the only one to see my pupils turn white. Don't, fucking don't tell me this is connected to me. I can't influence her mind, but I can fuck her up with a kiss? Bullshit.*

There is no way she is like this because of me. It can't be the reason. Damn it! It's the reason.

She's like this because of me. Well, look at the hole you created, Bennett. Now I fucking do have to fix it. If I don't, I'm fucked with this movie. The last thing I need is a quack job actress picking fights in post-production. I mean, I could leave her like this, and when she goes batshit enough times, she'll get locked up, and that solves her talking about my eyes. That could put a damper on revenue. It could also boost it…

"Put your arms up. You're not leaving this rooftop without a shirt on." I palm my hands over my eyes, and I sigh. "Come with me."

"Why are we at your trailer?"

The old, white, and basic piece of metal is a sleeper—as in, it looks like shit, but it's nice where it counts. Why would I purchase your top-of-the-line fabricated box when I don't fucking need it? I have this damn thing towed everywhere, and it sits in my yard the few weeks a year I'm at the home base. I own one property with a small house on it, along the west coast. It is a place to blend in and disassociate. I bought it after my first book hit—before the movie adaptation.

"I'm going to help you. Don't ask me any more questions. Come inside and so you know, Justin isn't openly welcomed into my trailer, which means you're special."

"Compares me to his assistant and proceeds to tell me I'm special." She tosses her honey-blonde waves to one shoulder.

"This way." I lead her through the kitchen, living room, and small hallway—an open rustic cabin from the inside.

"Your bedroom. Really, B? You brought me here to take advantage of my issues." She walks two fingers up my arm as she stands behind me in the doorway.

I flick the light on and point to the black diamond-stitched comforter hanging off of my queen bed. It's lined with three matching pillows and black sheets only seen by my eyes. "It's not like that. Sit." She crosses her arms, glaring at me. "Cherry, sit on the bed. It's not a request." Her attitude tests my patience. "If you want my help, you will sit your ass down."

She will be the death of me in one way or another.

Finally, her reluctance fades. She leans against the side of the bed and kicks her shoes off, pulling her weight up and crossing her ankles in front of her like she's in a kindergarten class. I sit in front of her, take her hands one at a time, and lay them flat, palms up on her thighs. With my fingers, I trace down hers and back to the tips. The friction manipulates the oxygen in my lungs. It turns ridged, and I shield an intense stabbing beneath my ribs.

"Look at me," I softly call to her. "I need you to breathe. Normal and calm. Don't hold your breath." She nods. With my hands above hers, I focus as her ribs flare. *I hope this works. If I kill her...I can't. I can't mess this up.* "Calm, natural breaths," I repeat.

She shouldn't trust me, yet she's composed, her shoulders are relaxed, and the burnish from her eyes has a death grip on my blackened heart. The terror of fucking this up ceases to ease.

*I take a deep breath in through my nose and slowly let it out of my mouth. I'm drawn to the unbalanced force. It's—*fuck, it's—*like when your leg falls asleep after sitting on the toilet scrolling on your phone for too long mixed with rubbing your fuzzy socks across the carpet and touching your sister to zap her. As uncertain as it began, it's gone. I lean back on my elbows, closing my eyes. Is that it? As I inhale, I choke, sinking into a blackout.*

Please don't let it go black. Please don't let it go black.

And that's how I learned of my third ability. I can heal—some people. And I can't foresee myself doing it again because it doesn't fucking feel great.

"Are you okay?" Her fingers skate across my arm.

"It's just a dizzy spell. I'll be fine. How do you feel?"

"Level." She crashes backward into my pillow, turning her head to the bedside table. "Is that Annie?" She asks, pointing to the single photo frame as if nothing abnormal had happened.

"Yeah." I smile, cashing in on the memory with my beautiful brunette best friend. "I broke into my parent's house for it."

She laughs. "That's a little suspish."

"My dear, what is suspish is this entire fucking night. This picture was mine—at least I had an identical one to it when I moved and I lost it. They can keep the boxes of my history in the attic. They can't have this piece."

"Don't they reach out at all? I mean, your name is everywhere." She stares at the ceiling, brushing her hair through her fingers and yanking out knots.

"It's complicated."

"Sure...About that...I don't know what happened and I feel like I should apologize."

Sliding to the left side of the bed, I throw my jacket to the empty dark-stained wood and roll the sleeves of my make-up-stained shirt. "I think you'll be okay, as long as you don't kiss me again."

She thinks I'm joking. "Awe, come on, B. A little bit of lip action." She pukers. "Can I earn bonus points for tongue?"

"Did you like it when I kissed you in the lobby?"

"At the risk of inflating your already enormous ego, it was kinda *euphoric*," she exaggerates, rolling her eyes. "I mean it. Are you sure we have to stay friends?" She pokes me in the ribs, but I grab her wrist before she can try to fucking tickle me again. "What's that?" Her thumb presses to the inside of my elbow, and her fingers hold the back of my arm as she tries to get a look at the tattoo peeking out of my sleeve.

"It says *no matter what, no matter where, let tomorrow pour*. Annie was obsessed with the late-nineties sitcom *Friends*. I didn't want anything unoriginal and this is kinda my take on friendship and my love for her." She was the only person who could love me unconditionally.

"What about that arm? Is it a full sleeve?"

"Yeah, to the top of my shoulder."

"Can I see it?"

"You're trying to get me to take my shirt off. It's not happening."

"You suck." She drops back to the pillow with hair flying everywhere. I'm going to be finding a strand of blonde on my blankets for days, but wait a damn minute...

"Whoa, what happened to euphoric?"

"I wouldn't call any of my friends euphoric, so I take it back, *friend*. That's like you calling Justin euphoric."

"He would probably have a panic attack. Hold on, hold on..." I clear my throat and drop my voice an octave, reaching for a raw, gruff sound. "Justin, that was fucking euphoric. Damn."

"Oh my god." She laughs, bowing over on her side and holding her stomach. Those big, fucking blue eyes close and reopen as broad, with a huge smile ending at the apples of her heated cheeks. "I dare you!"

Shaking my head, I stray from her charisma. "I can't put my PA in the hospital. Surviving without the guy is impossible."

"You have healing energy." She leans forward, shaking her head all sassy. "Fix him like you fixed me."

"That's a little different."

"You don't want to tell me?" She asks.

"I don't. Some things are better left unsaid."

"You're a mystery, Bennett." She tucks her hands behind her head and dreamily looks back at the ceiling.

I'm scatterbrained, intently locked on her face with too many parts to take in. Her soft lips beckon my desire, and her beautiful jaw should be felt by hand. Her eyelashes curl outward, becoming less heavy toward her nose. "Pizza," I declare, quickly finding my way out of bed and to the light switch near the door.

"Pardon?" Her eyes carelessly follow.

"Are you hungry?" I flick the light switch and walk out of the dark room, expecting her to join. Opening the fridge, I grab a glass container with a slice of pizza in it and remove the silicone lid. "I'm glad you decided to join me." I take a bite and hold the slice out to her. In swallowing most of what I bit off, the acrid remark meant to hound her slips out a little more playful than I intended. "Cold pizza is the best. Fight me."

"I won't argue." She grabs my hand, takes a bite, and bedroom-eyes me. "Mhm, the best."

"Screw overloaded toppings too. Pepperoni only." I take another bite when she lets go of my hand.

"That's where I have to correct you." She overlaps her hands, holding this in a stop signal between us. "Because pizza is always, *always* better with mushrooms."

"For a minute I thought you were going to tell me you like pineapples."

The never-ending pineapple debate: you don't put sweet acid on top of supple salty like that. It's a hard fucking no. This is unnegotiable.

"Oh oh—" She sways back and forth on her heels. "Tacos with pineapple are *life.*" She nabs the rest of the slice from my hand.

"On tacos?"

"Chicken or steak tacos—it's chef's kiss. Don't knock it, pineapple hater."

"Well, you're not going to believe it, but where do I sign up?" I set the container in the sink, turn around, and find her doing a little happy dance as she chews. Whatever I did to her, she's certainly more fun now and it's rubbed off on me. Fuck, I'm not fighting the smile. So what if she sees it.

"Oh." She holds up a finger as she swallows hard, twice. "They have cubed pineapple in Freedome and leftover rotisserie chicken."

"I have soft taco shells." I shrug, pulling open a drawer and slapping the package onto the counter.

"Let's go," she insists.

"Right now? It's almost ten."

"You have one slice of cold pizza that we are sharing." Her deadpan glare freezes on me. "Here, you can have the crust."

"Fine. Go grab one of my hoodies. I'm tired of seeing you shiver every time the wind blows in your direction. It's fucking annoying."

"You own something other than dress shirts? Shocking." Too often, she makes that outrageous face—big wide eyes, pinched lips, and a stupid tilt.

"Don't fuck with my vintage tees."

"Can I have a designer suit?" She jokes and turns the light on. As she opens the closet, she pages through the hangers. "*Gamer Mode.* You play video games? Nerd."

"Baby, I used to *own it.*" I lean into the doorway, my hand pressed against the frame, while I finish off the two bites of crust she left me. "Chicken dinners every night." I couldn't escape a few parts of the old me.

"What the hell is a chicken dinner?" She side-eyes me, pulling the hoodie off the hanger.

"Winner winner, chicken dinner." I act like she should know what I'm talking about. With no fortune, it's been so long that I don't know if anyone would understand the reference.

"We're playing." She adjusts my hoodie she's swimming in and pulls her hair from the collar. "Chop chop!" With a push past me through the threshold and back into the living room/dinette, Cherry is at the door, waiting.

"I know I have something smaller in there."

"They don't say Gamer Mode on them!" She calls.

"For Bennett's sake! What are you doing?" She yells into the microphone of her headset. I look between Cherry and the big screen, shaking my head at her antics.

"You good?"

What in the fuck is in my heal mojo? This woman is on another level tonight, and between me and you, it's refreshing. I'm a kid again, having fun and not thinking about tomorrow. I don't know when I'll be able to do this again—if I ever do.

"This guy sucks. Stop shooting at me, dumbass!"

"I don't think he's on your team, Cherry." I slide forward on the couch, my plate resting on my lap as I pick up the taco and take a bite.

"He's definitely on my team." Her brows furrow as she argues with me.

"Whatever. Take him out."

She wrinkles her nose, glancing at me and down at my plate. "Do you need more light?"

"Between the strip of cabinet LED lights and the TV are enough."

"And it's good?" Her teeth press to her lower lip.

"Fucking bliss," I answer and take another big bite, trying to keep it in my mouth.

"I told you!"

"You played this before, haven't you?" My sarcastic remark hits at the perfect time.

"Son of a bitch! I'm dead."

"Yeah, been there." I shrug, glancing back at my notepad. She sets down the controller and leans closer to me, trying to sneak a peek.

"What are you writing?"

"I don't know what it's called yet. I guess it's suspense, maybe mystery."

What do you call a book about a dude that dies, comes back to life, and fucks shit up? Fiction, ah yeah. That's the simple answer.

"I always see you writing in the little notepad. Wouldn't it be easier to write on your phone?" She picks a plastic bottle of water up off the floor near her foot and twists the cap open.

"Too many distractions...the apps and notifications. I don't know why I have an assistant if these fuckers are going to email me."

She nods. "What's the story about? Three-line synopsis." Replacing the cap, she sets the bottle back in front of the couch, wiping her lip with the side of her hand.

"A man who dies and returns to life."

"Like you." The corners of her mouth turn up.

"What?" I shove the rest of my food in my mouth, averting.

"You said you got shot and died and they revived you."

"Oh." I smugly laugh under my breath. "Right."

"What happens to him?"

I start to smile, my teeth playing against my bottom lip as I feverishly hide it. "I don't know. What do you think should happen to him?"

"He should befriend an incredibly awesome chick and go on an adventure."

"An adventure like making chicken pineapple tacos and playing Xbox when they should be sleeping like the responsible adults they are?"

"That's kinda lame." She pulls her legs up onto the couch and tucks one under her ass. Then she leans forward, resting her chin on the ball of her knee. She clasps one hand over the other and resumes. "They should go on a heist spree. Hit as many places as they can in a twenty-four hour period."

"That lovely couple has been done before." Even today, TV shows, movies, and song lyrics point discussion at the infamous couple. They weren't even fiction, but then again, neither am I.

She sits upright, her legs and arms stuck in the same position. "I never said they would be a couple."

"There is always a love interest. Even if it's unrelated to the plot, someone is married, dating, or lusting on the sidelines. It's the common hope that a viewer roots for. Fuck, it could be the love of a child or sibling."

"Okay, then he falls in love," she suggests.

"No. He definitely doesn't fall in love."

"Why not?"

"This is raw...not a fucking fantasy. It's not Red Tape or Lost In Nirvana."

"You're saying, you spit out these love stories but you don't believe in what you're selling?"

"There are no happy endings. That's why we write them. It's a way to grasp what we can't achieve in this life."

"That's quite sad." She chews her lip, looking past me. The idea hits her, and the muscles below her cheeks flex, beaming brightness. "Then for your story, make it a sex interest."

"That's a...interesting take, but—" I fluctuate my head from side to side. "I don't see it turning into a ransack." I could write sex. I don't plan on robbing any banks or supermarkets anytime soon though and if I'm keeping this true to my life, I should stay clear of overzealous attributions.

"Suit yourself. You're the genius." She turns back to the TV, her feet falling to the floor as she reaches for the controller. This has been an interesting night, to say the least.

It's Okay To Love A Vampire, Cherry

I f only I could be as focused as Samantha right now. I lit two vanilla ginger candles, set the white noise on my arm clock, and double-checked the locks. My trailer is dark and cozy. The only interruption is my brain. What haven't I tried? Clamps?

I pull the bedside drawer open, blindly reaching until I find—clamps. Yes. The pain edges my body closer to the brink, pinching and tugging at my nipples. Yet, it's not enough. I should have put my freaking vibrator on charge last night.

Stop. Forget about it. I need to clear my head and think only of his hands—masculine, veiny hands all over my body. His warm mouth falls from my neck and tugs my nipple. Oh yes. He tugs hard. His presence makes me clench around his fingers as he pulls them out and slams them back into my pussy.

"You make me so wet," I mutter.

I slide my fingers over my slit, back and forth, until they're coated.

"I want you, Ames." *His* fingers trace my clit and press between my legs. They slide inside, immediately finding the soft spot that rapidly builds pleasure. He bites my nipple, pulling it tighter between his teeth. His thick fingers slide in and out between my thighs.

He steals the orgasm away from me, withdrawing his soaked fingers and throwing my legs over his shoulders. He squeezes my ass in one hand while one wet finger toys at my other hole. With a slow motion, he takes me to the first knuckle. I buck, overwhelmed with sensation as my finger takes my pussy.

"That's it, baby," he coaches. "Tell me how bad you want it."

I pull my dripping fingers out and grab his throat, wishing for his lips. His finger deepens, the pressure makes my stomach tense and I clench my walls, grasping for more. Sliding my hand to the back of his neck, I pull his face down.

He looks up at me, but his blue eyes turn to white, and he's not the man I started this with. My fantasy of Ames becomes that of Bennett.

The man I never wanted to feel anything for is the one I want between my legs. Bennett Larson, it's you. I want your stupid hands squeezing my thighs. I can feel your dick sending me to the edge.

I push my left hand on top of my right as hard as I can, hammering my fingers as deep as I can get them. With a quick release, I do it again and again. The third time, I moan for him. I beg him with sounds. My heavy long breaths sync with my racing heartbeat and falling chest. The heat rushes over me as I peak. My sporadic moans break free and the red behind my eyelids turns into Bennett's hooded glare. His wispy dark strands hang in his face as his upper lip glistens and he holds himself above me.

I drop my tired arms to the mattress and exhale.

Damn it!

Half of the day, I avoided Bennett with success. Now it's time to move on and do what I do best—pretend. I fantasized about sleeping with him. It doesn't need to be anything more.

As I march to his trailer, I open six tabs on my phone each with a different tabloid headline.

"Benny, open up. It's me." I knock, rattling the door. "Bennett!" My obnoxious yells will get him off the couch. I try looking in the opaque window, but it's no use.

I lied to him again. That night on the rooftop I knew I could get his reaction. I knew I could mess with his head and make him think he broke me. I had to test time and see what he could do. There is a lot I know about Bennett Larson. Probably more than he knows about himself. The things he is capable of...

As soon as he swings open the door, I ignore his cold, stony look and push past him into the trailer. He's probably mad I called him Benny again. "Did you see Ames' face?" I ask with excitement before turning around to face him.

He nods, pulling the door closed. "Yeah. What did you say to him? You took off pretty quick earlier."

"Did I make you nervous?" I taunt. "Don't worry, I know you need him." I spin around walking sideways as I talk to him, moving toward the couch. "I explained that we were seeing each other, but not exclusively. I gave you the ultimatum to commit to just each other or we were done. I didn't mean to string him along and I did like him. It's just, you and I have *something special*." Holding my hand over my chest, I bat my lashes. "You didn't agree initially and when you saw him kissing me, well, you knew you had made a mistake."

He slouches against the counter with his arms over his chest. "I'll remember if I'm ever stuck on a romance scene to give you a call for some ideas."

"I like the sound of that — co-written by Cherry Kaas."

"No. Absolutely not. Pick a pen name," he complains.

"You're an asshole." And I will take it to my grave that I saw you between my thighs this morning. Bennett's vision comes first. He's not a man you can expect to catch you when you fall and if he's ever had a meaningful relationship, he lost that with his sister. How would he please a woman with deep-rooted selfishness?

I doubt he's ever loved anyone else or felt remorse for the people he has used to get this high on his pedestal. He hides behind lies and mystery, yet he's let me in and I've seen parts of him that I can't bury. Those little flecks of gold make me reconsider my goals...and I hate that. I like to tease him, but hooking up with him would defy my promises.

"You're a stripper."

"Screw you." I grab the black throw pillow beside me, chucking it at his head. *I suck.* He catches it, not even close to where I was aiming. "Would Cherry Larson sound better?"

He walks slowly over to me and bends down on one knee in front of me. My heart drops into my stomach for a second, and the vision of his hands on my legs, his face buried between my thighs creeps back into my thoughts. He's on one knee, looking up at me and I want to see the white cover his irises. He presses the throw pillow onto my lap, shaking his head. *Ugh.* He's such a douche. "You're going to try to take this fake dating as far as a fake marriage?"

"Maybe even a fake baby," I say, leaning forward. "And later it will turn out to be planted by your secret twin, who tricked me into believing he was you and now you have to decide if you will raise it as your own or divorce me." He closes his eyes, burying his chin into his chest before he stands up and moves to sit beside me.

"I don't write soap operas, darling."

"You got any cold pizza in there tonight?" I nod upward toward the fridge.

Standing back up, Bennett walks to the fridge and opens it, arching down. "Nope. Just cheese, jelly, butter, peanut butter, water, and beer."

"Who puts peanut butter in the fridge?" I sass, kicking my shoes off and hanging my feet off the arm of the couch. Laying my head on the cushion, I revisit his stone-solid expression that begins to crease at the end of his mouth and the corner of his nose.

"It's the stir kind, the real deal, not that fake shit. It's thicker when it's cold."

"Oh, is the thickness of your butter important?" I sneer. "*Fake* peanut butter is the plague, but those disgusting cancer sticks you put in your mouth are fine."

He straightens. "I haven't had any since you threw my last pack off the roof."

I smile arrogantly, proud of my actions, but I wonder why he never bought more or sent Justin for them. "Okay, peanut butter and jelly. You have bread, right? Peanut butter and jelly and a cold beer. Our first official date."

"Well shit, the ladies are going to be so jealous."

"It sounds like a good time to me." I kick my dangling feet back and forth.

He sets the peanut butter, jelly, and two blue and silver cans on the counter, then opens a cabinet to the right at face level, pinching the plastic bag and dropping the load beside the jars. "I wouldn't ever bring a woman back to my trailer, yet have a first date here," he grumbles.

"Where would you take them?" Once in a while, he says these things that remind me not to trust him. It's the never-ending mental war of wanting to screw him, wanting to be his friend, and wanting to do my job. None of that lines up.

"A rental or hotel, after a date at a five-star restaurant that doesn't deliver a beer to the table in an aluminum can." He pulls a few paper plates from the cabinet.

"Okay, I get it. You want to impress them, but you seriously never had a woman in here?"

"No." He turns around and slouches, pressing his forearms to the counter. "This is my space. It's not for anyone else." He glances over his shoulder. "I'd love to know how you get me to talk."

"I remind you of your dead sister." My vague expression jumps into a smile.

"Ames dodged a bullet. That little bitch could never handle your dark humor."

"You don't have to call him that. It's not like I wanted to date him. I'm saying, he's not a malicious person. He was hurt and lashed out."

"He did that to cause you pain. He wanted you to feel what he had felt. I think that could be classified as malicious intent."

"You of all people should know, that nothing is as simple as black and white." I sit up, studying Bennett as he paints the bread with strawberry jelly. "And if anyone asks, he had nice lips and good press."

"And that's where you fucked up." The muscles in his forearm flex and trying to revert my eyes is pointless. I love a man's back. The curvature of the muscles beneath their skin is somehow appealing. It can be slightly toned or heavily; both are attractive. Bennett isn't one or the other. He's lean and his ass is...firm. I widen my eyes, quickly looking away. Mhm. "You separated yourself from my sweet big sister." Well, no fake B. I'm not you're perfect sister and I certainly hope you don't feel that way when you think about touching me.

"I'm more of a Boondock Saint."

Face to face again, his lips pressing to his thumb and with the flick of his tongue, he licks the peanut butter from his skin. "Are you a killer, Cherry?" I'm the rough-cut hero; vigilante if you will. I spare lives if I can, but sometimes evil can only be stopped one way. "Are you here to see if I'm a bad guy and take me out if I am?"

I walk over to him and reach around his shoulder to dip my finger into the peanut butter. I bring it to my lips and hush him before a suck it clean. "What do you think, Benny?"

He steps forward, closing the gap. "Bennett." I roll my eyes at his correction. "I'll let you in on another secret...I'm the bad guy."

"That's not a secret," I reply.

Leniency. Mercy on the helpless women and the innocent children. The irony. It takes me back to Chris—this kid in the apartment across from mine. He would come over to escape the arguing outside of his bedroom door. He was nine or ten—five-ish years younger than me. My place wasn't always better, but that's what separates the good and evil. I became his safe space while in my own agony. I want to always be *that person*, not *just a woman*.

"That doesn't scare you?"

"I never worry." I smile, playing my part. "So, since I'm your first house guest, I think you owe me a tour."

He looks around, his open hand waving to the side. "Living room, kitchen, bathroom. You don't even need to move to see it all."

"What about your bedroom?"

"You saw it already."

"Oh yeah, you did your witch doctor magic on me." I grab the beer with my name on it, crack it, and take a sip before walking to the dinette. "You have a picture on your bedside table. How come you don't have any out here?"

"That's the only photo I own." He joins me, setting our gourmet dinner on the table.

"And you stole it." His tongue swipes over his teeth, loosening the stuck sandwich pieces. "Can I see it again?"

He swallows. "Why?"

"I need an excuse to get in your bedroom." I press my forearms to the table and wink.

"Again, why?" He takes another forceful bite.

"To seduce you, why else?" His chewing slows and his hostile gaze drives into me as his eyes rise from the plate in front of him. "I'm kidding. I'm exhausted and I'm pretty sure Carly is stalking my trailer so she can parade me around Freedome like she's going to be a bridesmaid in Bennett Larson's wedding." He doesn't know who she is. At least not by name. "She's one of the assistants for the stunt coordinator, Andreia. You told her, and I quote *blow some more shit up* yesterday. What was the saying? *Go big or go home.*"

Straight-faced, he swallows. "You want to sleep in my bed? Fuck no."

"Language," I annoy him. "It's a bed, B. Why are you making it weird?" It's all the secrets he has hidden in the walls. "Stay in the room if you don't trust me."

"Fine. One hour."

"You really don't let anyone else in your bed?" I finally pick up my sandwich and take a bite, looking at his empty plate.

"It's not that bizarre." His finger's inner lace in front of his face as he leans on his elbows.

I push the food in my mouth to one side and talk between chews. "You go out of your way to take a woman somewhere else." I gulp back what's left in my cheek. "To avoid her coming back here. It's a little bizarre." I rinse it down with another ounce of my beer. "It's the eye thing, isn't it? Do they glow while you sleep or something?"

"No," he growls. "You're never going to let that go are you?"

"What are you? A vampire?" As unladylike as it seems, I take another bite and shimmy my shoulders, dancing to the music in my head. The peanut butter is good. I won't take that from him.

"Vampires. You believe in that?" That look, ugh; that know-it-all glare with his one stupid raised eyebrow like he suddenly knows what's cooking. "You believe in good vs evil and Heaven vs Hell. Logically, vampires vs werewolves are next."

"I'm not talking about glitter and intoxicating beauty. Late seventeenth-century European stories of people being attacked in their sleep and drained of blood."

"Those myths most likely started with the plague and I'm pretty sure none of them had white pupils signifying they were the undead."

"Evolution." I raise my can, tipping the end to emphasize my point.

"Blame evolution for everything. I'm pissed I never got to meet a raptor." He bows his head, only looking back up when he hears my voice again.

"That's not the same thing and it's still somehow better than blaming the ever-lusting vampire romances."

He sighs, seeing less humor than I did. "I have no fucking clue what I am."

"You admit you are *something*, right?"

"I have freaky eyes. Can't we leave it at that?"

I chug the rest of my beer and pick up both of our empty plates with my can, walking to the garbage can at the end of the counter, and tossing them in. Paying no attention to Bennett, I walk down the short corridor into his bedroom, sitting on the end of the bed and peeling my combat boots off. I haven't worn them since I got here and it felt like it was time. The zipper on the left gets stuck and I give up as usual trying to yank it off my foot. It breaks loose and thumps to the floor. I advert my eyes, standing to untuck the blanket.

"You're loud."

"*I can be louder*," I mutter. "Well," I speak up. "I'm taking a nap now, so don't get your panties in a bunch."

"You should be nice to your host." He peers around the door frame and I step into his space.

"I'm always nice, B."

"You're nicer to other people." The deep guttural sound that comes from his throat sends chills over my arms, radiating down my body. He has no idea what he does to me when he talks like that. If he knew—if only I told him I masturbated to the thought of his thick fingers, he'd bail and I'd lose all the progress I've made.

I get lost so deeply in his eyes that I question my sanity. Is it possible to see a person's soul through their shield? If Bennett Larson has a soul, I would have seen it. That's how deeply lost I am in his hypnotizing blue eyes.

I foolishly listen to the pulsing between my legs, pressing my chest against his as I arch to my tiptoes. I touch his chest, skating one hand up to his neck where

I dig my fingertips into his skin and my thumb takes his jaw. My mind escapes back to this morning. I follow his gentle touch as he caresses my arm, stopping at my hand. He peels my fingers away and steps back, letting me go.

"We're not dating, Cherry."

"It's not that serious," I assert, taking a step back toward him.

He shuts me down. "I'm doing you a favor."

"The favor I was hoping for started with *oh* and ended with *yes*."

He chuckles, the deep evergreen rumble sending me into a spiral of cringe. I've lost my freaking mind. I should hate him. I did hate him. I'm going against everything, all the promises I made before I came here because I can't get past my attraction for this man and he won't admit he wants it too. Even if neither of us would let it happen, I'm still dying to make him admit he wants me, over and over again because it makes me feel better. "You're starting to annoy me with that laugh."

"Good, Cherry. Do you want me to walk you to your trailer now?"

"Don't patronize me." Asshole. Asshole, asshole.

"I don't have a problem admitting that first kiss was fucking—" The airy sound leisurely breaks from his mouth. "Hot. I wanted to rip the shirt right off your chest—" That tenuous chuckle again. "And I could have." His jaw hardens. "You're the only one that knows who I am, Cherry. If I cross those boundaries—" He draws an invisible line with his finger between us. "There's no going back. I don't care if you tell me it's not a big deal. I know how women get attached. If I fuck you, then you'll catch feelings or ones that preexist will grow, and I'll break your heart. Then I'll lose the one person I like talking to. I like having someone to share my secrets with."

"You're a selfish bastard. Probably a selfish lover too."

There he goes again. Stop with the laugh! If my jaw tightens anymore I'll grind my teeth to pieces. "It doesn't matter. You'll never find out."

I wiggle my boots on, not bothering to zip them, and push past him, walking into the kitchen. I hate his stupid face.

I look over my shoulder. *Stupid face.* I shouldn't have said a damn thing and fingered myself in his bed while he cluelessly sits in the kitchen. I'm running out of time. I have to make the choice. If I can't get him in a vulnerable situation, I'll have to go with plan B.

"I thought you wanted to take a nap?" He follows behind me. "Take one. Don't be dramatic."

Dramatic...Ha. "You're...ugh!"

"Tell me." He nods with a stupid little smirk on his stupid freaking face. "Lay it all on me. What do you want to say?"

First, I want to call his six elementary names. Then, I want to spit on him. And then, I would apologize and put my adult pants back on.

I take a deep breath in through my nose, looking at the window to my right. I'm looking at a wall, blacking out the graying sky. I lower my wrathful glare over to him. "I..." My gaze falls to the floor. I want to tell him everything. It would be a mistake. "I'll sleep on the couch." I kick my shoes back off, plopping down on the sofa flat on my back, and refuse to look at him.

"Cherry..." He murmurs, standing beside me. "You don't want to go down that road with me."

No, B...we're already on the road and I have to choose which path to follow. The right or the left. He walks away and I close my eyes, breathing deeply in and out until I feel recentered. I want to fight it—the tranquility. I want to cry...and I can't.

I finally start drifting into a dream state when I feel the fabric draped over my body. I've lost my focus. I don't know what I'm doing here anymore. *He's not redeemable. I can't save him. I can't keep him. I can't sleep with him.* I wish I could get off this rollercoaster, but it's human nature to fight for the good in humanity. It's my nature to shake hands with demons and greet nightmares, dress them up, and drink sweet tea.

I can't stop until Bennett Larson either surrenders or dies because I know he's not a vampire. I know exactly what he is.

Perfectionism Might Be Your Next Death, Bennett

I could use a fucking cigarette. I should have stopped for a pack on my way to this podcast interview.

Relationships are messy. Women are a fucking nightmare.

Delete that. Have I looked at my analytics lately? *Women.*

Do I remember the first person I killed?

No. Sorry?

I remember the first time I didn't blackout. It was this guy that kept trying to interview me. He was short with a shaved head, he had a gold filling like he was special, and a strong handshake that I avoided half a dozen times. He would come to my house every day—every fucking day. This was my old rental that I got right after Red Tape, the book, hit. It was in a nice little suburban community and likely the push I needed to purchase a property.

I strangled the little fuck with a pair of old shoelaces—real thick ones from my boots. And you could guess it; that little neighborhood had cameras on every house.

It wasn't the first person I had to bury, just the first I didn't blackout for. The idiot broke in at two or three in the afternoon, and I found him standing in my bedroom holding Annie's photo. That's one way to pull the trigger.

To his misfortune, I left the old laces from boots on top of my dress earlier that week. I didn't intend to do it. The laces were there. He broke into my single-bedroom home. He picked up Annie's picture. The demons in my think space didn't like it.

I smoked half a pack of cigarettes that night. You could say it became my coping mechanism. My conscience wasn't heavy. It was more of a realization. The bodies I woke up to before were my doing. There was no escaping the reality. I'm a killer. It wasn't a conscious decision at first. Then it became a way of survival. Anyone who got in my way went overboard. I killed them all.

I know—it's heinous. It's what separates a monster from a man. I walked away every time with only the fear of getting caught—not being shamed or punished.

I spent a good three hours talking to the neighbors and working my mind magic, clearing their cameras, having them erase anything on the cloud, and then disposing of the body. It was still easier than the one that I found after I woke up in the cabin. It looked like I tried to strangle the guy, but said fuck it and slit his throat. It was a fucking mess. I'm talking paintball splatters and finger paintings. I couldn't tell you what triggered that one. I must be too sweet on the women I've encountered. I haven't found one of them yet. Maybe I felt something and hid them before I came to. I don't know.

It's been two years—over two years since I've taken a life.

Why? Why would I stop if I can get away with it?

Any more questions?

Why didn't I use my mind powers, maybe?

I'm a bad guy, darling. Sometimes people deserve to feel pain, and people like me are dedicated to administering it. Morally, you would think, sure, B, if a man is taking advantage of the girl, he deserves to have his balls fed to him, but you wouldn't take it in your hands to deliver that promise. You would let the proper authority handle it. I'd do worse without thinking twice because I don't need to. Do I run around looking for sad boys and hurt girls to save? Of course not, and that's what divides the vigilantes from the villains.

Cherry is right. I'm selfish.

And I'm content with it.

"We hear you're a taken man?" *The first fucking question.* I eyeball Justin from the other side of the plexiglass window. What did he sign me up for?

I adjust my headset and take another sip from my coffee. Today is not the day. I haven't slept much all week and I'm excelling at my normal level of crude.

"Yeah, that's true." I talk into the mic, rubbing the stubble along my jaw.

"And you didn't initially hit it off, right? What's the story here?" The bearded man continues—whatever the fuck his name is. Slicked with oil, his mustache curls at both ends. His long, slicked-back hair aesthetically fades to his groomed beard. I eyeball his gray hooded sweatshirt with a phrase I don't understand. When the first topic of discussion is my love life, he's already lost my respect. I hoped this one would be more colorful than every other predictable interview.

"She showed up late. It was fucking annoying," I reply, impassively.

"We'll beep that out in editing." He lets out a nervous short laugh. "Okay, yeah, that's annoying." He bobs his head like a chicken. "Is she a diva?" This guy fucking sucks.

I adjust my mic, flatly staring at him. "She is not."

"What's it about her? We know you have a lot of women around. Why Cherry Kaas?" Notorious manwhore, cool. I'm also an outstanding writer and director, so let me know when you want to talk about that since it's the *reason I'm here.*

A breathy exhale consumes me as a slow smile pulls at the corner of my mouth. "She doesn't run through the forest trying to slaughter all my demons. She's out there trying to make friends with them...like their cute little hell kittens." I glance between the bearded man and Justin outside the window, rolling my thumb over my chin.

"Oh, wow. Okay. That's a visual. So let's talk about this new movie."

I smirk, taking a sip from my cup. Wow is right. Let's get to what I actually came here to talk about.

After the other evening, I'm not sure I should have let Cherry back in my trailer. I'm fighting for her. She doesn't seem to understand that.

We're almost in post-production and I won't see her again until reshoots. What happens when I lose her? What happens if I keep her? When she cheats or decides she's bored and breaks up with me? You know what happens. We both fucking know what would happen.

First possibility: I would hold her against her will and never let her go.

Second possibility: I would fucking kill her.

Two years as a sober psycho would be ruined because I became obsessed with the one woman I couldn't contain. I make a lot of dry threats these days, but I know it's a matter of time until I get set off.

I told her she could come over. She asked, and I said yes despite being able to write for the first time in days. The thoughts are finally coming through clearly. I've spent the last three nights typing and erasing. Then I decided to stop whining about Cherry. I went back to the middle of the story and rebuilt it.

High school is a place where you start to discover yourself. You get the confidence kicked out of you. You explore the state of lust. It's where friendships change your outlook on the world.

"Ames said hello." Cherry pulls the door shut, breaking my reverie.

"Ames? He wanted you to tell me he said *hello*?" I catch myself chewing at the edge of my nail.

"Yeah. He was out for a run and I bumped into him on my way over here." I side-eye her, trying to stay focused on my screen. "B."

"What?" I ask breathlessly.

With a stir of commotion, she tosses her bag onto the bench. "Am I an inconvenience?"

"No." With the flick of my wrist, I wave. "Sit. Continue."

"I'm not happy with his actions either. Nonetheless, I'm not going to feed into a hostile environment while we're working together." The keys click beneath my fingertips. "Wouldn't you do something just as petty if you saw your superior kissing the girl you've been flirting with for weeks?" *I'd do worse.* Much worse.

"Coming from the woman who wanted to kill him." Hah. "Stop trying to fool yourself. The act isn't working, Cherry."

"I'm trying to forgive and move forward," she insists.

"No, you're not." Her glare burns a hole in my forehead. "You're putting on an act for me. We're past it. Tell me how you really feel."

"I'm over it. Don't turn a mountain into a molehill." She finally slides into the booth and leans over the table to sneak a glance at my screen. "What are you doing?"

"Writing. That's how *I* move to get over it."

"Can I read your therapy replacement?" She kicks her shoes off and crosses her legs under her ass, leaning on the dining table with her forearms.

"*Yeah,* no." I'm a perfectionist. I could change this chapter six times over before I'm I call it a first draft. I'm not letting her see it.

"Come on," she badgers. "Are you taking time off after filming wraps?"

I glance up from my screen to search for my notepad. "A few weeks. Justin's sharing more information than he's permitted."

"Take it easy on him." With a hypnotic stare, her blue eyes soften me.

My notebook is looking rough, and some of the pages are testing to understand. This is the only chaos that works for me.

Cherry slides out of the bench seat, walking the foot to the kitchen, where she starts exploring and opening cabinets. "If you're going to work, you could at least let me help?"

"What are you looking for?"

"Don't you have any candles? Incense?" She continues looking in the empty cabinet after cabinet.

"No."

She takes my word for it. "Oh, I can proofread!" She grabs her *tiny* backpack from the bench and unzips the pastel purple child's toy. Her hand shoots up with a small circular tin between her fingers. "I almost forgot I had this."

"Is it normal for you to carry around candles?"

"Cindy—she's kinda like a second mom to me—she gave me this before I left." Her fingers slide over the label, and she removes the lid. "Smell it." She holds it under my nose, giving me no choice. What is that? Cinnamon. It's also nutty, and a hint of...vanilla?

"It smells good."

"It's called Find Me. It's my favorite and there's only one company I know that sells it."

I bury my smile into the crease of my arm, erasing it before I reply. "That's an odd name."

"It's warm and...seductive. It has all these multifaceted notes. You always catch something different, kinda like little secrets." One candle brightens her day. "Where's your lighter?"

I lift my weight to one thigh, reaching into the pocket of my jeans and pulling out the silver Zippo. "You know how to use this, right?"

"It's a lighter, Bennett."

"I'm partial to this trailer." I lift my shoulders and groan. "*Fire bad, Cherry.*"

"I grew up at a young age, B."

"I don't think you lost your innocence."

She lights the candle and places it on the counter, rejoining me at the table to sit in the same childish position. "So, are you going to let me read this dead boy story?"

I press my tongue to my cheek and give up. "One paragraph." I turn my laptop for her to see the screen, a single paragraph highlighted for her to read. Her eyes work from left to right, her thumb flickering over the ring on her pointer, and her face remains indecipherable.

I could have been one of those kids who got caught with a hitlist in high school. I kept more of a mental note though, locked away in the back of my brain, which is the same place I could have easily put a target on the assholes who bullied my best friend. None of them said shit to me because I never gave them a reason to. I kept quiet and stayed below the radar. I don't know if it was a survival instinct or if it was the crippling anxiety that I didn't know existed until years later when my secret weapon was no longer a short walk away.

She looks over the top of the screen, giving me the smallest smile. "B, I want more."

"That's enough." I press my fingers to the back of the screen and reach for the bottom of the keyboard with my other hand, bringing the lit document back to me.

"Come on, don't leave me with just that."

"What's with the ring?" She glances at her hand, clasping the opposite over it. "You do that a lot."

"What?"

"You touch it. Does it do something?" *A sentimental value?*

"It's like a fidget ring. It helps with anxiety, stress, hyperactive stuff I guess." Her lips softly turn up. "You understand what it's like, don't you?"

I avert my gaze, blinking back to the screen. "Why do you say that?"

"You can't write about something without doing the minimal research. What's the main character's name?"

"Beckett." I clear my throat. "Beckett Landon."

"He has an anxiety disorder." She pauses. "Amongst other issues. He chose to be friends with the kids being shamed for their differences."

"That's one way to look at it," I admit. It's not how I saw it when I wrote it.

"Was it supposed to be perceived differently?" She scooches around, fixing her twisted flare legging.

"Do we choose our friends or do they come to us because they see past the surface? There's that shitty old saying of you can't pick your family, but you can pick your friends. I think...like everything else, it's not as simple as this or that, yes or no...black or white. It's in the gray. I didn't want you. I didn't choose you."

Her gaze is unsettled. "You did choose."

"Did I consciously choose or was it gravity that demanded I stop trying to deny intermolecular force?" I look down at my screen, then back to her. "You can read one more." I highlight a second paragraph and turn the screen toward her. "One more, but then you let me work."

Mike wasn't like me. He was always outgoing and didn't give a fuck. He ignored their torment. Carter, on the other hand, was the kid undeniably filling out his bulletin in the back of study hall. Beckett's joking about school violence. He's sicker than I imagine. That's not what I'm saying, darling. *I had one weapon neither of them had. Allie—my popular, older sister. She deserved to be noticed, and I was meant to be invisible. Carter felt the only thing keeping him safe was a piece of paper with the names of people who threatened to kill him because he walked with a stiff limp. They threatened to kill his stepsister because he wore hand-me-downs. They threatened to string his little wire-haired mutt from the power line because his fucking hair was too long. He wasn't athletic—they talked shit. His fucking piece of paper was his lifeline. He was a good kid. He wanted your help, and you wrote him off, ignored his calls for help, and what if he took his life instead? That was always the plan.*

I spin my laptop back to her, studying her face. This time it's different. She's colder, looking me over, and her nose twitches, the little silver stud catching light. "B—" She finally says.

She sucks her lower lip into her mouth.

"What?"

Her head drops back and her eyes wander the ceiling before she lowers her chin, finding my eyes. "This isn't fiction...is it?" Her arms pebble. "Did..." She swallows.

Nothing in me hesitates. "The next chapter is too obscure to not call fiction."

"It's partially fiction?" Her eyes narrow.

"It's entirely fiction. Why would you think otherwise? Do you see me as this weak, worthless guy?" I peer at her catatonically, slouching until I hit the backrest. "I'm not him, Cherry. Why do people always assume the author must be fucked in a certain way to write deep shit? Harry Horror never gets dissected for this twisted gore."

"The dead giveaway is the older sister who outshines the brother, asshole. And I don't see that character as weak and certainly not *worthless.* I hate that word. My mom's ex would yell it all the time." She straightens her shoulders, and a slight red glow highlights her cheeks.

I blink away, not knowing what to say. "It's one similarity. They say *to write what you know.* That's the part I knew."

"And if you know nothing?"

"Pull some crazy shit out of your creative dark think space and make millions off of it?" She looks away, shaking her head, and I find myself smiling. I wipe it off my face and straighten, finding where I left off.

"How much do you have left to write?"

"I don't know. I'm a pantser, darling. It might be ten more chapters; it might be twenty. Whenever it screams, this is the end, I close it."

"When it's done, I want to read it."

"And you can buy it just like everyone else." I re-read the last paragraph on the page, not taking the time to look up.

"Seriously?"

"Yes, *seriously*." *Oh, fuck.* I catch an error and hit the back button five times. "I spend hours of my life…" I finish typing my correction and find her eyes. "Hours of lost sleep and missing out on Netflix binging for this. I'm not giving my hard work out for free. You wouldn't do your job for free, would you?"

"Easy Cujo." Her blue eyes send in a full circle. "I'll buy ten copies if I must to be one of the first people to read this one."

"Suit yourself." I glance down at her hands, noticing she's not messing with her ring anymore. She reaches out and brushes the strands of hair dangling over my right eye.

"What does that mean?" Her voice softens. "Does it get darker?"

"It's brain chemistry alternating," I smirk. "It's not like my other contemporary pieces. You won't find Samantha in this one."

"Speaking of Samantha, I didn't come here to talk about your book." *Great.* "Justin is screwing Rochelle and Dawson."

"What?" I utter the word. "I knew he was flirting with Simon." I laugh. The sly shit is a player.

"Wait, what? Did Simon tell you? I haven't heard him talk in—I've never heard him talk. What's his voice like? He has a sexy Russian accent, doesn't he?" She nods, pressing the tip of her tongue to the corner of her mouth.

"He's not Russian. He's Canadian and that's the furthest I know. Do not ask me any other questions about his personal life." My entire trailer smells like her seductive candle at this point, and I'm tempted to tell her she can blow it out now. "That's what you wanted to tell me? Why would I care that Justin has multiple fuck buddies?" Fuck. She's going to get me on the double standards. I made a fuss over her and Ames. This is a trap.

"Because there may be a small riot in Freedome. Dawson is married and Rochelle called his wife to tell her he was cheating and was entirely dissatisfied when the wifey wasn't as upset when she mentioned it was another man—allegedly."

"Mel can handle it. Babysitting the children in adult bodies is in her job description. If they can't get it together, I can replace them."

"You could replace Justin?"

"If I had to—everyone is expendable. I'd start with the other two." I exhale loud enough for her to understand I'm tired of talking and want to get back to work. Of course, it's not that easy.

"That's not all I wanted to talk to you about."

"Yeah?" I grumble.

"I have another job opportunity. A series. The part is Tulip Dean. She's like this stuck-up pretty chick in a group of seven *travelers*. That's what they're called." Her voice fluctuates. "She's the most hated female character in the series, as far as I've read."

"Sounds unforgettable. Take it." I glance between her and my screen. I hope this conversation is over now.

"But—"

"Cherry, I type two words and you start talking again and about stupid shit. What's the real problem?"

"I...I'm scared. What is my identity becomes attached to her and for the rest of my career, viewers expect me to play this *bitch*."

"I'm not a security blanket." I sternly glare at her. "Don't come to me to convince you to take the role."

"I don't want you to save me," she bites. "*I* saved myself when I turned eighteen and *I* am the reason I'm sitting across from you now. You need *me*, and I need the company, so stop being a *douche* and let me vent. Be supportive like a friend should be. Then I'll shut my mouth and read lines while you write. If you can't, tell me to leave."

"I'd never tell you to leave." My phone buzzes on the table, and for a brief second, I consider ignoring it. I shake my head, grabbing the vibrating device and answering it. "Hello? Okay, yeah. I'll be right there." I hang up and slide it into my pocket. "Except for now. I have to go deal with something, but come back later if you want."

She blows out the candle, leaving the warm tin on the counter, and grabs her bag, following me out of my trailer. Peace only comes at midnight.

Recap ladies, gents, and aliens: I'm an undead writer/director. I like to cry about my sister, who died a decade ago. I have the ability to influence minds, control light, and apparently mentally heal select people. I'm a bit of a man whore. I'm in a complicated, sexless relationship with a woman who is immune to me. And one of my previous thirsty flings decided to flash her way onto set. Yes — Cassie's back.

I had to go deal with something alright. Something I already handled once, or so I thought. This is what I get for being lenient.

A storm is going to hit at some point tonight. It's already dark and gloomy. The last thing I want is more drama, more stupid questions from the press, and less focus on what's important—my fucking movie.

"Nobody saw her," Simon's harsh voice calls as I approach. Cassie swings her arm free from his grip; her little purse flies across her body and slips down her shoulder. She adjusts the strap and tugs at the hem of her lacy top.

"Cassie," I mutter.

"I know the tabloids are lying," she sasses. Oh, here we fucking go. "The Bennett I know—" I cup my hand over her mouth.

"That's all I need, Simon. I'll handle this and see her out."

He nods, never a man of many words. His large body disappears back into the building, through the rear door.

"What are you fucking doing here?" I grab her arm above her elbow, the same place Simon had previously been containing her. She contorts her body, protesting, while never actually fighting me.

With every angle in mind, I pull her toward my trailer, making sure nobody sees us. I keep fucking up lately. I'm starting to wonder if I end that streak of mine—if it'll reboot the no-fucks-given section of my brain.

I need a fucking cigarette...or a punching bag.

"I want what you owe me." She chews her bubble gum obnoxiously.

I stop, turning back to her, and contort my face. *What?* "I don't owe you a fucking thing." She freezes. Abruptly pulling on her arm, I continue toward my trailer.

"Do you love her?"

"Come on, Cassie."

As soon as I get her back to my trailer, I'm setting her straight, if you get my drift. I swear if she fucking tracks me down and shows up again, she's dead.

You won't do it, B.

Stop. Don't act like Cherry. One goody-two-shoes hover over my neck is enough. I swear I'll do it if it comes down to her or me.

"Cherry Kass. Do you love her?"

A sinking feeling burns in the pit of my stomach hearing Cherry's name come out of her mouth, but I don't stop walking.

"Are you that naive? You know I only love two people. One of them is me and the other is dead." Cassie's knowledge exceeds all of my other flings.

"Then why can't we keep our arrangement?" I continue reeling her along, catching her eye roll.

"Did you run out of money or run out of sugar daddies?"

"Patrick's wife came back and she made him cut me off."

"Yeah, exactly," I counter.

"Bennett, please. It's a win, win."

I quickly face her. "I'm bored with you. Don't you get it? It's not a win for me. You served your purpose. Move on."

"You sure about that? How many other women have you taken from the back in a graveyard? Next time maybe I could meet your sister."

Bitch.

Heat pours to my face, and a noise catches my attention. I pull her back to my chest, wrapping my hand around her mouth, as my back takes the rear of my trailer. *Erh. Fuck. Do you know how wildly I want to snap her fucking neck right now?* Three women cackle as they jog past, oblivious to their surroundings. "If you mention my sister again, I will gut you. I will tear your fucking intestines out through your mouth. Go inside." I draw my hands back to myself. I follow her to the front, vigilant as she takes the steps.

Telling Cassie about Annie was a mistake. It was her birthday. I liked the false danger I put myself in. Why else do you think I let her stick around for three months? The foolish part was thinking she would move on when the fling was over and forget everything without being forced.

You're Quick With The Tongue, Bennett

"When are you going to shut the fuck up?" I've been banging my head off the table for over an hour, waiting until it's quiet enough to escort Cassie the fuck out of here. I don't want to hear another word about Penny's new titties—whoever the fuck Penny is. I'm not funding new tits.

If I listened to Annie, would I be here entertaining Cassie kookhead? She has to be on something to think I'm going to say *"Oh sure, baby. Ride me for ten minutes and I'll give you another two grand."*

Look, this shit is getting out of hand. Everything is so fucked. I'm burnt the fuck out. We're wrapping production up, I have a deadline for the first ten chapters of this book via my editor, and I have two women fucking up my life. One wants to exploit me and the other...I don't know. She wants me to admit I'm in...

What am I?

I vigorously rub my brow bone and forehead, running through my plan.

"Please, baby?" Cassie stands between my thighs, pressing her palms against my jeans.

"Cassie." I deeply chuckle, leaning my head against the back of the couch. "Fucking look at me," I demand, grabbing her chin. "I'd kill you right now if I wouldn't get caught." The panic is all over her face because she knows I'm not lying. "I'm not giving you a fucking thing and you're not going to ever walk in the ten-mile radius as me again. Do you understand?"

"Hey, Benny—" Cherry swings my trailer door open, shutting it behind her. She halts dead in her tracks. Her face pales, eyeing Cassie straddling me on the couch. "What the fuck is this?" She looks between me and Cassie, and then I know she sees it. *My fucking eyes.* "What the fuck!" Son of a bitch. "You want a prostitute over me?"

"Cherry, it's not—"

"You!" She yells, cutting me off. I slap Cassie's hands off of me, prepared for a screaming battle, but Cherry suddenly becomes calm. She's terrifyingly calm, and an airy, high laugh escapes from the back of her throat. Her eyes roll up, and then she stares directly into me. "You fucked up, B." Her flat monotone remark is short-lived before she attacks in a violent rage.

She charges forward, fisting her fingers through the back of Cassie's curls, and she drags her by the head with one hand to the floor. Cherry steps over her, kneeling above her abdomen. Her knees press into the carpet on both sides of Cassie.

Is that...ginger? Shit, it's the candle Cherry left on the counter.

Everything enhances as my heart pounds faster, an airy laugh escaping my lungs as I watch Cherry pull Cassie up by the hair. She slams her head to the floor twice before her knuckles connect with Cassie's jaw, knocking her out cold. As entertained as I am, this ends now.

"Cherry!"

She turns around, heavily exhaling with rage as she lunges at me and tackles me to the floor.

Oh fuck. She slammed my head to the floor, and that was it. Darkness.

No, she didn't kill me. You know that already. It's the cold nothing I've found myself lost in before. You know this is my assumption because I didn't see shit from the point where my head collided with the floor.

It feels like seconds later I regain consciousness. My eyes snap open to the water surrounding me. It's fucking running water. The cold shower waterboards me as I come to, lying in the bathtub. I latch my hands around her wrists, using my strength to lift my head out of the waterfall. Managing to spit, I beam her in the face. It pisses her off more. A guttural scream pierces my ears like a raging fury.

Fuck. Fuck, oh fuck.

Rush of water become mutes as she pushes my head back underwater. She's trying to drown me, not wake me. I gasp for air, pulling myself up again, and look past her to see Cassie standing behind her.

Son of a bitch.

She's going to—Cherry follows my eyes. She releases her grip on my shirt, and I lose her wrist, falling backward into the tub.

"Cherry!" I howl, struggling to climb out of the tub. I get my foot and stand, water dripping from my soaked jeans and a see-through button-down. The blood pools around Cassie as she lies lifeless on the floor. "Move!" I order, opening a cabinet to the right of her head, and grab a towel. I mop the edges of the pooling blood, attempting to contain it.

"Oh my god." She panics and begins to lose her balance. She walks backward into the side of the tub, damn near falling in.

"Get another towel. If this transfers to the carpet, I'll never get it clean."

"That's what you're concerned about?" She stands there staring at me.

"Towel, fucking now!" She turns, pulls another white towel from the shelf, and hands it to me.

"Is she...dead?"

"You don't lose this much blood and continue to breathe," I snap bluntly.

"Oh no," she pants. "What...what are we going to do?" She whispers through thickening breaths as she begins to panic. Her eyes are glossed over with stuck lids, not blinking once.

"Maybe you should have thought about that before you decided to attack her and then oh yeah, try to fucking drown me." I arrange the towels while kneeling above the blood and glare up at her.

"I wasn't trying to…" Does she think that if she sticks that lip out, I'll feel sympathetic? I didn't do this myself, knowing it was going to be a pain in the ass to seamlessly get away with. And look at all the fucking blood. "I just got…so angry."

"I'd say you are way past anger management, darling. You want to explain?" She keeps quiet, looking between me and her hands. "Stop pacing. Nobody saw her come in here and the only person who knew she was on set is in my pocket." Simon won't ask any questions. "Cassie didn't have any family either."

Ladies/Gents/Aliens: This is your answer to question number two. Who did I fucking kill? It doesn't matter because Cherry is responsible for this one and I'm guessing by her face, this is the first time.

"That was her name? I—killed her." Here we go. The reality is finally setting in. "I…I killed her." Her breathing quickens, and I watch her unravel in a panic attack. Her chest visibly jumps and falls over and over. She pushes her back to the wall and slides down to her butt, where she sits inches from the bloody gold digger. She exhales hard, opens her mouth again, and somehow makes coherent words come out in a ramble. "What was she doing here, Bennett? We have to call the cops."

"First, don't fucking start with this jealousy shit. We are not together." I stand, shuffling around both the dead girl and the living one to get to the sink. "Second, no fucking cops." Her eyes shadow, physically appearing ill. "I was seeing her in Arizona. I broke up with her, and she didn't take it well. I cut her a break and sent her on her way with a nice paycheck." I should have just mind-fucked her.

"You paid her off?"

I glance over my shoulder at her, continuing to wash my hands.

"I helped her out." I grab the drying towel and pat my hands. Facing her, I squat down. "Look at me." With two fingers, I point to my eyes. "Inhale on a six-count. Okay?" She nods, and I begin counting. "1, 2, 3, 4, 5, 6. Now exhale on ten," I continue. She follows my hand as I drop it and rest my forearm on my bent thigh.

Her eyes move up my chest, over my skin-tight shirt, hiding nothing, including my nipple piercing. I doubt she'll notice how panicked she is, but if she does, she's going to go off on me for nagging her about the nose ring. I never said I was anti-piercing. A lump moves down her throat, and she returns to my eyes. "Again." I stand, wiping the excess moisture from my hands. "Anyway, Cassie saw the tabloids—about us—and thought she could get more money out of me if she tried to make me feel bad or blackmailed me with some made-up shit. You two would have gotten along. You know, if you didn't kill her." She swallows and glances at the body. "I don't know or care what she wanted. It wouldn't have worked. I was trying to set her straight, but a raging Cherry bomb came in, full-on psycho. Now her mouth is no longer a problem. Her body is." I nod my head to the right.

"What are you going to do?"

"No, baby doll. What are *we* going to do? You got us into this shitshow. You're going to help get us out of it."

"How?" Her lip trembles. "We should call the cops."

"That would lock you up for a very long time. You're smarter than that. What would you do if I wasn't here?" I return the towel to the bronze bar and adjust it.

"I...um, wait till dark." *Thatta girl.*

"That's a good start. Can you stay calm?" She nods. "Keep this blood contained. I need to make a phone call." Without questioning her again, I step over the body. "What did you smack her head off of anyway?"

She hesitates, softly answering. "The sink, I think."

"Not a bad choice." I smile at her and walk into the kitchen. "Simon, I'll be needing the Rover tonight. No, I'd like to take Cherry out. Just the two of us. Yeah, leave the keys in the console." I hang up, sliding my phone back into my pocket.

"So...we're going to wait until dark and put her in the car." She strains an exhale, trying to grasp reality; she's a killer. Hah. She's not the only one in this room and she's about to find out. How's that for trauma licorice? "Where are we going to take her?"

I pull my wet shirt over my head, settling on her gapping lips as she unfolds in the slightest way. Her eyes sail over my chest to the line of dark hair below my navel. She blinks, looking away, the rising and falling of her chest barely easing as she leans her head back against the fiberglass wall. "Don't worry about that."

Walking around Cassie's empty shell, I stand in front of Cherry, one foot on each side of her legs, and reach above her to drape my wet shirt over the tension rod. My dick is essentially parallel to her face and I have nothing better to say than — "How's the view down there?" She looks directly up at me. She blankly stares, and I don't fucking move besides the twitch in my lower lip.

"There's a sheet in here..." I reach for the top shelf of the cabinet. "Get up. You're helping." I grab the sheet and lay it beside the body. "Grab her feet."

"These are cute shoes," she mumbles.

An airy huff of a laugh emanates from my nose. "She doesn't need them anymore. Take them."

"I'm not taking a dead girl's shoes," her attitude revives.

I unfasten my belt and pull it from the loops of my pants, waiting for her to get up. "Dead girl because you murdered her. Have you done this before? You're doing really well." I raise my brows.

She stands, wiping the running mascara from her under eyes. Blood covers her shirt. I automatically look to her hands next, finding her swelling fist. Good thing that ring is on her left hand. "What do you mean?"

"Cherry, she's fucking dead. Her blood has soaked my white towels red, and you say *cute shoes*. That's kinda fucked."

"I..." Her jaw hangs while she searches for the words. "I've seen a lot of shit. I'm not a bad person. I...I'm desensitized, okay?"

"Swearing again. You bad girl. Maybe I don't know the real you after all. I'd highly suggest looking into therapy after this. I don't want to wrap you in a sheet in three months."

"Can you save the snide remarks and just tell me what to do." Her little growl and hostile gaze earn another chuckle.

"You want me to tell you what to do?" I point two fingers to my chest that drip with slick crimson from shuffling the towels and step over the mess.

"Yes, Bennett. What do you want me to do now? Okay? I don't know how to fix this."

It's too much fun pushing her buttons. I smile, looking down as I stand in front of her. "What do I want you to do?" Hah, baby.

She rises and her devious eyes meet mine. "Yes, Bennett!"

I reach out with hesitation, catching her off guard as I grab her neck with my bloody hand, constricting her breathing. Her delicate hands clasped around mine.

"I want you to tell me you understand when I tell you if you ever try to drown me, injure me, or in any manner attempt to murder me, I will squeeze and squeeze and squeeze until you drop to the floor, unconscious. And when you come to, I'll do it again. I will do it again and again until you don't return to the land of the living. Do I make myself clear?"

Her nails dig into the back of my hand, and her eyes steady with icy hate. There's not even a speck of fear in her, almost like she wishes I would do it.

"Tell me you understand." I press my fingers harder around her already constricted throat. Then loosen my hold. Her gasp is a symphony to my ears.

"Put the fucking white eyes to rest. You know they won't work...I understand."

"Without the attitude." I let go of her. "This is the only warning you get. You can cry and plead all you want, but there will be no turning back if you try something stupid again. I will not be able to stop."

"You're so dramatic," her voice shakes, but I can't tell if it was the slight taste of fear or if she's still reclaiming the oxygen I stole.

I shake my head, knowing that somewhere inside that cold reflection, she knows I'm not playing. "And another thing, Cherry...make sure you check her purse. I want every dollar."

"You're going to rob her now?"

"Dead has no place for money. Plus it was mine first."

I hold Cassie's folded, sheet-wrapped body to my chest. Her arms and legs are pinched together and hanging across my left arm, while her thighs and ass are tucked between my right bicep and forearm. I told her she'd regret chasing wealthy men. "I got her. Just open the trunk," I say, walking to the trailer door. "By the way, you look better in that shirt than I do. Keep it." I knew I kept that black THRONE collection for a reason.

Cherry cuts in front of me without replying. She opens the door and looks around, walking outside, and I follow. It's a coincidence that I was once in this position. Well, not exactly *this* position. Unfolded and lifeless in a trunk. I could have been folded.

It's come full circle now, hasn't it? I was a good guy once. The one who never won anything in life and always got passed over.

I started getting little shadows of memories from the day I woke up, defining what happened. I've been waiting for the perfect moment to reveal this as it's unclear. It's like one of my blackouts emerging from some hidden place in my brain. Two days ago, I had a dizzy spell and then flashes of glass shards on this blinding white floor. I never saw a white floor before. There were only trees, a brick building, and mysteries in the dark. It was bright at first and then got dark, but all I saw were the shards of glass scattered about. I don't fucking understand it. All I know is that I tried to warn you. I've known it in my core since I woke. Something evil controls me, and Cherry should have saved herself before it was too late.

"Hey, Bennett." *This shit.*

Cherry puts the weight of her body on the hatch, slamming it shut as Ames rounds the vehicle. "I wanted to say no hard feelings. Cherry explained everything to me. I get it." He nods at her with a little bitch smile.

"It's fine." I look around the lot and back at him. "I thought you were heading back to the city tonight?"

"Decided to leave in the morning. I figured I'd get a late run in and—did you hear yelling?" He lifts his brows, looking Cherry over. The fucker had to be running around here for a while if he heard something. Chances are he's making it up because that little *no-hard feelings* jab is bullshit. You can't tell me that it doesn't piss him off that Cherry chose me over his perfect six-pack and baby blues. Maybe it's the monster in me that can't see good in anyone, or I'm fucking right and he's not past jealousy.

"A little improv acting," Cherry answers. "You know Bennett. He never stops working," she adds.

"What's in the trunk?"

Oh, this fucking *douchebag*. I can thank Cherry for adding that one back into my dictionary. I've had it with his shit. I tried to be nice. He filmed everything we needed him for and I sent him on his way early, but he just couldn't leave on a good note. No. He had to give it one last go with *my* Cherry. He came here to pick a fight with me.

"Donations. Cherry talked me into some improvements in the ole trailer."

"Oh, I didn't know you were into design. I bought a house a few months ago and I was planning on hiring an interior designer to spruce some things up, but I would be open to your suggestions before I bring them in."

"She's going to be too busy," I answer for her.

"Did you get cast in another movie already?" *He's fishing.*

"Yeah. I signed an NDA or I would tell you more." She's quick on her feet. Good girl. She looks at me as if she heard my thoughts and glances at my fidgeting fingers.

"When did you audition?" Shut up and fucking leave.

"I sent the footage to my agent a few weeks ago, not that it's any of your business."

"I was only asking. Didn't see you leave the set. I did see a woman enter Bennett's trailer earlier though. Did you know about that?" Oh, this fucker. Hah, yeah. *I fucking told you.* He's been lurking and trying to find an excuse to sweep in.

I laugh, shaking my head as I rub the tips of my fingers to my heated forehead. "Stop making up rumors to try to get Cherry to leave me. Even if we broke up right now, she would never let you in her pants. Not like you could please her either. That ego of yours, well, it screams I only care about getting myself off." Cherry rolls her eyes at me. She may have said something similar to me.

"You don't know anything about me. I'm a pawn to you, as is Cherry. You're lucky I don't beat the shit out of you for that disrespect."

Another deep chuckle rolls through my grin. *Oh, I fucking dare you, pretty boy. Give me a reason.* "You? Beat the shit out of me?" I egg him on, pointing two fingers straight up.

"Look at me and look at you," he replies and I stiffen. "One jab to the jaw and you wouldn't be getting back up." He takes a step forward. His shoulders are drawn back and puffs his broad chest out.

As he taunts me, a smile drags up half of my face, and I can feel the obsession slowly creeping in—the need to knock him on his back boils to the surface. "Okay. Let's find out then." I furrow my brow.

"Bennett." Cherry scolds me.

I shrug. "He won't do it."

"Right here? You want to fight me outside of your trailer in the dark?" Ames points, then holds his hands out to his sides. He half spins, acting as if it's the most unorthodox location someone had picked a fight with him at. He's probably used to gloves and face gear in a cushiony ring. I can't say I would have stood up to a bully in my previous life, but these days…Well, go ahead and see what the lanky kid has got. "This is white trash."

"Scared?"

"Shut the fuck up. This is pathetic." *Oh, he can bark.*

"I'll make it simple for you. Punch-for-punch. We go until the other doesn't get back up." I pull my sweatshirt over my head, holding it out to Cherry. She stares at me for a moment with her arms folded. Finally she sighs, taking it from me. "Afraid to bruise that pretty face? Look, Cherry, as my witness, I won't hold you accountable for any of your actions tonight. You're done filming. You obviously have some anger toward me. Now's the time."

"Alright. Let's do this." He stretches his arms over his chest and cracks his neck. *How fucking intimidating.*

"Come on. I'll take the first hit," I reply.

Cherry walks behind me with my hoodie looped over her arms. She leans into me and whispers against the back of my neck. "Are you sure this is a good idea?"

"Nope." I glance back at her with a haunting smile. She purses her lips and returns to guard the trunk.

The cool breeze makes the hair on my arms stand at attention. I don't brace myself. I don't flinch. I watch and wait…and *bam.* Uh, ouch. Fuck.

His knuckles rock me, driving into my mouth, and I stumble backward with the impact. As I smile, deep crimson streams crease my teeth.

"Okay." I nod, licking the blood the travels down my lip. My recovery time doesn't exist. I swing back at him and his ass falls to the asphalt. He doesn't stay down long, stumbling back to his feet. He locks eyes with me, lines up, and hawks blood in my face.

Don't do it. Don't fucking overreact.

His fist makes contact with my jaw for the second time, and I stumble backward, losing my balance. Cheap shot. *Like Shifter.* Cheap fucking shot.

He bends down, whispering as I wipe my face with my hand. "When I knock you out, I'm going to take your girl back to my place and knock her against my headboard until she forgets who you are. She'll be begging me for it."

I tilt my head back, my deep laugh nearly echoing. "Thanks for reminding me where I came from, swine." I spit a pool of red on the ground and push my knees to the asphalt, finding my footing.

Cherry grabs my wrist, noticing my laugh has faded and I'm turning to stone. I want to knock every tooth from his stupid grin down his throat and then fish them the fuck out so I can strangle him with the pearly necklace he fucking deserves.

"You need to stop this," she tries to whisper.

"Is the tart in charge now?" Ames yells, lengthing his arms to his side.

"What did you call me?" Cherry yells back. She throws my hoodie at the vehicle, where it slides off and lands on the ground. She lunges at him, wrapping her hands around his throat.

Fuck.

I grab her by the waist, pull her off him, and she repays me by smacking me across the face. *Cherry.* I stare at her, pissed.

"Eyes," she whispers, actually whispers this time, yet not quiet enough. I look back at Ames, and something is wrong. He looks like he witnessed an unbelievable magic trick. *Son of a bitch.* Why is this fucking happening!

"What the fuck is wrong with your eyes?"

"I don't know what you're talking about," I deny. "You must've hit your head too hard."

"No fucking way." He tugs at his pocket, pulling out his phone. I talk myself down at he tries to unlock it. *Don't do it.* I reach for the phone, struggling with him. Fuck! *Fuck this.*

My fist meets his jaw, then his nose, and his mouth. He doesn't loosen his grip and I punch him again. After the fourth or fifth time, I don't stop. I want that phone. I don't want him to have it. I don't want him calling anyone. I don't want him taking pictures. I want the fucking phone!

It falls from his hand and I keep driving my fist into his face over and over. Cherry's nails dig into my shoulders as she tries to pull me off of him. I turn around, shoving her by the shoulders to her ass, and hit him again.

"Bennett! Bennett, stop!" Her screams make it into my head, but I don't listen. I can't listen. I see nothing, besides the need to stop him, to end any chance of him fucking me over or taking what's mine. Cherry puts her body in between my fist and Ames' face, straddling his limp frame. I dodge and weave around her, trying to meet his flesh with my fist. The warmth of her hands takes my jaw and brings my attention to her parted lips. Her chest rises and falls, and her eyes search mine.

"Benny," she whispers. "Come back to me." I slowly blink, dropping my coiled fist to my side. "Stop."

"Okay," I agree. I look around her and instantly sense the depth of which I'm fucked. I did it this time. "Shit. Check his pulse."

She steps over him and kneels to his side, taking hold of his wrist. With two fingers, she feels for a rhythm. "I don't—there's nothing."

Now I have two bodies to get rid of, and this one is going to be more of a pain in the ass to conceal. I'm quick to my feet and back away. Cassie was a jealous, raging psychotic accident, but Ames was all me—all monster—and I don't fucking regret it...besides this part.

"Go back inside. Get the other sheet from the top shelf." She stares at me in utter shock, and I'm not prepared for another panic attack or a conscience meltdown. "What now?" I groan.

She shakes her head in disbelief as the rest of her body is cemented. I suck on my swelling lip, losing her in the distance.

Damn it. I could try the thing. If I...I don't let the thought marinate.

"Fine. Let me try something."

I walk back to his body and crouch next to him. Holding my hands over his chest, I focus on what I want. It's the same thing I did for Cherry. I did it last time, granted she wasn't flatlined. It's as simple as closing my eyes and feeling the buildup. The static that surrounds me is the same feeling I've felt every time I manipulate someone and when I fuck with the lighting on set. It's the feeling that overwhelmed me when I tried to fix Cherry. It's the same pain.

A gasp breaks my trance, and my eyes spring open, looking down at the rising chest of the man I killed and brought back to life.

No fucking way.

KEEP IT IN YOUR HEAD, BENNETT

"It wasn't supposed to happen like this, Bennett."

My faint laughs might disguise my irritation for a second, but they evaporate like my patience. "Cherry! Where the fuck are you going?" She stomps up the hill in her size seven and a half combat boots, her arms swinging with tightly coiled fists, one still wrapped around the middle of the shovel pole. The dirt indents leave a trail behind her. I keep yelling, but I don't care if she stops. I'll keep chasing—slow and steady—waiting for her to slip up. "You asked for this! It's not my fucking fault! You're in it now, Cherry, whether you like it or not."

I run up the hill after her, holding the cold air in my lungs until I reach the top. "You got us here, remember?" I scold her.

"I didn't try to—" She yells, before suddenly stopping to whisper. "Kill her." She looks around the heavily wooded path. "You did. You intentionally killed a man...and he's Ames Heart. And then you—I don't even know what you did. You killed him and brought him back to life. What if it messed with his brain?"

"He wasn't out that long."

"Why didn't you bring the girl back?" She returns to yelling.

"I didn't know I could. I was a virgin. Ames popped my cherry, Cherry." I wait for a smirk that never comes.

She's filled with fucking sorrow. It's all over her face and I have nothing to offer her. As Ames cracked my cheekbone with his knuckles, I laughed. I encouraged the pain. I fucking wanted it. With one word, the depths of my body twisted with wrath. He wasn't going to enjoy the pain I inflicted. Remorse never occurred to me—until now. In taking a life, Cherry may have destroyed hers...and I don't want that for her. It's my fault for letting Cassie get as far as she did.

Her eyes well. "You could have tried."

"She bled the fuck out. Was I going to restart her heart and then give her a blood infusion?" I blink away my frustration, caught between annoyance and defeat. "Not to mention, it wasn't a few minutes. She would have been a vegetable and guess who would end up responsible for paying for her."

She hugs her chest tighter. She's mad at herself and needs someone to put the blame on. Give it to me. I can tolerate it. I accept it. Your mistakes can be mine. The fucking anguish—you can *pretend* it's on my shoulders. I will never be heartbroken by Cassie's disappearance.

"You're insane if you think you'll get away with this."

"Me?" My palms stick to my chest. "If I'm going to get away with it?" I laugh—breathing out that deep chuckle she deserves. "Darling, I'm not the only one that's guilty." I walk off through the woods and head towards the car. "There's a shitty dive bar about six miles down the road. I wasn't joking about that drink, but Cherry..." I look back at her. "I will get away with it."

"You don't even have the least amount of remorse?" She yells, likely throwing her hands up.

"Says the jealous fake girlfriend who tried to drown me and killed my ex," I sneer, inches from her face.

"I wasn't going to drown you." She blinks away.

"Of course not, because I wouldn't have let you. Cassie didn't have to distract you. I could have stopped you." I lean in closer. "Any time...I wanted."

She doesn't back up. Her eyes run up and down my face. "Are you trying to say that you let me hold your head underwater?"

"I liked it." I wrap my hands around her waist, pulling her hips to mine. "Did you like how it made you feel, Cherry?" My breath warms his jaw. "The power behind knowing that you get to choose when I come up for air?" Her dilated eyes widen.

Is she appalled or questioning her sanity? This is the part of the story where you think I'll reach a turning point. Cherry's influence will make me see the error in my ways. She's not the monster I am. It was a freak accident fueled by a jealous rage. She never intended to smash her skull open. She's a little delulu baby who needs a mental facility and guided direction. She's worrying about the all what-ifs and I'm still waiting on that beverage.

You know damn well, I have feelings for this woman. I want to bear her burden. And I see through all the bullshit that you let slip by.

"I'm not you," she insists. "I'm not cold and lonely."

"Oh, you're right. You aren't me, but you are cold. You are the ice queen, baby. You're frozen to the fucking core. It's just hidden—" I press my fingertip to her nose. "—underneath layers." I tap her again. "And layers of lies."

"I'm a good person," she declares. "I would never intentionally harm someone. I have to live with this for the rest of my life. I can't do the right thing—go to the cops or something. Someone is going to miss her, and I took her away from them because I went...*manic.* I should be in an institute. I should have gotten help before and I could have spared her."

"Do you think I wanted to kill Ames?" My grip tightens around her.

"You started that fistfight knowing you would be the one to end it."

"You're right. I did know that *and* you had to point out the fucking eyes to him. If you didn't say it. He wouldn't have noticed it. They never notice it. The common denominator is you."

She shakes her head, her eyes static. "You said you didn't know."

"I didn't and they didn't. I never had a problem until I met you." I let go of her waist and grab her by the throat. I press strictly through my fingertips, taking in the pulsating rhythm against the length of my fingers.

"Do it. Squeeze. *Kill me*, Benny," she taunts.

"Stop calling me Benny." As much as it pisses me off when she calls me that, I do exactly what she wants. I squeeze with my palm, not just my fingers, and her heartbeat thickens against my skin. Fear is nowhere to be found on her face. "You're a fucking cocky little thing. Not even the least bit afraid?" She swallows hard against the v of my thumb and pointer. Her oxygen is simply restricted. I wouldn't cut it off. I held on tighter in my trailer.

"I've been in this position more times than I remember. I'm not afraid to die."

"You know that's not what I want. Is that why you're spitting such nonsense?"

"Death is final. It's the ultimate escape."

"Killing you would make life really difficult for me. Cassie, she's nothing. I got lucky with Ames. You—you're the star. I need you."

She wraps one hand around my wrist and the other over the top of my hand. "It's all about what's best of interest for Bennett Larson."

"Okay, sure," I nod. "And I'll let you in on a secret since you seem to already know me so well." Lowering my voice, my grumble deepens. "It was satisfying. Every single punch was *fucking* satisfying." I drop my hold, and as I step back, branches crunch beneath me.

"You would be as so selfish to grant me a life of misery and despair in order for you to continue telling yourself that you have a friend. Now you have someone who cares about you?"

"You don't want that." An ardent teardrop rolls down her cheek. She looks away. "I don't want to lie to you."

Her beauty snaps to me. "Do you want to kill me? If you didn't need me—if I wasn't the star— would you kill me?"

"No."

She adjusts the hood on her sweatshirt—technically mine—and tucks her hair back inside. "Good because I've never found you more attractive than I do right now. Covered in dirt and blood, with bruised knuckles and a fat lip. And even though I'm certain you didn't have a pulse when you collapsed on the ground fifteen minutes ago or if you are even human." Her bedroom eyes destroy me. I return to her, take her hips, and hold her body against mine.

"Do you want to fuck me, Cherry? Is that so? You want it that bad that you're willing to overlook the facts?" I'm begging her to admit it. "You want to fuck a dead guy?" I need her to tell me. I'll ignore everything—every tingling sense underneath the tightening in my core that's heating my body and the blood that's rushing below my belt if she still says no. "I said I don't want to lie to you, but the truth…" My wispy laughter evades her ears. "It's been in front of you the whole time. I'm dead, baby doll. I fucking died…and I was reborn, and I'm not talking about some type of religious shit. Not breathing, no heartbeat kind of death that lasted over a year—not eternally. I was shot and I was *not* revived. You were on the right track with vampires. I'm not one if that wasn't clear, but I don't know what the fuck I am either."

"Do you have a heartbeat now?"

"Yes." I take her hand, draw up my shirt, and press her cold palm to the center of my tepid chest.

When she feels the pounding, her eyes meet mine. "When you passed out and I didn't feel a pulse…Did you die again?"

"Cats have nine lives. I guess I have an unpredictable amount. Sometimes my heart races unbelievably fast when it happens. I blacked out. Didn't think I flatlined, but never had an outside party check on me when it happens either."

She pulls away. "How is any of this possible?"

"Ask the mad scientists and greedy pigs who messed with nature. Mankind did this. How exactly, I don't know. I took a good ole death nap and woke up like this." I lean back into her, my breath heating her ear. "You know what I am. Are you still attracted to me?" With a swift dip forward, I lower my voice. "Do you want to fuck me now, Cherry?"

"I've fucked you more times in my head than I can remember."

Her fingers drag along the sides of my head, threading through my hair, and she pulls me to her lips. Her tongue flicks into my mouth, grazing my teeth. I embrace the pain as she presses into my sliced lip. I don't care if it messes with her again. If she becomes an emotional disaster, I'll heal her. I'll take the hit for her. "How's that taste?"

"Like metallic," she says, pulling me in for more.

"Oh, you're vastly fucked up for this."

My words linger while she sucks at her lip. *I wish I could read her mind.* She stares at me for the longest time before turning away—thinking she can walk away now isn't cool. I wrap my hand around the back of her neck, dig my fingers in, and reel her back to me. Her lips return to mine, ever the sweetest—*Fuck! You bitch.*

I withdraw with crimson pain taking my tastebuds.

"Cherry!" With a growl, I rub three fingers over my lip. The blood collects on my skin, and I suck it off. She thinks she can control me with a bite.

"It's not happening, Bennett."

As I rub my jaw, my head falls back, and I roll my neck to one side—staring at her.

"Your eyes are white. Calm down."

"You don't understand how this works. If I don't get what I want…" I heavily exhale, continuing to pace. "It will eat at me and eat at me until I give in. It does not ease up. It will consume my every thought until I get what I want."

"Have you killed women for refusing you?" She asks, deadpan.

"Women don't refuse me. One look into my eyes, and they agree. It's not just women though. Anything…I can become obsessed with anything, and I don't have a choice. If I don't see it through…" I trail off. "I can't stabilize my emotions like a normal human being can. Everything is to an extreme. You have no idea how hard it is to control."

Her face goes blank, and her body becomes tense. She's smart—very smart. I know her mind is twisting and she's finally putting the pieces together. "You *mesmerize* women?"

"I'm quite convincing."

"That's how you do it…" She veers off, dreamily. "That's why people either warship you or fear you." Her eyes flick to the ground and then back to me. If it wasn't for the brightness of the moon and the tree clearing, I wouldn't be able to make out her expression. "Have you done it to me?"

"I can't."

"Why?"

"I wish I knew, but lucky you. You're the first one immune to my…manipu lation."

She steps back defensively. "You rape women."

"Not exactly." I take a step toward her. She needs to stop. I won't be able to see her face if she walks back into the thick.

"Yes, you do. You twist their thoughts into thinking they want it when they don't. You're a rapist and a murderer. *You can't be saved.*" Her voice softens.

"I don't do that. I tell them everything *they want* to hear, not what I want them to do. I know women. They're easy if you understand what they want. I'm not searching for a challenge. I pick the predictable." I move closer to her, and she shuffles but doesn't get far. "The woman who wants someone with integrity, someone respectful, someone with a sense of humor without being *a toddler.* He has to be confident and lead her. She wants to be told she's beautiful, but more than that, she wants to hear exactly how he can please her. I'm clear on the things I want to do to her body and where I'm willing to take her—a place she's never been. A man could whisper dirty words in your ear and get you rowdy; I can do that and more with a single look because I don't waste my time on closed minds and gold diggers. All you have to do is consent to me. Everyone knows what they're getting."

"I don't believe you."

"Good." I turn around, crushing sticks carelessly as I walk back to the lit clearing in hopes she'll follow. "I don't want you to trust me. *I don't trust me.*" She doesn't follow me. Instead, she turns to the darkness and takes two more steps into the deep neck of the woods. "I'm not done with you, Cherry."

She swings her arms out, taunting me. "Oh, the big bad Bennett doesn't get what he wants for once. What are you going to do?"

"Big bad Bennett, huh?" I laugh. "I'll huff and I'll puff and I'll tie you down." I'm not laughing anymore, lamb. "I don't know what kind of games you like to play, Cherry, but I have a few I like too. You better run while you have the chance." The sharp, sudden urge to let loose hits me like the imposing raindrops that fall on my cheek. "Cherry, you better fucking run."

I warned you, but you fell in love with me, didn't you? Little lamb to the slaughter.

I trick. I take. I kill. Abilities or not, I will break her down fragment by fragment until she wants to be mine because she will. She already knows what she wants. She will eventually give in to her desires. As much as I hate to admit it, she owns part of me now, and she's mine. I'm not letting her go—to next week, not in two months, and not in two lifetimes—starting now.

There's the fear! I knew she had it inside of her. Show me who you are.

As she steps backward, the blood drains from her face. She trips over a log and falls to her ass.

I own her with a single glare. "You look even better on your back, darling."

"You'd look better in the ground next to your dead ex-whatever."

Hah! I nod, continuing to laugh. "Ouch. Spicy in the face of danger. Call me *douchebag*, would you? I might even beg for your degradation."

"Don't you fucking touch me." She kicks her legs. Her feet awaken the dirt as it loosens in her flail and she scoots her ass back.

"I'm not going to," I continue forward. "I'm going to talk."

"I'm not—"

"Shh." I crouch to the ground above her and hold my finger to her lips an inch away. "I know, I have to be careful with you..." I sigh. "Like a dried rose. One wrong move and the petals flake to the ground. Tell me, who hurt you the most? We can go hunting. They should pay for their sins."

"And what about *your sins*? You don't have to pay?" She argues.

"I pay every day. I'm paying right now, but this isn't about me. It's about you—the sexy, smart, badass woman with more natural talent in one strand of her hair than most carry in their entire body. Do you see it? How fucking amazing you are?" I reach out, wanting to touch her skin, but I hold back, tussling my fingers through my messy hair and falling to my ass. I sit on the cold forest floor in front of her and crack my knuckles. My slow gaze lifts. "I want you around me all the time. I'm handing you all my secrets. You wanted to kiss me. You wanted to fuck me. It's undeniable. You still do. Do you see past attraction? That's your secret." Her eyes darken, admitting it silently. "No strings, Cherry. You get what you want. I'm only going to do this if you agree."

"What happens to you if I don't?"

"I don't know." I stare past her into the dark. "It's not your problem. I guess it could become..." The weight of her hand on my thigh quiets me.

"If I don't make the choice for myself, you'll make it for me when you can't handle it anymore. You said it yourself. It only gets worse, consuming you. I know you don't want to hurt me, but it would be a lie to believe you couldn't."

"Have I mentioned how smart you are?"

She returns my smile for a brief moment. "Only fifty times. Is this part of your thing?"

I lean forward, taking the curve of her waist in my hands. Lifting her onto my bent legs, she sits on my thighs with her knees pressed to the dirt.

"You're not like the others."

"That's cliche, B."

"It's the truth. The same goes for your attraction to poor decisions."

"You're the worst decision I'll ever do. Trust me."

"Be a good girl then and try not to bite me again." I run my lips across the side of her neck.

"I thought you liked it rough."

I hum against her skin. "Is that the impression I give?" With an authoritative touch, I trace her jaw. "Tell me what you like." She murmurs as I trail my fingers under the sleeve of her hoodie. Small, raised bumps coat her arms. "Do you like this?"

"Mhm," she hums again.

I pinch her chin between my thumb and pointer, forcing her to look at me. "Tell me you like it."

"I do." She wrinkles her nose full of attitude.

"No. Say I like it," I challenge.

She stares at me hard, then lets out a short exhale. "I like it, B," she admits.

The rainfall thickens the air. I ignore it, tracing the tip of my tongue down her jaw. My palm settles on her upper chest and my thumb presses into her neck. "How does it feel when I do this?"

"Good."

"Do you like it when I suck on your neck?"

"Yes."

I stop, narrowing my eyes. "Excuse me."

"I like it." She glares. "You're making this difficult."

"Good. You don't get to dead fish it." She mockingly giggles as I slide my hand to her lower back and pull her tighter. "What if I suck a little lower? Would you like that?"

She looks down at me, her lashes coated thick in mascara. "Yes, B!" She outrageously yells. " I would like it."

I laugh off her antics. "I want you. Let me help." Taking the hem of her hoodie in my hands, I drag it up, pull it from her body, and let it fall. As I slip a finger under the shiny beige strap of her bra, I stroke her skin and tug the strap until it snaps enough to jolt her. Shockingly, she doesn't hit me or come at me with a witty remark. I press my lips to the defined contour below her neck. "How does it feel when I suck here?"

"It feels good." Her voice is beautiful and genuine. "I like it. Keep going."

I run my hand up her lithe spine, sucking at her chest. With a twist of the wrist, her hair is wrapped around my hand. I swiftly unhook the two prongs holding her bra together. "Are you cold?" In a subtle swipe, I run my hands up and down her arms and back to her shoulders, letting the straps fall. She pulls it down to her wrists and drops it on top of my hoodie. "You can't lie. Your nipples could cut ice."

"You did that."

"Bullshit." She tips her head back, moaning as my mouth warms her skin. My suction pebbles her nipple harder. Then I take the other and make sure it matches. "That was me. Look at them, begging for more. What do you think? Should I give them what they want?"

"B..."

"I bet you're soaked." I take her crested nipples one by one, back into the heat of my mouth. As I lean forward, I lift her off of my legs without letting go. I reach for the hoodie with my free hand, flattening it on the ground at the edge of the log behind her, and set her down. Pressing my fingers into her shoulder, I force her back to meet the log.

"Do you see what you're doing to me?" I kneel before her, once again finding my dick at her eye level. The hardened silhouette stretches along my thigh, pressing against my jeans. I grip the length. "This is all because of you." She's fucking proud. Her eyes climb my body, a hunger within them. "I don't want to go slow and I'm trying incredibly hard for you. You deserve it. A good girl like you."

"I'm not a good girl, Benny."

"Ohh," I groan, rolling my eyes. "Anything, but Benny, *anything*," I stretch the word.

"You're both." Her hands warm my thighs, teasing centimeters from my cock. "The quiet, soft, nerdy gamer, and the rich, arrogant, powerful *director*." She reminds me with disgust.

"You cute thing. So naive." I tower over her, forcing her against the log again. My eyes fall over her exposed chest, and the increasing raindrops run in streams down her body. I wipe her tits dry, cupping my hands over them and rewetting them with my tongue. Past being warmer than the drops, she still shivers underneath me. I slip my hands behind her to the firmness of her lower back and drag her in an arch. While I trail my mouth down to her navel, I kiss and free her again. With a tug, the stretchy fabric of her pants allows me to insert two fingers along her hip. "Fuck. Why don't you have panties on?" I tug at the black fabric covering my shoulder, reeling my shirt up over my head, and toss it to the ground.

Her eyes run across my bare chest, wondering about the scattered tattoos I have or surprised by my pierced nipple. She never answers me as to why she's not wearing panties. Instead, she lifts her ass, pushing her pants to her knees, and widens them. The tension of the fabric makes her work to keep them spread as she runs a finger over her slickness.

"You—oh, you are making me..." I roughly exhale, the cold air sharp in my lungs. The heat between us defeats the cold night. Neither of us cares. Not about the rain, not about the midnight woods, and not about what happens when this is over. "Fuck, we need to get these off. Now." She loops her thumbs at the waistband of the fabric pushed to her knees, but I stop her. "Touch yourself. Rub it for me." I wrap my hands around her legs, forcing her pants to her ankles, pull her boots off, and yank her pants free without ever losing her glistening fingers.

"Open it up for me." She stretches her fingers until they hit her walls, and I wish it wasn't this fucking dark out. Folding my hands behind her knees, I pull her toward me, lifting her legs over my shoulders as I bury my face into her pussy. Her socks caress my skin, drying patches of water as the rain runs over the ridges of my back. Her fingers never stop; they easily move to her clit. I glance up, but her sight doesn't meet mine. "Eyes right here," I demand.

"Ah, yes," she moans.

"Close your eyes and I stop."

"Don't. Mm—don't stop."

Putting all my weight on my knees, I wrap my arms around her lower back, pulling her tight and unburying my face. Her legs tighten over my shoulders and as I lift her she gasps, threading her fingers through my hair. I exhale warm air, blowing both her hair and mine from my face. *Fuck.* Here we go.

I place my foot out in front of me, bracing to use the strength in my legs to stand with her on my shoulders. *Fuuck.* I exhale, blindly stumbling until her back is pressing against a massive oak. I kiss her inner thigh, and catch her eyes just before I bend, slipping her legs off my shoulders. I hold her wrists to the tree above her head and take her lips deeply.

"That's right, baby." The left corner of my mouth curves up, and I unfasten my jeans, letting my dick jut free. "Spit on it."

She catches me off guard, her fingers digging into my neck. *Fucking choke me out. Do it, baby, come on.* "How long have you wanted to give me a necklace? You are a bad girl. A very bad, dirty girl. What do you want?"

"You spit on it," she retorts. *Fuck. That's hot.*

I gaze directly into her glacial eyes, cocking my head to the side. "You want to go drown me again? There's a lake around here somewhere," I pant.

"You'll freeze."

"I don't mind and you like to see how much I can take."

"You're so screwed up."

"Is that a no?" I spit into my hand, holding it in front of her. Her eyes deaden, and then she adds her spit to mine.

Fucking hell. God damn, the heat in my body could cause a nuclear explosion. She sets my world on fire.

Running my hand over my cock, our collective lube coats with each pump. I grab her leg with one hand and wrap it around my waist, pushing my jeans lower with my free hand. Pressing the head of my cock to her opening, the heat engulfs me, and I can't take it slow anymore. A single thrust puts me deep inside her, and I pin both of her wrists in my hand against the tree, pumping in and out of her wet pussy. "Ah, fuck. Oh...mhm, baby." My moans are intertwined with a deep chuckle and a heavy growl against her ear. I can feel the beating of her heart against my hand that pins her wrists—it's rapid. Her moans are soft and airy, and I'm dying to hear her get loud. "Go ahead, wrap those pretty hands around my neck." I let go of her wrists. "I know you want to."

"Ah uh, slow down," she pants. Her dainty nails cut into my neck. *Holy shit.* I wrap my free hand around her throat, applying the lightest pressure.

"That's right, tell me. I want to hear you. Mm, tell me what you need." I thrust in and out, feeling the rising heat build. Fuck the rain. Fuck the cold. I'm sweating, working my ass off to hold her.

"Right...ah, there. Right there. Oh," she moans. Her grip around my neck tightens, and I groan deeply, wanting to yell at her for closing her eyes for a second.

"Fucking...tight," I pant, losing my preserved oxygen.

I look down to see her standing on her tiptoes, and I squeeze her thigh as she tightens it around my ass. It's...getting hazy. My vision darkens to spots and fuzzy lights. I find her eyes again, fucking iced over and greedy. My head drifts forward, and I start to sink to my knees. Cherry's open hand wakes me, slapping against my cheek. I slam into her, hitting that spot she likes over and over, fighting my spotty vision. I can't hear her moans or the sweet reminders of her wet pussy wrapped around my cock. I move in motion as I fall out of consciousness. Knowing that she's getting off—that she's coming all over my dick—is the only thing that keeps me alive.

None of that happened.

It was the obsession taking over my think space.

I didn't fuck her stupid against a tree. I didn't tell her anything I'd regret. I vividly fantasized about it while standing in the rain. I stared her down and tried to talk myself off the cliff of strangling her or ripping her fucking clothes off. I have a detailed imagination. I'll be rubbing one out when I get back to my trailer and hoping it suffices...at least for the time being.

Now, where was I? Oh yeah.

"Big bad Bennett, huh?" I laugh. "Cherry, you better fucking run."

"No. I'm not running and you're not going to do shit. You need me. You have to figure it out, whatever it is. Figure it the hell out, B."

"What part of it will *eat at me* don't you understand?" I tighten my fists, wishing she wouldn't fight me on this. I hate this game. She wanted me to fuck her, and now she doesn't? Now that I'm dying to make my fantasy a reality—her fantasies a fucking reality.

"Seeing as you brought a man back to life by hovering your hands over his body, I think you can figure out how to control your freaking impulses. And if you can't, then maybe it's time you find yourself in a padded room."

Shit!

Renew, Cherry Blossom

B ennett rushes to my side, walking down the asphalt toward the set building. He left me at my trailer right before dawn, a few hours ago.

"Where's Ames?" He searches the lot.

Bennett hides his face beneath his hood. It's a usual choice for him on a workday. His sweatshirt matches the black hoodie that hangs in my bathroom, a reminder that no matter how long I soak my skin in the scolding shower, I can't wash off the night. I can't take back what I did. It will be there when I return and I'd rather him sneak into my trailer to steal it.

"He's fine." Without a glance in his direction, I continue towards hair and makeup. "I left his trailer five minutes ago." Then had a miniature meltdown, collected myself, and transitioned into character. "The last thing he remembers is the fistfight. He thinks he got rocked." I cut him off with my body, forcing him to look at me.

Gees, Bennett. His lip has doubled in size, and his cheek is swollen with a matching shadow below his eye. He looks ten times worse than Ames. "You look like shit." He should have used his voodoo on himself. "Come with me."

I tug his hand, quickly parading him to the side entrance and into the beauty room. It's early and nobody is in yet. I flick on the lights and explore the counters, open drawers, and shuffle through samples. It may be rude to mess with Kayla's ensemble, but it's not like anyone will complain or remember if they walk in on me painting Bennett's face. He'll do his trick and make them disappear.

With his hands in his trouser pockets, he stands at the door. Finally, he tugs his hoodie over his head and tosses it to one of the vanities. Now he looks more like himself—white button-down, black belt, black slacks, and ridiculously expensive shoes. I pull my dark fleece jacket off and hang it over the rail of one of the black swivel chairs.

"Get over here." He takes his time, strolling over, and uneagerly sinks into the closest seat. "Did you sleep?"

"Did you?" He leans back, stretching his arms behind his head. It's not as easy to avoid his eyes when I have to look at his face to fix it.

My heavy sigh drains the air from my lungs. I thought I lived every nightmare the world could give me. I did. I have a sickness in my head that's no better than Bennett's. Unlike him, I've never stopped fighting it, and I never will. I'm going to do everything I can to balance the tables and repent. The plan remains the same. It has to.

I could move forward—pursue a career with no strings attached. I could do that—leave this set when it's all said and done, forget Bennett, heal my soul in holy water. Yet, deep down, destroying that monster is all I'll ever be able to focus on. Last night proves it. My actions were the result of him. I fell into his trap like everyone else and it hurt immaculately to find him with another woman. I want him to pay and I keep finding myself consumed in his unfortunately beautiful hooded eyes, his smooth voice, and the tiny pieces of him that don't feel like the man I came here to end. He did this. He made me weak and emotional. I've made up my mind. When filming wraps, I won't go my way. I'll make the final move—for everyone he hurt.

"You should learn how to fix this with your voodoo," I mumble, pulling a package of right triangle sponges out of the drawer.

"Voodoo? Do you understand how this shit works? Because I don't. I do know it doesn't feel good when I try to fix people." I return his dark glare, dropping the sponges on the lit countertop. "Don't give me that fucking look. I can't give you the answers you want."

"You can, you just won't." I storm around him, pulling another drawer open as I search for a matching concealer. Nestled to the left is a stack of clear palettes. I take one, smack it to the counter, and force the door shut. I pull another open, look for the foundation, and slam it shut. I open the next, and nothing, slamming it once more. "What?" I snap at him and circle back to the left side, drawing another drawer open. Finding a collection of concealer and foundation samples, I shuffle through them to finally manage what seems to be a match.

I didn't think he'd have it in him to heal Ames. He was...*Ames Heart was dead.* The curveball not only knocked me off track but gave me some insight I've foolishly wanted to find. The goal wasn't to turn him...or attain him. It was to destroy him. But what if I could use him? Bennett can do things that the others can't. It's not fair that he gets to live with such gifts nor would it be fair for me to let them go to waste. I swear—I'm not going back on my word. I'm going through with this. I might change the route a little. That's all.

God! Why is this so hard? Why can't I turn him over and know I did right by Jack and everyone? He would be killed and dissected, studied and buried only to be unearthed again and re-examined. They wouldn't risk him staying alive despite the good he could bring to the world. That's what he deserves—to be a lab rat for the rest of his life.

I was drowning. My demons weigh me down like an anchor. The orange reflection of a buoy calls me to safety and for the first time in years, I see hope. Now, I'm drifting away every time I close my eyes and see the girl's face. I see everything all over again and I hate him for it. Until I look into his eyes and I read his story. It twists my internal organs in ways I can comprehend and I want to know why. Why does he have this beauty within him when he should be pure monster? He should be easy to hate. After everything he's done. He's the reason the happiness I fought for was ripped from my hands.

I'm here for the wonderful, caring, giving man who saw me as more than a number and in the name of vengeance for every life that Bennett Larson took. Tearing him apart from the inside should be more satisfying the closer I get, yet that's the same thing that makes every day with him a battle beneath my skull.

I grab three shades that appear to work and hold them up. They should do the trick. His deep stare compels me to lower my hand, losing myself in his beautiful almond-shaped eyes. It's like driving by a car accident along the brim and instead of moving over like an intelligent person, you stay in the same lane and intently check out what's going on. He sucks me in with adrenaline and keeps me with desire—over and over and over. The hold he has on me...

"Damn, Bennett. Did you get into a fight with a sludge hammer?" Mel walks around the corner, startling me. Both Bennett and I ascend in her direction. "I can have Kayla or Shell come do that."

"No. Nobody else needs to know about this." He nods at me, and I tear open the pouch and grab a flat brush from the vanity. It's fairly thick, so I'm hoping it does the trick. I've seen the girls use color correctors for blemishes, but I wouldn't know where to start. Is it the orange shade or the green? He should let Mel call one of them.

"What happened on that date last night?" She jokes, looking between us. I glance at her, pretending I didn't hear anything as I try to paint Bennett's face. He doesn't flinch.

"Nothing worth mentioning," he answers.

I dab the brush around, trying to mimic the techniques makeup artists have used on me. "How's it look now?"

"Better. Looks like he needs a nap instead of an ice pack." She's not wrong. This is a mess.

"I'll take it." He rises. " You can go, Cherry. I'll see you over there."

I stare at him, irritated by how he simply dismissed me. I have the urge to pick up after myself, but I let everything sit and play it cool. "Oh, okay." I walk around them, smiling with a polite goodbye to Mel.

I stop outside the door, pressing my back against the wall.

"Alright, what's up?" Mel's words are clear as crystal as if she didn't care if she was overheard.

"What?" Bennett sneers back.

"What does she have on you? Something fishy is going on and after the last girl you kept around for a few months, it looks like you're forming a habit of pissing women off."

"It's none of your fucking business."

I spin my ring around my pointer and glance around. As the conversation behind the wall heats, I become nervous for her.

"You know it's really difficult for anyone to give a shit about you when you act like a dickhead," he retorts.

"Don't state the obvious. You can get back to work."

The sound of muffled footsteps puts me in a panic, and I rush down the hall. *Screw this.*

"Hey, girl," Kayla greets me as I reach for the pot of coffee. The hazelnut aroma wraps me in a blanket of comfort and eases my exhausted mind. I could inhale it for an hour. Considering the steam coming off the glass, I'll have to stand here for twenty minutes until it won't scold me. That will suffice. "You look exhausted."

I hold the pot up with a blank stare. Then sit it back on the base. "I didn't sleep well last night." *I didn't sleep at all, but you don't need to know that.* I place a lid on my cup and put a smile on my face. "I'm going to need six cups of coffee and the best makeup you've ever done in your life."

"You're with Lillian today, right?" She scans the table of assorted carbs.

"Yeah, that scene should be it. I'm hoping it's a quick day."

"Yeah, I'm tired of looking at this place too. Shell always does Lillian's make-up. I heard she's going to daytime TV." She picks a sesame seed bagel from the tray and continues. "Tell me you have something coming up."

"I do and I can't share...yet." She struggles to open an individual packet of fig jam and reaches for a knife.

"If you leave me hanging and I have to find out through the grapevine, I'm going be so disappointed Miss Cherry Kaas."

"When I can talk about it, you'll be at the top of my gossip train."

"Can you give me the slightest hint, though? A little teaser, if you will? Is it with Bennett? You two are a dream team, after all."

"No...and—" I sigh. "I don't know if it's going to work out between us," I admit. "I'm going back to California, and I have no idea what he's doing next."

"He hasn't told you?" She asks, swallowing the food she pushed around her mouth to talk. "If he's not communicating now, it's not going to last. Take it from me—the traveling wife. But hey, was he at least good in bed?" She bats her falsies.

"I wouldn't know," I again admit, steeling her gaze.

"What! What are you waiting for?" She starts humming *Pony by Ginuwine* and circles her hips. Then she throws in a lasso while holding her bagel and I crack an authentic smile.

"It's complicated."

"If you're going to break up with him at least sample the pony and let me live vicariously through you by telling me all about it." Scratching the back of my neck, I giggle for her amusement. "First you skipped out on Ames and now Bennett. My friend, you are missing out on your vital youth and fame privilege."

"Ames wanted to take things slow." I point. "That wasn't my fault."

"That's actually a good thing if you think about it." She reaches for a cup. "Less male ego jealousy."

"How are you late to the gossip?"

"What gossip? What did I miss?" She smacks her cup onto the table. "I'm legitimately upset that you beat me to it."

"Well, I was there so..."

Kayla crosses her arms over her chest. "What did you do?"

"It was not my fault. Ames made a snarky comment to Bennett and...he challenged him to a...*fistfight*." I question the term as I say it.

"They fought over you?" She coos. "Oh my *gawd*. You're living my dream. Why in God's beautiful name did I marry my high school sweetheart?"

"Because true love doesn't need the dramatics."

"Honey, you are the queen of dramatics. I've watched for the last four months on and off set. You are a fantastic actor and that goes all around." She turns back to her cup and grabs the pot of coffee. "You control those men. Even Bennett." She sets the pot back and places a lid on her paper cup. "You liked the hot and cold moment you and Ames had going on and whatever hush-hush relationship you had with Bennett."

"I honestly hate how observant you are." I frown. "Calling me out is such a friend move."

She wraps her arms around me, and I hug her back. "I'm going to miss you," he squeals. "But hey, we're not done yet. I'll catch you in a little. I have to run over to Freedome. Don't forget to show as Samantha tonight for our wrap party, as we discussed." She points, juggling her bagel and checking the time on her phone.

"I wouldn't. It's my final chance to raid her wardrobe."

"Mel! What the fuck." For the second time today, I find myself hiding and eavesdropping on Bennett. *Wonderfully*, I'm also half-naked.

I drop the heather gray skirt to my ankles and step out of it, quickly rushing to pull on a pair of joggers. Hopping around, I tug on my sneakers. Panic sets in and my pulse races as I shuffle behind a moving rack of clothing and peer around the silver bar. In my defense, I was here first. I thought I could change quickly and rummage through Samantha's wardrobe. The dress from the ballroom scene has to be in here somewhere.

"You can handle it on your own. I'm tired of canceling my plans for you," Mel fires back.

What are they arguing about? He's been more douchey than usual today. He's miserable and has been pushing everyone to their limits. I'm drained too. And it's like he doesn't care how far he drives them. He hasn't used any of his charms. He purely wants to piss everyone off.

"I pay you *damn well* to be available when I need you."

"*Damn well* isn't good enough to put up with an asshole for another year." Oh man, is she going to quit on him?

"What are you saying? You're quitting?" *Oh, called it.*

I jump back, sinking to the floor. *Did he see me?* Dang it.

"I can't quit, I'm under contract, but I don't need to be here right now." Peeking around the bottom of the rack, Mel's black clogs come into view.

"You're not leaving. *Stop.*" She keeps walking and I can't see either of them anymore. "I said stop." He gets louder.

Nope. No freaking way. I'm not going to sit here and wait for him to snap her neck. He can't treat people like this. They're not objects.

"Bennett!" I chastise him as if he were a child, causing Mel to freeze in her footsteps. His eyes inadvertently roll upward as he hesitates to look at me.

"What do you want, Cherry?" He grouses, turning away.

I march up to him and thread my fingers through the hair along the nape of my neck, grazing his ear with my lips. "Apologize," I whisper.

He turns his head, forcing me to lean back. His narrow eyes meet mine, and I'm tempted to tell him they're illuminated. Instead, I widen my eyes exaggeratingly, hoping he gets the hint. "Don't try to stop me," he mutters.

"Why do you have to solve all your problems this way?"

"In what fucking way? In the way that makes logical sense, and I've built an entire career because of? In *that* way?" The heat of his sweaty hand captures my wrist as he clasps around me. "I thought we were on the same page." His hand constricts. "This affects you too. I need her on this project, fully, and not with one foot out the door until it's finished and perfected."

I look between Bennett and Mel, shuffling my bottom lip back and forth. "Fine, but don't you dare touch her." I step to the side and he approaches her.

"Mel," he calls. "Please—" I can feel the grinding of his teeth. "Look at me."

"There's nothing else you can say, Bennett."

"There is. You see, I know you're overworked and I acknowledge that. And you're the only one who can keep us on schedule. You're the best at what you do. We need you. We can't survive without you. You want to keep us thriving and successful. You want to make sure everyone has a job and a paycheck to take home to their families. You want them to be able to feed their babies and puppies." He glances over his shoulder, rolling his eyes at me. "You want to work late today and secure those paychecks. "I may be a tyrant, but you're the hero saving the day and one day I might admit it too."

"As I was saying, I'll check with Justin and we can work together to handle this tonight. It will be done before I leave. I know you need me," she replies in an impudent tone.

Bennett scowls with his nostrils flaring.

I'm not dealing with him right now. I find my way to the door without paying him any attention. Bennett suddenly grabs me. He takes my chin in his hand, pinching my lower lip between his thumb and finger. I become slammed against the door and pinned beneath his strength. "Don't *ever* interrupt me again."

I grab his wrist, digging my nails into his veins.

"I'm growing tired of your antics, Cherry."

"Go take a nap, you miserable beast." My nails deepen, and he lets go of my jaw. I hold on to his wrist, and he stares at me until I free him.

"Fuck it." He dips his chin. "Enlighten me. What do you want to say that you're holding back? Go ahead and say it, Cherry. This is where we're at. You know too much, and I know enough, so hit me."

"What happened to you?" Unsettled, I press him. "You used to be a good guy, didn't you?"

"I wasn't anything. I was alive, going through the emotions." He inches closer. "I've never felt more contempt." The minutes stand still, and neither of us speaks.

"You have empathy. I've seen it." His eyes zigzag over mine. "When did you die, Bennett?" The warmth of his hand blankets my mouth, quieting me. He holds me beneath his palm with my back tight against his chest. Then the chatter of approaching team members fades. They make their way down the corridor, and he releases me. He shuts the door and locks it.

"October seventeenth—three weeks after my twenty-fourth birthday." *They had him that long?* "Why do insist on fucking—" His voice cracks and he fists air. "Why do badger me for my story?"

"Am I supposed to forget what I've witnessed?" I yell. "And more than that, do you expect me to move on after last night?" My breaths become labored as my lips remain parted. "I need something—explain to me why all of this is happening."

"I can't do that." He shakes his head. "I'm done talking about this here. I don't have the time to escort everyone off a ledge today." His hand falls to the door and twists the lock, opening it again. He throws it open and storms off.

"You didn't deny it! Having empathy," I shout as he walks down the hall. "Stop fighting it."

Give up now, while you have the chance.

I've struggled in these heels the entire length of the ladder, finally making it to the top and swinging my leg over. I knew he'd be up here.

I take his attention as he hears my clicking heels. "Don't drool," I call out.

His eyes scan every inch of my contoured body, taking in my Samantha ensemble. I'm decked out with wide pleated crisscrossed off-the-shoulder straps and a v-neckline with a peak of cleavage. The form-fitting bodice ends right above the knee. It's difficult not to play the character when I'm dressed like her. Sophisticated and—these are twelve hundred dollar pointed-toe pumps. "Cat got your tongue?"

"Where are you going dressed like that?"

With a hand on my hip, I strike a pose. "Home with you."

"Black looks good on you." He glances back at his laptop screen. His fingers tap keys at an alarming speed before he turns to me again. "It's not exactly your style."

"I'm versatile." I wink and sit next to him. Sliding off my pastel pump, I hang my legs off the side of the building. "It's chilly tonight." I pull Samantha's fuzzy black shawl over my shoulders.

"How was the wrap party?"

"It was fun. You couldn't get out of your miserable mood to stop in for a few minutes?"

The last gathering at Freedome ended about thirty-five minutes ago. We said our goodbyes and most people left for the city, considering it was only six in the evening. Kayla has my number, so I expect gossip updates on her half while she expects an update on male accessories. Bennett could've said a few words to the people who worked on his film during and beyond the last four months.

He gives me a one-word reply. "Writing."

"Does it have a title yet?"

"No."

"Aren't you going home tonight?" I badger.

"Why? Do you want to come with me?" He stares at me. "I'm surprised you're up here after expressing your feelings earlier."

"Where else would I go? Take me home with you."

"You do know I don't own a mansion?" All of the nights we spent up here talking over the past few months, I've almost become accustomed to looking for the good in him, but now I can't get the image of his bloody hand around my neck and the threats he would deliver. I have to be the one to make sacrifices for the greater good.

"You own a cozy acre of land with a ranch-style gray house in Minden—1281 Stanton Road sound familiar?"

He freezes in expression—stunned. It lasts mere seconds before he blinks, coming to terms with my knowledge. He repeatedly said that I'm always surprising him. "How did you find that out?"

"I like to read."

"Is this the next step in your ultimate plan?"

"Yeah. Do you have a twin I don't know about?" *Because your split personality makes me believe you should.*

"You should know. It seems like you've thoroughly investigated me."

I roll my thumb across my ring, preparing to take the leap. "I took that job. I have six weeks until I need to be in California."

"Where are you staying until then?" A smile tugs at my mouth, and I look away, covering it.

"A hotel or a few." I shrug.

"How about 1281 Stanton Road?" His buttery words come out better than I imagined, and I know I have him hooked.

Pressing my hands against the cold surface, I stand, slip on my heels, and pull my shawl over my shoulders once more. "I'm not going there and neither are you."

"Where am I going then?" I walk to the ladder, and he jumps up, closing his laptop. He slips it in his case, zips it, and throws it over one shoulder. "Hey," he calls out, running after me. "Cherry..." He yells out as I near the middle of the ladder. "Where are you going?" I smile up at him, watching the frustration cloud his face. As I reach for the next step, I slide my hands down the cold metal. He continues to follow me, fighting to keep up as I scurry toward his car. Simon was easily swayed when I requested vehicle arrangements for this evening. He followed the order, parking Bennett's black SUV at the rear of Freedome and tucking the key under the visor. "Cherry, where are we going?" He eyeballs the vehicle.

I stop when I reach the rear driver's side door and open it. Quickly reaching for my backpack, I unzip the pouch and turn back to him. "I have the name of a doctor. You can choose to go see her or you can choose to hang out next to the ex-girlfriend."

"What are you talking about?"

"It's not rocket science. You have two choices. Doctor." I hold one hand out. "Or death." I show him the other.

"Are you fucking serious?" His feet are concrete as hatred fills his eyes. I stretch my arms behind me, reaching into the open pouch. With my fist tightly bound, I wait for his guard to fall. "Is that a threat, Cherry?"

"Considering I said doctor or death, it very much appears that I'm threatening your life — if you make the wrong decision, of course."

"Is this my fault? Did I somehow warp you into another mental breakdown?" He comes closer.

"You don't even know how dangerous you are." The wind takes my hair, wrapping it around my face. I brush it out with my free hand and adjust my shawl. "The things you're capable of doing—nobody should have that power."

"And you know how dangerous I am?" His chest closes in on mine, and his scowl buries into my flesh. A hell-like fire runs through my veins, breaking in the center of my chest where it profoundly beats. "You don't know half the shit I could do to you right now."

"And there are *so many* things you don't know about me, B," I calmly reply, jerking my arm out and stabbing a needle into his thigh.

His eyes stagger between the needle in his leg and my face. His tongue runs across his lower lip and he inhales. Shock and confusion pinch his brows together. "Cherry," he exhales with an empty breath.

I pull out the syringe and drop it to the ground as I fight to hold him up. His legs shake, weakening and turning limp. He falls to my chest, reaching for my arms. I pull him into the backseat, struggling beneath his weight.

How do I manage this? Oh, I can...

I slide across the seat, opening the opposite door. As I jump out, I close the door and run around to the driver's side. My heels click off the blacktop.

Where's the cap? Damn it. Damn it! I can—wait, there it is.

I grab the cap from the floor and pick up the syringe from the ground, snap it together, and place the syringe in my backpack. The door sounds louder than it is as I close it. Then my heels click again. It's the last sound I hear as I hop in the driver's seat and reach for the key above me. Everything turns mute as I place the key in the ignition and the engine turns over.

Escaping into the starry sky, I drive on with only the words of Mom in my head; *Baby Girl — we are born fighters. We fight until we don't want to fight anymore.* Passing Bennett's trailer for the last time, I know I'm doing the right thing.

Taste Your Own Medicine, Bennett

"**B**oth of us are going to be dead by next week at this rate, Cherry."

Yeah, that's where we're at now. You recall her saying something along the lines of "We're not going to your house" right? She must've changed her mind or lied. The fuck if she tells the truth about anything. The woman is an absolute wild card.

I woke up in the basement of my own fucking house about twenty minutes ago. I can't fathom her thought process behind this—tying me to a chair? Was it supposed to hold?

I might not spend a lot of time here, but the ten-acre lot hidden at the end of my private driveway is surrounded by woods that I've explored often. The living quarters are on one floor and there's a few ways out of this basement.

Life lesson time: Always have an exit strategy. In this case—a fire exit.

"Cherry!" I stomp through the foyer, searching for her.

"I'm not the problem," she yells. A black marbled vase flies across the living room into the wall half a foot from my head.

The familiar monotoned box I call home doesn't resemble much more than a showroom. And while I only reside here a month or so out of the year, it would be great if she could stop destroying my shit.

"Too far left, darling." I tilt my head. "You know what, fuck this. At least I admit that I'm not a good guy."

Her fingers dance along the back of the dark leather sofa in the center of the room, and she slowly walks around it. "You have two choices. Surrender or die."

"Surrender to who? A-A-" I stutter. "What? A fucking government lab that can put me under a microscope and milk me for their benefit while I whither away? Is that the kind of help you think I should get?" She takes her eyes off me for a second too long, giving me the advantage. I rush her, shoving her against the wall. She fights back as I pin her hands above her head. "You want to know everything, Cherry? I'll fucking tell you everything. Although you know me so well, you should already be aware." I adjust my hold, taking her wrists with one hand and brushing the blonde strands from her eyes. She clenches her teeth, baring them angrily. "I didn't get shot and revived, you know that. Fifteen long empty months, and then I woke up fucked because of these people you claim can help me. Boom, they created a supervillain—a monster from hell walks the Earth." I stray from her eyes to her mouth and release her. With my hands surrendered above me, I back away. "Turn me in, but at least let me finish writing about it first."

She rubs her wrists, staring me down. "I knew that book wasn't fiction."

"Congratulations," I obnoxiously call, taking a few more steps backward. "You're cute and smart. Too bad I can't *fucking stand you.*"

"What happened when you woke up?" She calls out. The irritability in her voice proves she knows and for her own twisted logic, wants to hear it from my mouth.

"I was covered in some kind of nasty thick black gunk, face down in the woods," I reluctantly groan. "My old apartment was locked, my car was nowhere to be found, and my wallet, ID, and everything was gone besides a few bills that I used to get a shitty motel room. Then I went to the bank, and it turns out I can control minds. That's it. Now I'm standing here dealing with the one person I've come across in three years that I can't convince to leave me alone."

"You died and then you woke up in the woods. That's all you remember?" She tucks her chin, convincing herself I'm lying.

"Yes, Cherry," I insist. "I remember standing behind my shitty car. I heard the gun go off and stared down the alley like an idiot. Then—lights out. Black nothingness. Then the lights are back on. Muck." I lean into my shoulder against the wall opposite of her and cross my arms and ankles. Nothing besides our voices echoing off each other exists, and the scent of that fucking candle she's obsessed with taints the air.

"Are you sure you didn't move from where the shooter dropped your body?" She presses.

"Was I walking around like the living dead? Maybe, but I don't fucking remember it." Letting my head fall back against the wall, I don't keep my thoughts hidden. I'm not keeping anything inside. What's the point? Cherry knows everything. "I would have rather died."

"You would have died instead of being given a second chance at life with incredible abilities?"

"Maybe I wouldn't have been stuck in the black abyss. I could have moved forward and found Annie. I think about how easily I could end it. One day I might. People don't care until you're dead anyway. Then they talk about how this and that you were. How it's such a tragedy."

"I would miss you," she whispers.

Her back never leaves the wall across from me, and her eyes never fall from mine. Fuck these mind games. She would miss me. She's also willing to kill me if I don't surrender to being poked with needles? I don't think she could end my life if refused. She'd drug me again and take me against my will.

"Stop playing the games, Cherry. You're not like Annie. You're like me."

"I'm not like you," she sneers.

I tussle my dark waves, leaving the wall. "You're fucking like me."

The downward curve of her lips disappears. "No, I'm not." Her jaw becomes tense, stretching to the veins in her neck.

"You're fucking like me," I motionlessly echo.

I've spent the entirety of the last four or five months trying to convince you I'm unforgivable. I spent how many years of my life convincing myself I was invisible. I was visible to the right people then and it's not black and white now. I'm not a good man, that's easy to see. I fucking have a wrap sheet of victims. I'm not as heartless as

I want to believe either. You've been right the whole time, haven't you? You always saw something in me. You saw me for who I am, but what about Cherry? Did she fool you like she fooled me?

"The villain always thinks she's the hero."

"I'm not like you!" She screeches. Her nails cut into my throat in her sporadic attack. I lean into the stinging sensation, accepting every ounce of pain she delivers.

"Show it to me, Cherry. Show me your hatred. Bring it all to the surface and take what you must to fucking break free." I pull her legs tight around my abdomen, and she locks them behind me. "Let me be the sail to your shipwrecked boat. Fucking drag me down with you."

I crave her taste to the point that I have no shame in begging. She's top tier in the crazy department and the little psycho is mine now.

If I'm lucky, I'll make it to the couch, as I dizzily search for its leather surface. I slam her back to the wall, her blonde waves splaying the bland paint, and with a jolt of her head, her hands leave me. "I fucking hate you," I growl.

"I should have shoved you off the fucking Freedome roof." She yells. "Who's the idiot that decided on that name?"

"God, yes. You fucking little psycho. Say it again, fucking say it again."

The dusting of stars flying around me begins to fade, and I want more. I pin her to the wall by the neck, pressing until my fingertips flatten. She attempts to pull me by the wrist, quickly giving up and flailing her arms until she connects with my throat again. *Fuuck.*

"Show me how fucking much you hate me," I groan. My knees weaken, and I unpin her, holding her as tight as I can to avoid dropping what's mine in my backward stumble. I slam into the bookshelf and arch my shoulder in pain. *Fuuck.* Desperately reaching for air, I gasp for an inhale. I blink as my body starts sinking and her evil, disgusting little giggle fills my ears, relighting my flame. I utilize the burst of oxygen, stand up, and crash into the corner table bordering the recliner, falling on top of Cherry. *Fucking hell.* I roll off of her, cowering to my side as I wheeze and choke on saliva. With a distorted deep chuckle, I spit and cough. As my airway clears, I continue laughing.

Cherry slowly crawls past me on one elbow while her other hand takes the curve of her lower back. She looks right at me and meets my laugh with her sinister giggle. I might die tonight...and I don't fucking care if it's by her hand, *but she's going with me.*

"Where are you going?" I call, grabbing ahold of her ankle. "You can't leave now, Cherry. It's just starting to get fun."

"Fuck you, B." She kicks me in the mouth, slipping out of my grip. *Fuuck!* I suck at my teeth, rubbing two fingers across my lip.

"You're gonna have to try a little better than that. You didn't even draw blood." I press into my hands and knees, sliding against the carpet until I reach the arm of the recliner and hoist myself back up. The floating lights blur everything around me. I blink them away, searching for Cherry. "Oh, Cherry, oh darling—don't worry, Benny will find you. That's what you like, don't you? You just fucking love to call me that. Or am I wrong? You don't want the softness of him. You want the fucking monster—the God damned dead man!" She's hiding somewhere around here. She's waiting. Listening. Panting. Her heart is racing a mile a minute, and she's spinning that ring in circles. She's planning her next move and anticipating mine. She's fighting her own mind, wanting to stop me and wanting to let me win. I'm already past that internal battle. *She owns me. I'd bathe my body in blood for her.*

A deep, rigid chuckle pulls from my lungs as I stand, walking into the kitchen. "Ready or not—"

Fuck!

I dip back, noisily sucking in air and saliva. The little witch cut me. She reaches around the island for a second time, trying to mark my leg with her blade again. I exhale a gruff breath and lower to her level, clasping my hand around her wrist and shaking the knife free. "You feel that, baby?" I yank her by the wrist and drag her across the floor, using her as a mop to collect the speckled drops of blood. Pulling her back up to my chest, I hold the knife to her, dangerously kissing right below her chin.

I had enough fantasies about this moment—about that fear in her eyes when I finally caught her. But it's not there.

"Oh, is the big bad Bennett mad?" The pressure of the blade restricts her range.

Let me guess...

I press my tongue to my teeth.

She's looking into my stark white irises, isn't she?

"Fucking do it, B."

"Now Cherry, I don't want to do that." I smooth her hair to one shoulder. "If I did, tell me, what's the one thing—anything—you could have before you died—right now, right here—what would it be?"

"Not your fucking cock if that's what you think."

I sardonically chuckle in the hollow of her neck. She's fucking perfect and more than I ever imagined.

Not two months, not two years, not even two lifetimes.

I hold the blade out in front of her face, grazing her cheek with a cut, and bring it to my mouth. Her furious iced-over eyes fixate on me as I toy with her, taking a sliver of my lower lip in with my teeth. Her eyes widen. Her back stiffens against me and her breathing becomes noticeably more shallow.

We all know what that means; she's seeing the stark white hell. I'm starting to get a hang of this now. Either that or her facial expressions are quite telling.

I smile, drive out an airy laugh, and press the flat of my tongue to the blade, licking the nearly three inches of carbon steel before tossing it across the room with the flick of my wrist.

"Raa!"

Fuck!

Her immediate screams pierce my ears as she chomps down on my arm. Somewhere between her squeals, I moan and shriek. She fumbles forward as I tear my arm from her mouth. Her quick recovery allows her to crawl across the floor and shuffle to her feet in the moment I take to study to indents of her teeth that border both sides of my upper forearm.

"Cherry," I growl, chasing after her. *Shit! The fucking knife.*

In a running leap, I crash into her, taking her down to the carpet. I crawl up her legs, reaching for her arms as she claws the flooring in front of her, wildly trying to reclaim the knife. I tack her arms down and blow the hair out of my face in a huff.

"How long are you going to fight it?" I bark.

Trying to get to her knees, she arches her hips, pushing her ass into my lower abdomen. She bucks and kicks, groaning. "Bennett!"

"Scream my name!" I deeply chuckle. "*Fuuck* yes."

I grab her hips, heat radiating from her skin, and flip her over. As I straddle her body, I hold her hands in place above her head. I glance up and reassure the knife is out of reach.

"Fuck you," she spits.

Literally, she fucking spit in my face.

Ohh...hah. Darling, oh, fucking darling. You need a lesson in mannerisms.

I snap, pinching her bottom lip in my hand. "You better fucking behave."

"You've already lost, B."

"Your math is different than mine. You got a couple of points, but I have the upper hand."

"You can't kill me."

"Oh, I fucking wish I could, but you're right...because you're mine. Not just right now and not for two days, not for two years, not for two fucking lifetimes, Cherry. You're mine forever. If you die, I fucking die—and I pity the bastard that tries to take you from me."

"And if I end my life?" Her beautiful blue eyes stare into the depths of my soul. I don't know if she's asking as my attempting murderer or if she sincerely wants to know what would happen if she would leave me, the only way that's left.

"I'd never leave this hell without you. I'd endure all that this world has to throw at me. But if you end, everything ends. *When everything ends, it ends with you.*" Her gaze travels between my eyes and lips as I hover over her. I dip down, taking my chances. Her soft pillowing mouth melts into mild, turning deeper and rugged. I wait for her to bite me again. I almost crave her pain. The heat rises in my groin as my heart rate jumps. "I could give you everything, Cherry," I breathe against her skin. With my weight on my knees, I let go of her. She looks over at the knife and back to me.

Hah...I don't blame her.

With a swift tug, I reach over my shoulder, pulling the shirt off my back. I toss it and wait for her next move. "What's it going to be? Do we die tonight, darling?"

She takes my jaw in her hand and her finger traces the length of the bone. I grab her wrist, sucking the curve of her thumb into my mouth. The thick silence between us rings louder than fireworks on a summer's night.

As I stand, I pull her up to her feet. Her mouth plunges into mine with the deepest suckling motions.

Fuck. She makes me so hard.

My hands border the curves of her waist, of her hips, straight to her ass. I grip under her cheeks and hoist her up until she wraps her legs around me. Her nails scratch and dig into my shoulders and neck as her body grinds and rolls against me in my shuffle toward the couch. No sooner than I back up and sit down, she pushes into the recliner, and I lean with its fall. She sucks at my neck as her hands search my body, finding one of my piercings. Her nails slip under each small silver ball on both sides of the bar.

"You're the most hypnotical man to walk this Earth. The way you acted about my nose ring—" She hisses, pulling the piece of jewelry. "For what? You have a piercing too."

"Piercings. Plural." Her eyes narrow as a gap forms between her lips. I tuck my hands behind my head and stretch before lowering my voice. "Just wait until you get my jeans off." I flex my dick against her ass and she retaliates, pressing down against me with the wiggle of her hips.

"You're lying...You don't." She studies my face. "You do?"

"Want to make a bet?" Between the hungry look in her eyes and the stuck shape of her lips, she questions me with the scan of my body. It's more than she's been picturing in her head for weeks. "If I'm lying, I'll let you cut me again—any location."

Was she expecting the sparse amount of hair below my navel or my shaven chest to bear a piercing? Is she happy she finally got to see the whole colorful sleeve that lines my arm and the small inked words on my opposite—the upper forearm that keeps Annie's spirit alive? Has she hoped I had enough lean muscle to sculpt the Adonis belt that she can't take her eyes off of while she wonders what the barbell below my belt looks like or how big my dick is?

I'm stuck on her little silver ring that circles her dainty finger as her hand falls over my arm, across my knuckles, and slides all the way down to the button of my jeans. She traces the ellipse with a hint of reluctance. Her hesitation ceases, and she undoes my belt, hastily tugging on my jeans and boxer briefs.

She edges to the floor as her eyes consume my frenum piercing.

"Did that hurt?"

"Worse than your nose. Less than a bullet."

"*Does* that hurt?"

"Some women have seen red while others are quite enthusiastic. I keep my barbel on the shorter side with concerns of my female counter." A smirk tugs at my lips. "Don't worry. I'm cautious. I'm Bennett Larson, after all."

"How long have—"

"It's been years."

"Can I..."

Her pretty blue eyes follow my hand as I run it down my shaft and back up again. She stops me, covers my hand with hers, and holds it in place.

"What are you waiting for?"

The tip of her warm, wet tongue flirts with the barbell. She propels the flat down the center to the apex of my head. The tip of her tongue traces the crown before her lips wrap around my dick and take my length in as far as she's comfortable.

"Do you like it, darling?"

She speaks with her eyes, drawing back up, only to repeat the movement.

"*Fuck.*"

I brush her hair back, threading my fingers through her honied strands. She hits my arm, not bothering to look at me. I fucking hate it. I rethread my fingers, tugging her hair back. Cherry jerks upward, slowly rolling her eyes as she glares at me. She sits back, unhooks my fingers, and stands up. She foolishly turns away. I grab her wrist, tightening my hold.

"Where do you think you're going? Quit acting! You know how bad of a mood I've been in since the woods, don't push me farther. Why are you fucking teasing?"

"This is wrong!"

"No, it can't be. It can't feel this right and be wrong."

She tugs her shirt off, throwing it at me and hitting me in the face. *There she is—my Cherry Bomb.* I reach for her again as I toss her top. As I fall to my knees, I wrap my hands around her thighs, pulling her close. I stare between her legs and pull the waistband of her leggings, pushing them, along with her panties, to her ankles. With both hands firmly on my shoulders, she balances, allowing me to rashly pull them off.

"You're beautiful." I slide my hands between her thighs and press a gentle kiss on her smooth skin. As I glide my fingers over her groomed pussy, my hums vibrate her leg. "Oh darling, you're—" I exhale a breathy laugh. "Fuck. I want you."

With one finger, I slide into her wetness. As she moans, I slip a second in. "I want you all over my face." I hold out my fingers before sucking them into my mouth. I deeply inhale, moaning between her legs as I squeeze her thighs. "Sit. Sit on the couch. That's it. Legs up."

I spin, trying not to lose my balance as my jeans constrict my calves. She swings her leg over me and rests her ankles on my shoulders. Taking her ass, I pull her closer. I trace her pussy with the tip of my tongue, circling her clit with my thumb, and then my tongue. "If they made a fucking candle that smelled like you, I'd buy everyone ever made, but since I'm guessing that's not your thing, now is a good time as any to tell you to expect a rather large package when you return to your trailer — from Homesick Candle Co."

She jerks upright. "Find Me?"

"Every fucking jar they had in stock, darling."

I run my middle finger over her slickness, up and down each side of her opening, coating my finger in her, and slip back inside. I curve at the knuckle, stroking that soft spot. Hers is impossible to miss. Her abdomen noticeably tightens as I feel it. She becomes wetter, rolling her hips with me. My tongue meets her clit and she opens wider, arching her back and gripping the couch pillows. I stop and remind her where she's at. "I'm right here. Close your eyes again, and I'm fucking done. You'll look at me. Your eyes stay on me."

She side-eyes, quickly changing her tune. Cherry stares me down, watching me suck two fingers in my mouth and drive them back into her as she tries not to squirm. I love her soft moans.

She closes her eyes, and I stop. Once she reconnects with me, she tilts her head. She reaches to her back, unfastening her bra, and her tits fall from the bottom. I move to take them, but she moves quicker, wrapping the fabric around my neck and pulling my back to her bare chest.

"Cherry. This is testing my stamina."

I struggle, slipping my fingers between the fabric and my neck as I inhale. She's strong, but her strength doesn't match mine. I overpower her, stretching the fabric and sling-shooting it across the room. After her antics, she earned my arms around her throat. I squeeze as I jerk her upward and laugh. "This is more fun than making tacos. *Was any of it real?*" She narrows her eyes. A silent glare accompanies the nails that mark my skin.

I kick my jeans off and dig my fingers into her hair until I have a grip at the roots. As I steer her off the couch, I make my way—bare-ass—to the sliding glass door. I glance back at her perfectly naked tits, taunt midriff, and faint thigh gap. "Is this what you want?" I slide open the door, forcing her out onto the patio. "To be on your knees, begging me to spare you—dying for me to take you on the numbing wood so you can pretend the pain masked the pleasure and you never enjoyed our time together?"

"I'm dying to do something," she mumbles.

With a prompt squat, I lean in and admire her. "What was that?" I tug on her hair. Then I let her go.

"Fuck you, Bennett," she yells, suddenly taking off. She runs down the two wooden steps toward the tree-covered section along the left of my property. I walk to the banister and press my hands against the grain. The rear spotlight catches intervals of ass bouncing as she runs into the dark woods. I know these trees, this dirt, the grass, and every inch of terrain on this property.

"Alright, Cherry. Hide and seek it is—for the art, my darling," I yell, walking down the steps and through the grass. "You should know, I'm rather skilled at this game."

I casually walk along the trail, listening for her heavy breaths or frantic scuffling.

I'm naked. She's naked. It's a week from Christmas and nippy out here. I don't her shenanigans lasting more than ten minutes.

"I have another little confession," I project my voice as I carefully avoid creating excess noise. "I've had this fantasy about fucking you in the woods and I never thought it would come true." Something snaps against the earth nearby. "You can't hide for long." I move closer to the sound, precise as to where I place my bare feet. "No matter where you run, I'll find you. And that's exciting to you. I know it is. It's quite obvious, Cherry bomb. Whatever this is, I expect you were never supposed to find me wildly attractive." I snatch her arms before she can take off again, holding her to the bark of a wide tree trunk like fifty-grit sandpaper. "I want you. Let me—tell me, please. Say the words and let me in. I need your permission. You have to admit. Tell me you want me, too." I press my lips to her jaw, humming. "I swear I'd kill you before I'd ever fuck you without your full and complete admission of desire."

"Is that supposed to be reassuring?" She grunts, clearly still furious.

"Stop. Don't let your anger—pride—get in the way. Tell me what you fucking want." I lock her wrists in place with one hand and trail a finger down her ribs, along her petite breasts. They spill heavier to her sides as her arms extend and her hard pink nipples tighten in the cool air. She has an inch-long scar below the right. What's it from? An accident? Did someone put it there?

"I shouldn't want this!" She calls out. "I shouldn't want you."

"But you admit it." The corner of my mouth turns up. "You want me."

A shaky breath turns her voice soft. "I want you, B." She utters the most flawless words a woman has ever uttered from her gorgeous lips.

With that, I'm cooked. I squeeze her thigh, and she wraps her legs around my hips. I don't know if she can see it, but I can't wipe the smirk from my face. My dick twitches as I press against her, kissing her neck. Her hand clasps around it, pressing it against her heat.

Fuck. "Fuck." *Fuck.*

Did I say that out loud?

"B."

"Yes, darling?"

"Do it before I change my mind."

I thrust into her, soaking the head of my dick. "Hold onto me." She drops a leg and I let one of her wrists free. "Stop holding your breath. You feel it—the barbell?"

"Mhm." She nods.

"You're dripping down my leg. You'll be fine." I ease in more as the pressure of my piercing deepens into her sensitive skin.

"I want it. I want it!"

I thrust, stealing a gasp of oxygen. Her toes curl against the dirt, and her thigh tightens around me. The arch of her back lifts away from the bark and my hands take its place, lifting her hips up and down, repeatedly.

"You smell so fucking good."

"You fucking stink."

"Fuck, I love your voice."

"I wish you'd shut up."

"No, you don't."

"Yes, I do," she argues.

"Then shut me up. Shut me up, Cherry."

Her upper back rubs against the tree, and she throws her arms around it, holding on for her life. Her tits bounce with every thrust between our bodies. I fight to reach her nipple, sucking it hard into my mouth, and the fucking sexiest moan pours from her lips.

"Moan for me, baby. Tell me what you want."

"Less talking," she moans.

"No." I shake my head, slamming into her as I squeeze her ass and pull her hips back into me. "No, you don't want less talking. You want less questions. You want me to already know what you want." I lick up her neck, stopping at her ear. "You won't believe how badly I've wanted you, so I'll show up for you. You'll see how good I am."

I pull out, shoving her body back against the tree and letting her leg fall to the ground. She's so fucking perfect standing there with her hands above her head, sweat glistening across her chest in the light of the moon as it finally breaks through the dark clouds. I turn away and walk back toward the trail with my erect cock coated with her.

"Bennett!" She yells.

I don't answer. I wait, walk, and hide my smug grin in the dark until she takes her control back because—that's what she wants. She wants to prove she holds all of the control. She's only letting me take her when she says I can. I'm her puppet tonight.

She reaches for me, and I turn around, forcing her to abruptly stop.

"Are you trying to grab my wrist? You think you can stop me?"

"You're not going anywhere."

"Fine." I run my tongue over my bottom lip. "What do you want?" I close the distance between our bodies. Her eyes drift down my body to my hard cock, where they sit for a moment before she pushes her hands into my chest. She steers my back into another tree and her hands take my shoulders. My brows lift. "On my knees?"

"On your knees, B."

"I knew you wanted to be in control."

"You're wrong."

"What would you call it then?" I press my lips to her thigh and find her blue eyes.

"I want...a guy that's going to challenge me," she replies. "A guy that treats as an equal unless I say otherwise."

"A guy that would hold *your* blade to your throat?"

With two fingers beneath my chin, she directs me to stand.

I meet her steady glare and her thumb runs down my Adam's apple. "Do you want me to make you listen, darling?"

"Do you think you could?"

"No," I smirk. "You're only going to listen if you want to." With a sudden prise, I wrap my hand around her throat. "I can hold the pressure on, but it's always up to you." My hand falls to her shoulder, pressing until she spins and her ass is against my dick, her back is against my chest, and my lips meet her ear. "And you want to listen to me, don't you?" I cover her mouth, quieting her reply. "Fuck—You know what you're doing to me. You always do this to me. Grinding your ass like that—it feels good, my little tease. Everything about you feels so—fucking—good. You're the boss, baby. Won't you be good to me? Won't you be mine?" My heated breaths caress her skin. "Yeah, hah—You're mine."

I pull her hips up nearly knocking her to her hands and stroke my dick. As I line up and slide into her, I thrust deeper, pass my piercing, and slip into her wetness. She almost loses her balance again, stuck on her tiptoes. "I don't want you to fall." I pull back out, leaving her empty. Snatching her by the waist, I toss her over my shoulder and walk a few paces until I find the landscaping rock near the end of the path.

I set her down and push her back to the cold stone. Shivers take over her body, and I pinch her chin between my fingers. "I want your eyes on me. Can you give me that?" I let go.

She puckers her lip and nods.

I spit in my hand and hold it out to her. She looks at it and then back to me, wrinkling her brows. "Spit." Her hardened glare dares me. I wasn't going to pass up the opportunity to play out some parts of my fantasy. "This one isn't a request, Cherry." She rolls her pretty eyes and purses her lips tightly, trying to hide her smile. "It's hot, right?"

She adds her spit to mine and her mouth curves upward. One day I'll get her to admit our similarities are inescapable. I pump my fist over the thickness of my dick, twisting my wrist each time I get close to the tip. Her hungry eyes intently study my motion.

I hike both her legs up, hooking them around my hips, and push on her knees. Her arms fall and the curve of her back shapes to the rock as I thrust. She drops her head and her eyes roll back. Every sweet moan to escape her lips makes me hold off on correcting her. I don't need her eyes on me when she falls apart so perfectly beneath my frame.

"Mhm, you feel good. Cherry, darling, open your eyes. Look what you're doing to me." With wide eyes, her lips part and she scans my body. I thread my fingers through my hair, pushing it out of my eyes and her gaze meets mine. Her beautiful lips tug into a defiant smile. She lets her head tip back as her eyes roll closed and she grinds her hips in a tight circle, begging for clit stimulation.

I thrust in and squeeze her ass. Pulling my hand back, she moans as I slap her ass. It pisses her off. She lifts her head and swings an arm, attempting to hit me, yet she gives up after the second swing, closing her eyes again. "You fucking like it." I thrust in again, slapping her ass harder, and she moans louder.

"Fuck you, B," she mutters.

"Don't be shy now. Nobody can hear you out here." I thrust deep and smack her ass harder.

"Fuck—" Her moan carries, cut short by a breathy inhale. As she pushes her hips into me, she grinds in half a circle. Her fingers claw at the rock, searching for something to grip onto—and that fucking moan—it sends me. *That fucking moan!* "I love the way you do that. Fuck, it drives me—" Hah, god. Darling! Fuck. "—it drives me manic."

She stares at me as if she has something smart to say. Nothing comes out. She grinds on me instead, and it's obvious she's close—as close as I am. I slide my hands up her back, lifting her from the rock. My thighs become frigid as I sit down, her wetness coating my balls. I shudder, dipping into her neck while I guide her hips to keep riding the wave. "Don't stop. Don't stop. Don't stop." Her walls tighten around me, and I want it as bad as she does. "Ride me, god, fucking ride it, baby." I unbury my face, desperate to see her eyes roll back and the moans from her lips when she cums around my dick. I grab her throat in one hand, applying enough pressure to excite her as I squeeze her ass in my other hand.

"Oh my god," she moans. Her hands leave my shoulder and slam into my chest. Her nails glide down my body and dig in as she reaches the peak of climax.

"Holy fuck. Oh fuck yes, baby." I pant.

Her lips part, and her head tips back as she rocks on my lap. I grab her hips, pushing in deeper as she unfolds. With every long, perfect moan her chest rises and falls. I don't want it to end. I want this—I want her to last for eternity.

I bow into her, taking her nipple between my teeth and sucking it into my mouth. As I near ejaculation, I run my hand down neck down to her shoulder blade and take in every smooth contour of her back before grabbing her ass and lifting it. I lift her up and down, using her pussy to stroke my dick. She wraps her arms around my neck in the most exhausting way, hanging on while I keep taking her wet pussy over and over until my abdomen becomes taunt and my movements turn sharp. I pull out, continuing to pump my hand. In a breathy exhale, I direct her. "Knees."

With the pressure of my free hand on her shoulder, she presses to the ground. Cherry takes over, shoving my hand out of the way to strike my dick with both of her hands. Her tongue runs over my piercing and twirls over my head before she precisely flicks the barbell, sending me into overdrive.

"Ah fuck, mm," I moan, coming onto the warmth of her tongue. With every pulse, I push deeper into her mouth, and she lets me until I'm empty and clean. I pull out, and she slowly smiles up at me, wiping her lip with the corner of her hand.

"You're fucking perfect."

"And you're a fucking idiot."

I see the rock out of the corner of my eye as she stands and smashes it off my head.

Son of a bitch.

Do As I Say Not As I Do, Cherry

"Wake up, B," I sing to him. "Oh, there you are, sleepyhead." His dazed squint begins to focus on me. "That was fun and all, but we have some more secrets to discuss and you need to keep your hands to yourself."

"What the—" His thought is cut short as he jerks his wrists. "Cherry."

Between the heaviness of his eyes, the quick breaths that inflated his chest over and over, and the fact that as he fought me inside that house until he almost blacked out, yet refused to let go of me, I wasn't taking my chances.

I slept with him, and it was wrong. I shouldn't have. I can't believe he has one of his nipples pierced. I can't believe he has that barbell on the underside of his dick. He's such a freaking hypocrite. It was easily a mistake—and I don't regret it for one second. It was arguably the best sex of my life. Granted, most men talk a big game and don't back it up.

It can't happen again.

It's out of my system.

It was pierced.

I clench at the thought of the barbell inside me. It's such a turn-on. I never slept with a man with one of those, and I don't know if I'd want to go back. The way it hit—maybe it was him. The thrill of the knife and the chance and the—I don't care.

It was the kind of good that I could think about two days later, and I wish it didn't have to end. Everything—all of it—has to end with Bennett. It must.

He blinks several more times, glancing around as he tries to piece together what happened and how he got here—a few feet deeper into the woods. "Why, *fuck*—" He winces. His head has to hurt. "Why am I fucking tied to a tree, Cherry?" The thick yellow rope holds his arms to the trunk of the tree while his ass is planted on the ground—semi-clothed—and he looks up at me for once. It's nice to be the tall one for once. By now, it's quite late, and I'm drained. It was enough of a hassle dressing him like an infant and lugging his buns to a tree I knew he couldn't break.

"Because you were too heavy to drag back into the house. Now, like I said, we have some secrets to discuss. It's kinda like licorice trauma, but I need you to dig deeper, hunny." I flip a pocketknife over my knuckles, between two fingers and back.

"What fucking secrets?" He yells. "I told you everything. Fuck, at least tell me you have some Aspirin."

"Tsk tsk." He should be glad I put his boxers on and bandaged his leg, but Bennett is above gratitude. "You're so predictable. Therefore, I'll lead. I have some secrets of my own." I sigh, squatting beside him. He was out long enough for me to redress, patch him up, and search the garage for some necessary supplies. "I know who you are—probably more than you do." I brush the pieces of dark hair from his face. "You were never B, or Benny, or Bennett to me. You were number zero-zero-one, sweetie."

"What are you talking about?" He groans low and deeply.

"Think, B—calling you number one would play into your ego, so I'm going to stick with your other pseudonyms—think *really* hard." I tap a finger on his temple. "You have all the memories stored in that big brain of yours some-where." I rise, looking down at him. "Where did you wake up?"

"In the woods, behind the plant. I fucking told you this already."

With force, I turn around, slapping him in the face. I grab ahold of his jaw and compel his attention. "That wasn't a plant. It was a lab." I leave him with nothing besides the sound of him spitting behind me as I walk a foot and a half away from him to sit on a stump. "Yes, you got shot. You died and you were thrown into those woods, but not everyone is as intelligent as we are. Those animals—the pigs that took your life over a few ounces of weed and various opioids—they must've been dealing and doing. They dropped you off and didn't see all the cameras."

"What? Since when was that place a lab?" His face has more creases than a man in his twenties should hold. "Wait, were they were caught?"

"Not exactly. You were an opportunity." His brows furrow even more when I didn't believe it was possible. "An experiment gone wrong." I shrug.

"Me? I—You're telling me, people know I'm like this?" He struggles to move with his arms tied down. "Someone did this to me and they haven't bothered to track me down?"

"They couldn't if they wanted to. *They're all dead.*" I study his glacial face. I don't know why I hoped for something more. "You killed them." He bites at his lip, his sight leaving me to stare at the ground as he chews at the skin. "Innocent technicians and scientists just following orders, dead at the hands of subject zero-zero-one. *The god that is Bennett Larson.* Jog your memory?"

"Sixteen." He cautiously glimpses back up at me. "I killed sixteen people that day." He's a freaking stone wall. I wanted to see more from him. I could beg for regret and sadness. I want to see it from him. He has to be better than all of this. He has too.

Why did I ever think he was capable of feeling?

"The blinding white—the room was so fucking bright. It overwhelmed me." He pushes his feet into the dark earth in an attempt to straighten his back to the tree. "I've been getting these weird…visions, I guess—memories—since you showed up. The shattered glass, the lights, the bright white flooring, and being strapped to that fucking sad excuse for a bed. I don't remember you being there. How do you know any of this? If everyone died, Cherry, how did you find me and who are you going to take me to?"

"I had a number just like you and if I didn't I'd be dead. I wouldn't be right here because you would have taken my life." I clench my jaw with the heat that pours into my chest like gasoline and anger that lights it on fire. "How do you feel now, Bennett? Does that upset you in the least? You wouldn't have met me. Does that sit well with you?"

"I—"

"How are the headaches going for you and the dizzy spells? Did you think I didn't notice?" I assert.

He shakes his head either in disbelief or disappointment that he didn't see what was right in his face. "Did you die?"

"No. I needed money. I volunteered...along with several others as test subjects. You were the only one they brought back to life—foolishly."

"Sounds like they got what they deserved." He chuckles.

"You're sick." I walk over to him and bend down, whispering in his ear. "But let me tell you the best secret I've been holding in—*I came here to kill you, B.*"

He looks up at me and smiles. *He freaking smiled!*

"I've been dead and stuck in hell for years. Death wouldn't hurt me if it's revenge you're after. Who was it? A boyfriend? A bestie?"

"It looks like you're living a pretty good life." I ignore his questions.

"Uncloud your judgment instead of twisting the fucking blade," he replies, unbothered. "Do you think what I have is happiness, Cherry? You ask me all these stupid questions, and I thought I made it crystal fucking clear that I'm not fucking happy. I'm alone. I'm still fucking invisible after all these years, but at least they see my art, right? Yeah, paint my name across that big screen. Do you think if I died right now, anyone would care? They'd talk and it would be a media frenzy, but actually fucking care that they'd never see me or talk to me again?" He deeply chuckles. "No...and I wouldn't fucking care either. I wouldn't miss anyone, *except you.* The only sunshine I've seen in years is in your eyes. If you're my death, so be it."

"You took *my light*! The sunshine that showed up in my life when the shadows had taken over—he was *my sunshine.*"

He leans his head back against the bark. "Who was he?"

"Jack." I quickly clear my throat. "Dr. Jack Malondo." I shield my eyes.

"Mm, yes. Malondo rings a bell. You're triggering a lot of memories tonight, Cherry bomb."

"He's dead."

"I figured that out. You two had a thing? Isn't that against a policy—doctor and patient? It's kinky. He was quite the good-looking guy, huh?" He shakes his head with one of those arrogant, breathy laughs that make me weak and resentful at the same time.

"Enough," I scold. "I promised him I wouldn't let you take any more lives. I have to stop you."

"Me? Stop me? You killed an innocent woman in what? A jealous rage over your boyfriend's killer? I should have fucking knew it then. I should have seen all the signs. You had dizzy spells right in front of me and the fucking rage—that's the worst thing for you isn't it?" He asks.

"You ruined our chances at getting rid of the side effects. All of the doctors are gone except one. How many people are buried in those woods?"

"Just Cassie, darling." He blows hair from his eyes and winks.

"You said you knew those woods." I stand, refraining from rushing him.

"I knew where *not* to bury a body. As in not near a nuclear waste plant or a *fucking lab.*" He scrutinizes me from every angle. "I haven't gotten rid of any bodies in two years, Cherry, but what have you been doing? I saw the scars. The one on your ribs looks older, but the one on your right forearm...not so much."

"I've been practicing, B. Did you really think I couldn't control my rage? *Oh, help me, Benny. Help me fix the cake. Teach me how to meditate, please. Let's count.* Come on. While you were out here playing the movie guy, I was exercising my abilities in a healthy way, understanding how to control them. I never needed you to fix me, but it's nice to know how much you bend to my will. I will say, whatever you did to me—it was one intense high." I stroll over to him and lean down. "Would you have tried to save Ames if I wasn't there?"

"I wouldn't have needed to if you weren't there." He slides his bare feet across the dirt and pushes himself upright. "Did you intend to kill Cassie?"

"No. That was a...mishap. I can calm my rage. I never said I've managed to get rid of it." *Don't think about it.* "That's beside the point." I flick open my knife and hold the blade to his neck.

"Was he the love of your life?"

I keep steady, then finally answer. "No. He was too professional to date anyone in the lab."

"He was a guy you liked and was what—your friend? So what was I, Cherry? Was I the same? You fuck me."

"He was the boss. You're the job," I insist. "It was only sex, Bennett."

"Ouch." He shuts his eyes and then looks back at me. "You felt something between us. It was the spark you didn't have with him, wasn't it?"

I push the blade tighter to his skin, and he leans back. "Beg me, B. Beg me to let you live."

He doesn't move and the way he looks at me makes me want to smack him. He has that dreamy, doped-up glimmer in his eyes as if I was the most incredible woman he's ever seen. I hate him. I hate him so much. I hate his smug face and his unaffected demeanor. I hate his blue eyes and his white eyes and his naked chest...*his naked chest*. His tattoos. His dance moves. His ancient gamer hoodie. His peanut butter. His stupid book.

I hate that I don't hate him—that I want to hate him and can't.

I move the knife to the rope, sawing at it until it snaps. "Don't fucking say it, B." *I can't do it.* I should be able to. Jack was a brilliant, sweet, wonderful man. Bennett is selfish...and he would burn bridges for me. Something in that is appealing. It's downright addictive, and I want to capture it. We're two of a kind—the only ones left. I can run from it, but I can't hide.

"Say what, Cherry?"

"Don't tell me I'm weak, because you of all people understand the obsession and how badly I wanted to end you." I drop the pocket knife and hold my hands to my temples, letting my knees fall to the ground. "I don't know what to do anymore."

"You're not weak. I've never met a stronger woman." He rubs his wound. "Did you bandage my leg?" He asks, pulling his body from the rope. I nod without looking back at him. "Cherry..." He caresses my chin in the palm of his hand. "Let me help."

"How can you help? You're the reason I'm here!" He doesn't flinch despite my screams.

"No, I'm fucking not. They did this, and it backfired. I finally try to move forward with my life, and I get fucking shot, and not a motherfucker noticed! Is it my fault? Maybe. I'll take the blame, fine, but I never asked for this. Do I feel bad that I killed them? No. Why? I don't fucking know. You tell me. I'm not the one that fucked with human DNA. It's not on me."

"Then why do I feel remorse? Why can't I live conscience-free too?"

"I'd tell you to ask them, but you can't." I press my hands into the dirt, mustering up the energy to walk back to the house. "Where are you going?"

"I need to make a call?"

"It's at least four in the fucking morning. Nobody is coming to your rescue." Bennett rushes me and throws me over his shoulder.

I smack his ass and back repeatedly, demanding he stop. "Put me down."

"No." He continues toward the house.

"Put me down, Bennett." He pushes open the sliding door and walks in, kicking it shut with his foot. "Where are you taking me?"

"You'll see." He opens a door and sets me down in the master bathroom.

Oh, he has a floor heated. It's wall-to-wall black marble tiled flooring. A huge fuzzy white rug borders a beautiful freestanding white bathtub in front of a window and off to the left is a glass-door shower. I haven't been in here. I used the half bath. "This is...beautiful," I mutter.

"It's not only for looks. Take your clothes off."

"What?" He doesn't answer me. Instead, he runs the bath and takes off his boxer briefs. I couldn't look away if I wanted. His body is as beautiful as this room despite his not being aroused.

He walks to the hamper, tosses his clothes in, and comes back to me. The pads of his fingers kiss my ribs as he peels my shirt off. "Turn around." I glare at him. "Please." I exhale, drop my shoulders, and turn. He unhooks my bra, and his hands skate across my skin. "Does this hurt?"

"My back?" I ask, well aware of what he's talking about. It occasionally stings, but I've been far too distracted to pay much attention to it.

"It's red." I look over my shoulder into the mirror at the scratches covering my upper back.

"Looks as bad as those marks on your chest." I point out.

He tosses my bra into the hamper. "Take your pants off."

I don't argue. I'm spent, having not slept in over twenty-four hours, and mentally destroyed. I still don't know what I'm doing—or how long it's going to last.

He takes my hand and leads me to the bath, shutting the water off and helping me in. I slowly lower myself into the warm water, and he kneels beside me.

"Did you put lavender in here?"

"Just a little. You like that kind of stuff, right?" I slightly smile and look away. "Can I wash your hair?"

I nod, closing my eyes as he begins to massage my scalp with shampoo and gently rinses it. His lips brush my forehead, then the tip of my nose, and meet my lips. I blink, feeling his leg brush mine as he lowers his body to the opposite side of the tub, leaning back and closing his eyes.

"Who are you?"

He chuckles. "I'm the same asshole, Cherry. I'm the same killer. I'm the same bad *bad* fucking boy." He tucks his chin, gazing at me. "I'm all of those things and I'm also—"

"I could kill you right now," I interrupt him. "I could change my mind and shove your head under the water."

"I could beat you to it." The water moves between our bodies. His hands rest along the sides of the tub and he appears taller as his legs bend on both sides of me. "But I won't because I'm fucking in love with you." I tense, unable to breathe. "I told you, I'm not letting you go. You're mine to take care of now. I love you."

Are You In The Morgue, Bennett

"Did you hear me?" I repeat.

Don't make me say it again. *Ah, come on, Cherry.*

Fuck.

Fine. I admit it.

I'm fucking in love with this dastardly woman.

The moment she laid her demons out on the table, she put every raw and broken piece of her soul in my hands, pulling on the heartstrings I thought I detached years ago. She walked into my life with that sweet, innocent act, then blinded me with her humanity.

Her imperfections pulled me in because I relate. Her laugh kept me because it's home.

Everything about her feels like home. She's where I want to be at the end of the day and who I want to talk to about everything. Her thighs are where my hands belong. Her arms are where my demons are welcome.

She splashes water everywhere, stands up, and steps out of the tub as she stabilizes herself with one hand.

"There's nowhere else to run, Cherry," I call while she searches for the towels.

This woman washed her peanut butter and jelly down with a cold beer with the joy of a broke college kid on a Saturday night, but that scar on her right forearm matches the one on her frozen heart. I'll chase her until she buries me six feet deep because I'd rather suffocate than breathe another day without her.

"I'll tell you anything you want to know. Just don't leave."

She wraps a towel around her body that matches the black cotton her hair is spiraled with, and spins back to me without coming any closer. "How many?"

"Blades are messy and guns are more work than I care to put in. This mind I have now—that's a different story. Have I talked someone into stepping off the ledge of a building? I fucking did. No clean-up for me ruled as a suicide. Have I talked someone into walking onto the tracks in the subway? I fucking did. My hands appear clean. How many? Enough to call me a serial killer. I've made a lot of bad choices, darling."

"How many?" She repeats.

"Twenty-seven...give or take blackouts." I push out my lower lip. "Have you ever blacked out? No idea what happened?" I lean my head back on the rim of the tub.

"Is that what happened at the lab?" *She didn't answer my question.*

"It just came back to me tonight." I roll my neck side to side against the cold rim. "It's pretty fucked...that I've gone years with no recollection of that night or morning? It was early morning hours, wasn't it?"

"What do you think we're going to do, Bennett? Live happily ever after, trying not to kill each, screwing and writing and acting and producing—living that elite life? I can't move on with you like nothing happened." She pulls the towel from her hair, rubbing the ends.

"I got all these abilities yet I can't do the one thing I want...to bring Annie back. So yeah, let's just fucking live. This is what we have now," I calmly continue. I could talk my way out of murder, and perhaps I have, but I'm not talking her off a cliff or over one. I'm letting her in. I'm letting her know she's not alone. "Do you think I wanted to move forward or that I don't know what kind of person I am? It's conflicting...I'll admit, *Benny* wants people to show him they care, and *Bennett* would rather force their eye and cut them if they refused. I feel like I'm two people fighting inside to see who gets a turn on the surface."

"I'm pretty sure I've read that one," she says blankly. Her lashes flutter, unintentionally flirting, before she looks away. "It's not the same. I don't want to worry about losing my temper and hurting someone again."

"Come here, darling." She slowly nears me. I reach for her hand and run my thumb across her knuckles. "How many people did you hurt, Cherry?"

"Hurt? Easily a dozen." She bows her head. "Kill? One."

"So wait." I sit up, rocking waves of water across the tub. "You thought I would be your first kill? Darling..." I close my eyes and spring them open wide again. "Were you going to beat me to death with those ugly chunky white sneakers at the airport? Did you change your mind *after* I told you I liked the pigtails or *before*?"

"The airport was a feeler," she admits. "But B, if you did anything, I mean anything remotely questionable that made me think you were going to hurt me, I could have stopped the blood from pumping to your heart without lifting a finger."

"We can do that?" I lower my chin and close the gap between my lips.

"Creatively, the same effect. You can do a lot more than you think you can. I wasn't exaggerating when I said you're dangerous. You could kill me. I know this, but what I lack in strength, you lack in knowledge."

I lightly chuckle, sitting forward and releasing her fingers. "Cherry, I need to know everything."

I step out of the tub, water running down my body in streams. As I push my slicked hair back, I edge closer, towering over her. She stares up at me and wraps her arms around my torso, burying her face in my chest. Wet pieces of her hair stick to my skin, making me scratch them away and push threads behind her ears. "Can you fill in the voids?" Her tears meet my core. "If you can you do that for me and I'll do what I can for you, okay?"

She sucks her bottom lip into her mouth and nods but quickly lets it go and her gaze falls. "You said you knew a doctor, darling?" I ask, refusing to let her attention leave me. "Tell me about him."

"She left the lab early that day. I don't know how to reach her without going back. They had to have an employee file."

"Then, let's go. Whatever you need me to do, tell me." She doesn't have to say it. If I kill again, I'll lose her. "I wouldn't do this for anyone else."

"You have no idea what it's going to be like for me..." She creeps backward, her eyes slowly drifting around the floor. "Going back there..." Her icy gaze hurts. Her tight lips pinch together with the smallest shaking over her jaw. "This isn't a field trip to build-a-monster. What I witnessed and...that town."

I grab her hand. "I'll be with you."

"No!" She scolds, smacking me away. "No." With the slow shake of her head, she returns to me, and she tilts her chin up, nearly touching my face. "You think because you lived where I lived that you can relate. You've seen some stuff, but have you felt it? Have you rocked yourself back and forth on the floor, listening to the hair-curling screams of the one person you loved, knowing you couldn't do a damn thing? You don't get why going back there is the farthest thing I want to do. Nothing good has ever come out of that town."

"We don't—"

"Yes, we do. We have to do this. It's the only way. I don't want to go...and it's the only way." She leaves me hanging as she walks toward the door.

"Cherry," I call out. "I don't know what you went through. I can't manipulate it into something better. I honestly wish I could because I don't want to go back there any more than you do."

She turns back, shouting and swinging her arms down like rapid hail. "You don't get it!"

"I fucking get it," I growl, rushing her. "I get it, Cherry! My best friend died! She fucking died! She's dead! I can't bring her back and it should have been me! Her husband spent more time consoling me and trying to keep me from going over the edge than he had processed his loss. It was his wife. His fucking wife. I wasn't going to pretend my pain was worse than his. So, I detached from him, just like everyone else. Nobody was going to be sucked into Benny's downhill vortex except Benny himself." I shrug, letting my cold glare capture her. "I don't want to get anywhere near them—my family. They already moved forward without me." I exhale a wave of calm, centering my heart rate. "I know, my family isn't from there, but I don't want the odd chance of running into Caleb or my parents." I dig my thumb into my brow. "Look..." I slip my hands down her towel-covered back and pull her to my chest. "I don't want to fight with you. We're both exhausted. Can we *please*," I stress. "Go to bed?"

She nods, and I grab another towel, dry off, and lead her into my room. I walk into the closet, pulling a shirt off a hanger. The front logo is faded beyond recognition. "Here's a t-shirt. I'll wash your clothes in the morning. Get your ass in bed."

"Can I have a pair of your boxers?"

"You won't be able to fill them like I do." She doesn't bother hiding the smirk that begins to take her lips. "Top drawer. Pick a pair."

I tear apart the bed, untucking the sheets. "Bennett."

"Yeah, doll."

"Why me?" She closed the drawer. "Is it because I'm immune to you."

"It's because you made friends with my demons. They didn't scare you away." I smooth down the silky black sheets. "Your fucked up matches mine."

"Does that mean you want to befriend the monsters in my head?" She asks.

"Are you lost?" I stare at her cock-eyed. "I'm in love with those manic fuckers."

It's after ten already.

With the blackout curtains shadowing my windows, you couldn't tell what time it is. Everything is a shade of black in here besides the gray walls—like the rest of the house. It doesn't appear lived-in or homey. It's a fucking monotone box.

Cherry is asleep. I've been awake for the last twenty minutes watching her chest rise and fall, wondering why such a beautiful woman had to get caught up in this. If she was ugly, would it change anything? Abso-fucking-lutely. Look, if you don't want to hear the truth, you picked up the wrong book. If I didn't find her attractive—if the casting teams didn't think she was—she wouldn't have made it to my set in the first place.

She has this natural ability to connect with an audience and make you like a character you have every right to be wary of. Oh, I see what I did there. I hired a double-edged sword. She's great on-set and she'll fuck you over off-set. That's her brilliant talent. It's funny because she talked her way into my film like I talked my way into directing and I never saw it coming. Neither of us would be in these positions if it weren't for whatever science experiment we became part of—willing or not.

I hope she doesn't hate me. I took away someone she cared about. I wouldn't have been as adaptable as her in my revenge scheme.

She rolls to her side, and I suck in my breath.

Fuck. Why am I anxious? I can say it.

I need you to tell me to chill the fuck out. It's not a guarantee that I'll listen, but maybe, just maybe it'll hit harder.

That doesn't make sense. They can't talk to me. I can only talk to them.

I draw a line through the section.

I don't want her to think I'm a fucking creep who watches her eyes rapidly flicker under her lids and her brow occasionally twitch as I brush the hair away from her mouth so it doesn't stick to her face in that little dribble of drool pooling out the side.

Fuck, that's a long sentence. Why can't I write today?

"B," Cherry mutters, reaching for my arm. I close my notebook and set it down on the bedside table. Her soft fingers kiss the hair on my forearm as she pulls me closer. I try not to sneeze as her hair tickles my nose and she wiggles her hips back into me. Are we...*fucking spooning?*

I've always felt like Cherry would want to be the big spoon, not that I ever had intimate thoughts of lying in bed with her like this. There have been plenty of masturbating sessions to the thought of her, and I tried to pretend that one chick was her in the woods. That was brutal. Nobody has her bite. Fuck, the way she handed my ass to me last night—I have the cuts and bruises to show for it. It wasn't much of a struggle. It was a battle for dominance, and we both won. I can push her right to the edge without breaking her. That fucking smile she gave me after slamming her to the wall—

Oh no...oh, shit. She's going to feel that.

The big spoon is now a fork. *I have a fucking boner.*

I try to back up, but she pulls at my arm and pushes her ass against my dick.

"You are not sleeping," I mutter, low and scratchy before clearing my throat.

"Shh," she hushes, tapping her fingers on my hand.

"How's your back?"

"How's your leg?" She retorts, forcing a smirk to curl from the corner of my mouth.

"Doesn't need stitches."

"I should have pressed deeper."

"Cherry..." Tucking hair behind her ear, I hope this comes out right. "Are you on birth control?" She snaps toward me, narrowing her eyes. I cover my vulnerability with a quip. "I don't know if I can make walking-dead babies, do you? I'm not trying to find out."

Tell me, you were thinking the same thing? Why do you think I pulled out last night?

"Didn't you ever want kids, B?" She taunts, smiling with a gap between her teeth. Turning away, she lays her head back on the pill. "I have PCOS."

"That—like painful ovary thing?"

"With all the words you have stored up inside that big brain, are you sure that's how you want to ask that question?" She rolls over, propping her head between her arm and pillow. "Yes, it's that thing. I've been on hormonal birth control for years."

"Do you go to a doctor annually?" It's not unreasonable to ask. If she was a test subject and now has abilities and side effects as I do, how can she treat her body like it's human?

"I used to, but it's pretty easy to access what I need now and I don't always follow the rules. Why?"

"Do they know about the trial?"

"I can't exactly give them any contact information for reference, so no." She moves around, trying to comfortably look at me. "I know the risks I'm taking when I walk into a doctor's office. They could find something unusual and it wouldn't end well for me. B, I can't do all of the things you can do. I can't *persuade* people."

"I bet you fucking can and don't realize you're doing it. If you think about it, people tend to fold for you. Nobody would put two and two together because of your pretty privilege." She scowls at me. "It's milder and you're charm covers it up because you talk to people so easily. Better?"

"I can admit the privileges I happened upon, but I won't blame them for any of my actions."

"I know, darling." I lay back, tucking my arms behind my head. "Tell me, if I'm getting this right, I'm stronger because I died. What did they do exactly?"

"I don't know if they gave you more or the same dose, but I got an injection three days a week for the first three weeks, then once a week for a few months. I had a diary. I kept a record of everything, but I left it—um—in my rush to get out of there. Towards the end, when I had finished the injections, they started testing what I could do. Can we...not talk about it right now?"I blow her hair back into her face. "Want to go kill some zombies on PlayStation? You got a kick out of the last game we played."

"Or you could kill the zombies and I could ride one." She wraps her fingers around the shaft of my dick, rolling her thumb over the tip through the fabric of my boxers. Her bedroom eyes float over my chest.

"Will you hold that little pink switchblade to my throat?"

"It's not pink. It's red. It's just really, really faded." Her lips meet the v-cut that draws her eye to my dick. She glances up at me. "Your eyes are finally blue again. That's the longest I've seen them stay white."

I suck in my cheek, not knowing what I want to say to her for once. I'm a little bitter about how she can point it out like it's not a big deal when clearly it could fuck me over if anyone else sees my eyes the way she does. "Why can you see it? How did Ames?"

"B—for today, can we skip the hard questions? I like that I can see the color drain from your eyes and that's all I can give you right now."

I nod. "I have the entire week blocked off to write. I've instructed Justin to only contact me if it's an emergency. Will one week suffice for searching this lab, tracking down this doctor, and getting—"

"Shh. Please." She flicks my nipple piercing. "Let's talk work later." She rolls over me and stands to the floor, marching out of the bedroom. I follow her, stalling as she freezes in front of me. "This place is fucked," she says from the doorway.

"Oh, say *fucked* one more time." She glares at me and walks away, picking up her clothes. "You said it, not me—for once." I run up behind her, snatching her clothes and throwing them down.

"Bennett!" She yells. I lean against the kitchen island, smiling. "Oh, you…" She smiles back and the tiniest dimple pulls at one side. "What's for breakfast?" My boxer briefs fall from her hips and she steps out of them.

"Pussy. Come over here and serve me." She crosses her arms and walks past me. *I fucking love these games.* She searches a drawer, pulling out a lighter and scissors. I spin, leaning my elbows on the counter, and keep my eyes on her. She picks up the glass candle jar and tilts it, cutting the wick, then sets the scissors down. Holding the lighter at the same angle, she waits until the flame catches before placing it on the counter.

"Why did you trim it?"

"I don't want it to tunnel." *Huh? Am I supposed to know what that means?* I blankly look between her and the candle. "The flame will get too long and too hot, burning more wax than it should need to."

"And this is the favorite one?"

"Yeah."

"I could smell it last night. It was the same smell the night when you—well, you know." I click my tongue off the bottom of my mouth, motioning a chopping hand at my throat. As I walk around the L-shaped island, I meet her with my fingers, trailing up her arm. I trap her between my hands, holding onto the granite. "Didn't seem to calm you down. That's more of a lavender job, right?"

Cherry dips forward, deepening her lips to mine. "Someone has picked up a new book." She nibbles at my lip, wrapping her arms around my neck as I hoist her bare ass onto the counter.

I kiss the inside of her knee, tagging down her thigh. The sizzling noise of a catching spark wheel draws my attention. She lowers the lighter inches beneath my chin, and her daring blue eyes dance over mine. I stick out my tongue and the flame pierces it as I gaze up at her. She holds the heat for a brief moment and throws it to the floor. I kiss her navel, squeezing her wrist as I lift and toss her over my shoulder. I wobble to the right and stop, taking in a deep breath.

I'm fine. I'm fucking fine.

As I sit in the recliner, Cherry's petite half-dressed body slides down my chest to my lap. I clench onto her thick ass and lift her back up. Leaning against the backrest, her knees press down on my shoulders. I can already taste her. I inhale her, the warmth of my breath coating her arousal. "This should be fucking illegal."

"What?"

I look up at her. "Smelling so fucking good." With a chuckle, I continue. "Is this what you want?" I lift her ass, pull her thigh to my mouth, and kiss her delicate skin.

"Maybe," she whispers.

"How bad do you want my mouth?" I breathe against her, moving my lips up higher without touching.

"I don't want you, B. I need you," she moans, toying with the hair along my neck.

My low chuckle vibrates against her, and she does this little wiggle—a mini-arch— curving her ass back in the slightest and relaxing. "This is all mine." I kiss her thigh once more, tracing the tip of my tongue around her clit and down the extent of her pussy lips before moving back up. She rocks against me, searching for ecstasy. "Easy, darling. I like your greed, but we have all fucking day."

I dig my fingers into her ass cheeks, tracing up and over. With the lap of my tongue, I intensify my pace to her liking. She keeps begging for more, grinding against me with no fear that she's going to drown or suffocate me and fuck, I love it.

Mm, I fucking love every time she suddenly jerks when I trace her clit, and as soon as I start lapping her again, she tries to ride my face. I slide my hand between her thighs while she rocks, and grasp her ass as I push the coated finger into her entrance. She slows her hips, steadily pressing her ass out and curving her back. She guides me to where it feels euphoric.

Fuck. Fuck. How the fuck am I not exploding right now? I'm incredibly turned on by her moans and how tight her thighs wrap my face.

I continue the same motions, rubbing and sucking at her clit while giving her deeper pressure and steadying my finger. She drips down my finger and her thighs are coated. I can't stop and she can't stop, grinding and riding and flexing her hips as I fuck her with my mouth.

Her knees pinch inward, and she lets go of my hair, stretching her arms up under her shirt. I fixate on her tits as she pinches her nipples. *Holy fuck—she's really tugging.* Her hips deepen long and hard, and she gasps. She's silent for half a second and then screams, rocking so fucking hard against my face I could suffocate. Her pussy pulses around my finger and my dick throbs to get a piece of it.

I don't wait for her orgasm to ride out. I fucking can't. I grab her by the waist, pulling her off of me, as I stand. She stares at me with her hands in her lap, unable to keep her thighs still. Her body shutters as her breath shakes out of her. I push my briefs down and my dick jets out. Her eyes fall to my rigid cock. "You're not spent yet," I remind her and push my boxers off my legs. I scoot her up in the recliner and pin both of her legs up.

Holy fuck. Am I even going to make it two minutes?

I let go of one of her legs to run my hand over my cock, smearing the precum over the tip and easing in. Easing in doesn't exist today. I slam into her and grab her other ankle. My thrusts hit over and over. Her pants and moans collide with the sounds of her perfect wet pussy.

She takes my hand, pulling it to her throat. I slow down, and she flashes me this sinister little smirk. "Oh, you're fucking crazy-crazy. And it's so fucking hot on you." She pulls moans from my throat. "Will you fucking burn me? Burn me again, darling. Where's your little lighter?"

"I'll leave you scarred," she mutters the sweetest words to my ear.

"Show me where you'd scar me first." I thrust, and she jolts, leaning forward and biting my nipple. She sucks the barbell in her mouth. "Oh, ho," I laugh. "That would fucking hurt." I huff a heavy exhale mixed with a moan.

"It would melt into your skin—a permanent reminder of mine."

"You can burn if I can make see stars. We both know what they look like by now." I tighten my hand around her neck, slowly losing control, the farther I bury my head into this ecstasy and the harder I slam into her soaked pussy.

"Tighter!" She orders as she clenches around my cock. Her eyes close, blinking rapidly before they slowly fade again.

I thrust again and again as my core tenses and my think space lights up so brightly I forget that we continue to exist on this earthly plain. I squeeze her throat in my hand as I cum inside of her warmth. My dick pulses and I breathe heavily, slowly awakening from my trace. As I come to, I notice Cherry's eyes remain closed.

"Cherry…" She doesn't move. "Cherry," I say louder. "Fuck, fuck fuck." I lightly slap her cheek and jaw. "Come on, baby. Wake the fuck up." She gasps, sucking in all the oxygen she can get with that same fuck-off smirk tattooed on her face. "Cherry?"

"Did I scare you?" She giggles.

I tip my head back. "Don't you fucking let me do that again."

My rugged breaths match her spent ones. "Nothing ended with you," she exhales.

I look back into her crazy blue eyes. "No, because you found me so everything could begin."

"B…I am *truly* hungry. Tell me you have more than beer and peanut butter and jelly because while it's a great meal, I could go for eggs with a side of cinnamon toast."

"Cinnamon toast?" I tilt my head, side-eyeing her. "Share your knowledge."

"So you can steal my recipes. I'll know when your next book is a cookbook."

"That a reach, my darling." I inhale and slowly breathe it away. "My cleaning lady is going to start charging me double."

Bennett, You Dirty Lab Rat

"I expected this place to be more of a disaster." I open a cabinet, not sure what I'm searching for.

It's surreal to think I was essentially born in this very room. Of course, I mean born again and as a killing machine. After two days cooped up in my house with Cherry, fucking and forgetting the world that spins around us, we took a flight and then a drive, ending up in the town neither of us is fond of. Cherry raided my library, resting her head on my shoulder the entire flight with one of my favorite YA novels in her hands. I managed a few thousand words that you've certainly read at this point. I fear for her as we take the steps through the threshold of a laboratory where she witnessed horrific death—by my hand. In my selfishness, I don't want her to hate me. With the way I feel for her, I don't want the immense pain to break her self-built metal plate protecting her heart.

"What were they trying to do here—design their own undead army?" I joke.

The moment we left my house, Cherry's humor was gone. I can't keep my eyes off of her. These dark wash jeggings—I think that's what she called them—those stretchy-as-fuck jeans hug her ass and she's making it a habit to steal my black hoodie over her tank top and her boots. She's either prepared to hide or kick someone's ass. The pigtails give her a less badass appearance. Yeah, those pigtails. You can feel my smug smile, can't you? Well, they're some kind of fancy braid—French or Dutch—I don't know. She has them tucked in her hood and the drawstrings pulled snuggly. I followed her example and haven't removed my hood since we stepped into this town.

I want to believe she's told me everything and somehow I have this aching feeling she left something out. I thought I knew exactly how my story was going to end, but I'm walking into that chapter. You know, the one I didn't see coming. That chapter you definitely didn't see coming.

"I watched you walk out of this building over three years ago; a disoriented killing device controlled by only the evil thoughts in your head. As I looked around me, bodies splayed left and right. Bodies of people I knew and talked to every day for months. They were people that had told me about their families and their weekend plans like the people I befriended on your movie set. Their bodies draped lifelessly over counters, frozen against red-smeared plexiglass, and drowning in their own blood on the floor. That image—it's not quite a photo. It's an entire reel that plays in my head. And now I'm here with *you*." She licks her drying lips. "I've seen too much blood."

I rush back over to her, taking her face in my hands. "That lifetime is over. Give yourself permission to heal." I sound like a fucking therapist as I preach words I refuse to follow. Kissing her, I lace my fingers between hers. "Come on, give me the tour." I raise my brows. "I know, it's fucked, but we came here for a reason. Let's find it."

She nods and leads the way.

It fucking stinks in here. It's like a medical-grade sanitizer mixed with bleach and musk. Someone cleaned up all those bodies and made it look like nothing happened here. Are we going to find this doctor's information? Someone went out of their way to make this place spotless. I'm waiting for a fucking skeleton to pop out of a closet from a pull string. It wasn't very hard to break in. Something is off.

"Cherry, where is their security system set up? The cameras you talked about—they're all over this place?"

She continues to tug me along. "East wing."

"Is there something you're not telling me?"

"No." She looks around, on edge and jittery.

"You're looking for something."

"Look." She pulls me closer, lowering her voice. "This lab is privately owned. Two research doctors, both that you killed, and the silent partner. B, you know what a powerful man can do. This man has everyone in his pocket. If the cameras are still running, we need to get out of here as quickly as possible."

"Because if we shut them off it will cause an alert of its own." I nod in realization.

"Bingo."

"You do know we're superhuman though, right?"

"You're too cocky. It'll be a death sentence."

"I'm confident and that will save my neck. It's something that happens to you when you come back from the dead."

"It's so quiet," she murmurs to herself as she walks down the east wing. It's like she's reliving a time in her past, and I'm watching a private showing from her head. I glance into the first room on my left, surprised that it reminds me of a tiny dorm. It's stripped bare, besides the twin bed placed to the left with crisp white linens. A very colorful painting covers the majority of one wall. It's a long, landscape banner in graffiti style—a sunset with all these tiny elements that I would have to study for quite some time to name.

"That looks hand sprayed." I stand with my hands in my pockets, taking it in as if every worry about this place is suddenly a memory. She stops, taking in the painting beside me. Then she finally gives me a quiet reply.

"It was." She begins walking again without any further explanation.

I chase after her. "Who's room was that, Cherry?"

Room after room, they're all the same—a white twin bed, a dark-tone leather-like recliner with a small table next to it and a dark rug underneath, a dresser, and a thirty-two-inch flatscreen hanging on the wall. Eight rooms border the hallway, and the ninth houses screen upon screen, a computer, and several upright cabinets.

"They're all off." She flicks the light switch, and the room stays dark. "The power is cut."

"Can someone access the system manually? I'm just a writer, but I would think you would need some sort of power source for them to work."

"It's been years," she replies. "They had to have come in, clean house, cover their tracks, and close up."

"Yeah," I nod. "Exactly, years ago. Don't you think this place is odd, though?" I press my tongue to my cheek. "It doesn't have a speck of dust."

"Maybe they have a cleaning service to maintain it," she suggests, trying to calm her worrying mind more than mine.

"Why would they do that and not monitor it? Something is off and I don't like it."

"Help me find what we need then and we can get out of here." She doesn't waste time sharing a dirty look, instead, she yanks on a drawer. Searching a filing cabinet, she pages through manila folders.

"Do you remember that idea you gave me? Uh, you told me that the guy in my story would meet a cool chick and they would go on a heist?"

"We are not technically stealing." She keeps flipping through files.

"We broke into a lab for data. That's several charges there. Do you also have the power of foresight? It's like you knew we would be doing this."

She giggles quietly. "I can also fly," she whispers in a sarcastic manner.

"This is kinda exciting though." I wrap my arms around her waist and nuzzle my face into her neck. "Are we going to get caught or...are we going to make it out to see the sunrise?"

"Bennett," she hums.

"We need code names in here," I murmur, pulling the edge of her hood back to kiss her jaw. "Safety first."

"Easy." She spins to face me, and I lock my arms, pushing my fingertips to the filing cabinets along both sides of her head. Her fingers toy at the loops along the waist of my jeans. "Little Red and the Big Bad Wolf."

"Say Red." I lean in to whisper. "When we get out of here, you want to play a game with me?"

She pouts, looking far more innocent than she's ever been. "But would grandmother approve? With eyes so big..."

"Better to see you with, darling."

"And teeth so...sharp." She closes her eyes, and I dip down to kiss her lips.

"Better to fuck anyone up that tries to touch you, *darling*."

The tip of her nose brushes mine, and she softly moves it up and back down. "You told me not to trust you, remember B?"

"Since when do you listen?" I lean farther into her.

She takes my face in her hands, fiercely kissing me.

"Oh, you fucking drive me wild." I lift her and push her back into the cabinets. Letting go of her, she's forced to latch her legs tighter around my waist. I slam my hands to the sides of her head. She jolts a hair and her lips slowly lift to a smile.

She puts her hands on my neck—one above the other—like she's going to ring me out. I deepen into her lips, taking her tongue with mine. As she unhooks her legs and slides off of me, she unbuttons her jeans and turns around.

I hastily undo my mine and push them to my ankles, bending her over the open cabinet. She lies on her stomach, pushing to her tiptoes. *Fuck foreplay.* She's always fucking ready for me—thinking about sex as much as I do. I rub the tip of my cock up and down, slide over her pussy lips, and push in. Her moans belong to me. I fight for more, thrusting in and out of her beautiful body.

You don't have to tell me. I already know what you're thinking. These two fuck like rabbits. I'd like to think it lasts a little longer than rabbits. Have you seen a rabbit get it on? They're a quick nut and run. The thing is, new love or lust is enticing and exhilarating. We wish the honeymoon phase could last forever. I wonder if it could with the right person. That one who is willing to push their limits in order to keep it an everlasting thrill.

Anyway, I'm going balls deep and getting tired of holding her up to my level. I lean my arm on the open filing shelf, and it creeks.

"Don't break it," she scolds, glancing over her shoulder.

I pull out and grab her hand without saying a word. As I lead her to the desk without any monitors, my hunger for her heat grows. The keyboard is underneath, leaving the surface free. She leans back, spreading those legs for me. My voice lowers an octave, and I chuckle. "You're too fucking good to me." I grab her hips, thrust in, and lean into her. Pushing up her hoodie, I kiss her navel. "You're going to cum for me. Right here, right on this desk." I kiss her breasts. "Cum for me."

"Make me," she giggles, running her fingers through my hair. I thrust in and freeze as her head falls back.

No, I'm not iced over for dramatic effect and dick-deep stimulation. I'm frozen because as I look up—directly at the open door—there stands a shadow with his back against one side of the frame, his arms crossed over his chest, and one leg bent while the other holds his poor posture. He pops his chewing gum and smirks at me. He's dressed like the two of us—well before we started undressing—with a black hoodie and dark jeans. His marbled-brown circular glasses are hipster chic, and his brown hair swoops to one side where it's longer than the other half of his hair.

"Don't stop on my account," he says. Cherry's eyes meet the stranger's. She screams like she saw a ghost and sits up quickly, pushing me off of her as she turns to cover her pussy. She dips behind the desk, adjusts herself, and walks around the desk while I shove my dick back in my pants. Luckily for her, I dragged her jeans with us when we moved.

"Are you kidding me? Are you kidding me!" She yells, excited.

The guy stands up straight, holding his arms out and pops another bubble. Cherry wraps her arms around his neck, giving him a big bear hug. I'm left with my fucking jaw on the floor and a wet dick in my fucking jeans.

"Would someone like to tell me what the fuck is going on?" I ask without losing my temper or moving from behind the desk.

She looks at me and back to the hipster. "I thought you were dead?"

Of course, she talks to the voyeur first.

"Whole wing survived, sweets. All fucking seven of us, including Slow—unfortunately." He pops another bubble and glances over at me. "Who's your friend, Cherry?"

I walk around the desk into slightly better lighting.

"Oh shit, I know this guy!" He points. "It's fucking Bennett Larson. The director. No fuck." He looks between us. "So you went through with that acting stuff you wanted to do and you made it all the way to a Bennett Larson movie." He tilts his head, widening his brown eyes at her. "Sweets, that's awesome. I'm proud of you." He hugs her again. My jaw tightens, wanting to break his fucking fingers. *Sweets? What the fuck is this?* "As long as I didn't just walk in on your payment plan to be in said movie," he nudges her with an elbow.

"Pig," she replies, smacking him in the back of the head.

"I'm just fucking with you. *He was fucking with you*—yeah." She nearly smacks him again, and I try not to smirk.

"He's patient one."

"Whaaaat?" He exaggerates, squatting to the floor and holding his head. "What!" He stands back up and looks obnoxiously between Cherry and me. "Bennett Larson is patient zero-zero-one? This explains so much." He shakes his head.

"Okay, now that we established who I am. Who the fuck are you?"

"B." She takes my hand, not wanting me to go white. "This is David. Everyone calls him Shifter. He was part of—"

"The east wing," I answer for her.

"He signed up for the lab trial right before I did. He's like a brother."

"A brother or step-brother?" I ask, rolling my tongue across my teeth.

"What's the difference?" She wrinkles her nose.

"Oh, there's a difference," *Shifter* inputs himself into the conversation with a wink.

"Anyway." I ignore him. "Is it safe to be here?"

"Yeah, yeah, yeah, yeah," he rambles off. "I disconnected all the cameras and Mr. Richman hasn't been to the lab since the massacre. He has no idea we took over—no idea we're alive."

"What about that doctor that survived, Dr. Feather Romberg?" Cherry asks him.

"We had a doc here whose first name was Feather?"

Oh, fuck me. Was this guy like this before the trial?

"I'll take that as a no," she asks. "I'm trying to contact her."

"Always on a mission, Cherry. What do you think? She can get rid of the side effects? One doctor? It's not gonna happen, sweets."

"Okay, fuck this. You—" I point to Shifter. "Stop calling her sweets. You—" I point to Cherry. "Find her info. It has to be in here somewhere. Let's get this shit and get out of here."

"Fuck you, Bennett," she groans. "He said it's safe. I trust him. I'm staying here as long as it takes. If you need to leave and regroup, you know where I am when you calm your jealous ass down."

"Yikes. You made sweets curse," he coos. "I think I'm gonna give you a minute." He slips through the doorway and down the hall.

"Don't start, B."

"Fine. I'm going for a walk too." I push past her, stopping to kiss her stony cheek. She refuses to look at me, walking back to the file cabinet.

The Man, The Myth, The Legend, Bennett Larson

"Well, holy shit! Bennett Larson is a lab rat."

This guy is a fucking trip.

I double-take, searching for an understanding of why the fuck he's talking to me. *Wait, what did he call me?* "A what?"

"A lab rat, a test subject, a little science puppet like the rest of us." He walks into the first room at the end of the hall with the painting. "You wanna hang? I wouldn't go back to Cherry for a while."

"I can handle Cherry." I walk into the room anyway, and he sits in the recliner, not giving it to his guest or anything. After a moment of sulking, I leer over the artistic wall. "Did you paint this?"

He glances up, admiring it. "Yep. That was my dream—to be an artist. Well, until my dad kicked me out." He pulls the handle on the side of his recliner, kicking his feet up. "But then I found this place and now I'm living rent-free and can change the channel with my hands behind my head."

"That's convenient," I agree. "Are you working on a piece now?"

"Nah. I haven't picked up a brush in a long time."

"Why?" I scowl.

"Lack of inspiration." He shrugs, not looking away from the TV.

"What was your name again?" I tuck my hands in my pockets. He's a shitty host. If he thinks I'm going to sit on his bed, it's not happening. I'll stand.

"Everyone calls me Shifter."

"That's funny. I used to game with this kid. That was his username. My sister loved to rag on him." Hah. Yeah, Annie had fun with him.

"Shifter1269?" He casually asks, tipping his head back.

"Uh, yeah." A perplexed wrinkle takes my forehead.

"That's me, bro." He looks over, flashing me his pearly whites. "What was your tag?"

"FuccBenny—with two c's."

Shut up, you. It's fucking cringy. I've moved past it.

"No shit." He looks at me for a second, then peels his glasses off and rubs his eyes. He replaces his goggles and stretches his arms above his head. "What the fuck happened to you? *I see* what happened to you, but you went ghost."

"My sister died," I reply, deadpan.

"Shit man...I'm sorry." He gives me the look that I've seen too many times. It fades quickly, and he continues. "And then you died too, I guess? Twisty."

"Not exactly, but I think that's enough of a history lesson for today."

"So, Cherry told you everything?" His brow lifts.

"She told me enough." I look him over, trying to get a feel.

"Girl is a handful—a sweetheart—and yeah, a handful."

"Tell me about this doctor she was into?"

"Doc McHandsome, I bet." He nods robotically. "Every broad in this place wanted him. I don't think he was the commitment type. *Player*," he whispers like someone else might overhear or give a fuck. "Pretty sneaky too."

"Oh yeah?"

"Nobody is a paragon." He glances up at me without moving.

"They didn't have anything serious then?"

"To my knowledge—the only thing that dude took seriously was his research."

Huh. It's not the understanding I got from her. "Alright. I'm heading out," I say, walking out the door and heading back toward the end of the hall to see if Cherry has calmed down.

Cherry sits at the desk with her back to me, typing into her phone. "Did you find it?"

"I did," she replies with concentration.

"Good."

As I walk up behind her, I rub her shoulders. "Do we have to stay here?" I was sure this place would be trashed, and we wouldn't find anyone living in it. I book a hotel past the town limits. Then *he* showed up. She's not going to leave now.

"I'm not forcing you to do anything."

I drop my hands from her body. "You're in a mood and it's this fucking place. I'm not going to hold you to it. It has to be overstimulating." She stares at me blankly, certainly telling me off in her head. "So, *Shifter*. Small world—we've met in a previous life."

"What? You're joking." She spins back, looking up at me. "Tell me you're joking."

"I used to game with him when I was a teenager. Annie would always tell him off in her subtle way. I don't think he remembers that part much. You can ask him. He gave me a little more information, as well. He recalled all the women wanted to date the dreamy doctor—the man you were willing to kill for."

"He was a catch. What else would you expect? We had a thing anyway, so it's not like it mattered." Her lip pulls at the side, and I try to figure out if she's reliving a moment with this *perfect doctor* or if she's doubting the *thing* she thought they had.

"*Had a thing.*" I huff. "Hah, is that like hooking up in the janitor's closet?"

"Shut up, B. I could talk to him for hours. He made me happy, and I felt a greater purpose with him. You don't have to be an ass because you're jealous. He's dead."

"Being jealous of a deadman sounds like my M.O." I kneel in front of her and touch her knee. "He told you whatever you needed to hear to keep you content for the experiment you signed up for. It's okay to be embarrassed."

"You're an asshole." She swats me away.

"Realist, darling. At least I'm honest." I rise, grabbing the file from the desk and opening it.

"What's that supposed to mean?" Her voice spikes with frustration.

"Forget it," I mumble. "Where are we staying?"

"*I'm* staying in my room. You can bunk with Shifter or go to your hotel for all I care."

"The fuck I am. Can we not do this? Fucking please."

If I'm less than charming, I'll chalk it up to this place too. Neither of us has fond memories here, and it's showing. She's returned to wanting to kill me and I've become less—what's the word?—*sensitive.*

"Knock knock," Shifter calls out as his knuckles rattle the door. "Are the newlyweds fighting?" I glance over at him, close the folder, and toss it back to the desk.

"Shifter," Cherry groans, amused. "Not now."

"Don't hurt me," he fictitiously begs. "I came with food offerings." He lifts his leg like he's The Karate Kid and flicks his ankle. Once he straightens, he uses an invisible fork to shovel nonexistent food into his mouth. "Dinner's ready."

"Who cooked?" Cherry picks up the file and walks around the desk, pages through the cabinet where she found it, and fits it in place.

"*Slow.* Charlie and Seth helped."

"Solomon and Charlie in the same kitchen? And they're both alive?" Well, at least he got a smile out of her. *How nice.*

"I said Seth too. Someone needed to supervise."

"Are these your friends, Cherry?" I interrupt.

"Fellow lab rats, friends, family," Shifter replies for her.

"I wasn't asking you."

"My bad." He surrenders with his hands raised.

"Bennett, can I talk to you?"

"No. Let's go meet these friends." I walk past Shifter and into the hallway.

✖

"Hey, guys. Look what the cat dragged in."

I trail behind Cherry as we make our way to—the east? Eh, I don't fucking know—one of the wings in this place. It's similar to a cafeteria. Besides it having the same bright white appeal and hospital stench, an industrial-like kitchen borders the end of the dining room. Okay, that's a lie. This room smells better because of the food.

Is that lasagna?

A long table, set for the meal, seats eight. Boring white linens cover the surface, and every seat has a placement. Fresh rolls and bowls of mixed salad are spread across the table.

And that is fucking lasagna in the center of the table.

Who's the guy wearing a wide brim brimmed hat with a soft crown and pinched front, like he's a two-thousand-and-two pop star? "Holy *fucking* shit. Cherry?" *2002 guy* has his hands on my girl now.

"Charlie." *2002 guy* is Charlie. Okay.

"We thought the zombie got you."

Let me guess—I'm the fucking zombie? The willpower it takes to not roll my entire neck...it's unbelievable.

"Lucky woman." *The six-foot wonder* approaches. "You didn't have to clean that mess," he jokes. "What happened to you?" *Sasquatch* has his giant hands on my girl. "And be glad you didn't come here sooner." He leans closer to her. "Those two in the kitchen," he mutters and rolls his dark eyes.

"Don't remind me." She looks around. "I didn't think anyone else made it. Where's Wes?"

"With Ronnie."

Who the fuck is the *tall guy*? There are two more? This is turning into a one-girl, ten guys porno.

"They hit the gym. No worries. They know what time dinner is," the *six-foot-six man* replies.

Once I get past the initial shock of his height, I notice there's more to him. And by more—I mean this guy looks like he stepped out of a smoke-filled van looking for Scooby snacks. At least 2002 Charlie has his dark hair slicked back. It's not a shaggy mess.

"Guys, guys, guys," Shifter's deep voice travels. "Guess who Sweets brought back to the fort with her."

Both of these guys stare at me with their brains bouncing around their heads.

"Is that Bennett Larson?" One of them asks, but I've lost track of who is who already. It might have been the guy in the kitchen.

"Yeah, AKA zero-zero-one." Shifter smirks.

"The fucking legend," a voice says from behind me.

"Wes!" Cherry screeches, allowing another man in this room to feel her body against his.

"Cherry, this is wild." I don't know where this one came from, but his face is as long as his accent. "Nobody knew what happened to you."

"Spend any time in Texas?" I interrupt.

"You're quick." He almost smiles. His face stays flat as he continues to play hard. He doesn't trust me. He's the smartest man in the room.

"I hear that often," I reply. "Maybe we should put it to the test. Do you think I could drop all of you dead in five minutes?" I smirk, fucking with him.

"Including Cherry?" A woman walks in behind *southern vocals*. She doesn't share the draw, but her tone is gritty, akin to sandpaper. She's tall, thin, and her long black hair covers most of her back. It's not her looks that stole the conversation. It's that she asked if I'd take Cherry's life.

"That's impossible," I answer her. "Unless one of you could manage to kill me. That's the only way Cherry dies."

"Oh, you got yourself a bodyguard now." She makes a pouty face at Cherry, asking for a catfight—possibly one that's been brewing for years.

"Ronnie, it's nice to see you're still the stick bug from hell." She bats her lashes and cheeks flush with her smile. Cherry is as cunty with *this* Ronnie chick as she was with Cassie. What's the story?

"That's so sweet of you to say." The room is full of sarcasm now, isn't it?

Wes—*Southern Whiskey*—wraps his arm around her neck and leads *Rowdy Ronnie* away from Cherry, toward the table. I pull out Cherry's seat, and she gives me another look that could kill. I get it. She's on edge here and she doesn't need a reason to look weak. I sit down next to her, across from her nemesis.

Shifter sits next to me, leans his elbows on the table, and whispers. "Sweets and Veronica have some alpha woman tension."

I nod and glance around the table.

These seven people volunteered to be self-titled lab rats. They all have some range of abilities that are similar to mine, but I'm the strongest—according to everything I have learned so far. I'm the only one lacking a typical conscience. I have more blood on my hand than a soldier. They're all sitting around this table thinking the same thing—why the fuck did Cherry bring the zombie into our sanctuary?

I stand, clearing my throat. "Let me see if I can get this straight..." I look around the table and back to the end when the 2002 *guy* sits. "Charlie, right?"

"Yes," he answers, dryly.

"What's your number?" I pick up a bottle of water from the table, crack it, and take a swig.

"Zero-zero-two."

"Nice, okay..." I look to the next seat. *Tall Scooby guy.* "Something with an S..." *Scooby-Seth.* "Seth?"

He nods. "Zero-zero-three."

"Right in a row." I let out an airy chuckle. "Cherry, you're four? Did you sit like this on purpose?" She glares at me, trying to assess what I'm doing. "And five—Ronnie?" I flex my brows. *Rowdy Ronnie.*

"You're good." Her eyes flash over me. "What else are you good at?" She flirts.

"Shifter—six." I pause as I try to remember *Southern Whiskey's* name. The silence is too good not to hold out a little longer. "Wes—seven...And they call you Slow? Number eight."

"Solomon. I have been dubbed with the unfortunate nickname of Slow." He's a decent-sized man. I'm betting he usually spends his free time at the gym with the other two or at least with Southern Whiskey over here.

"Do you want to explain that one?" I smirk.

"I'm always last?" He blinks.

"He's last at everything including jokes," Shifter blurts out. "I told this fucker a joke one day and two days later he finally comes over to me and says he gets it."

"That's out of context. I got the joke later that night, but I forgot about it until two days later when I ran into you."

While this place is fucking creepy, it does not lack entertainment. I'm out-doing myself with the names, though. This has to be some sort of record for me.

"You all know who I am. I'm Bennett fucking Larson." I hold my arms wide. "The legendary number zero-zero,-one. Whatever you want to call me, I don't care. You all know what I'm capable of. My body count is higher than sixteen now. I'm here for Cherry and at the risk of her biting my dick off tonight, I'm going to say it—if anyone touches her, I will make you regret it. That's all. Don't touch Cherry and we won't have any problems. Especially you, Miss Rowdy." I gesture toward Ronnie. "It's nice to meet everyone."

I sit, slide my chair in, and the table remains quiet. Except for Shifter, who gives me a fucking thumbs-up with a huge grin. I shake my head, at a loss for words for this one.

"You always need a man to fight your battles don't you, Cherry?" Ronnie opens her mouth.

Ah fuck. She's going to try to kill me again.

"Give it a rest, Ronnie," Swifter chimes in. "Everyone knows you're just butthurt because Doc would only fuck you, but never have a meaningful con-versation like he did with Sweets." He takes a bite of his roll as if this was open knowledge. He was mistaken. Cherry stares at the woman across from us like she's about to eat her last meal.

Oh, here we go. Cassie 2.0.

"You lying little bitch."

It's the calm. Fuck, oh fuck. It's the calm. Abort!

Despite the weight of my arm draped over her shoulder, she presses forward. "You said you would never."

"So I lied, Cherry. It's not like he was going to ever date you or marry you. Did you think if you held out he would make that commitment? He wasn't that great of a lay. You didn't miss much," she gloats.

"I held that man's hand while he took his last breaths. I spent years making the right moves to avenge his death."

"Looks like it went well for you. You're shacking up with the zombie."

For fucksake, why am I the zombie?

As Cherry stands, she slams her hands to the table. With moving, I patiently watch for a cue that she needs me. That's one thing I know—Cherry is capable of taking care of herself.

"How much blood is on your hands, Ronnie?"

Wait. What is she doing? What in the actual fuck is Cherry doing?

I grab her hand, and her glare settles on me in a way I haven't seen before. It's with great disdain and it would be in my best interest to let this one play out.

"I know what I'm capable of now. Don't fucking test me." Their staring match creates a tension in the room that nobody is immune to...except Shifter, who won't put the fucking bread down. Cherry finally finds my eyes and sits back down. Slow—the notorious last-place lab rat—is the first to take a roll from Shifter as he holds out the basket.

PROTECTIVE OR OBSESSIVE, CHERRY HAS HER HANDS FULL

A roll flies across the table and pegs Bennett in the head. It bounces straight up in the air and a silence stills the room. My surroundings slow to point eight—slow motion. I'm a passenger in my mind as my body flies through the air. I dive across the table, slamming Ronnie's head to the floor. Blood pounds in my ears, drumming loud and louder until Wes pulls me off of her, and I instantly regret everything.

"B! *B!* Bennett!" I yell before he even gets to the side of the table. "Shifter!" I scream out, begging him to stop this. *Stop Bennett.*

Shifter sets his fork down, untucking his napkin from his shirt. His casual demeanor twists my stomach into knots. I thumb my ring in a panic. He should have Solomon's nickname at this point.

A switch flips Bennett's brain, sending him on a mission. Destroying Ronnie becomes his obsession. In a blink, he's suddenly in front of me, holding both Wes and Ronnie by the throat with iced-over eyes.

"I told you not to fucking touch her," he growls.

"There is a lot of tension in here. You're doing too much. Can we all just chill the fuck out for a hot sec?" Shifter holds his glasses in his hands, letting the light shine through them, and then wipes the one lens with the bottom of his hoodie.

"Shifter!" I scold him, a desperate attempt to kick his butt in gear.

Bennett is about to find out that I skipped part of the story. I left out one key component. It sets Shifter apart from the others. He flatlined.

He's a zombie, too.

"Fine," he shrugs. He rushes Bennett, stepping to his face. "Enough." Bennett lets go of his victims and closes the space between them.

Bennett studies Shifter. His lips part for a brief moment. Then they close, his jaw becomes stiff, and he glares at me. "Did you know?" He asks with a finger pointed in the air.

Saliva runs down my throat as I swallow. "Yes."

Shifter's eyes match Bennett's. *White.*

His abilities are not the same. He's as strong and I'm immune to his control. Nobody else can see it unless I point it out. The ability I didn't understand until Bennett.

It's not that crazy. Eight different humans with eight different medical histories all took an experimental injection that we had no idea what it was designed to do. We're imperfect and made choices that landed us in this position—an unpredictable freak show.

Some of us are okay with it because we think we can control it. *Some of us* hide and live the best we can in solidarity. *Some of us* think we're invincible, and *some of us* refuse to let this be the end.

One of Bennett's deeply alarming—and somehow comforting—chuckles spills from his lungs. He walks back to his chair and sits down.

He doesn't say a word the entire dinner. In fact, it's quite silent throughout the entire table. Besides a few polite exchanges, Shifter doesn't even speak.

I've done a lot of bad things. Maybe Bennett's right. Maybe I'm not a good person. I lie to everyone. I thought he was the exception. Is omitting parts of the truth the same as lying? I had no reason to explain the situation with David.

I roll to my side, finding Bennett's shadowed jaw. As I run my pointer across it, he stares at the ceiling. We barely fit in my twin bed. It's weird sleeping in it again after all these years.

"Bennett, I..." I trail off. "I'm afraid to close my eyes," I whisper, unsure if he heard.

I don't know what to say to him. I kept something from him that left a stain of betrayal. He thought we had this undeniable connection because I could see the white in his eyes when nobody else could.

He turns to me, answering my muted cries. "Do you need me?" No matter what I say, I'm walking on glass and I'm bound to be cut.

"That's a complicated question."

"No, it's not. I've always felt a void—not in the way you'd think. It was a me problem. I wasn't a person others strived to be around. Then you made it your mission to get close to me. *Do you need me?* Is that why I'm here?" His thumb traces my lower lip. "Or would you find me in a sea of souls every time?"

"Bennett—" *Do I love him? Is that what this feeling is? I...All I know is, I don't want to be without him.* "I'd choose to find you. That's the truth." I grab his hand, intertwining our fingers. "I have to believe everything I've gone through has led me to this moment for a reason." As I press my lips to the back of his hand, his fingers comb through my hair. "The way you write, I want to read everything in your notebook. I'm hoping I find a long grocery list in there." I smile, and he wants to do it back. "B—I want to stitch you up when I can't control my crazy. I want to see your blue eyes every morning and your white ones every night. I want to be with you because you make me admit I'm not an angel. I'm a liar. I'm a murderer. I'm just as wicked as you. I'm *worse than you.* And you accept me for everything dark and deprived."

"Don't make me laugh." He pinches my chin between his pointer and thumb. "Everyone knows I'm the worst thing to come out of this lab. Not you, darling."

"Want to try to be less of a terrible human with me?"

"Promise me, no more secrets. Nothing. Not one. If you fucked anyone else in here, tell me now. Did you have something with Shifter?"

"Oh, ew." I smack his arm. "No. Shifter is my favorite person here. I would never."

He traces my fingers, kissing my hand. "I'm glad you said that because I might like the guy. I would hate to have to kill him."

"Thanks, man, but I'm pretty hard to kill."

"Shifter!" I whisper-yell. He slipped into my room so quietly that neither Bennett nor I noticed him open the door. "What are you doing?"

He pops his bubble gum and peers around the door frame, down the hall. With a gentle push on the door, he closes it and walks over to us. "Get dressed, A-sap." He pulls his phone from his pocket, scanning the screen. "*They* do these periodic raids, checking for squatters. It's been too long, and I had this feeling earlier." He holds up his phone, and I grab it.

"You have your own cameras?"

"At entry points. The only one that's not breached is the far wing. So you might want to move your ass."

I hand the phone back to him and pull on my jeans and hoodie. Bennett beat me to it, already dressed and going over Shifter's plan with him. I should have listened to Bennett instead of being stubborn in my ways...for once. The hotel sounds nicer by the minute.

"What about everyone else?" I ask.

"Already on the move. You didn't forget the rules, did you, sweets?" He smiles.

"Divide and conquer."

"I'm not dividing shit." Bennett grabs my hand.

"I wouldn't expect you to. Stay close," Shifter orders. It amuses me how Bennett listens, walking tight against the wall behind him.

"B," I whisper. "Do not use your abilities unless you have no choice. It will start a chain reaction."

He nods, ducking into the storage room. "Fuck."

"What?"

"I lost him. I can't see for shit. Night vision would be excellent right now."

"It's fine. Let's keep moving. I'll tell you where to go." I look around the dark building, creeping slowly behind Bennett.

Long, bony fingers wrap around my wrist, and I look back. Dressed in all black, a masked man hastily tries to snap restraints around my arm. I thrash out, kicking them. My movement flows through Bennett's body and before I can exhale, he slams the creep into the wall. The man falls and groans in pain. It gives us enough time to make a break for it.

"Freeze!" Another yells.

They're everywhere and hard to spot. It's the shuffle feet that announce their presence before they call out. In my rush to get away, I separate from Bennett. He continues straight, and I dip into the pharmacy.

As I reach around, touching shelves and opening cabinets, it's empty. Someone cleaned it out. *What's going on?* Something isn't right.

"Red!" My big bad wolf calls. I run to him, grab his neck, and steer him into the pharmacy. As I push him into a wall, I hold in silence, listening for the others.

"We have to stop meeting in such violent situations," I murmur. "Shut your loud mouth. They'll hear you."

"They won't divide us. Come on." Amusement laces his voice and he takes my hand as we inch back into the hallway.

With a scream, I stop, letting go of B. "Son of a bitch!" As I claw at my shoulder, I yell out. "I got hit with something." Bennett wraps his arm around my back and suddenly pulls his hand away. As the security light blinks above us, it catches the liquid on his hand—blood. I'm bleeding.

"Fuck. Let's go." He pulls me toward the exit despite his rage. He wants to fight back and he doesn't. He runs. *We run*—until I can't. "Let's go." He takes my jaw. "Use the adrenaline, keep running."

"It's the stars, B. It's always the most terrible when a blackout sets in." I laugh as if it's funny and fall sideways. He catches me. "Easy, darling. I got you." He hugs me tight and lifts me to his shoulder. The pain shoots up my back and I fight the urge to scream.

"What the hell are they shooting?" He yells in a whisper.

"Bennett, just go. Put me down. I'll hide or something. I'm not worth you getting caught too," I plead. "Divide and conquer. I'll be able to hide easier without you."

He sets me down and grabs my face between his palms. "Look at me. Fucking look at me. I'd never tell you to leave, so don't fucking tell me. You are worth the last breath in my body. You are so fucking worthy," he insists. If he could manipulate my mind to believe his words, he would. His kiss takes my lip as if he'll never get to do it again. "Suck it up and stop trying to save everyone else. I'm not fucking leaving without you. It's time to save yourself. Be the determined, intelligent woman who survived decades of agony. Stop trying to save everyone else. *Save yourself.* Okay? Tell me you understand, Cherry."

"Yes. Yes, I understand." I hang on to him, digging deep inside to find my fight.

I'm a born fighter.

"That's my girl. I'm going to help you up, and we're going to run like hell. Ready?"

I nod. "Yeah."

"The pain will not control you. They will not control you."

"I'm not done fighting, B. Don't worry."

He pulls me up, and I run harder than I ever imagined I could. I don't know if we're going in the right direction or how much blood either of us has lost. I could blackout at any point and never make it out. None of that matters as long as I hold onto him and keep running. The *what ifs* and the *I coulds'* will fall to my feet and become buried in the dust.

"Sweets, we doing okay?" Shifter wraps his arm around my waist.

He didn't follow the rules. He came back for us.

"She's hurt. What are they fucking shooting?"

I feel my legs turn to Jell-o and I try to kick it, pulling the weight of my head back up every time I start to drift away.

"She'll be okay," he tells Bennet. "Cherry, it's Shift—it's David. Listen to me. You have to push past the shooting stars. It's home run time."

Tell Your Story, Bennett

"Hey, gorgeous. I fucking love you."

"I know you only said that to get me to stop and you could check out my ass," she rebukes. "I love you." Her mind never rests, seldom allowing her to sit in the sun for a consecutive twenty minutes.

Are you surprised my story leaves in a micro cliffhanger? I'm Bennett Fucking Larson. You can't sum up my existence in three-something pages.

Did we make it? Don't make me be the bad guy today. Yes, we fucking made it. Our supernatural dream team found sanctuary—a hotel for the night. Those wounds are looking better as I type, thanks to hidden knowledge.

I'll let you in on a secret. I'm excited. For the first time, in a very long time, I'm excited to learn what I'm capable of and why. I'm skeptical of Shifter.

I don't trust a soul. It's a matter of time until they let you down. Every time I get my hopes up, I become excited and overwhelmed with joy. Then I'm shot down with a single, silent lightning bolt. That's the kind of people I attract. They talk the talk and walk the walk. They find out what would hurt you the most. Then, they subtly attack and walk away like it never happened. I never happened. A small blip on the radar of time. Someone to fill the vacancy.

I won't make that mistake again.

These secret ties and electric pellets are only the beginning. I trust Cherry and until she tells me it's time to leave, these rats are where we find answers.

"Shifter." I meet him on the balcony.

He wets his lower lip and steps to the side. "Yeah."

"Are you coming with?"

"Traveling to the East Coast on a mission to find the last doctor that can help us? Is that even a question?" He rocks his fist into mine.

"Look, I'm not that same kid you played games with over the internet." I lean against the stucco, folding my arms.

"Sounds familiar."

"We have a long drive. I'm open to hearing how much things have changed on your side." I'll make an effort.

"You sure about that?" His brows drag up and his forehead creases.

"I didn't choose this like the rest of you." I cross my arms. "You signed up for this, right?"

"I did...at first." He looks at the graying sky.

"What did they do to you?" His lip twitches in silence. "Why the fuck did you all stay?" I shake my head in disbelief.

He adjusts his glasses, looking down and then back to me. "I'm gonna need that long drive."

"I need you to do me one favor if you're coming with." He intently listens. "Try your best not to walk in when I'm getting my dick wet again." I break from the wall as he steps closer to the door.

"That's kinda bullshit." He tilts his head, and it's hard to get a read on him.

"If you're looking for artistic inspiration—you paint, right?"

"Yeah. I appreciate a live model." He smiles, walking back into the room.

None of us are evil to the core, are we? We have all made decisions that fucked someone else over, whether it be selfishly or foolishly. We have troubled pasts. We stack more trauma and toxicity on top of our existing hell instead of searching for healing.

I was invisible by choice. I shut everyone down by choice and buried my head, acting like I was a victim and a villain at the same time. Someone could have seen me, helped me—they could have saved me. That was the past. I'm the one in control now and I always knew, deep inside, what I was doing.

Cherry sees me and we're a perfect curse. To be loved by her might make up for it.

I thought I was writing the story of my life. A boring wallflower who isolated himself until he died and became a monster who forced the world to their knees. I was wrong. This is where everything begins.

Who knows where this road will end? Maybe I'll be dead this time next week or maybe I'll finish my story with Cherry by my side and I hate to admit it—I might make some fucking friends. I don't know if I'm there yet. I'm Bennett fucking Larson, darling.

Afterword

Get all K.R. books, updates, and future releases by signing up for my mailing list at **www.krbrendlinger.com**

Find me on social media **@kr.brendlinger**

About Author

A quirky free spirit, K.R. resides with her family on the east coast of the United States. Her favorite form of caffeine is chocolate, she's unapologetically awkward, and multi-tasking is her way of life. When not writing or reading an alternative reality, K.R. can be found seeking out laughter, music, or something with a motor.

K.R. classifies her writing style as easy to digest and raw between the lines. Her stories are character-driven with the same packed and fast-paced pep as plot-driven stories. K.R.'s undeniable Pisces energy emotionally steers her when the pen hits the paper, writing stories with realistic characters you can relate to and plots that submerge you.

ACKNOWLEDGMENTS

To my husband and sister: Thanks for listening to me through every emotion and stage of my journey.

To my supportive family: I don't think you should read this book, but I feel blessed that you all care and want to.

To my readers: Thank you for picking up this book, giving me a chance, and falling in love. I appreciate you so much.

www.ingramcontent.com/pod-product-compliance
Lightning Source LLC
Chambersburg PA
CBHW030001010826
48973CB00007B/2108